FOOD FOR THE GODS

FOOD FOR THE GODS

by Karen Dudley

Published by Ravenstone
an imprint of Turnstone Press
Artspace Building
206-100 Arthur Street
Winnipeg, MB
R3B 1H3 Canada
www.TurnstonePress.com

Turnstone Press gratefully acknowledges the assistance of the Canada Council for the Arts, the Manitoba Arts Council, the Government of Canada through the Canada Book Fund, and the Province of Manitoba through the Book Publishing Tax Credit and the Book Publisher Marketing Assistance Program.

This novel is a work of fiction. Names, characters, places and incidents are either the product of the author's imagination or are used fictitiously, and any resemblance to actual persons living or dead, events or locales, is entirely coincidental.

Cover Illustration: Doowah Design

Printed and bound in Canada by Friesens for Turnstone Press.

Library and Archives Canada Cataloguing in Publication

Dudley, Karen

Food for the gods / Karen Dudley.

ISBN 978-0-88801-401-6

I. Title.

PS8557.U279F66 2012   C813'.54   C2012-904931-X

To Dr. Robert J. Buck, who always said that there were no new stories under the sun, just different ways of telling old ones.

FOOD FOR THE GODS

Chapter 1

Not surprisingly, everybody stopped short when the girl screamed.

For a brief moment, there was complete silence in the kitchen—a stillness broken only by a single startled *yip* of the household dog, which had been lurking underfoot since my arrival. I waited, listening carefully for further sounds from the dining room. Had it been a cry of terror, or something else?

A spate of giggles followed a few moments later, some deep and masculine, others distinctly higher and much more musical. There was another delighted shriek and a burst of feminine laughter.

Ah. Something else, then.

I had been reprimanding an imbecile of a kitchen slave—a man so lacking in perspicacity he could not, apparently, tell honey apart from olive oil. I uttered a few more choice words then waved him away and glared impartially around the room. The remaining kitchen staff resumed their duties with a sneering reluctance that had seen me grinding my teeth since early this morning.

To say that I was unused to such conduct would be an understatement. My lineage alone would normally preclude contact with any such feeble-minded individuals. Sons of kings—even late, unlamented and foreign kings—did not generally consort with lesser slaves. That I did so now was due to unanticipated, unwelcome and, ultimately, immutable circumstance. But even without taking my exalted antecedents into account, my authority in this kitchen should have been on par with that of Zeus himself. I am, after all, a celebrity chef. But Athenians, I was discovering, had their own thoughts on the matter, and I lacked the great god's thunderbolts to reinforce my own.

Nicander's slaves were pretending to bustle around the kitchen now, the clangs and crashes, mutterings and grumblings effectively drowning out any further exclamations from the dining area. Satisfied for the moment with their industry, I turned my attention back to the dessert trays, which the aforementioned slave had very nearly ruined with his stupidity. With infinite care, I began tucking almonds into the soft flesh of fragrant dates, replacing inedible pits with lightly toasted nuts. Once I'd finished doing that, I would drizzle the confections with gently warmed honey and garnish them with finely chopped fresh mint. They would be ... perfection.

Another cry. Even louder this time.

I grimaced and made a quick decision. The dinner party was getting out of hand. Clearly it was up to me to calm things down.

"Go!" I ordered a house slave out of the kitchen. "Stop cluttering the room. Go in and set up second tables."

"I done that already, didn't I?" he objected.

I counted slowly to three, holding on to my temper with an effort. "Well … go sweep the floor then."

"I done that too, guv. After first tables."

"You are to address me as Chef," I snapped. "Not 'guv.'" I dragged the word out, making it sound like something you'd toss on the midden. "Now get in there and sweep that floor again!"

The man pulled a sour face, rolling his eyes as he slouched over to the broom and fumbled it off the wall.

Unbelievable!

I took a step towards him, ready to plant my sandal soundly in his lazy ass, but he saw me coming and scooted nimbly out the door. His outraged "Fuck me!" floated back into the kitchen followed a moment later by "Chef." The two dishwashers snickered behind greasy hands and I ground my teeth together again. Zeus and Hera save me from these mouthy Athenian slaves!

I scowled at the dishwashers, then shook it off. There were more important things to worry about than slaves with attitudes.

Dessert was late.

I snatched up another almond, crammed it into the last date, then dumped honey over the lot before ordering a kitchen slave to finish the garnish. All that was left to do now was arrange the cakes. It only took a moment, but it was a moment too long.

"Chug, chug, chug-a-lug…"

I could hear the chanting—and a sloshing sound that could only be the wine splashing to the floor.

Quickly, I slid the final sweet triangle onto the platter. "They're ready," I told the serving girl. "Go, go! Take them in. Same serving order as first tables."

She stepped up to the tray with a perky jiggle.

"And re-pin your chiton," I added, disapproval colouring my tone. The clothing in question was slipping from her left shoulder, revealing the soft smoothness of her skin, the swell of her breasts. How could anybody concentrate on food if the slaves were jiggling about in such a fashion?

"Oops," she said insincerely and shrugged the shoulder, which made the chiton slip even further.

More shouts of laughter boomed out from the dining room, mingled again with naughty feminine giggles. The serving girl winked, picked up the trays and grinned back at me with a flirty flick of her chiton.

She did not come back for the fruit bowl.

"You." I motioned to another slave. A young boy this time, with dark eyes and long lashes. "Here, take the fruit in for them. Can you carry this? Good. Set it down in front of your master. Be careful, mind!"

He did not come back either.

I'd sent in extra lamps, tasteful entertainment, and slaves to keep things clean. The last of the food had been served. I had now officially done all I could.

Weariness suddenly set in, and I surveyed the mess in the kitchen, absently rubbing my shoulder. Herakles himself might have found the task daunting. The household slaves would clean the bulk of it, but I disliked leaving my hired crockery for slaves to attend. Too often, the pots and pans ended up chipped or cracked or …

Crash!

… even worse.

Mentally, I added the cost of a fruit bowl to tonight's mounting tally.

I was rapidly coming to the unpleasant realization that I'd made a rather strategic error when I agreed to cook for Nicander's symposion. Oh, Nicander himself wasn't a problem—the man was a fine upstanding citizen, owner of a prosperous shield factory. Any of the celebrity chefs in Athens would have been delighted to provide the culinary entertainment for his symposion. But a number of his invited guests had less than stellar reputations when it came to the sober, philosophical discussions of Homer which are supposed to make up the Athenian male's dinner party. And the gatecrashers, who'd breezed in shortly after the grilled tuna had been served, were even worse.

I took a sip of well-watered wine, sighed heavily, and began scraping off the casserole dishes. All the while trying—and failing—to ignore the increasingly raucous noises coming from the andron where the guests had gathered, ostensibly to dine.

Inviting Proteas had been Nicander's first mistake. Proteas may own one of the largest silver mines in the country, but even the slaves knew him for an ass—and the man drank like a Thracian. Including him among the dinner guests had been bad enough, but I couldn't imagine what had possessed Nicander to name him symposiarch for the evening.

Proteas as symposiarch. It would be laughable if it weren't so horribly, horribly real.

The symposiarch is the life of an Athenian dinner party. A jolly sort. The kind of fellow who keeps the conversation moving and directs the entertainment for the evening. It's his job. It's also his job to water down the wine so the partygoers don't get dung-faced, annoy the neighbours, and generally find themselves unable to converse in a coherent, philosophic manner. But while Proteas might be able to keep a conversation clipping along, watering the wine was not proving to be one of his strengths.

"We're sinking! We're sinking!" several voices cried out.

"Oi! Clear th' decks!"

"Dump the ballast!"

Great Hera! What were they up to now?

I stepped out of the kitchen and saw a dinner guest stagger across the courtyard, one of Nicander's carved serving tables clutched under his arm. I gaped at the sight—and was nearly run over by Nicander and Proteas shouldering one of the dining couches between them.

"*Wha ... what are you doing?*" I demanded shrilly.

"Bloody trireme's sinking, isn' it!" Nicander explained with slurred urgency. "Mus' be th' storm. Been told t' clear th' decks!"

Trireme? Storm?

There was a crash as the small table splintered onto the street, followed quickly by the muffled thump of the couch with all its cushions and coverings. I had to dodge aside as another group of guests with another set of dining tables marched past. Recovering myself, I ducked across the courtyard, past the curtain and into the dining room. Two more couches were following the first out the door. I flattened myself against the wall and blinked to adjust my eyes.

Oil lamps flickered in the dimness, their untrimmed wicks sending black curls of greasy smoke toward the ceiling. The sweaty stench of a dozen diners had long since overwhelmed the delicate scent of the flower baskets, and the air was hot, heavy with stale perfume and the fruity fumes of wine. Only three couches remained in the room. One was vacant. On the second, a man was busily throwing up in one of the wine kraters. And on the last couch, I saw the serving girl who had disappeared earlier. She lolled against the cushions, her eyes distant and dreamy. Her chiton had slipped even further, but she didn't seem to mind. Neither did the citizen who was fondling her rosy-tipped breasts.

"Ho! Pelops!" A voice boomed out from behind me.

I started and spun around.

He was tall for an Athenian, with broad shoulders and a magnificent beard. One of the gatecrashers, I guessed. I didn't recognize him.

He leaned in close. His wine-soaked breath leaned even closer. "It's me," he hissed. "Dionysus."

It took a moment for the name to register. "*Dionysus!*"

"Shh!" He hushed me and bent his head to my ear. "I'm in disguise," he whispered gleefully. "So's Hermes."

"I, uh … Hermes is here too?"

Dionysus chuckled and gestured with his beard. "He's found love."

I glanced over at the couch. The serving girl looked very happy. And so she should. It wasn't every day a girl got to make love to a god.

"Brilliant party, yeah?" Dionysus elbowed me back to myself. "Gods, I'm good."

"*Brilliant?*" I sputtered. "They're *destroying* the place. They think they're on a bloody warship. They never even touched my desserts! How much drink have they had?"

The god of wine looked affronted at my tone. "Several amphorae, I think." He belched long and loud, then offered me a blissful smile. "I may have lost track."

"*Several* amphorae!" I choked off the rest of my words.

"It seemed best," Dionysus was nodding eagerly. "We've all been told to keep an eye out for you, haven't we? You know, to make up for—" he waved his hand around airily, "—things."

I scrubbed at my forehead. My knees were urging me to sit down. "But, what … why … how did you know I was here?"

"Well, you could say … I heard it through the grapevine!" He slapped his knee and burst into peals of boozy laughter.

I managed a feeble grin. When a god thinks he's funny, you'd better think he's a scream.

Dionysus threw an arm around my shoulder and gave me a friendly shake. "Pelops, *relax!* Hermes and I just thought we'd, you know, smarten things up a bit. Help you make a name for yourself in Athens."

I dropped my gaze, certain my dismay was all too apparent. "Oh, I'll have a name for myself all right," I muttered under my breath. "Whether I'll ever have work again is another matter."

"Ah, bollocks!" Dionysus brushed it off. "You worry too much, my friend."

I should have known he would hear me.

He clapped me on the shoulder. "You should have a drink. Piss about. I promise you, by tomorrow all of Athens will know about this party. You can't *buy* publicity like this! Just look! *Look* at them!"

He spread out his arms to encompass the scene and laughed in unadulterated delight.

"Mortals are so much fun! I've got to get my lazy arse off The Mount more often. Well, must be off. Things to do, people to see, tables to toss. Cheers, yeah? *Ho! Nicander! Wait up, mate!*"

And with that, the god of wine jumped back into the fray, helpfully grabbing one end of a couch, which was making its way speedily out the door.

I bit back a string of oaths. Dionysus *and* Hermes! No wonder this dinner party had descended into chaos. My eyes had finished adjusting to the darkness. Now I could see the bowls of carefully selected fruit upended on the floor, the discarded clothing lying in wine-sodden heaps in the corners. A citizen was savouring the delights of a flute girl on a bed of leftover honeyed shrimp.

The dog was eating my pastries.

Deflated, I stared at the ruin. This dinner party was supposed to have been an important step for me. Another rung in the ladder of professional success. I was one of the best chefs in Athens. An up-and-coming foreigner with a wealth of new and interesting recipes for jaded Athenian palates. A person of importance! *A man in demand!*

Hermes lifted his mouth from the serving girl's bosom and gave me a mischievous wink. I offered him a sickly smile in return. How do you tell a god you don't need—or want—his help? The crash of breaking crockery startled me from my stasis.

My dishes!

I moved quickly then, darting around a half-clad cithara player, stepping over another writhing couple, slipping on a forgotten tuna steak. I tried desperately to rescue my hired dishes. Dinner guests in search of more "ballast" wheeled and swerved around me, their eyes red with the wildness of wine. Another table—an elegant gem with ivory inlays—was hoisted through the courtyard and sent tumbling into the street.

By the time someone finally reported the civil disturbance and the archons arrived to investigate, a crowd had gathered in front of the house to enjoy the show and to pick through the windfall of household possessions. With the gravity that comes only after imbibing large quantities of drink, Nicander informed the officials that the trireme he was on was sinking in the storm, and that the pilot had instructed him to dump the ballast. It was a task, he explained solemnly, he had almost, but not quite, completed. And then, after imparting this information to his disbelieving, but highly amused, audience, Nicander collapsed with a small sigh into the street on top of all his furniture.

Or so I heard.

Long before the archons got there, I'd gathered up my pots and pans and what was left of the hired crockery and slipped out into the hot Athenian summer night. As I guided the mule towards home, I tried out a number of different excuses for the state of the pottery. None of them involved gods. All of them sounded contrived. When Meidias saw his dishes, he was going to be upset. He'd probably charge me double. He might even threaten to kill me. The last didn't worry me too much. I was still one of the best chefs in Athens. Still a man in demand.

And besides, I'd been killed before.

Chapter 2

I don't remember being dead.

Not surprising, I suppose, but one would have thought I'd recall the River Styx or, at least (and possibly, more likely), Cerberus, the three-headed dog. But no. I have memories of neither Stygian darkness nor multi-headed mutts.

Which is probably just as well when you think about it.

My troubles began with my father. I do remember that. A slippery customer by the name of Tantalus, he did little of note besides father my sister Niobe and me. Oh yes, he was a king too—I have to give him that—King of Sipylus in Lydia. He was a good enough king, as kings go..But as a person? Well, let's just say that in the great olive of life, he was the pit.

I suppose he was not always thus. After all, while I was growing up, gods were constantly popping by for a cup of wine and a bit of a hobnob. Poseidon, in particular, was a regular visitor, and I remember even Father Zeus, himself, coming to visit when I was about nine or ten. He'd chucked me under the chin, told me how big I'd grown, and offered to bounce me on his divine, if somewhat knobby, knee. For someone who had produced so many children you'd think he could have been a bit more inspired, although my mother sent me to my room when I commented on it. But Zeus did bring me small gifts. A box of iridescent shells. A pouch of honeyed almonds. A terracotta centaur. These were happier times.

My father was fortunate enough to enjoy the friendship of the gods—a fine thing to have, to be sure, but Tantalus let it go to his head like unwatered wine. When the gods started getting chummy, he started thinking that maybe being king of some backwater mountain in Lydia wasn't quite enough. That perhaps he ought to be kicking back on Mount Olympus with the rest of the lads. That's when the troubles started.

You see, friend though he was to the pantheon, it was a long while before anybody thought to invite him up to the Mount for a spot of supper. Oh, he dropped hints like apples in autumn, make no mistake about that.

"Ambrosia, eh? That must taste incredible."

"Boy, I bet the view from Olympus is pretty amazing, huh?"

"Plans for the weekend? Oh, nothing really. I'll probably just sit at home by myself and read a scroll."

But the gods ignored his broad hints even as they continued to share his wine and inquire after his family. And when Tantalus was finally invited around for a sip of nectar and a taste of ambrosia, was he honoured? Humbled? Not a chance. As soon as the gods' backs were turned, he slipped a jar of nectar under his chiton and smuggled it off the Mount.

Only my father could "forget" what had happened to Prometheus after *he'd* stolen something from the gods.

Back in Sipylus, Tantalus strutted around impressing his mortal friends with the stolen drink, but he impressed himself even more. Zeus the All Wise hadn't mentioned a thing about the missing jar. Surely, that proved Tantalus was as good as Zeus was. Or, could it be he was even … *better*?

Personally, I think Zeus knew all along what he'd done—knew, also, of the foul hubris that invaded my father's soul—and he was waiting for that perfect moment to smack him back down to size. But before he could do so, Tantalus decided to invite all the gods to a special banquet at the palace.

They say the smallest pebble thrown in a pool can still produce multiple ripples. The pebble in this case was an empty larder. My father really should have checked his food stocks before planning a party, but … well, he'd never been the brightest lamp in the pottery shop. The upshot was, on the day of the party, the palace cook informed him there really wasn't enough food for the gods.

Now gods, as you might guess, possess quite healthy appetites. To invite them for a meal and then skimp on the comestibles is simply not done. So Tantalus decided to kill two quail with one stone. He'd provide adequate food for his little repast all right and, in doing so, he would prove his superiority once and for all by pulling the wool over the gods' divine orbs.

He chose me as the instrument of his deception.

I've been told what he did. I don't remember it. As I said before, perhaps that's for the best. On the afternoon of the feast, without a qualm, without even a flicker of an eyelash, my father took his bronze battle-axe, chopped me up into convenient bite-sized pieces, and tossed me in the stew pot.

Well.

I simmered all afternoon. I've been told I smelled quite tasty. Rich and meaty with a smash of garlic and a hint of oregano. I would have made my mouth water.

The gods arrived more or less on schedule (immortals have a rather odd sense of time, so you can never be quite sure that this will be the case), and Tantalus's little dinner party got underway. He must have been chuckling into his beard as he greeted them with fine kraters of honeyed wine. If so, he did not laugh for long.

The gods recognized immediately what was in the stew of the day—namely me—and were first horrified, then enraged. Punishment was swift and decisive.

My not-so-loving father was sent straight to Hades to be tortured with everlasting thirst and hunger. Chained forever to a tree, he stands up to his chin in water, but each time he bends to quench his thirst, the water recedes from his parched lips. Branches heavy with fruit dangle enticingly over his head, but each time he reaches up to pluck one, a gentle wind blows it just out of his reach.

A fitting end, most would say. Divine retribution. My father was punished not because of what he did to me, but because he abused the gods' friendship. It doesn't exactly do wonders for my self-esteem, but I am, above all, a pious man and the end result is such that I don't complain.

After Tantalus had been uncomfortably settled in the underworld, the gods, very thoughtfully, scraped the pieces of me back into the stew pot and remade me. I emerged from the cauldron "cloaked in radiant beauty." At least, that's what they told me. Myself, I was a little distracted at the time. They also told me I was so stunning that Poseidon fell instantly in love with me.

That I remember.

The Sea God had always been friendly to me. As boys (for he usually appeared as slightly older than myself), we'd raided the palace larder together, played tricks on the royal steward, and ridden the wild hippokampoi, the fish-tailed water horses of the sea. When I was older, he'd taken me on my first fishing trip, given me my first sip of wine, and introduced me to the delights of women in general, and Nereides in particular. He was like a brother to me. But when I stepped from that cursed cauldron, there was nothing at all brotherly about his love, and I felt both shocked and betrayed by his intensity.

Though the god of the sea is also known as Poseidon Earthshaker, I had little desire to see if he'd make the earth move for me. When you've been chopped into stewing meat, cooked, eaten, and remade all in the space of a day, sex—even with a god—isn't exactly high on your list of things to do. But if I did not wish to love him, I had even less desire to anger him, and so I turned down his generous offer as politely as I could. He was, to put it mildly, unamused. The royal dining hall did not well survive his initial ire.

In hindsight, it was foolish of me to believe that would be the end of it. I thought he would simply retreat to his watery domain, perhaps console himself with an obliging nereid. I have since been thoroughly disabused of that notion. In fact, Poseidon's anger was proving both deep and abiding, despite the sacrifices and prayers I offered up to him on a regular basis.

There was another unforeseen and unfortunate consequence of Tantalus's barbaric behaviour. It had to do with my left shoulder.

Yes … my shoulder. You see, Demeter, goddess of the Goodly Crops, had been invited to that feast. So had her daughter Persephone, but the young goddess was nowhere to be found, having fallen into the hands of Hades (though it was a while before *that* story came out). Desperately worried about her missing daughter, Demeter had accepted Tantalus's invitation, taking respite from her gruelling search to rest and revive herself. But her attention was definitely divided and I paid the ultimate price of that distraction.

The gods knew what Tantalus had done. Knew even before I'd been dished up in the special red-figure Athenian bowls. They all knew, and so did not eat—all, that is, except the goddess of agriculture. Preoccupied, and certainly not expecting deception in this of all places, she tucked into her portion of the meal. My left shoulder, to be exact.

Oh, she was mortified, of course. Promised me wheat and barley for life. And she still apologizes every time I see her (which makes me feel a little odd). When the gods, in their divine kindness, remade me from the pieces, my missing shoulder had to be replaced with a nub of ivory. A valiant effort, really. And most of the time, it works well enough—though not quite as well as the original. But when it rains, when the damp settles into the joint, then the truth of what my father did washes over me anew.

Now, barley rolls and porridge for the rest of your life is all very well and good. And Hermes and Dionysus had been conscientious (perhaps a little *too* conscientious) about helping me make a name for myself in a new city. But as a lonely bachelor on those long, dark nights in Athens, I often find myself wishing it had been the goddess of love who owed me a favour...

Chapter 3

"Pelops! You lazy son of a one-eyed goat! The day's half over." I felt a rude smack on my behind.

"Clear off," I groaned, pulling the blanket over my head.

"Not likely. Come on. Up you get!" Gorgias yanked the covers off me.

I cracked open a crusty eye and glared at my friend. "It was a late night, Gorgias," I protested. "Give me a break."

"No breaks. You've got a customer."

Suspicious, I opened the other eye slowly. "Who would come looking for a chef at this ungodly hour of the day?"

Gorgias shrugged his powerful shoulders. "A slave."

"Whose?"

He frowned at my peevish tone. "Do I look like a sodding scribe, then? I don't recognize him. He asked for you and he's bloody waiting in the courtyard."

I dragged myself into a sitting position and scrubbed at my bristled face. "All right, all right," I grunted. "I'm up. Don't go getting your cloak in a knot." I smoothed my sleep-creased chiton. It was still stained with wine and oil from the previous evening.

Gorgias was also looking at my tunic. His lips twitched in disapproval. "I'd think about changing that if I were you," he advised.

My ears pricked up at his tone. "Wealthy?"

"His slave's certainly well-sandalled," Gorgias nodded.

I rolled off my sleeping couch and began rummaging around in the wooden chest for another chiton. "I'll be right down," I told him.

Hoping to wake myself up, I tipped some washing water into a basin and splashed my face. A massive shiver shuddered down my spine. The bloody water was freezing! This, despite having sat out all night in the warm summer air. Icy droplets ran off the end of my nose as I regarded the basin sourly.

It seemed I often had problems with water these days. Poseidon's way of letting me know he still cared. I routinely spent a small fortune on sacrifices to him, and he still refused to forgive me. Spiteful bugger. Still, a rich man's slave was waiting for me downstairs. Things couldn't be that bad.

Right. I almost forgot. This is *my* life.

Gorgias's only female slave was on her way up the stairs as I was going down. Her sharp eyes took in my dishevelled appearance, and she pursed her thin lips and gave a disdainful sniff as I bade her a polite good morning. Everyone knew her as Irene.

I called her The Gorgon. Whatever you named her, she did not care for me.

She brushed past me without acknowledging my greeting—a rudeness I would not have tolerated in my previous life. But I was no longer a prince, she was not my slave, and it wasn't my place to correct her behaviour. Besides, I knew full well why she did not care for me.

I was, quite simply, a foreigner. Nothing but a drachma-less intruder who had taken sly advantage of her master's generous nature. Gorgias was not a wealthy man, but he was respected, having fought in his late twenties with Archestratus at Potidaea. He had also built a small but successful pottery business in the twelve years since the battle. And now I had wormed my way into their well-ordered home, subverted Gorgias's nine-year old-daughter with my barbaric ways, and ousted Irene from her role as family cook. My sins, in her eyes, were both myriad and grave. I shrugged philosophically and continued down the stairs. The Gorgon's opinion of me was yesterday's news. Right now I was far more interested in what a rich man's slave might have to say to me.

"My master wishes you to cook a feast for him the day before the Great Panathenaea," the slave announced when I made my entrance.

I blinked at his peremptory tone. Even in Athens, slaves usually showed a bit more deference to a celebrity chef (as long as that slave's name was not Irene, of course). I sharpened my gaze on this one … and realized he was better dressed than I was.

His tunic was fine wool, dyed a cheerful orange. The colour

set off his dark curls, which were oiled and freshly scented. His fingernails gleamed from what must have been a lengthy and meticulous buffing, and he looked plump and well fed. This slave must have a wealthy master indeed. I cursed Gorgias under my breath. He could have warned me.

The slave's sandals were grey with dust from the road (which made me feel a little better), but his nostrils flared as he took in my appearance (which did not). My clean chiton tried to sneer, but was clearly wishing it was back in the chest.

I raised my chin and, with a loftiness that needed only a little encouragement, I did not apologize to the slave. "Out of the question," I said instead, giving him a taste of his own attitude. "Your master wants me to cook for him with less than two days' notice? At this time of year? Impossible!"

He blinked, clearly unfamiliar with the concept of refusal.

"My master requested you specifically."

"And I'm grateful that he honours me with his request," I said, softening my tone. The poor fellow looked like I'd smacked him upside the head with a sea bass. "But the Great Panathenaea comes once every *four* years. My tablet's been filled for months."

The slave was still trying to find his tongue.

"Who is your master?" I asked.

The man pulled himself up to his full height and aimed a glance at me that took a long detour down his nose. "I'm not at liberty to divulge that," he said snootily.

Actually, he wasn't at liberty at all, but I kept that to myself.

I shrugged. "Suit yourself," I said. "Starting the day after tomorrow, I've got engagements every single day until the festival ends—and for quite a few of them afterwards. If your master wants me after that, then come back and we'll talk."

I started towards the kitchen, my thoughts turning to breakfast. A cup of wine and some cool grapes would do quite nicely. Maybe a small dish of olives and...

"I've been instructed to offer you five hundred drachmas. Plus expenses."

I froze. Five hundred drachmas! For one evening's revelry? You could buy a highly skilled slave for less than that. It was more than double what Apollodorus was paying me—and he was more generous than any of my other patrons. Five hundred drachmas.

The slave thought he had me. I could see it in his eyes.

"Why does your master want me so badly?" I was curious now.

It was the slave's turn to shrug, the gesture somehow managing to imply that his master's wishes in this case were quite beyond him. "You are the only cook—excuse me, *chef*—in Athens who specializes in foreign foods," he said. Then, as if realizing his response needed more explanation, he added, "My master enjoys experiences that are ... new."

New. My cooking was that all right. Full of unusual combinations and exotic spices. I had the gods to thank for my success. As Prince of Sipylus, I hadn't thought much about the kitchen, beyond knowing that one existed somewhere in the palace and that it produced food to fill my belly whenever it rumbled. But my stint in the stewpot had left me with a certain appreciation for kitchens as well as a superior talent for the culinary arts. When I decided to make a new life for myself in Greece, I quickly became a hot item on the Athenian dinner party circuit. It was not a reputation I was willing to soil by tossing over one patron for another.

"I am sorry," I told him. "Any other time, I would be happy to come and cook for your master. But I can't play favourites—even for five hundred drachmas. Apollodorus booked me two months ago. How would it look if I cancelled on him now?"

"But it's *five hundred* drachmas!"

"The answer would be the same if it was a thousand. I'm not a slave," I said softly. "I don't need to buy my freedom."

It hit home, like I knew it would. Offended, he drew himself up and thanked me for my time. I started to apologize again, but he cut me off with a cool goodbye and strode from the courtyard.

I sighed as I watched him go. The morning was still a bit chilly, but the back of his orange chiton was stained dark with sweat. He had an attitude problem—like every other slave in this city—but I was sorry to send him home with only my refusal for a reply. I hoped his mysterious owner wouldn't take it too badly.

In fact, he took it very badly indeed.

Chapter 4

"Sorry, guv," the skinny slave said again.

Hearing the words a second time didn't help.

"How could ... why ... why did Apollodorus change his mind?" I finally found my voice. "His banquet's tomorrow! The pastries are made! The eels are marinating! *I've already bought the sacrificial lamb!*"

The slave licked his lips. At least he looked sorry.

I passed a hand across my eyes. "Perhaps I should speak with him?"

The man shook his head mournfully. "Won't make no difference, will it? He's already done a bunk. Porter says he were headin' for Rhodes."

Rhodes! The slave nodded, though I was fairly sure I hadn't said the word out loud. I clamped my teeth together and fought to control my temper.

"Thank you for passing on your master's wishes," I said at last, my voice as cold as Boreas. The man didn't deserve it, but I couldn't bring myself to sound any friendlier. Not after receiving such news.

The slave bobbed his head and scuttled off on stick-like legs, leaving me pale and fuming in the courtyard.

Apollodorus had left the city.

Apollodorus. Mr. Responsibility. Mr. Next-In-Bloody-Line for the city's archonship. Why would one of Athens's most important statesmen, one of Athena's most devout followers, "do a bunk" the day before the Great Panathenaea? It didn't make any sense! I smelled a rat—and it wasn't my cooking. I never serve rodent.

"What was he banging on about, then?" Gorgias asked, sauntering into the sunny courtyard. His chiton was fastened at one shoulder the way a tradesman or peasant would wear it. His hands still bore the chalky traces of his morning's work. He was devouring an apple with noisy gusto.

"Apollodorus just cancelled."

Gorgias choked on a piece of apple, coughed, and spat it out, narrowly missing the household altar. I noticed Irene lurking behind the well. She was ostensibly sweeping the courtyard, but I could tell from the satisfied smirk on her face that she'd overheard every word of my conversation with Apollodorus's slave. I scowled at her and she flounced off, sliding me a huffy backwards glance. Nasty old gorgon.

"You're joking!" Gorgias said.

I turned my attention back to him. "Do I look like a bloody comedian? Apparently he's buggered off. Gone to Rhodes."

"*Rhodes!* But—"

"I know," I cut him off. "Have you been 'round the Agora yet? Did you hear anything about this?"

Gorgias frowned and tugged at his beard. "I was at the market earlier, but I heard nowt about Apollodorus." And then, as he realized what the news meant to me, his voice softened. "Ah bollocks, I'm sorry, Pelops. You were counting on this one, weren't you?"

"Yes." I sank down dejectedly on one of the benches. "Yes, I was."

In fact, I'd been cooking for the event all morning and had only just stopped for a quick bite to eat. Needless to say, all thoughts of lunch had fled with the messenger slave. I couldn't believe Apollodorus had done this to me. His banquet was to have been a sumptuous feast. The perfect prelude to the Great Panathenaea. I'd even beaten out The Sicilian for the job.

Gorgias sat down beside me. "You think Mithaecus had anything to do with it?" he asked, his thoughts obviously on the same path as my own. "I mean, it wouldn't be the first time that dodgy git tried to bugger up a job for you, would it?"

I sniffed at the name. Mithaecus the Sicilian was considered the best celebrity chef in Athens—or at least he had been until I'd burst onto the scene. Why the Athenians were so enamoured of him was quite beyond me. He was a flashy little prat, I suppose, with that bright yellow chiton he always wore. And he did have his own line of cookery scrolls. And he served all his banquets on the newest red-figure pottery, which he'd had decorated with pictures of tuna and rays. Oh, he was showy all right, but did he have it where it counts? Not to my mind. The recipes in his much-vaunted scrolls read like a child's writing tablet, each one a three-ingredient wonder. As in, I wonder why anybody would want to eat it.

I sniffed again just thinking about him. Could Mithaecus have convinced Apollodorus to change his banquet plans? That he would *want* to do so, I didn't question. My culinary creations made his look like something the household dog would spew up—and he was a jealous little Phthonos of a man. I almost lost out on a job last month because he'd been slandering me. Then there was the time he'd tried to bribe Krysippos to sell me week-old eels instead of the fresh ones I had requested. And the day he'd stood up in the Agora denouncing my roast lamb as an affront to the gods. Of *course* he'd be tickled if Apollodorus cancelled his party. But could Mithaecus have engineered such a thing?

"I don't think so," I shook my head reluctantly. "Even if he did persuade Apollodorus to fire me, what could he possibly have offered him to miss out on the Panathenaea?"

Gorgias was silent for a moment. "He's a right bog-eyed sprat though," he said, unwilling to let the Sicilian off the hook.

"He is," I agreed.

Gorgias sighed heavily. "Well, at least you've still got the other festival parties."

"Right."

The other parties. Symposia for middle class misers. Cheese-paring drachma pinchers who insisted the hired waiters eat before they arrived. Whose tables were set so high, their guests could barely reach up to snag a morsel of food. Whose stewards were always sent around afterwards to argue about the size of the bill. Such ilk were hardly worth my efforts.

Apollodorus's symposion had been my coup, my introduction into the kitchens of the Athenian upper crust. Perhaps my other clients weren't quite as miserly as they seemed at the moment, but they couldn't hold a lamp to a patron of Apollodorus's standing. And besides, none of them would pay me enough to buy my own set of crockery—not after I'd reimbursed Meidias for the ones that had been broken the other night.

I sighed. Gorgias reached over to pat my shoulder.

"Fancy a bite of lunch?" he asked. "I found some nice olives at the Agora. I think even you'll approve."

I nodded glumly and followed him back to the kitchen.

It had been just over a year since I'd staggered off a merchant ship at Piraeus, alone, unknown, and very, very seasick. It had been a calculated risk on my part to board a ship bound for Athens, though I'd made sure to sacrifice a black and white bull to Poseidon before doing so. After all, having rejected his advances, it was unwise of me in the extreme to attempt to sail his oceans. The Sea God can only kill with salt water, though he could—and did— make my life challenging with fresh. Ever since I'd turned down the offer to become his lover, I had made a special point of staying away from oceans and estuaries. But for whatever reason (I did not fool myself into thinking he'd actually accepted my sacrifice), Poseidon had not despatched me on that particular voyage, though the waters had been so turbulent, I'd found myself wishing more than once that he'd just drown me and be done with it.

I'd never sailed before, never even frequented dockyards, and upon landing at Piraeus, I'd found myself utterly bewildered by the clamour of the busy port. Sailors shouted for their pay, merchants bawled their wares—*Onions! Anchovies! Leeks!*—while flute girls called out merchandise of a different kind in high, musical voices. All of this over the constant clatter of oars and the deafening clang of pipes and fittings.

It had been Gorgias who had noted the unsteady steps of a foreigner. Gorgias who had offered a kind word and a helping hand. He had been at the port supervising the loading of a shipment of his amphorae. One look at my green face, and he'd helped me over to the nearest taverna for a cup of wine. Upon discovering I had neither friend nor family in the whole of Greece, he had offered me the hospitality of his home. A potter showing kindness to a prince. Though he was almost ten years my senior, he was the best friend I'd ever had.

"Hey, Dadias. Hey, Pelops." Ansandra greeted us as we entered the kitchen. "How's it hanging?"

Gorgias gave her an incredulous look. "*Dadias?*"

Ansandra giggled impishly. At nine years of age, Gorgias's daughter was a cute little thing, all mischievous eyes and dark curls and gangly limbs. Her knees were always skinned or bruised, her fingernails always chewed to the quick, and her hands were usually filthy with some unsavoury thing or another.

Right now, she was feeding bits of grain to the household pet, a tame quail she'd saved from a fiery fate some months before. I'd named him Kabob, in case we ever had to eat him. Ansandra called him "Bob" for short, and if she had any say in the matter, we'd boil our sandals and eat them for soup before we ever got a chance to tuck into Bob. A pity, really. Under Ansandra's tender ministrations, Bob had become easily the fattest quail I'd ever laid eyes on.

"All right, Sprout?" I greeted her. "Helloooo, lunch," I cooed to the quail.

Ansandra stuck her tongue out at me, then grinned and dashed a few more seeds on the ground for Bob. He gobbled them up, making happy chuckling noises.

"Whoa, whoa! Slow down, sunshine!" Gorgias caught Ansandra's shoulder as she made to run past us. "Where are you off to in such a hurry, then?"

"The Amazons have just attacked the Greeks," she explained, trying unsuccessfully to shrug off his hand. "They sneaked up on us at night while we were sleeping, the dirty great buggers. But don't worry, we've got better swords. Shields too." She squirmed. "Let go, Dad, or I'll miss the battle! Hermogenes is waiting!"

"Ansandra, I thought I told you not to be playing about with slaves. And Hermogenes is too old to be playing games."

"Da-ad!" she wailed. "Hermogenes is only a couple of years older than me!"

"More like five years older," her father corrected.

"Plus he's the only one who lets me be a soldier! I don't want to be a dumb wife sitting at home with some stupid loom. And I don't want to be an Amazon, either!"

"Who says you should be an Amazon?" Gorgias asked, sidetracked.

"Elpinice does. And Damo."

"Nico's daughters?"

"They say if I'm not going to be a wife, then I have to be an Amazon. Damo says it's not *appropriate* for me to be a Greek soldier." Ansandra rolled her eyes with undiluted disgust for such obvious irrationality. "But I *don't* want to be an Amazon, or a wife, and Hermogenes doesn't make me." Her expression was mutinous.

Gorgias hesitated. His own wife, Helena, had died almost six years before in the same plague that had taken out a third of Athens's citizenry. Ever since then, Gorgias couldn't seem to bring himself to discipline his only child. He did keep Irene to watch over her, but The Gorgon was almost as indulgent as Gorgias was when it came to her charge, and Ansandra ran circles around them both. I thought Gorgias was probably setting himself up for more trouble further down the road, but he never asked my opinion on the matter and I kept my thoughts to myself.

"Where's Irene?" he asked now.

Ansandra shrugged under his grip. "Weaving," she answered, injecting an impressive amount of distaste into the word. "Again."

Gorgias frowned at her. "We need new cloth. It's important. Maybe you should be helping her. That's what women do. They help with the household weaving."

Ansandra scowled right back at him. "I'm not a woman! I'm just a girl. And I asked if I should help with the weaving—I did! But Irene didn't want my help. She said she doesn't know how I always manage to get the threads dirty even when my hands are clean and that even if I managed to stay clean I never pay attention enough to get a nice tight weave because I'm always getting distracted by thinking about battles and fighting and stuff and she doesn't know what the world is coming to these days when girls would rather play war than weave clothes. I told her the Amazons were all girls and they sure didn't sit around on their bums all day weaving, but if they had, then we wouldn't have had anybody to fight except maybe the Spartans and we wouldn't have any stories to tell by the fire and then we'd all just sit there looking at each other and that would be dumb. Then she gave me a honey cake and told me to go and play."

Gorgias regarded his still-squirming daughter, then he sighed and lifted his hand. "Go!" he waved her off. "Save us from the Amazons then. Did you want some lunch first?"

"I already ate," she called over her shoulder. "Thanks for the olives, Dadias! Bye, Pelops!"

"Cheers, Sprout."

"I hope you saved some olives for us!" Gorgias bellowed after her.

But she was gone. She had not, in fact, saved any olives for us.

I set the now empty olive dish to one side and rubbed my chin thoughtfully. "How about some scallops for lunch, Dadias?"

"Now, don't you start!" Gorgias scowled, pointing a warning finger at me. He continued to grumble under his breath while he poured us each a cup of watered wine.

I grinned to myself and started heating a pan of white wine and herbs to poach the scallops. I'd purchased the shellfish for

Apollodorus's feast. There was no sense in letting them go bad. Gorgias laid out the bread while the scallops simmered.

I had learned not to poach anything in water anymore. Too often, the water would boil over or turn unaccountably tepid, resulting in soggy, undercooked food. Poseidon was clearly not ready to forgive me anytime soon. The unintended consequence of this was that my cooking had actually improved, for most fish and shellfish were more flavourful when poached in wine rather than the plain water utilized by other chefs—a little fact I hoped Poseidon would never have cause to discover.

I brought the pan, steaming and fragrant, into the andron and drizzled some olive oil over them for added richness. We tore off chunks of hard bread and began eating.

"You know, these aren't half bad," Gorgias said after a few bites. "You should think about doing this for a living."

"Ha, ha."

We both went after the same scallop. I won. Gorgias consoled himself with another.

"Truly, these are cracking," he said. "Thank you, my friend."

My mouth full of scallop, I contented myself with a bulging smile. We finished the meal in companionable silence.

"So, what do you say to a supper of eels and pastries tonight?" I asked casually as we mopped up the last of the scallop juices with our bread.

Still chewing, Gorgias raised his bushy eyebrows.

"I've got the eels and the cakes." I tried to sound nonchalant. "I'm not about to toss them on the midden."

He swallowed his mouthful before answering. "Don't be daft," he protested with a stern rumble. "A few scallops are one thing. But eels, those are pricey, them. You can't afford that!"

Gorgias was a fine potter, but without a wife to manage things, his household was expensive to maintain—even with The Gorgon running the place. When he was between commissions, he and Ansandra choked down sprats only a peasant would consider edible. As far as I knew, eels had never graced the tables of *his* andron. All the more reason to treat him.

I waved off his objections. "Don't worry about it. What else am I going to do with the food? I can't unmake the pastries. Krysippos is hardly going to buy back his eels. And—" I leaned back and sighed heavily, "—what are my chances of finding another customer this close to the festival?"

An hour or so later, I was thinking seriously about a post-lunch afternoon nap, when I found myself summoned to the courtyard.

"My master wishes you to cook a feast for him the day before the Great Panathenaea."

Him. Again.

I narrowed my eyes at the well-groomed slave. His orange chiton seemed overly bright in the mid-afternoon sun. I was beginning to dislike the colour.

"What makes you think today's answer will be any different from yesterday's?"

"News of Apollodorus's little 'holiday' is all over the Agora," he smirked. "Unless you've had another offer, I'm willing to bet my savings the answer will be *very* different."

I wanted to wipe that supercilious smile off his face. Wanted to tell him to take a flying leap off the Parthenon. But a job was a job, I needed the coin, and besides, Athena probably wouldn't appreciate his pampered corpse mucking up the foot of her earthly home.

"Well, I guess it's your master's lucky day then," I said, turning away so I didn't have to see him smirk at me again.

I motioned the slave to follow me into the room where I kept my writing tablets. An altar to Athena and Hestia dominated the space, with a smaller altar for the household gods beside it. A short table leaned in the corner, its mended leg barely supporting several stacks of wax tablets. There was a folding stool against the far wall.

I picked up an old tablet, smoothed the wax with the end of a stylus, and settled myself on the stool. The slave scanned the room, taking in the modest altars, the bare walls. He flared his nostrils (he seemed extraordinarily good at that) before drawing himself up haughtily.

"Shall we discuss the menu first?" I asked him. "Does your master have any personal preferences? And how many people has he invited?"

"It will be an intimate party, ten at the most. As for the food," the slave laced his fingers together as he prepared to recite, "he wants to start with the usual sort of thing. Fresh fruits, olives, some grilled vegetables. But he'd like the shellfish in a spicy sauce."

I nodded and started taking notes.

"Then you'll serve appetizers of figs along with roasted thrushes. He's fond of sea bass, and he wants eels, of course, done up with wine and cherries. And for the main course, your famous roast lamb—the one with plums. Now, for second tables, he's ordered cheese and sesame sweetmeats, quail eggs, cheese, dried fruits and nuts, and several platters of those almond pastries you make."

I had stopped writing after the roast lamb. "Is this a joke?" I demanded, trying to keep my voice calm and reasonable.

The slave looked outraged at the implication. "I never joke," he replied stiffly. He paused and smoothed the folds of his chiton before continuing. "In addition to the food, my master wishes you to secure the services of a certain hetaera. If you'll present yourself at his house later this evening, he'll give you more information about her."

I regarded the slave steadily. He was staring at a point just above my head, his nostrils still slightly flared.

"And where does your master live?" I asked at last.

He told me.

"I'll be there at dusk," I promised.

The slave nodded and left with a swirl of his vile orange chiton.

I remained seated on the stool, staring down at my nearly blank tablet.

I hadn't printed out the whole menu on it because I had already written it elsewhere. The slave with the mysterious master had just requested every single dish that I had planned to serve at Apollodorus's cancelled dinner party.

By the time twilight was falling, I was more than ready to have a sharp word with my new employer. Ready to demand answers to questions about an all-too coincidental menu and a certain ill-fated dinner party.

Then I walked into his house.

For some unfathomable reason, Greeks disapprove of luxury. Any kind of comfort—cushioned chairs, carpeted floors—is seen as fit only for barbarians like Persians or Egyptians who are, presumably, so soft that they require such debauchery. As a result, most Athenian homes are small, simple dwellings. Rectangular in shape, they consist of a series of small rooms wrapped around a modest central courtyard. Floors are of stone or packed dirt, roofs of red clay tile, and walls are constructed with unbaked mud brick. Simple. Functional. Plain.

Well, there's simple and then there's *simple*.

My employer's abode was a rectangle, and the roof was covered in red tiles. But the walls were made of stone rather than mud brick, and the silent porter, who had been waiting for me at the column-flanked door, led me into the courtyard on plastered floors that had been painted with a deep ocean-blue wash. Several very expensive Lydian carpets covered the walls, and even the walls of the smaller rooms boasted painted scenes of gods and heroes. Hanging bronze lamps flickered the frescoes to life. The furniture was sparse—as it was in all Athenian homes—but the few tables and chairs I could see were beautifully decorated with inlays of ivory, silver, and gold. Silver bowls of flowers and scented leaves perfumed the air.

It had been a long time since I'd seen such luxury.

The citizen was in his courtyard, a lovely space with a pink stone floor and an elaborate marble altar to Zeus the Protector. There was a well in the northwest corner of the yard. A lush garden with several dozen small trees and shrubs refreshed the eye, while aromatic plants gave up their sun-warmed scent to the cool twilight air. In Athens, water is a precious commodity. Only the very rich could afford to waste it on lush pleasure gardens such as these.

As for my client, he had seen a few summers, though they hadn't been hard on him (a healthy supply of drachmas probably helped with that too). Dark and handsome in the way of most Greeks, he was dressed less flamboyantly than his slave, but the linen of his white chiton was very fine and its purple border had been woven with an intricate pattern of leaves and vines. His cloak, too, was purple, the sort of pure purple achieved when dyers use rare snail shells rather than the more common (and much less expensive) combination of indigo and madder. He was seated on a marble bench, the pelt of some spotted cat protecting his rump from the chilly stone.

"Ah, Chef Pelops. Come in."

His voice was deep and commanding—and he had a presence to match. Briefly, I wondered if he'd ever been in the theatre. But no, I couldn't imagine him slumming in such a fashion. I guessed he must be among Athens's most influential citizens, likely one of the many statesmen seeking to fill the void left by Perikles's untimely death.

"Good evening," I greeted him politely, then hesitated. I still did not know his name.

"You may call me ... Xenarchus," he said.

"Greetings, Xenarchus."

Now that I was standing in front of him, I found myself utterly incapable of asking my questions. I hated myself for it, but the house—and the man—intimidated me. Me! An ex-Prince.

"I understand Simos has provided you with the menu," he was saying.

"He has."

"Do you have any problems with it?"

I shook my head, hating myself even more. "No, sir. It shouldn't be any trouble. All very fine choices, with some unusual combinations. I think your guests will appreciate your creativity."

Xenarchus waited a few moments. Then, "You are less ... verbose than your competitor," he remarked. "Do you not wish to lecture me about diet? Or expound on your vast culinary talents?"

I shook my head again. "I let my cooking speak for itself," I told him. "And I leave the pontificating to Mithaecus."

It had been the right thing to say. Xenarchus threw his head back and laughed in delight. "I like you, Chef Pelops," he said warmly. "I'm looking forward to your feast."

There didn't seem to be much I could say to that.

"I will, of course, expect only the very best quality—both in ingredients and presentation."

"Naturally."

He paused and stroked his beard.

"Simos tells me he broached the question of the ... entertainment?"

"He mentioned nothing of cithara players or dancers, but he did tell me you wanted a hetaera and—"

"Not just any hetaera!" Xenarchus interrupted.

I closed my mouth.

"I want one in particular. Daphne of Megara."

I frowned, unfamiliar with the name. "I'm not sure I—"

"She's very new, just in from the north. And—"he lowered his voice "—still a maiden."

I blinked. A virgin courtesan. What a concept.

"She's glorious," he continued, his eyes softening at the thought. "Her skin is like the finest honey, smooth and sweet. Her hair is so black, it's almost blue. And unbound, it falls to her waist. She smells—" He paused and breathed in. "—like hyacinth."

I chewed the inside of my mouth as I considered him. He appeared to be in something of a bad way.

"Forgive me, sir, but … why do you need me to hire her?" I asked, bringing him back to reality. "You seem to know more about her than I do." At least he'd *seen* the woman.

He rubbed his nose uncomfortably. "Well, that's the problem … I can't find her. I know she's still here in Athens. I would have heard if she'd left."

"Uh …" I hesitated. "You know I am a chef, yes? A man who prepares food?"

Xenarchus's eyes hardened. "You have a *problem* with my request?" His voice had lost its friendly tone.

"Of course not," I hastened to say.

"Good. I would hate for you to lose any other commissions."

I gulped.

"You are a professional chef. That means that you are in and out of all the best homes in Athens. You see and hear things that others would not. Daphne has a sister here—a hetaera named Neaera. I understand she's been hired for Lysander's festival banquet, and that you are to prepare the food."

I nodded, feeling a little sick to my stomach.

"Then I would imagine it would be best for you to start with her."

"Lysander's symposion is two days from now," I protested. "I won't be able to talk to Neaera until then."

He inclined his head. "I don't expect Daphne to attend my festivities tomorrow. But eight days from now, I want you to prepare a second banquet for me. A special feast to celebrate the end of the festival. You'll be well paid. And you *will* see to it that Daphne is present."

It was not a request.

I swallowed hard, sketched a quick bow, and left Xenarchus to his fancy courtyard. I already had a job booked for the last day of the festival, but it didn't take a philosopher to figure out that Kallias, like Apollodorus, would be overcome by a sudden urge to see the sights in Rhodes. Xenarchus knew a little too much about my business affairs—and he had power enough to affect them. Who was he? Just what kind of influence did he wield in the city? And why had he fingered me to help him find this Daphne of Megara?

THIS IS KINDYNOS!

At the Theatre of Dionysus...

ALEXANDROS: Thank you, gentlemen, and welcome to KINDYNOS, the Peloponnesian game show sensation that comes to you all the way from distant Messenia! For those of you who are joining us for the first time, my name is Alexandros, son of Trebekeos, and I am your host. This is the first round of today's contest. And these are the six categories the contestants will be dealing with: **CITY STATES**, **STATUES AND SCULPTORS**, **WINES OF THE WORLD**, **SEA BATTLES**, **INDOOR PLUMBING**, and **KNOW YOUR GODS**. Diomedes, as returning champion, you have the honour of first selection. Choose a category as well as an amount.

DIOMEDES: Thank you, Alexandros. I'd like **KNOW YOUR GODS** for 100 obols.

ALEXANDROS: Very well. **KNOW YOUR GODS**, it is. The Big Twelve are easy, but how well do you know the lesser deities? The first answer is: I cover the sky with my raven dark wings.

DIOMEDES: Who is Nyx?

ALEXANDROS: That is correct, sir. Nyx, the goddess of night. Mother of Sleep, Death, Strife, Pain, and the three Fates.

Applause

ALEXANDROS: Select again.

DIOMEDES: **KNOW YOUR GODS** for 200.

ALEXANDROS: My fingers are the colour of roses and I like to sport a saffron robe.

DIOMEDES: Who is Eos?

ALEXANDROS: The goddess of dawn. Right again, Diomedes!

Applause

ALEXANDROS: Select again. You're up to 300 obols.

DIOMEDES: I'd like **KNOW YOUR GODS** for 300, please.

ALEXANDROS: I rule over the dream spirits and often appear in the dreams of kings and rulers.

DIOMEDES: Who is Morpheus?

ALEXANDROS: Very good! You're up to 600 now.

Applause

ALEXANDROS: Select again, please.

DIOMEDES: I'm going to have to go with **KNOW YOUR GODS** for 400.

ALEXANDROS: Right you are then, **KNOW YOUR GODS** for 400. My wings are purple and my beard is spiked with ice.

DIOMEDES (pausing): Who is Boreas?

ALEXANDROS: You are correct again, Diomedes! Boreas, one of the four directional Anemoi, or wind gods. Good work! That was a tricky one.

Applause

ALEXANDROS: Now Diomedes, I want to take a moment to caution you here. You're up to 1000 obols. That's almost 167 drachmas. You'll have 1500 obols—250 drachmas—if you can wrap up this category. But any wrong answer will be deducted from your score. Go ahead and select, please.

DIOMEDES (nervously): I'll take **KNOW YOUR GODS** for 500, Alexandros.

ALEXANDROS: Okay, for 500 obols, the answer is: I am the spirit of envy and jealousy and have been known to disguise myself as a winged love god.

DIOMEDES: Who is Nemesis?

ALEXANDROS: Oh, that is incorrect! You lose 500 obols.

DIOMEDES: Who is Zelos?

ALEXANDROS: I'm sorry, you only get one try, Diomedes.

DIOMEDES: Who is Momos? Who is Oizys? Who is Eris?

ALEXANDROS: Oh, you *are* grasping at straws, aren't you? You're wrong again. And let me remind you once more, you only get one shot at each question. The correct answer is Phthonos.

DIOMEDES: Phthonos! Who the fuck is Phthonos?

ALEXANDROS: Please, sir! That kind of language is not permitted in the Theatre. For future reference, Phthonos is the god of envy. A minor god, I'll grant you, but still a deity.

DIOMEDES: A minor god! A minor god? I've never heard of a fucking god called Phthonos! Where do you get these sodding questions from anyhow?

ALEXANDROS: Please control yourself, sir!

DIOMEDES: This is bullshit! This is all bullshit! Give me back my 500 obols!

ALEXANDROS: I'm sorry, sir. That's not possible.

DIOMEDES: You son of a bitch! I want my money back! Ouch! What are you doing? Leave me alone! I'm not going anywhere till I get my money. Ow! Get your sodding hands off me! Fuck!

Chapter 5

With so many unanswered questions, I did what I've been doing ever since I fetched up in Athens. I went to find Gorgias.

Like all his clay-slinging mates, Gorgias maintained a house and adjoining shop in a neighbourhood named after Keramos, the hero of potters. A son of Dionysus and Ariadne, Keramos won Athens's lifetime achievement award by single-handedly founding the Athenian pottery industry. His special emphasis on the production of wine-vessels had secured him both fame and fortune, as well as the position of number one son in his father's grape-loving heart.

Located just northeast of the Agora and bounded on one side by the Panathenaic Way, the Inner Kerameikos is filled with the one- or two-storey houses and workshops of Athens's potters, as well as her sundry metalsmiths, tanners, sculptors, and other craftsmen. The neighbourhood also boasts a fair number of prostitutes, though *they* tend to congregate around the main entrance of the city. From there they can service any not-so-weary travellers passing through the double-arched Dipylon Gate. These little houses of Aphrodite—more like tiny stalls really—spring up all along the Way and, for an obol or two, you can find true love for as long as the mood is upon you.

The evening was cool for a change and I wasn't weary, but the mood was most definitely not upon me. Although our street is only a few blocks east of the city's entryway, I left the Panathenaic Way well before the Dipylon Gate's cluster of curtained stalls and turned onto the tanners' street. This was narrower than the main road, and it took me slightly out of my way, but it was considerably quieter and, though the fumes from the tanneries could be truly noxious, they were somewhat less so at night. I often came this way after a job.

I gave the Herm at the beginning of the street a friendly pat as I passed by. There were Herms all over Athens. Essentially rectangular columns with an erect phallus halfway up and the head of a grinning Hermes on top, the Herms marked entrances, roads, and crossroads. In fact, there were so many of them at the northwest entrance to the Agora that most people referred to the area as simply "The Herms."

Probably the most famous Herm stood guard at the entrance to the Acropolis. Carved by the talented Alcamenes, it bore an uncanny resemblance to the god it represented, and I often wondered if Hermes had modelled for it. The Alcamenes Herm was particularly well-endowed, and I suspected that even if Hermes had not actually posed for it, no doubt he heartily approved of it.

But if the Herms in the Kerameikos were less accurate or refined than the one on the Acropolis, they were still just as cheerful and perky, and many people touched them in passing for good luck.

Because the house I shared with Gorgias was located at a crossroad, we had a Herm right beside our door. The marker had a decidedly odd cast to its face, as if wondering how it had ever ended up in such a strange place. Our street was narrow, dark, and not terribly clean, but then so were all the other neighbourhood streets in Athens. Ours, at least, had the added benefit of its proximity to the Panathenaic Way and from there to the clay pits outside the city boundaries (for Gorgias) and the Agora (for me). In order to get first pick of the freshest ingredients, most days I was up and at the shops even before the bell had sounded to signal the market's opening.

Nyx had long since covered the land with her ink-dark cloak, and even with the lamp, it was difficult to see where I was going. I jumped over the visible filth and grimaced when my sandals squelched through some of the less obvious bits. I saw only a mangy cat (which I avoided), a couple of the Scythian archers who guarded the streets (I nodded politely to them), and a boisterous group of late-night revellers on their way to crash some poor sod's dinner party. I shielded my lantern and hid in the shadow of a Herm until they staggered past. I did not want to think about dinner parties at the moment.

Fortunately, Gorgias had not been thinking about parties either. I found him relaxing quietly at home enjoying a last cup of wine before bed.

His house was surprisingly large and airy, a holdover from the pottery shop's more prosperous times. The front door opened onto a corridor, which led into a south-facing courtyard bounded on three sides by pillars. The floors were packed dirt, but the pillars supported a sturdy wooden balcony, which wrapped around the courtyard and gave access to the upstairs bedrooms and the women's hall. A wooden staircase led from the courtyard up to the second floor. There were, several storerooms, a kitchen, a modestly decorated andron, and a separate room, accessible only from the street, which served as Gorgias's workshop. Walls were painted a tasteful red, the golden wood of the trim provided a nice contrast, and the white baseboards lightened any dark corners. Despite my upbringing in more noble surroundings, I found I far preferred the easy comfort of this home to any palace I'd ever lived in.

Gorgias's garden was the heart of the house, and it was here that most of the living took place. His courtyard might not have been up to Xenarchus's standards, but it did have its own well and enough room for a decent herb garden. There was also a small but fine household altar in addition to several comfortably cushioned benches—one of which was nestled amidst a lush patch of pink geraniums which Helena had planted before she died. Gorgias was lying on it (the bench, not the patch of geraniums) when I arrived.

As soon as he heard my step, he took one look at my face and waved me over to one of the other benches. I slouched down with a sigh and rubbed my ivory shoulder. It had started aching as soon as I'd left Xenarchus's house. Gorgias nudged the cup of wine toward me.

"Rough night, then?"

I picked up the cup and took a healthy swallow. "You have no idea," I told him.

He waited.

"Are you familiar with a citizen by the name of Xenarchus?" I asked after a long moment.

His bushy brows crowded together in a frown and he propped himself up on his elbows. "*Xenarchus* is your mystery patron?" His tone was odd.

I sat up quickly. "Why? Is that bad?"

Gorgias hesitated. Then, "Nooo," he said, drawing the word out.

"I would have preferred a nice, resounding, unequivocal 'no,'" I told him.

He shrugged. "Sorry. There're a lot of stories about Xenarchus. That's all."

"And they're all bad?"

"Nooo."

There was that squishy "no" again.

"It's just that they're conflicting," he explained. "He's a bit shadowy really. Nobody seems to know much about him, do they? His mum was from Athens. No, she was from Argos. His dad was at the battle of Salamis. No, it was Marathon. He's a citizen. He's not a citizen. He engineered the alliance with Megara. No, it was with Corcyra."

He paused. A faint note of reproof had entered his voice. I knew it was meant for me and I scowled. I cared little for Athenian politics—past or present—and my apathy irked Gorgias's democracy-loving heart. Having grown up in a monarchy, I found the Athenian concept of government a strange one. All that everybody-gets-a-vote nonsense just seemed wrong to me. After all, how much did your average Jason really know about mounting a festival or foreign policy or waste management? In addition, as a foreigner, I wasn't even permitted to participate in her much-vaunted democratic processes—all of which, I kept telling Gorgias, explained my lack of interest. What I didn't tell him was that all those alliances and rebellions and factions and infighting reminded me far too much of my old life in Lydia. A life I had resolved to leave behind me.

"So where's the truth?" I asked, ignoring his unspoken reproach.

"Zeus knows," Gorgias shrugged. "The only thing I could tell you for certain is he's bloody stinking rich. Judging from all the public works he's sponsored."

"What kind of works?"

"The usual." Gorgias sat up and splashed a little more wine into the cup. "Putting on plays and building temples. Holding sacrifices, outfitting triremes, entertaining and feasting other citizens."

"Yes, he certainly does that."

"He wants you to cook for him?"

I nodded.

"But ..." Gorgias frowned again, puzzled. "Isn't that what you were after? Xenarchus may be a bit dodgy, but he's hardly the type to get takeaway from a sprat bar. He's even more powerful than Apollodorus."

I swirled the wine before drinking it down. "It may be," I agreed, passing the cup back to him with a nod. "But I don't think much of his way of hiring chefs. And if he's such a pillar, why does he need me to find him a hetaera?"

Gorgias blinked. "He wants you to get him a woman?"

I nodded morosely. "Yeah. Some Daphne of Megara. Apparently her sister Neaera's a hetaera too."

"Neaera!"

I looked over at him, but the lamp had burned low and I couldn't see his face. "You know her?" I asked.

"Every red-blooded male in Athens knows Neaera." He said her name respectfully, almost reverently.

"Well, I don't, and last time I checked my blood was as red as yours."

"Oh, you know Neaera," he assured me. "She's got a statue in the Agora, hasn't she?"

"She has a *statue*?"

"A bronze. Commissioned by Diodotus." He nodded. "Phidias did the work," he added, naming the most famous sculptor in Athens.

I was still trying to get my head around the original concept. "Are you telling me a hetaera—a courtesan!—has a statue in the Agora?"

"And why the chuff not?" Gorgias shrugged, mystified by my reaction. "You'd rather see a statue of some poncy politician standing there with his tackle hanging out?"

"Of course not! But—" I shook my head slowly. "I'll never understand you Athenians."

"She's a right looker," Gorgias explained. "The woman could give Aphrodite a run for her money. Not that she would win, of course," he added quickly. "No mortal could. Not against a goddess. But it would be close, Pelops, very close."

I knew better than to read too much into his tone. As far as I knew, Gorgias hadn't even glanced at another woman since Helena had died—though he claimed that Aphrodite had paid him a visit one long, lonely night.

He filled the cup again and took a slow sip. "You know," he leaned closer and lowered his voice, "they say Neaera invented Lion on the Cheese Grater."

"Lion on the *what*?"

"Cheese grater."

"What in Hades is that?"

He sat back with a huffy sigh. "Bollocks, don't you know anything?" he demanded testily.

"I'm a foreigner," I reminded him. "Remember?"

He opened his mouth to retort, then changed his mind and stroked his beard thoughtfully. "That's true, isn't it?" he conceded. "I keep forgetting."

"So?" I prompted.

"So, what?"

"Lion on the Cheese Grater?"

"It's a position."

"A position."

His frowned at my flat tone. "You know, for flute girls and hetaeras. They charge different amounts depending on the position."

"I know that," I said loftily, though I knew it only because I'd overheard several patrons talking about it. Apparently something called The Racehorse was all the rage in Athens this season.

"So what is Lion on the Cheese Grater?" I asked. Again.

"Well," Gorgias cleared his throat. "You'll have to ask Neaera, won't you."

"You don't know!"

"Oh, I know," he assured me. "But I wouldn't want to spoil your ... surprise." His eyes twinkled in the moonlight.

I waited patiently.

"It's very expensive," he added after a moment. "The *most* expensive."

"But *what* is it?" I insisted.

Gorgias lowered the wine cup and looked around the courtyard. We were alone. The slaves had long since sought their sleeping couches. He bent his head to my ear and I leaned closer. He glanced around again, took a deep breath ... and burst out laughing.

I sat back and gave him a disgusted look. "You know you really are juvenile sometimes, Gorgias."

He chuckled into his beard, quite delighted with himself, and passed me the cup again. I took it and slouched back on the bench. We sat in easy silence. The night air was soft, scented with the herbs from my garden. A whisper of a breeze ruffled the feathery fronds of the dill. Kabob foraged quietly in the plants.

Finally Gorgias stretched and pushed himself off the bench. "Well, that's it for me, my friend. Are you ready to turn in?"

"In a bit. Leave me a lamp, will you? I still need to check

the pantry to make sure I haven't forgotten anything. I've got a thousand things to do in the next few days—not the least of which is to find Xenarchus his hetaera."

"I never knew Neaera had a sister," Gorgias said, shaking his head.

"Well, I hope you're the only one who didn't—" I paused, stifling a mighty yawn, "—because, lions on cheese graters or not, I need to find the woman before the end of the Panathenaea. I've a nasty feeling this shadowy citizen of yours does not tolerate failure."

After Gorgias shambled off to his sleeping couch, I stretched out full-length on the courtyard bench and wedged a cushion behind my head. I had a lot to think about.

It was during quiet moments like these that the course of my life seemed wildly improbable to me. How was it possible that I had gone from prince to celebrity chef? The question still teased at me, though at the time, it had seemed my only option.

Despite Tantalus's abrupt departure for the underworld—and the consequent royal job vacancy—I could not have assumed his rule even if I'd had the support of all the factions among the nobility (which I did not). After all, how could anyone respect a king whose own father saw him as entrée rather than heir? I would have been laughed off the throne. Or forcibly removed from it. No, I had known almost immediately that I would have to leave Sipylus—leave Lydia entirely, for that matter—and try to make my own way in the world.

Unfortunately, being a prince doesn't exactly prepare one for any sort of gainful employment should one's fortunes reverse so dramatically. Oh, I was able to throw a mean spear, handily skewer any enemy with my sword, and order slaves running about from dawn until dusk. But having experienced death firsthand, I did not wish to be a warrior and, while motivating slaves was well within my skill set, the role of slave supervisor seemed decidedly beneath me.

It was the palace cook who set me on my present path.

While wandering aimlessly through the palace in the days following my demise, I overheard a conversation between the cook and the steward. They were discussing the relative merits of the stew that Tantalus had fashioned, and were arguing whether or not his choice of herbs had been entirely appropriate. It gave me an odd feeling to hear described in such terms what was essentially myself, but these concerns quickly fell away when the import of the cook's words sunk in.

"I would've used dill," he was saying in a superior tone. "With much more garlic. To mask the gaminess, you know."

"Are you mad, man?" I interjected, striding into the kitchen.

All colour drained from his face. "Your Highness! I did not mean … forgive me … I …"

"Dill?" I repeated, not bothering to hide my incredulity. "In a stew of red meat? Don't be absurd! Even oregano would be a better choice than dill. But rosemary would have clearly been the way to go, complementing the meat without overwhelming it." I gave a scornful snort. Dill, indeed.

Having had my say, I swept out of the room, leaving the two men standing there gaping at me, their eyes agog. It was only when I was halfway down the corridor that it occurred to me to wonder how exactly I had known what the perfect seasoning would be for such a dish. I had never so much as chopped an onion in my life, how could I know how to flavour a stew?

But somehow the knowledge was there, fully formed in my mind.

That night, while the palace slept, I crept down to the cavernous kitchen and began to cook. Breads, stews, soups, roasts, tarts and dainties, appetizers and casseroles. They flowed from my hands as if I had been preparing food my whole life. Suckling pig stuffed with apples and herbs, eels with sour cherries, deep-fried fritters drizzled with honey and dusted with cracked peppercorns. The air was redolent with myriad scents each, to my newly discerning nose, both succulent and distinct. By the time the palace cook burst into the kitchen the following morning, jaw falling open in disbelief at the sight before him, I had found my new career path.

And so here I was in Athens, the culinary centre of the world, building a life for myself as a celebrity chef.

I lay on Gorgias's bench and stared up at all the sparkling heroes in the sky, pondering the vagaries of life (specifically mine), the demands of the wealthy (Xenarchus), and the nature of divine beings who, while apparently meaning all the best, somehow still managed to bugger up my aforementioned life. I was afraid—very afraid—of what Dionysus and Hermes might make of Xenarchus's well-planned and elegant symposion. Nothing good, I was certain.

I couldn't even have a word with them about it either, sorely though I might be tempted. Some of the northern barbarian tribes argued or bargained with their gods. Their gods enjoyed it. Expected it. My own? Not so much. My gods could destroy a mortal's life out of simple irritation, I wasn't about to risk offending them outright, especially not after my father had given it the old Akademia try. I suppressed a shudder, thinking of his fate. No, the gods' ire was not something I wished to arouse. The best I could hope for was that Dionysus's gossipy grapevine would fail him and my two deities of delight would not hear about Xenarchus's party.

The party.

The food, the wine, the servers, the … hetaera. I sighed, tallying up the tasks ahead of me. Once preparations for both of Xenarchus's symposions were underway—not to mention the preparations for all the other dinner feasts—I would have little time to inquire after the reputedly ravishing Daphne (let alone large cats on kitchen utensils). First things first, though. Which meant planning for tomorrow's feast. I pushed myself off the bench, caught up the small oil lamp and padded over to the kitchen.

Most of the ingredients had already been purchased, some of the pastries had already been made—I had, after all, expected to prepare them for someone else—but I would need to pick up more shellfish first thing in the morning to replace the ones Gorgias and I had eaten for lunch and…

Without warning, my feet slid out from under me.

"*Ares's balls!*"

The lamp flew from my hand, crashing down and plunging

me into darkness. Wildly, I clawed at the door frame, wrenching my bad shoulder, and just managed to catch myself before I fell. I straightened, still clinging to the frame.

What in Hades…?

The kitchen was as dark as a blackened fish. I couldn't see a thing. I bent down and lowered my hand to the floor. It was wet. I rubbed my fingers together. Slippery. With a sick feeling in my stomach, I brought my fingers up to my nose. Could the gods be that cruel?

I sniffed … and closed my eyes in despair. It appeared they could.

I had slipped in olive oil.

Slumping against the door frame, I dropped my face in my hands.

Olive oil is the mainstay of any civilized cuisine. The one essential ingredient upon which all celebrity chefs agree. Personally, I always use the best quality, preferring the pressings from an early harvest. It's expensive, naturally, but no self-respecting chef would use anything else. Two days ago, I had purchased the largest amphora available. Clear, golden, with a heady, fruity scent, it was oil of the finest quality. Given the sort of clientele I was anticipating, it was more than worth the drachmas I had paid for it.

And now my olive oil—my hideously expensive olive oil!—was soaking into Gorgias's kitchen floor.

Cautiously, I slid my feet across the stone tiles, feeling my way to the table where I kept several spare lamps. I lit the wicks and turned to look around me. Perhaps I hadn't lost it all. Perhaps only a small dish of it had spilled.

But of course, this was *my* life.

"Fuck!" I swore crudely as the flickering lamps illuminated the kitchen.

The entire kitchen floor shone greasily in the light, the small yellow flames from the lamps dancing merrily with their reflections. This was no spill from a dish.

"Ares's balls," I cursed again, closing my eyes against the sight.

Strabo and Lais had struck again.

I'd spoken to Gorgias about these two slaves before. Men so hopelessly inept in the kitchen, they could barely hold an olive between two fingers, let alone arrange one on a platter. So foolish, their minds had never been disturbed by an intellectual thought. Unfortunately for me, they were quite skilled at various aspects of pottery making which is, of course, why Gorgias kept them around. At that moment, I cursed him roundly for it.

I could see at a glance what had happened. Some imbecile of a slave had stupidly hung a large three-handled hydrias on the wall hook above my amphora of oil. It was *not* where the jug belonged, and the hook had not been designed to hold its weight. The shattered hydrias lay on the floor beside a fair-sized chunk of the wall. And as for my precious amphora, it had completely tipped over in its stand. A large crack now split its smooth side. The last few drops of oil clung to the jagged edges like a row of golden tears.

I swore again, hoping it would make me feel better.

It didn't.

I righted the amphora, hoping that some oil was still resting in its base.

It wasn't.

I spent the next several minutes reeling off unflattering descriptions of cretinous slaves and cruel, capricious gods. It still didn't help.

The Great Panathenaea only comes around every fourth year. Everybody in Athens celebrates this most important of festivals, which essentially means that everybody in Athens eats themselves bog-eyed for seven days. And because Athena, in addition to all the other gifts she bestowed upon her people, also gave them the olive tree, olive oil is an integral part of the celebrations. Every lamp burns with olive oil. Every winner of every race and contest receives a prize of olive oil. Every single festival dish requires ... olive oil.

I'd been warned to buy early to avoid disappointment. To buy quantity to avoid running out. To buy quality to satisfy the wealthier patrons. And I had! But now here I was, with a thousand things to do before Athena's biggest birthday bash, utterly olive oil–less.

Chapter 6

The Agora is *the* place to be in Athens. The place where all the beautiful people go to see and be seen, and to sneer down their noses at those less attractive than themselves. The place where slaves and working women come to fill their jugs with water and their ears with the latest gossip, and where men come to do the same, though in the case of the latter, it is referred to as "taking part in democracy." Beside the law courts, bread-wives perch like harpies behind their baskets of barley rolls, cackling abuse at customers and non-customers alike. On the marble steps of the Painted Stoa, philosophers share their views on life with any who care to listen (and quite a few who don't). And of course everywhere there are statues of gods in all their different incarnations.

The gods are ridiculously multi-talented, adopting different roles depending on situation or whim. Athena, for example, is the goddess of wise counsel, war, the defence of towns, heroic endeavours, and various useful and elegant arts such as weaving, pottery, cooking, and the like. Each of these incarnations naturally requires separate and select prayers, titles, sacrifices, and statues. And that's just Athena. The other gods are equally gifted—and equally demanding of worship in all their aspects. As a result, the Agora is so saturated with bronze and marble gods that even on a slow day, it always seems quite crowded.

Each time I go to the market, I pass by one of the most famous of these figures, an especially well-rendered bronze of Athena Ergane (the patroness of craftsmen). The statue is a favourite of artisans throughout the city, and it is here that cooks far less talented than myself shuffle behind their displays of ladles and spoons. These second-rate heroes of the kitchen like to boast loudly of their skills and specialties to all who stroll by, the volume of their cries increasing in direct proportion to the girth of the passing citizen.

"Cleanse your stomach of foul winds with my special appetizers!"

"Eat my swordfish and skewer your lover with your fish sword!"

"Increase your stamina! Watch your love stick stand up all night! Try my steamed clams and drive the flute girls wild! Satisfaction guaranteed!"

An easy promise to make. After all, who would admit that their love stick had *not* been up to an all-nighter?

The only cook I recognized was a great bear of a man from Macedonia named Castor. Indeed, he was so large and hairy that few in Athens *wouldn't* recognize him. But although he towered over every man in the city, and possessed enough musculature to handily sacrifice an ox, he had a personality as gentle as a dove. I did not consider him a rival (frankly, he was not skilled enough for that) but he was a good enough cook for the lower-middle classes. Given a few more years of experience, I suspected he might rise even higher, though he would never attain my status. He had, however, always been pleasant to me, offering none of the challenging gibes accorded to me by lesser chefs, and I nodded to him as I passed by. Castor beamed back, obviously pleased by my acknowledgement.

Nestled below the temples and shrines of the Acropolis, the brightly coloured awnings of the Agora beckon to all to mingle, socialize, and shop. And although the renowned statue of Athena Parthenos (Virgin Athena) is tucked out of sight in the Parthenon, the enormous bronze figure of Athena Promakhos (She Who Leads in Battle) stands atop the Acropolis, spear and helmet glinting in the sun, gazing down in approval at the commerce and activity below.

Everything is for sale at the Agora. There are grains from Euboea, baskets of sweet almonds from Naxos, and fine wines from Chios, Lesbos, and Thalos. Under the saffron awnings of the cheese sellers' stalls, pots of soft cheeses are lined up like offerings at a temple. At others, wheels of harder, aged cheeses are wrapped in leaves to keep them fresh. Under the fishmongers' blue and white awnings, fresh fish of every size and shape sparkle in the morning light, while the not-so-fresh fish add their own pungency to the air, overpowering the fruity scent of sun-warmed plums, apples, and dessert grapes.

Normally I take my time going through the market. I stroll past the wreaths and baskets of the perfume sellers' stalls, stop to examine the wares of a tanner or metalworker, trade insults with the bread-wives, and pause to hear the latest scandal. In many ways, I thoroughly enjoy my new life. But I had no time for the sights and smells, or even the gossip of the Agora today. I needed olive oil, shellfish, and a hetaera. Not necessarily in that order.

Athenians like to think they're people of leisure. The sort who use "summer" as a verb. Frowns of disapproval follow those with a bustling gait. Socrates, though respected for the agility of his mind, is the butt of many jokes due to his unfortunate habit of swinging his arms about vigorously whenever he walks anywhere. Despite my hurry, I was careful not to commit that particular sin. Here in Athens, foreigners are closely scrutinized and quickly satirized. When your livelihood depends on your reputation, you learn to adapt to new customs. So instead I sauntered past the stalls and barrows, cloak arranged in the latest style, arms hanging decorously at my side.

I was accompanied by a slave, Ansandra's playmate, Hermogenes. He was a small, wiry lad, on the mouthy side, but bright for all his brashness. Ostensibly he belonged to Gorgias, but the boy was a veritable bull in the pottery shop and, after a disaster involving several specially commissioned funeral urns, he had been summarily banned from the workshop. Gorgias was too softhearted to sell him, so he had foisted him off on me. Fortunately, Hermogenes had proved less of a disaster in the kitchen than in the pottery shop. In fact, most of the time he was quite helpful, and his fresh sense of humour often helped me through the more stressful days. He'd attached himself firmly to me, having apparently decided that his first, best destiny lay in earning his freedom and becoming my disciple, and perhaps one day, becoming a celebrity chef himself (this, right after chariot racer, discus thrower, boxing champion, and hero, of course). As a result, whenever I went shopping, Hermogenes was my impudent shadow.

The stalls and shops had not yet been dismantled and shifted to make room for the Panathenaic procession or the games that would follow, but I could see stacks of lumber on the northeast side of the Agora waiting for the carpenters to hammer up into temporary stands from which the spectators would view the festival. As usual, Hermogenes and I entered by way of The Herms, strolling past various statues and several shrines before we began mingling with the early morning shoppers.

"Where is the statue of Neaera?" I asked suddenly.

Hermogenes glanced up at me as if surprised I didn't know. "At the far end, Chef. Between the Painted Stoa and the Spring House."

"Show me."

Following Hermogenes, I wove my way through the crowd. It was already hot, but the plane trees that line the Agora provided a measure of shade, and the grove of laurel and olive trees around the Altar of the Twelve Gods was a cool resting place for weary shoppers and young men with nothing else to do but posture and make rude comments about passersby. Already small groups of these adolescents were gathered in the grove, carefully positioned to show their nascent musculature to its best advantage.

Hermogenes and I ducked around a donkey cart, flirted with a group of tired-looking flute girls and hopped over several of the open stone channels, which carry overflow from the Spring House to water the Agora's trees. Although many houses have small wells or cisterns, most of Athens relies on water from the Spring House. The spring originates on the slopes of Mount Lycabettus, and its waters are pure and cool and sweeter than any well water. Not coincidentally the building also provides a handy meeting place for the women of the city who fill their jugs each morning from the lion-headed spouts and linger to exchange the news of the day. The statue of Neaera stood by a solitary laurel tree beside the Spring House. The tree, Hermogenes informed me, had mysteriously appeared fully formed one morning. But Hermogenes was known to enjoy a good joke, so I ignored his outrageous claim and concentrated my attention on the statue.

The bronze hetaera was half-clad, with hair cascading down her back and a small, secretive smile playing across her full lips. It was slightly larger than life, with proportions that seemed equally exaggerated: the eyes that much larger, the breasts and hips that much rounder. It was a gorgeous piece, exquisitely crafted. If the real Neaera looked anything like her statue, I no longer doubted that every red-blooded male in Athens knew of her. I wondered if her sister was as lovely. All of a sudden, Xenarchus's commission seemed like less of a hardship.

After admiring the statue for an appropriate length of time,

Hermogenes and I plunged back into the bustle of the market. I had too much to accomplish this morning to spend any more time ogling statuary.

Back in the crowds, I greeted those I knew (not all of whom I liked), paused to sample a ripe plum (it had worms), and stopped to listen to a story (probably untrue) about a certain citizen and a long-haired she-goat. Hermogenes enjoyed this last bit very much. We had to hide briefly behind a cock-eyed statue of Herakles when Meidias and two of his overgrown slaves strutted past. I wasn't in the mood for a loud, lengthy lecture about the importance of taking care of other people's property—especially while his goons stood there flexing their overdeveloped muscles and underdeveloped intellect. I'd pay him for his broken dishes as soon as I had the coin. Until then, it seemed best to avoid him. After Meidias had passed, we moved casually but directly to the green and gold awnings where Talos the Oil Seller had his shop.

Talos was one of the lucky few who could afford a permanent space in the Agora. His shop wasn't huge, but it was nicely situated next to one of the larger plane trees.

"Location, location, location," he liked to say. "It's everything for a businessman like myself."

Maybe so, but the fact that he carried the best olive oil in Athens didn't hurt. Or perhaps I should say he *usually* carried the best olive oil in Athens.

"Sorry, Pelops," he said now with an apologetic shrug. "I'm completely out of first pressings. The Panathenaea, you know."

I knew.

"I've got some fairly decent second pressings ..."

I was already shaking my head. "Not for this crowd."

"Ah, then you've found someone to replace Apollodorus, have you? Excellent news, my friend! That was a rotten trick he played on you."

I pulled a glum face. "You heard about that."

"Heard about it? Everybody heard! And nobody knows what the truth is, so don't waste your breath asking. There are more tales flying around than there are owls in Athens." He gestured toward Hermogenes. "Your slave here could probably tell you more than I can."

"Oh, he has," I said dryly, slanting my shadow a sour look.

Hermogenes grinned, unrepentent. He had, in fact, regaled me with all the stories and speculations surrounding Apollodorus's hastily arranged holiday. Most involved well-endowed women or long-lashed youths. All were wildly implausible. As far as I knew, nobody could explain the man's behaviour. Even his friends in the Assembly were stumped. As for me, I had my own suspicions, though I knew better than to voice them.

Talos clapped a friendly hand on my shoulder. "I'm so happy you found another client on such short notice. It must be that lovely lamb of yours."

"Which won't be quite so lovely if I can't find some decent olive oil."

"True, true." Talos frowned and tugged at his beard. "I hate to suggest this, but I've heard Lamachus still has some first pressings left."

I wrinkled my nose.

"I know," Talos agreed. "But, I don't think you'll have much choice in the matter. Pickings are slim right now." He gestured at a handful of empty stalls. "You see? Many of my colleagues didn't even bother coming today. Tell me, how is it *you* are out of olive oil? Did I not sell you a very large amphora a few days ago?"

I told him about the cracked container and he clucked in sympathy.

"You'd better find yourself a nice goat while you're here," he advised. "Make a sacrifice. It sounds like someone up there has it in for you."

I thanked him for the advice—and the referral—and Hermogenes and I moved over to where Lamachus conducted his business.

"How can I help you, honoured sir?" His voice was as oily as his product.

Unlike Talos, Lamachus had never quite grasped the concept of location. Too cheap to spring for a better spot, he had set up his stall on the very edge of the olive sellers' section, far from the cooling shade of the plane trees. His green and gold awnings were tattered and thin, and did little to keep the amphorae shaded from the hot sun. It was one reason why I never bought from him. The fact that he had a personality to go with his voice was another.

"I need some olive oil," I said. "Preferably from an early harvest before the olives were fully ripe. First pressing. And no windfalls."

Lamachus's eyes opened wide in feigned astonishment. "Of

course," he assured me. "I wouldn't dream of selling such a fine gentleman as yourself an inferior oil. Only the best for the best chef in Athens—"

"Yes, yes," I said, irritated with his obsequious tone. The man was such a toad. "And I'll need to taste it first."

"Of course you do, fine sir. A chef such as yourself should never buy oil without tasting it first—even though I'm sure you'll be delighted with the quality. So light. So fruity. And look at the colour!" He poured a small puddle onto a dish. "Liquid gold, it is. Like the finest honey." He placed his right hand reverently over his heart. "You don't find olive oil of this quality just anywhere, you know."

I dipped my finger in the oil and sampled it. It wasn't as bad as I'd feared. The olives had been a little riper than ideal, but it was rather nice. And it hadn't been sitting in the sun long enough to go rancid.

Lamachus was still extolling its virtues.

"I'll take it," I interrupted him. "I need your largest amphora. Hermogenes here will carry it, if you can spare one of your slaves to help."

"Oh, I'm afraid I didn't bring my *largest* amphorae here today," Lamachus oozed regret. "I have only these small jars. The larger amphorae are at my brother's farm. But for such an important gentleman as yourself, I can surely arrange to have them delivered. There is a small cost, of course, but this is nothing to a man of your means—"

"Yes, alright. I need it today."

Lamachus cringed. "Oh no, sir, the earliest I can have it

delivered is tomorrow. My brother, you see, he's not close to the city and the mules must haul it in and—"

"Fine." I gritted my teeth. "Give me one of your smaller jars for tonight. Tomorrow I need the amphora. I'll be cooking for Lysander, son of Prodicus. Have your slaves bring it directly to his house. As early as possible."

"As early as possible. Of course. A great chef like yourself cannot be without olive oil during the Great Panathenaea and—"

"Without olive oil?" The voice behind me was loud and carrying.

I knew that voice.

"Dear me! *Without olive oil* the day before the Great Panathenaea?" The voice rose in both tone and volume.

I grimaced and turned around to see the dreaded yellow chiton. The Sicilian.

"My dear Pelops," Mithaecus chided, "it makes one wonder if your culinary talents are not grossly exaggerated. If you can't even plan ahead to have enough *olive oil* for the Great Panathenaea, how can anyone expect you to cope with the precise timings involved in a truly fine feast?"

He was surrounded by sycophants—slaves, really, but they fawned over him like flute girls, tittering at his remarks, brushing specks of dust from his splendid yellow garb.

"Mithaecus."

"Pelops, Pelops." Mithaecus shook his head and leaned toward me. "The elite, you know, are very particular about their food and—oh, but wait." He straightened and tapped his beaky nose thoughtfully. "Didn't Apollodorus cancel on you? Yes, that's right. It seems to me I *did* hear something about that. Well, I expect the middle classes are not quite so *exacting* about their parties." He brushed at his spotless chiton and aimed a helpless smile at his entourage. "I mean, if the tuna congeals while waiting for the barley rolls to finish baking, why, it isn't such a tragedy for those who don't know any better, is it?"

His sycophants snickered on cue. So did Lamachus. Hermogenes took a step toward The Sicilian, and I gestured him back sharply. The last thing I needed was my slave attempting to pop Mithaecus in his pointy nose. Much as I might like to see such a thing, I didn't have time for a lawsuit. Besides, Hermogenes was half his size.

"But really, my dear Pelops, to run out of olive oil? One can only hope news of this doesn't find its way around the market."

One was quite sure that it would—now.

A small crowd had gathered around, but I wasn't about to explain myself to Mithaecus.

"I heard Agathon wasn't too impressed with your ribbonfish," I said instead.

The Sicilian chuckled into his well-oiled beard. "Middle classes." He waved it off. "I only cooked for him as a favour. Old friend of another patron, you understand."

"Of course," I said through my teeth.

"Alcibiades was quite complimentary about my ribbonfish." He dropped the statesman's name effortlessly.

"That's not what I heard, me," Hermogenes piped up. "They say his pecker went limp as your ribbonfish afterwards. Even Neaera had to give it up as a bad job."

The crowd burst out laughing. The Sicilian's face darkened and his hand came up.

Hermogenes squeaked in alarm and darted behind me.

One of the sycophants began whispering in Mithaecus's ear. The Sicilian's mouth worked as he struggled to get himself under control, then he lowered his hand. It was, after all, poor manners to beat another man's slave.

He satisfied himself with a sneer instead. "Market gossip," he scoffed.

I shook my head sadly. "Out of the mouths of slaves ..." I said with a commiserating smile. Everyone knows slaves hear everything. I often wondered if that was the reason the Athenians kept them.

His face flushed again with anger.

I started to turn away, then stopped. "Oh, and that cancellation you mentioned earlier? Well, it turns out it was a good thing Apollodorus decided against his little soirée. I'm cooking for Xenarchus tonight—maybe you know him?—and let me tell you, *my dear* Mithaecus, he is *much* more generous than Apollodorus." I paused for effect. "Provided, of course, one doesn't serve ribbonfish."

The crowd roared again, and with a last regal nod at The Sicilian, Hermogenes and I swept away with a grand swirl of our cloaks. I couldn't help glancing back as we walked off. The sycophants were fluttering around Mithaecus like birds at a grain seller's stall. The Sicilian seemed oblivious to their attentions. He looked like someone was holding a month-old sprat under his nose.

Feeling much better about life, I allowed myself a small inner smile before turning my attention to my slave. "Did you really hear that bit about his ribbonfish?" I asked curiously.

Hermogenes looked up at me, a mischievous grin lighting his face.

"Ah, I thought not."

"But now it'll be all over the Agora," he said with a certain amount of smugness, before adding innocently, "It's what a good disciple would do."

I had not yet named him disciple. For that he would need to become my right hand, an invaluable assistant who thought as I thought, who could anticipate my wishes before I had a chance to articulate them. Despite his own feelings to the contrary, Hermogenes was not there yet. I ignored his pointed comment.

"Indeed," I said instead. "Come, Hermogenes. You look like you could use a honey cake."

I bought Hermogenes several of the sweet confections before steering my now sticky slave in the direction of the blue and white awnings of the fishmongers' section.

"More eels for you, my cook friend?" Krysippos asked as soon as he saw me. "I have some nice congers today. Very fresh."

Krysippos was a decent enough chap, but his pallid skin and large, watery eyes looked so much like one of his fishes that my fingers always itched to toss him in a pan of sizzling oil.

"No, I need some shellfish," I told him. "*Fresh* shellfish."

Krysippos tried to palm off some day-olds on me, but I was familiar with his slippery ways and he knew it.

"What kind of chef would I be if I couldn't tell fresh from

old?" I inquired. The question had become part of our routine. A cue for him to bring out the real goods. He didn't disappoint.

"A very bad chef," he answered. "As bad as Mithaecus."

I would have been gratified if I hadn't been certain that he said the same thing to The Sicilian about me.

Looking furtively around him, Krysippos bent down and pulled out a basket from underneath a pile of crates. It was filled with silvery oysters—even Xenarchus couldn't complain about the quality—and we got down to some serious haggling.

We had settled the question of cost and were assuring each other of our mutual regard when I remembered the other task I was supposed to complete.

"Neaera has a sister?" Krysippos's surprise seemed unfeigned.

I sighed inwardly. If nobody knew of the woman, how in Hades was I supposed to find her?

"Apparently," I replied. "She's new to Athens, from what I've been told. I've got a client—a very important client—who would like to employ her. I'm sure he would be extremely generous to anyone who could help me find her."

Greed warred with honesty across his fish belly face, but after a few moments, Krysippos shook his head regretfully. "I wish I could help," he said. "But I only know Neaera by reputation. I have never heard of a sister."

I suppressed a sigh, thanked him, and sent Hermogenes home with the shellfish.

"Mind you go straight back to the house," I admonished my slave. "No sloping off to the Kolonos Hippios to watch the charioteers."

"I wouldn't have done that," Hermogenes protested, full of offended self-righteousness.

"And no lingering by the gym either, hoping some teacher will be so amazed at your athletic physique that he'll immediately offer you a place on the wrestling team," I added.

"Che-ef!" He dragged the word out in such a way that I knew he'd planned on doing just that.

"I'm serious, Hermogenes. In this kind of heat, those shellfish need to go directly into the ice pit. And besides, slaves aren't allowed into the gym. You know that."

He heaved a long-suffering sigh. "I know," he mumbled.

I watched him scuff off and, satisfied that he'd follow my orders, albeit reluctantly, I continued with my search. But the bread-wives hadn't heard of Daphne of Megara either. Neither had the wreath sellers. Or the fruit sellers. Even the flute girls at the Spring House couldn't help me—not that they didn't offer to help with something else. But the life of a celebrity chef seldom involves fast chariots and loose women. I turned down their kind offers and started to retrace my steps back to the Kerameikos, wondering gloomily how I was going to find a hetaera that nobody had heard of.

MITHAECUS BITES
Cooking with the Phidias of the Kitchen

When I first served my Ribbonfish Showstopper to **PERIKLES**, the great statesman and (though many were not aware of it) a true gourmet, second only to myself, he took a single bite, then had me called from the kitchen to compliment me on the fine flavour of the dish.

"Mithaecus," said he. "You are a true **PHIDIAS** of the kitchen. You have created a wonder. A dish fit for **OLYMPUS** itself! Truly, you have honoured my house with such superior fare."

Drachmas rained down upon me in a shower of silver as all fortunate enough to be present that night showed their appreciation for my succulent creation.

NOW YOU TOO CAN EXPERIENCE MY TRIUMPH BY FOLLOWING THIS ELEGANT RECIPE.

FOR BEST RESULTS, BE SURE TO USE ONLY MITHAECUS'S WONDER CHEESE BLEND.

Ingredients:
Ribbonfish
Mithaecus's Wonder Cheese Blend*
Olive oil

Method:
Gut ribbonfish and discard head. Rinse and fillet. Add cheese and oil. Pan-fry over a hot fire and serve immediately.

Mithaecus's Wonder Cheese Blend available only from Kleisthenes's Cheese Shop

Chapter 7

There was one more stop to make before I could go home, but it was for pleasure rather than business, and I had been looking forward to it all morning. I needed to shop for a gift to give Gorgias for the Panathenaea. He was proud, I knew he wouldn't accept anything too costly—and, quite frankly, I couldn't afford it—but times had been lean for him since the plague. In addition to losing his wife, Gorgias had also lost several of his shop slaves to the wasting disease. He worked hard and he'd done a lot for me this past year. He deserved a treat.

I wandered through the Agora, considering and discarding any number of pricey foodstuffs. Things like sturgeon or cinnamon bark or fresh Levantine dates were beyond my present means, and none of the other fishes or fruits seemed special enough for what I had in mind. I ended up in the wine sellers' quarter where, after much debate and a certain amount of negotiation, I purchased a small amphora of wine for my friend. It was a superior Chian, with the faint scent of violets. A vast improvement over the raw swill he normally sampled.

Happy with my purchase, I paid the shopkeeper and started on my way home. I was taking a long detour through the spice sellers' section when I noticed the shouting. The Agora, being the largest market in the civilized world, is naturally a noisy place filled with voices raised in barter, anger, laughter, or just plain exuberance. Quarrels are common, as is shouting, but the quality of these hurled insults caught my attention as did a familiar booming baritone. I drew nearer.

"You're just walking bollocks, you are!"

"Well, you're so ugly you'd make an onion cry!"

"You're a goatfucking little tosser with delusions of adequacy."

"Oh, yeah? Well, you couldn't count to twenty-one if you were barefoot and naked!"

"Well, you … say, that's not bad! Ha! Barefoot and naked! Ha, ha!" The wine seller, a broad-shouldered individual with a luxuriant beard, clapped the other man on the back, their disagreement dissolving in the face of his hearty laughter. "That's pretty good, is that. Ha, ha!"

I hung back, waiting politely for them to finish their transaction. There was more laughter, an exchange of a few more good-natured (though less impressive) insults, a shared cup of wine, and some serious haggling. Then coins changed hands as did several of the larger amphorae. The wine seller was still chuckling as his now satisfied customer sauntered off, amphora-laden slaves trailing behind him.

"Pelops!" The merchant gestured me over. "All right, then?"

I tucked my own amphora more securely under my arm and stepped up to his well-appointed stall.

He'd cleverly set up shop in front of the wall between the Tholos and the Bouleuterion. The former was where those city council members on duty (no fewer than fifty at a time) ate and drank at public expense. The latter was where all of Athens's five hundred council members met to discuss public affairs—discussions which were, presumably, facilitated by the contents of the wine stall outside.

On each side in front of the stall's central counter, large wine amphorae, almost a man's height, stood partly embedded in the soft ground. Several sizes of smaller amphorae and jars lined the shelves behind, while a stack of sampling cups sat on the counter ready for use. A purplish-red awning protected the goods from the sun and another purple cloth curtained off the back of the stall, likely to block off more exclusive vintages from the envious sight of those who could not afford them.

"I'm fine, thanks," I replied to the seller. "And you?"

He patted his ample belly and beamed at the bustling crowds. "Couldn't be better, my friend, couldn't be better. Nice surprise, seeing you here."

"You're a god," I told him. "You're not supposed to be surprised."

"Figure of speech." He waved it off, then leaned forward and lowered his voice. "Makes you lot feel more comfy-like," he said with a broad wink.

"Ah, that explains it."

Today, Dionysus was wearing a form familiar to me. Having grown up with gods as house guests, I could generally recognize most of them on sight (when they weren't disguised at dinner parties, that is), for gods tended to keep to a few favoured, presumably more comfortable, forms. No other mortal I knew appeared to have my facility for identifying gods, but then my past experience was not exactly typical.

"Say, did you hear what Leander said to me?" the god of wine asked.

"About not being able to count to twenty-one?"

"Hee, hee," Dionysus snickered gleefully. "I can't wait to use it on Ares! He'll be all day trying to puzzle that one out. Duuuuhhh!" He made a face indicating his impression of that god's intellectual prowess. "Too many hits with the bronze battle sword, if you know what I mean," he said in a whisper that carried effortlessly over the noise of the crowd.

I grinned uneasily. It was one thing to laugh at a god's jokes, but quite another to laugh at a god himself. Even if Ares wasn't in the immediate vicinity, gods had an unsettling habit of seeing and hearing precisely those things one did not wish them to see or hear.

"So, uh … how *is* the family?" I asked, trying to change the subject.

Leaning against the counter of his wine stall, Dionysus closed his eyes and pinched the bridge of his nose. "Beastly," he moaned with a long-suffering sigh. "Simply beastly."

Dionysus could be a bit of a drama king. Seeing how he was the god of theatre, I suppose it made sense.

"I tell you, Pelops, the egos alone are enough to drive me to drink!"

"You're the god of wine. Everything drives you to drink."

"True, true," he conceded, stroking his curled beard thoughtfully. "How about the egos are enough to drive me sober?"

"Better," I agreed. "More shock value. So ... a little full of themselves, are they, your family?"

"Full of shite, you mean!"

I winced.

"Athena's the worst." He scowled and started chewing on a hangnail. "Stupid cow thinks she's the mutt's nuts just because she sprang from Dad's head instead of his leg like I did. Bollocks! That's what I have to say about that. Bollocks! Heads wouldn't get far if legs weren't there to move them around." He nodded forcefully. "And now we've got the Panathenaea happening—*again*. And why? She's bloody needy! That's why. Needs to be the smartest. Needs to be the best. Needs to have the most chuffing festivals. And it's not enough to call it the Panathenaea either, noooo ... we have to call it the *Great* Panathenaea! Bunch of bollocks!"

"Well," I began weakly. "She is the patron goddess of the city."

"Only because the Athenians decided they liked her sodding olive tree better than Poseidon's spring. Well, of course they did! It was the bloody rainy season, wasn't it? If they'd had that match in the summer, we'd be celebrating the Great Poseidea ... or Poseidonaea ... or some other rubbish!" He brooded on this for a moment, his expression dark, then he looked up and shook himself. "Speaking of Poseidon ..."

"Yes?" I said cautiously. I was always cautious around any mention of the Sea God. Having offended him once already, I had no desire to do so again, and given Dionysus's present mood, I wasn't sure what might come up.

"He's still mighty pissed at you," he told me soberly. "You watch yourself. He may be my uncle, but he doesn't have my sunny disposition, does he? When it comes down to it, he's a right vengeful bastard."

I pulled a face. "I know."

"You think you know," he corrected, waggling a finger in my face. "But you don't know the half of it, do you?"

"What do you mean?"

"I mean, why are you here?"

"What?"

"Why are you here?"

"Because I didn't feel like staying in Lydia after my father decided I was done like dinner—"

"No, no, no, bog eyes! Not here in *Athens*!" Dionysus interrupted impatiently, waving his arms around. "I mean, why are you here in the Agora? Today! When presumably you should be in a kitchen somewhere, stirring and chopping, and ... all those other things chefs do."

"I had to get more olive oil," I told him, struggling to hide my annoyance. Why couldn't he just come out and say what he meant? "I had a large amphora of it, but Gorgias's moron of a slave hung the hydrias right over the amphora and the hydrias fell and broke the ..." My voice trailed off as I realized the implication of what I was saying.

"Exactly!" Dionysus smacked his hand on the counter, rattling the sampling cups. "The hydrias—a *water* pot—broke your amphora of olive oil."

My knees were suddenly wobbly. I dropped my head and pinched the bridge of my nose much as Dionysus had done earlier. "Poseidon?" I asked, already knowing the answer.

Dionysus was nudging a cup of wine towards me. "He's not big on you, my friend. Trust me when I tell you that trident of his spends more time up his fishy arse than in his hand. Too much water in his wine, if you ask me. And to tell the truth, he doesn't get on with any of us, really. Anyhoo, Hermes sniffed out what he'd been up to and we thought you ought to know."

I slumped against the counter and nodded, unhappy but ultimately unsurprised. It was not the first time I had had trouble with water and, I thought glumly, it was not likely to be the last. I prayed to Poseidon, I offered him sacrifices, but one did not turn down a god's affections without repercussions. "Thanks," I said. I took a sip of the wine. It was very good.

"Don't mention it."

Dionysus *harrumphed* meaningfully and I straightened up, noticing only then what he had already seen.

A high-class hetaera was passing the wine stall. Deeply coloured veils hid all but her rich, dark eyes, though the thin draperies clung to her slim form in a most salubrious fashion. Clouds of perfume swirled around her as she swayed past, entourage in tow, perhaps on her way to her next assignation. Dionysus and I stood without speaking for a few moments, admiring the view. She glanced at us just before passing by and the god of wine saluted her respectfully. She gave him a saucy wink in return.

"I don't suppose you know of a hetaera named Daphne?" I asked hopefully after the woman had moved out of sight. "From Megara."

Dionysus frowned in thought, then shook his head. "Never heard of her."

Of course he hadn't.

Dionysus took in my glum expression and clipped me on the shoulder. "Cheer up, mate!" he said bracingly. "Your life's not so bad. Don't you go worrying about Xenarchus and his poxy tricks. Even if you don't find his hetaera for him, there are plenty of rich, hungry Athenians just panting for a taste of your cooking. Besides, Hermes and I are on the case, yeah? We'll make it right."

How had Dionysus found out about Xenarchus? Horror-struck, I stammered, "But ... um ... I—"

"Of course, we do have all those sodding family obligations over the festival," he mused. "But they won't take up *all* our time. We should be able to nip out, crash a few parties, drop your name, and Basileos's your uncle."

I smiled weakly. "Lovely."

"Probably not till closer to the end of the festival though," he amended. "Hera's a bit of a pitbull for the whole happy bloody family thing." He rolled his eyes expressively. "But Hermes and I'll find a way to slide on out, don't you worry. We wouldn't let you down."

"No," I agreed helplessly.

"And in the meantime …"

He didn't do anything. Just looked at me. Maybe the sun shone a little brighter. Maybe not. But suddenly the amphora I'd tucked under my arm felt heavier. Surprised, I looked down.

It was not the same amphora that I'd purchased.

The Chian I'd bought had come in a lightly decorated vessel: black geometric shapes circling the plain reddish clay, a wax seal indicating its island of origin. The amphora I was now holding was much larger and far more elaborate. The entire vessel was burnished black, with red figures depicting the harvesting of grapes and a beaming Dionysus overseeing the production with a paternal smile. Whatever wine this amphora held, it was not Chian. And it was not in my budget.

"A decent enough likeness," Dionysus conceded, looking over my shoulder at the painting. "Though I don't think he quite got my nose right." He fingered the appendage in question.

"I … I don't know what to—"

"Oh, Chian's fine for everyday use," the god of wine said dismissively. "But you need a little something special, don't you?"

I turned the amphora to see the seal. "Thasian! You're giving me Thasian wine?"

Dionysus nodded vigorously. "Rare stuff, yeah? Expensive— if you have to buy it. Good thing you have a friend in high places. Take it, Pelops! Drink yourself bog eyed! Or use it to impress your next client. Lysander, isn't it? There's a man who likes the finer things in life. He'll piss purple when he sees it. More tips for you, eh? More contracts! Hmm, but you still need a bit of something for yourself too, don't you? Here …"

And then I was holding two amphorae of Thasian wine. I bowed and stammered my thanks, but the god of wine waved them off.

"Least I could do," he told me. "Least I could do. Go! Enjoy the Panathenaea—oh, excuse me, the *Great* Panathenaea. Hermes and I'll jolly along as soon as we can."

Hugging the two precious amphorae protectively against my body, I made my way back to the Kerameikos, my thoughts vacillating wildly between gratitude for the extraordinary gift, and apprehension for the unwelcome promise of assistance. But even after I arrived home, amphorae safely intact, there was no peace of mind to be found.

"Who's Daphne, then?"

She was sitting stiffly on a kitchen stool, one leg crossed over the other. A shapely, sandalled foot peeked out from under a fetching turquoise chiton. Her complexion was pale enough that she didn't need the white lead makeup favoured by less fortunate women, and her soft brown eyes were lovely enough to rival those of ox-eyed Hera (though I would not risk offending the goddess by making such a comparison aloud). She had dark hair, which tumbled down her neck in artfully arranged curls, and her mouth, while too wide by conventional beauty standards, tended to quirk up delightfully on one side. At the moment, however, the mouth was pulled thin and tight all the way across and the liquid brown eyes were glaring at me with a gaze that was anything but soft.

"Zeuxo!" I exclaimed warily, setting my precious amphorae down in a safe corner. "I wasn't expecting you."

"Oh, were you waiting for *Daphne*? Sorry to bugger up your plans, I'm sure."

I sighed inwardly, knowing better than to roll my eyes.

"Zeuxo," I chided her gently. "I need to hire her for a client."

"I know you need her for a bloody client, don't I?" she snapped, her eyes sparking. "What about *me*? Aren't I good enough for your sodding client?"

"It's not my fault," I protested. "He requested Daphne specifically—very specifically! I would have recommended you if I'd been given half a chance. Gods, look at you! You're beautiful, talented, intelligent. What man *wouldn't* want you at his symposion?"

It mollified her.

"I'm just a flute girl," she said sadly, dropping her eyes, inviting further compliments.

I hastened to comply. Zeuxo and I had been friends for the better part of a year. I knew she was putting it on now, but she had helped me out of a few tight spots in the past, providing last-minute entertainment for my wealthier clients. They had all been exceedingly satisfied. Quite simply, I owed her. It also helped, of course, that she really *did* possess all the qualities I was extolling. She was, in fact, well on her way to rising above the status of mere flute girl to become a hetaera, versed in the arts of pleasing men through refined manners and skillful conversation (in addition to the requisite music and sex offered by flute girls).

After judging herself suitably flattered, Zeuxo cast me a side-long glance. "Are those your honey cakes?" she asked with studied innocence. "Over there on the side table?"

I could, and did, roll my eyes then. "They are," I confirmed, unable to suppress a smile. "Shall I fetch one for you?"

My cakes are a particular specialty: honey-soaked pastries studded with lightly toasted hazelnuts and walnuts. The secret is in the fine Attic honey, which I infuse with a mixture of rose petals and exotic cinnamon bark. It gives the confections a unique flavour, quite new to Athenian diners, who consider them a lascivious—even barbaric—dessert. Needless to say, they are among my most frequently requested creations.

I was fairly sure Zeuxo was fond of me for more than my pastries, but she was a woman who liked her sweets and I ... well, I was a man who liked her. A lot. I cut her a generous slice and perched on the stool next to her while she ate. Her pleasure was palpable.

Just then, a small whirlwind blew into the kitchen.

"Hi Pelops, hi Zeuxo you look beautiful today I like your chiton has anyone seen Bob? Oooooooo are those honey cakes?" she said all in one breath.

She was filthy—even for her—and it looked like she'd been playing in Gorgias's clay pits.

"Hello, Ansandra," Zeuxo greeted her. "They *are* honey cakes and they're wonderful. But ... where have you been to get so dirty?"

Ansandra screwed up her face as she considered the query. "You probably don't want to know," she said at last.

Zeuxo laughed. "Probably not," she agreed.

"Have you seen Bob?" Ansandra asked me.

"Not since this morning when Hermogenes fed him."

"Oh, good! I thought he might've forgotten. I didn't want Bob to get hungry."

I refrained from mentioning that Kabob could probably live off his hump for a month.

Ansandra twisted a lock of her hair around her finger and smiled winsomely at me. "So ... can I have a honey cake? Zeuxo's having one."

It was my turn to laugh. "Do you think you might want to clean up a bit first?"

"I'm okay with it," she assured me. "Besides, I'm not done, um ... doing ... what I'm doing yet."

I regarded her for a moment, then shrugged and cut her a piece of cake. "Okay, here you go, Sprout, but you'll have to take it outside. I don't want you mucking up my kitchen. And don't let The Gorgon see you!"

Her eyes sparkled when she saw the size of the piece I'd cut for her. "I won't! That's cracking! Thanks, Pelops! You're the best! Bye, Zeuxo!" she called as she skipped out the door. "I really like your chiton!"

Zeuxo and I shared a smile. I noticed she'd finished her cake, so I cut her another piece.

"So ... who is this Daphne when she's at home?" she asked, licking a dribble of honey from her fingers.

The weight of my task descended on my shoulders once again, distracting me from the luscious sight of Zeuxo's pink tongue. I sat up straighter and blew out my breath in a heavy sigh. "I don't know," I said moodily, throwing my hands in the air. "Some hetaera from Megara. According to my client, she's

Neaera's sister, but he seems to be the only one who knows about her. Oh, and she's supposed to be a virgin, too."

Zeuxo made a noise as rude as it was disbelieving.

"His words. Not mine," I assured her with a lopsided grin. "I've been all over the Agora. Nobody even knew Neaera had a sister—let alone where she might be found."

"Well, certainly not in Megara!"

"Excuse me?"

"Neaera's not from Megara. Your client's misinformed. Neaera came from Thessaly."

"Thessaly!"

Zeuxo nodded.

I didn't question her knowledge. As a flute girl with higher aspirations, she'd made it her business to know everything there was to know about the high-class hetaeras. Through her, I'd heard all about them: Aspasia, whose beauty, wit, and intellect had resulted in her being more wife to Perikles than hetaera; Timarete, who owned her own house, kept dozens of slaves, and claimed the unheard of privilege of selecting her own lovers; and Metaneira, whose legendary skill caused three citizens to bankrupt themselves before she retired in decadent splendour to Naxos. Zeuxo knew every minute detail of their lives, from their long list of lovers, to how many drachmas they spent on perfume and jewellery. If Zeuxo said Neaera was from Thessaly, then it must be true. I brooded on it, swearing inwardly the longer I thought about it.

Zeuxo was licking the last of the honey from her fingertips. "So, where's Gorgias, then?" she asked casually. "He's never about when I come 'round."

"Who knows," I shrugged off the question, not really paying attention.

A mistake, as it turned out.

"Who pissed in your olive dish this morning?" she said, her eyes flashing.

I paid attention then.

"I'm sorry," I apologized quickly.

"You're not the only one who has problems, you know."

"I know!"

"Don't be such a selfish bastard!"

"I know, I know! I'm a total boor. I'm sorry, Zeuxo. Here, have another bit of cake."

She seethed for a moment before deciding to accept my peace offering.

Her eyes still flickered dangerously. I caught her gaze and held it. "I'm sorry," I said again. "It's just ... I've spent half the day asking about Daphne from *Megara*. I don't exactly have copious amounts of time, here. I've got food to prepare, there's the banquet tonight, and my olive oil was—" I choked it off. Zeuxo didn't need to listen to my "to do" list.

"Well, it's not my fault you don't know enough to come to me with these little difficulties, is it?" she replied with a tartness that indicated I'd not yet been entirely forgiven.

"You're right," I told her. "It isn't your fault and I don't know why I didn't think to ask you right off. You always know these sorts of things. I'm a total idiot. Friends?"

Zeuxo relented almost as quickly as she'd flared. "Friends," she said with a quick smile.

I breathed a quiet sigh of relief. We were all right again.

She finished her cake, then stood up and brushed pastry crumbs off her chiton. My mouth was suddenly very dry. Oh, to be a crumb on her chiton!

Zeuxo must have known the effect she had on me—she was professional enough for that—but her friendship meant more to me than a quick once-around the Acropolis. Don't get me wrong. It had been a long while now since I'd been chopped into stewing meat, eaten, and remade. I was ready for sex again. More than ready. But the truth was, I wanted more than that with Zeuxo.

She'd become a flute girl after the plague had killed both her parents and her new husband. With no extended family to rely on, she'd parlayed her charm, wit, and unusual good looks into a successful new life for herself—one that was noticeably deficient in husbands (at least, of her own). I was willing—desirous, even—to assume the title of Husband Number Two, but what could I possibly offer a woman who had achieved a measure of financial independence? I was still trying to build my career. I didn't have enough drachmas to finance a set of my own dishes, let alone a house for Zeuxo and me to live in. I must admit, there were times in the murky hours of night when I wondered if I'd been a little too quick to give up my birthright and all that that entailed. But when rosy-fingered Eos lit the sky once more with her saffron robe, I would remember that if I'd stayed on as Prince of Sipylus, I might have been pampered and wealthy, but I never would have met Zeuxo. Or Gorgias. Or Ansandra.

One day I might actually tell Zeuxo all this. See if she could be persuaded once again into the matrimonial state. But in the meantime, I wasn't willing to risk the relationship we did have by hiring her services. Though, I reflected, as she smoothed her chiton over her hips, there were times … there were times …

These frustrating thoughts led to others. As in, how in Hades was I going to find time to make inquiries again about Daphne of *Thessaly*? My slate was so packed I'd be lucky to find time to sleep. I scowled and rubbed my shoulder absently. It had been aching since this morning.

"Cheer up, Pel," Zeuxo said, giving my sore shoulder a friendly little pat. "I've not heard of Daphne, but tell you what. I'll ask 'round and see what I can find out for you."

"Really?"

She laughed at me. "Really. What are friends for?"

"Zeuxo, if you can find this woman for me, I'll … I'll make you a banquet's worth of cakes," I promised.

She smiled and ruffled my hair fondly. "I know you will."

"So, where are you off to in such a hurry?" I asked as she wrapped herself in a turquoise himation that was a shade darker than her chiton. It was really too hot for a cloak, but Zeuxo, like the high-class hetaeras she envied, always covered up in public. She said it set her apart from the lower-class flute girls. The quality of her clients had certainly improved in the year I'd known her, so perhaps her strategy was paying off.

She patted her curls before answering my question. "The Trireme. I've got a contract for tonight which is good, but Mithaecus is cooking, so the food'll be shite." Zeuxo was nothing if not loyal.

My automatic frown at The Sicilian's name grew puzzled as the rest of her words sunk in. "The trireme? I didn't realize the fleet was in."

She stopped fussing with her hair and gave a little tinkly laugh. "The Trireme's not a real ship, silly," she told me. "That's what they're calling Nicander's place now. Ever since the other night."

"The other night...?" I began before it hit me. Oh. *That* other night.

"All Athens is still laughing about it," Zeuxo chuckled, genuinely amused. "I was on my way home when the archons arrived, you know. You should have seen Nicander trying to talk his way out of it with them. They were all for hauling the silly bugger up in front of the bloody ekklesia, weren't they? Drunk and disorderly, and all that."

"Really. How did he get out of it?" I asked, curious in spite of my worries.

"Well, I'm not sure he would have done if it had been someone else's property they'd tossed out, but seeing as how it was his own ..." She shrugged, then her expression darkened. "The problem is, it wasn't just the furniture that was damaged, was it? Aphrodisia's going to be out of commission for days. She was there that night, you know. Had Prodicus pumping away on top of her—it takes him forever, and he wheezes like a bloody bellows, it's all we can do not to laugh—anyway, there she was waiting for him to find his bit of Olympus and somebody goes and tips a sodding dining couch on them. I hear he's worse off than she is, but she's the one who has to make a living, isn't she? And now she's ruined for the Panathenaea."

I made sympathetic noises.

"I know it's a hazard of the profession, but I'm solid booked for the festival," Zeuxo said uneasily. "It's a lot of cash, Pel. I can't afford for things to get out of hand like that tonight."

"They won't," I assured her.

She shot me a quizzical look. "What makes you so certain, then?"

An image of Dionysus and Hermes trapped at a family get-together rose up before me. "Different guest list," I told her as I escorted her to the front door. "You know, I'm really rather astonished Nicander has enough furniture left to entertain."

Zeuxo's eyes twinkled in merriment. "He didn't. His slaves were scrambling 'round the Agora all morning trying to find replacements. I'm surprised you didn't see them."

"I had other things on my mind."

I sounded morose even to myself. Zeuxo reached up and gave me a quick peck on the cheek. "Must be off now, Pel. I don't want to be late, and I've just got to do something with this hair."

I smiled at her fondly. Her hair was perfect, and she knew it.

The scent of her lavender and violet perfume lingered in the air long after she'd gone. I could still smell it when I realized that I'd forgotten to inquire after my other (admittedly less important) concern. I hadn't wanted to destroy my street credibility with Hermogenes by asking the girls from the Kerameikos about Lion on the Cheese Grater, but it had been niggling at me since Gorgias had told me about it. If Zeuxo didn't know what Lion on the Cheese Grater was, I'd eat ... well, I'd eat Mithaecus's revolting ribbonfish. If I were lucky, she would tell me what it was. If I were really lucky, she'd *show* me.

Given the state of my fortunes these days, I wasn't holding my breath for either.

Dinner Parties for Dummies

A GUEST SHOULD:

1. Spend a certain amount of time each day at the public toilets. In addition to maintaining healthy bowel habits, you never know when an invitation to dinner will present itself.

2. Never accept an invitation to a symposion and then fail to appear. You may find yourself immortalized in literature or, at the very least, liable for the costs of the banquet.

3. Visit the baths on the day of the banquet. A malodorous guest is unlikely to receive a second invitation.

4. Be effusive when praising your host's atrium. He has deliberately paraded you past the richest space in his abode, the least you can do is remark with favour upon his gardens.

5. Take a slave to the banquet in order to wait upon you, but do not allow him to serve or clean up the tables, as this is the job of the household slaves. Direct him to sit on the floor in front of your dining couch, or to stand behind you. If so moved, you may toss him a scrap or two after the other guests have eaten their fill.

6. Refrain from collapsing on the dining couch like a limp ribbonfish. Instead, slide gracefully onto your couch, straighten your knees, and pull yourself into position. Lie only on your left side propped up by your left elbow. The left hand may hold a dish, but use only your right hand to pick up food to eat.

7. Remember to compliment the host on the décor of his andron, even if it is insipid, repulsive, or laughably pretentious. This includes wall paintings, couches, and flooring as well as the imagery on cups and dishes.

8. Eat and drink in moderation. Do not appropriate favourite dishes for your personal consumption. Share with your dinner mates.

A gluttonous guest is never a popular guest. It is acceptable to take some leftovers home with you, but exercise restraint in this as well. It is poor form to cart home an entire banquet and doing so may result in fewer invitations in the future.

9. Take a poor friend to the banquet on occasion. Your host will expect this—such a person is known in civilized circles as the "ghost" at the table. By bringing such an individual along, you have the opportunity to demonstrate your own magnanimous nature.

10. Tip the cook when the food is exceptionally fine. Not only will this be construed as a compliment to your host for securing the talents of such a remarkable cook, but it will illustrate your own superior breeding and should result in future dining opportunities.

11. Wash hands between courses so as not to repel the host and the other guests. Remember, a considerate guest is a future guest.

12. Never steal the napkins.

13. Never try to seduce the host's son.

Chapter 8

As a celebrity chef, I wasn't as uninterested in Athenian politics as I usually led Gorgias to believe. What he didn't understand was that I didn't need to know where the Athenian fleet was on a daily basis, or what the Spartan army was up to now, or who was allied with whom. All I really needed to know was that Athens had been at war with either the Persians or the Spartans for more years than Meidias had dishes. And ever since the terrible plague six years ago, Athens had become a city of party animals. Popular thought ran along the lines that if you were going to die anyway, you might as well die happy. For a chef-for-hire, it was a good time to be in business.

Not all Athenians were wild hedonists, of course. There were still some levels of Athenian society in which the golden age of culture and refinement had not yet begun to tarnish, where the rules of a dinner party were innate knowledge rather than something one gleaned from a well-fingered self-help scroll. Xenarchus clearly inhabited these spheres.

His stately abode proved more luxurious in the light of day. Even the kitchen was impressive with large indoor and outdoor hearths, numerous tables and shelves, and a full set of exquisite red-figure dishes. I examined these enviously. They were beautifully decorated with scenes of musicians and their various instruments. Xenarchus, it appeared, had a certain appreciation for the melodic arts. It was one of the few things I was able to discover about him before the feast.

When I'd arrived, focused and ready to create a sumptuous banquet, a small part of me had been hoping also to get a better sense of this citizen, this man who had such power over my life. And so, during the course of the morning and into the afternoon, Hermogenes and I managed to pop into almost every room of the house—including those used for storage. There had been just one uneasy moment:

"What do you think you're about, then?" a voice behind me had demanded.

I was crouched down in one of the storage rooms examining a basket of Anatolian figs. I straightened up and dusted off my hands before turning around. It was Simos, of course. The superior slave in the orange chiton. His curls were still freshly oiled and perfumed, his nails still meticulously clipped and buffed, and his fine wool chiton still managed to sneer at my own inferior garb. But I was no longer simply a foreigner with a frying pan. I was the contracted chef for his master's symposion and, as such, I outranked him for the day.

"My job," I replied haughtily, flaring my nostrils at him before he could do the same to me.

He stared at me for a long moment before dropping his eyes. I thought I saw a flush on his cheeks but he turned away without another word, so I couldn't be sure.

Simos was not quite out of earshot when Hermogenes piped up from behind a stack of baskets. "He's a great smarmy bugger, isn't he?"

"Probably because he's the most important person in the house apart from his master," I said tartly.

"Well, he's sure not much on you."

"Hmm. The feeling's mutual."

"You know, Chef, he looks like a right wanker. I could thrash him for you—"

"No."

"But—"

"No!"

"Che-ef! A good disciple would—"

"No, Hermogenes, no! What is it about the word you don't understand? You're not my disciple yet, and even if you were, I would never set you to such a task! How many contracts do you think I'd secure if you went about thrashing the clients' slaves? And the head slave at that! The point is to develop a clientele, not alienate it."

He mumbled something unintelligible.

Like many boys his age, Hermogenes spent far too much of his time daydreaming. When he wasn't playing Greeks vs. Amazons with Ansandra, he was Herakles sweating over his legendary labours, or Jason sailing the seas in search of the Golden Fleece. Lately, he'd become obsessed with chariot-racers. He had taken to tying a green victory ribbon around his head in the style of Damokles, one of the most popular charioteers and the one voted most likely to win the Great Panathenaea's chariot race (this despite the fact that he hailed from Thessaly, traditionally one of Athens's sworn enemies). But Hermogenes didn't care where his current hero had been birthed. He also seemed to forget that not only was he himself a slave, rather than a hero or an athlete, but that he was a young, very junior slave, and exceedingly undergrown for his age. A prize bull in a scrawny calf's body.

"I've too much to do to rescue you today," I told him severely. "Do you remember Dromon? I remember Dromon. Your nose looks like a flattened barley roll because of Dromon. As I recall, you thought he looked like a wanker too."

Hermogenes fingered his nose resentfully.

"No," I said again. "Besides, I've got more to worry about than some snarky slave who may or may not be a poncy little tosser. Now come, leave your nose alone and lend me a hand with these figs. *That's* what a good disciple would do!"

With Simos rendered temporarily harmless and Hermogenes busily employed with figs, I was able to explore the rest of the house with impunity. I ducked into living rooms and vestibules, porches and the richly appointed andron. All I could tell from this was that Xenarchus was even wealthier than I'd realized, and that he had a marked fondness for silver bowls incised with swans and, if the exquisite lyres which hung on the walls were any indication, for music. He was also a man who liked his figs. There were five large baskets of the fruits in the storeroom, and I decided to double the number of fig and cheese appetizers I'd planned for that evening. It never hurts to oil up the customer.

Apart from its epicurean appointments, the house yielded few clues about its owner. In fact, the place seemed like a normal, albeit high-class, Athenian household. The sole exception to this was the slaves who—not including the supercilious Simos—were not only efficient, but remarkably deferent.

"Can I help you with this, Chef?"

"Please, Chef, may I carry that?"

"Chef, you shouldn't be troubling yourself with this. Allow me."

For once, all was as it should be.

With such ready assistance, my own impressive culinary skills, and a total absence of revelsome gods, Xenarchus's first dinner feast came off beautifully. The wine was carefully watered, the guests were elegant and well-groomed, and the only sounds from the andron—apart from the tasteful background music provided by Athens's most talented cithara player—were the rise and fall of male voices in measured intellectual debate.

I served scallops in a spicy Lydian sauce, Krysippos's oysters lightly steamed with a drizzle of garlic-infused olive oil, and thrushes roasted in a crust of ground cumin seeds and coriander. The crust ensures the juices stay in the delicate meat, while the spices flavour both flesh and juice with their fragrance. My fig appetizers were particularly well-received.

I'd taken fresh figs, stuffed them with a mixture of goat cheese and mint, and wrapped them in the thinnest slices of salted pork. Then I grilled them over a hot fire until the pork was crisp and the cheese mixture inside was soft and creamy. I finished by drizzling them with warm honey—from Mount Hymettus, of course—to which I'd added a few crushed thyme leaves. The dish was new to my repertoire. The idea had come to me unbidden and fully realized one morning—a gift from the gods, apparently. The serving slaves informed me Xenarchus had eaten almost a dozen of the creamy morsels and every fine red-figured plate had come back licked clean. There were no leftover appetizers for guests to take home which, though perhaps disappointing for the guests, is exactly what one desires as a professional chef. Always leave them wanting more.

After the party had finished with second tables, I was called in for applause. Before stepping into the andron, I paused for a moment to prepare my "blush." In a city where chefs are ridiculously grandiose about their talents, a modest one stands out.

"Ah, and here he is!" Xenarchus gestured me over magnanimously.

I bobbed my head and took in the room with a quick glance.

Xenarchus's andron was large and quite tastefully appointed. The walls were frescoed, decorated all over with a palm leaf motif, and the dining couches were placed neither too close together nor too far apart. For the symposion, lamps had been situated alongside silver bowls of flower petals throughout the room. Incense burners stood in each corner in perfect combination for the air was pleasantly scented without being overpowering. I recognized almost all of the men on the well-cushioned couches though I had cooked for none of them before now. In the same way that Zeuxo knew all about the high-class hetaeras she wished to emulate, I knew much about the men at Xenarchus's table. I did not want to *be* them, but I did want to cook for them.

As befitted well-behaved guests, these men had all arrived freshly bathed and perfumed for the feast. There were no grubby necks or greasy heads here. They reclined gracefully on their dining couches with silver water bowls placed close at hand so they could rinse their fingers after each course. There was the brilliant young politician, Alcibiades, with his friend Socrates sitting beside him. Everything I'd heard about the philosopher appeared to be correct. Even at such a symposion, the man wore a plain tunic instead of a chiton, and his himation (left on, no doubt, to cover up some hole or another) was worn and frayed. Socrates may have had an agile mind, but he looked like an unmade sleeping couch—albeit a clean one. It was said that he consumed only bread and water except when dining out. If that was the case, then he was certainly making up for it tonight. Although all the other guests had finished with their meal, Socrates was still eating, seeking out every last meagre crumb on the serving platters. His attending slave, who by tradition might have been assumed to be the recipient of any leftovers, looked thin and ill-tempered.

The sculptor Kritias, a surprisingly wealthy man for an artist, was far more richly dressed than Socrates and wore a fine blue chiton edged with yellow. His infamous artistic temper was not

in evidence this evening, possibly mellowed by the refined surroundings and the superior food. He reclined easily in the arms
of his lover, the model, Charmenides—a tall, long-lashed youth
with the body of an athlete and, according to Hermogenes, the
morals of a cat.

Across from Kritias were the Parthenon Pair, Iktinos and
Kallikrates, architects of Athena's newest temple. A nice-enough
duo, if somewhat given to mumbling about columns and tri-
glyphs and metopes and the like. They enjoyed spicy food and
I had prudently ensured that they'd received the spiciest of the
cumin-crusted thrushes. A true chef needed to be sensible of all
such matters.

Xenarchus shared a couch with the historian Thucydides,
who had a bad stomach (no thrush for him) and had required
more bland dishes than the rest of the party. The lack of spice,
however, had not stopped Socrates from reaching over and
picking at Thucydides's leftovers too. Honestly, the man was as
bad as Kabob.

And finally, Palladas, an elder statesman, dignified and superior, sat beside the only man I did not know. He was a greying man in a grey chiton—the token ghost presumably, judging
from his inferior garb and unfashionably long hair. Apart from
the ghost, Xenarchus's guests were among Athens's greatest poli-
ticians, thinkers, and artists. I was impressed despite myself.

My employer lounged against the cushions of his dining
couch, relaxed and red-cheeked with contentment. A wreath of
palm leaves adorned his head, and a lovely, ox-eyed serving slave
was carefully dabbing the remains of dinner from his face with a

fine linen napkin. Another comely slave stood at his side adjusting his draperies. He sent them off with a wave of his hand.

"The man of the hour!" he said, suppressing a long belch. "A fine meal, Chef Pelops. Indeed, truly exceptional. The lamb was superb, and those appetizers! Your cheese-stuffed figs were the best dish I've eaten in a very long time. Well done, man, well done! I must say, I look forward to your next feast now with an even *greater* anticipation."

On cue, I blushed and murmured my thanks but I'd caught his deeper meaning and the whisper of threat implicit in it. All the delicious fig appetizers in the world would not placate him should his hetaera of choice be absent from the feast. It took some of the glow from the moment, though I continued to smile and bow as the other dinner guests added their praise to his.

The congratulations were sweet, the tips pressed upon me even sweeter. And the not-so-subtle inquiries as to my availability promised many contracts in the future. At this rate, I'd be able to pay Meidias for his dishes in no time. I started to cheer up. Most of these men were the golden egg glaze on the upper crust of Athenian society. Even the ghost pressed a small, worn coin upon me, though he did not inquire as to my availability.

To top everything off, when I returned to the kitchen, I discovered that a kitchen slave by the name of Ajax had taken charge of the cleanup and had the job almost done. You just knew a slave like that would go on to greater things.

All in all, I was feeling pleased as I quit Xenarchus's house with a fat pouch of drachmas cheerfully clinking at my side and a sleepy Hermogenes stumbling behind me. The evening had been a professional success. Perhaps I had overreacted earlier. Perhaps Xenarchus wasn't so bad. Perhaps, I mused, he would prove to be the best thing that ever happened to me, my first step into a larger, more affluent world.

The Fates, however, had other ideas.

Chapter 9

The first day of the Great Panathenaea dawned hot and bright—too hot and a little too bright for me if truth be told. It had been a very late night. Indeed, it seemed as though Morpheus had just begun to bathe me in dreams when Gorgias was tipping me unceremoniously from my sleeping couch.

"Goooood morning, merry sunshine!" he boomed cheerfully as I slid off the now vertical couch and onto the floor. "The birds are singing, the sun is shining, and the sky's as pink as a godlet's little bottom."

I groaned and pulled the blankets over my head.

"Come on, then." He poked me with his toe. Gorgias has very large toes. "Get a move on! It's time for all little chefs to be chopping and cooking, cooking and chopping. Such lazy little chefs! Not like potters. Potters have been up for hours! Mixing and firing and throwing pots. No lolling about for poor potters."

"You're a bastard," I croaked. "Did you know that?"

Gorgias just laughed and with a last ungentle nudge of his toe, he wandered off singing some off-colour song about nymphs and centaurs. In full voice, naturally.

He was annoying, but effective. Awake now, I fought my way out of the covers and went to wash up.

Despite Gorgias's colourful description of the sky, dawn was barely on the horizon when Hermogenes and I met in the court-yard. He was bleary-eyed too, though I noticed that he'd still taken the time to tie one of his jaunty green ribbons around his head. I regarded it with resigned tolerance. Youth! I took a moment to thank the gods I was no longer so fresh and foolish.

We were bound for Lysander's house, which, as befit his upper middle-class status, stood in the district of Melite, near the base of the Hill of the Nymphs. Despite the earliness of the hour, the courtyard just inside the Diplyon Gate was almost impassable. It was here that participants in the Great Panathenaic Procession were to gather before beginning their parade at first light.

The Great Panathenaea was eight days long, and normally the Procession was held on the sixth day, after all the athletic and artistic competitions had ended. But for various reasons (which Gorgias had tried to explain in detail to me and which I had ignored), the city council had decided to shake things up this year. This year, the Procession was to kick off the festival, followed by the torch race (normally held on the fifth day), fol-lowed by all the various athletic and artistic competitions. Most Athenians seemed fine with the change in schedule, though some of the older men muttered darkly about messing with tradition. Tradition or not, it seemed an odd decision to me to have the big party at the beginning of the festival, and I wondered if the athletic events would suffer for it, as all the athletes would be obliged to compete after whooping it up at an all-night bash.

Regardless of old men's dark forebodings, the crowd of people around the Dipylon Gate that morning seemed happy enough. There were priestesses with their acolytes, athletes with their trainers, and musicians with their citharas and aulos. All milled about in a disorganized cacophony. Grizzled commanders of battles long forgotten strutted about in freshly polished armour, made young again in their memories. Armed warriors wiped non-existent smudges off the shining chariots they would soon race around the field that had been prepared for them outside the city's walls. And women bearing wine and flowers for the goddess juggled gifts and draperies as they tried to avoid the fragrant turds of a hundred sacrificial cows. A tall, stick-like man clutching a fat scroll, clearly some kind of organizer, kept consulting his scroll and hopping from one foot to the other, red-faced from bellowing orders at people who were not listening to him. I pitied the man. Great Zeus and Hera, I'd no idea there would be such a crowd!

"Keep to the edges," I shouted to Hermogenes, shaking his shoulder to get his attention. "It's the only way we'll get through."

He nodded, sparing a last, longing look at the group of charioteers before squeezing past a cluster of sacrificial sheep and making his way over to the side of the courtyard walls.

It wasn't much better on the sidelines. Flower-garlanded

women held precariously balanced jugs of holy water on their heads, while resident foreigners waited beside the women, protecting offerings of cakes and honey with the folds of their distinctive purple cloaks. Though the sun was barely in the sky, it was already hot and I felt the sweat running down my back as we pushed through the crowds. We paused briefly to admire Athena's new peplos. Nine months in the making, the special tunic had been intricately designed with scenes of the goddess's victory over Ecceladus and the Giants. It would decorate the venerable statue of Athena Polias, whose golden owl and diadem would be polished to a blinding shine for the occasion.

Hermogenes tugged on my chiton and pointed behind us. I craned my neck back and then up, gaping in amazement. A second, much larger peplos had been hoisted up and suspended from the yard arms of a full-sized ship that was itself mounted on wheels. Gorgias had told me of this ritual, though I'd never witnessed it myself.

Countless heavily sweating men heaved and strained to pull the ship up to the Dipylon Gate. People shouted, livestock bellowed, and everybody scurried to get out of their way. These men would drag the ship through the city and up to the Acropolis, where most of Athens waited. There, the priestesses of Athena would clothe the larger-than-life-sized statue of Athena Parthenos in her giant new peplos. I say *most* of Athens. The rest of the city's dwellers, myself included, would be far too busy working to watch the goddess change her kit.

I spotted Castor the Macedonian as well as several other chefs gawking at the sights as they made their way to the day's assignments. It was a timely reminder. Hermogenes would stand here all day watching the show if I let him, but Lysander's festival symposion beckoned and we needed to be on our way. I nodded pleasantly to Castor, who gave me a wide smile and a friendly wave in return. Then I yanked on Hermogenes's arm and gestured him onwards. He moved reluctantly, but I ignored his reproachful looks and we made our way past the Dipylon Gate's courtyard and the seething mass of the waiting parade.

Even past the gate's entryway, the city streets were already noisy and crowded as peasants shoved and shouted their way to the best viewing spots for the procession. My head, I quickly realized, had started to ache.

In all the chaos, I certainly wasn't thinking about omens or portents. In my defence, I did notice the black crow above us flying unluckily from right to left, but Hermogenes had dropped my ladles in a puddle of urine and, in my anger, I forgot about the dark warning. Even the most devout man can be blinded by the frustrations and concerns of everyday life.

I stumbled on the threshold when I entered Lysander's house. That, too, should have alarmed me. But one of my jars of salt tunny—an expensive delicacy from Byzantium—slid from my basket and rolled onto the floor, distracting me from the unlucky stumble. At the time, I thought it fortunate the jar did not break.

Fool.

At first, everything appeared to be going well—except for my ladles falling in donkey piss, of course. A good scrubbing in boiling water had sorted that problem (though Hermogenes had complained bitterly about the temperature of the water). As I said, everything seemed to be going smoothly. Krysippos had sold me some unusually fat eels, the greens were crisp, cool, and fresh, and through Dionysus's beneficence, I had an amphora of rare Thasian wine as a surprise treat for my client and his guests.

Even the unsavoury Lamachus came through that morning. His slaves delivered the olive oil to Lysander's kitchen just as Hermogenes and I began setting out the raw ingredients for the feast. The oil arrived in a huge globular amphora—easily waist-high—and the scrawny delivery slaves huffed and groaned as they wrestled it into the room. Hermogenes watched them, a superior sneer wrinkling his nose.

I thanked the two men and slipped them each a barley roll with cheese. I knew Hermogenes thought they were putting it on, but the amphora was very large and the men were extremely thin, especially for a foodseller's slaves. Lamachus, it would seem, skimped on more than just the cost of renting his stall. The slaves were pathetically grateful for the food.

"Tha's a treat, tha is, sor," the first said, bobbing his head up and down and clutching the roll with both hands.

The second slave bowed and smiled grotesquely, treating me to a view of stained, blackened teeth. "Righ' gen'rous of you, guv."

I averted my eyes from his mouth. "Come back this evening if you can," I told them, cutting the grovelling short. "There'll be food and obols for you both if you help me get this amphora back home."

Hermogenes tried to hide his disgruntled surprise, but not before I saw it.

I waited till the two slaves had bowed and bobbed their way out the door. "You can't possibly carry that monster all the way back to the Kerameikos yourself," I pointed out.

"But I thought Strabo or maybe Lais would help," he whined, naming two of Gorgias's more muscular slaves.

"*Strabo or Lais?*" My voice went up an octave. I suspected Strabo of breaking my other amphora. The man had a brain as thick as his non-existent neck. "You thought wrong," I told Hermogenes. "You know Gorgias. He'll have given them both the afternoon and evening off to see the Festival. If you think I'd allow those two anywhere near this amphora after the drinking they'll be doing, then I've got a trireme to sell you. Cheap."

"Oh, and those wankers'll be any better?" Hermogenes muttered, gesturing sullenly in the direction of Lamachus's now cheerful slaves. "Like *they* won't they be out pissing it up."

"On what Lamachus tips them?" I snorted. "Not bloody likely. What's your problem? At least they seemed eager for the work, which"—I slid him a significant look—"is more than I can say about some."

Hermogenes ignored the look. "It's just not done, Chef. It's not right that you use someone else's slaves. It's ..." he paused and wrinkled his nose, searching for the right word. "... foreign."

I regarded him for a long moment. As Prince of Lydia, in my eyes, all slaves had been created equal. Athens had introduced me to a reality that was quite the opposite. Here, slaves were not only cognizant of, but extremely competitive about their status. Kitchen slaves were lower than serving slaves, who were lower than bath slaves and so on. Zeus above, they were worse than nobility when it came to rank.

"Tell you what," I said to Hermogenes. "When they come back tonight, you can be in charge. Supervise them. Boss them around. Whatever. Just get that amphora home. Safely."

It appeased him, though he tried not to show it. "Supervising! That's about all I'm good for, me," he grumbled, then added, "with these fingers near poached in all that boiling water."

"Truly, your life is a tragedy," I agreed, before setting him to chop vegetables. "It's a wonder you're able to get up each morning."

"It's bloody heroic, it is."

"Indeed. I am most impressed. Very disciple-like behaviour. Now perhaps you can see your way to committing some heroic acts on those greens."

Hermogenes had started chopping the greens and I'd just begun slicing the mullet into thick steaks when a voice interrupted our industry.

"All right, then?"

I turned and looked down. Far down. A very small man was standing in the doorway. At first glance, he looked like Eros. I'd only seen the god of erotic love only once before and I had to look again to make sure it wasn't really him. I did, and it wasn't. My shoulders dropped in relief. This man was definitely mortal.

He was almost as round as he was tall, clean-shaven with a crop of wheat-coloured curls, and pale eyes. His plump cheeks looked like a pair of spit-polished apples, though I would hesitate to say that to his face as, upon closer inspection, his bulk proved to be more muscle than fat. With his colouring, I guessed he was from one of the northern islands. Thasos, perhaps. Or maybe Samothrace.

"And you would be…?" I inquired.

"Name's Geta," he said, sticking out a plump hand as he beamed up at me. "Lysander's steward. I'd've introduced myself sooner, but I've been running my arse off for the Missus. She's got her own little shindig happening, y'know? Not sure if anyone told you. Lysander's orders and all. Not orders that we shouldn't tell you. Ha! No, orders for her to have herself a bit of a hen party after the race. Smart man, Lysander. Keeps the Missus happy while he's about his own business. No flies on him, eh?" He winked broadly and elbowed me. "And keeping the Missus happy? I'm all over that. Got a bit of a temper, that one. Touched by Ares, if you ask me. Likes to take it out on slaves. Not so fond of that, let me tell you. Hope it's not a problem. Cooking more food and all. There'll be twelve more for dinner, but her bunch don't eat much. More interested in the bread dildos, if you know what I mean. Ordered those myself this morning so you won't have to worry about them—not unless the master'll be wanting a few. Ha! Not likely, with all the fluties he's invited. Should be a regular boink-fest around here tonight. So anyhow, slaves are all under orders to work their butts off today. If you see any of 'em sitting around with their finger up their arse, you let me know and I'll fix 'em." He flexed his arm muscles meaningfully. "So, all right then?"

The sudden silence caught me by surprise. I struggled to collect my thoughts after his verbal assault (the man *must* be from

Samothrace!). But one piece of information stood out quite clearly from the rest. "You're telling me I need to prepare food for twelve more people?" I inquired carefully.

He nodded once, his chins jiggling. "You got it."

"And nobody thought to inform me of this ahead of time?" I struggled to keep the edge from my voice.

"I got nothing." Geta shrugged. "Didn't know myself till late last night, did I? Zeus on a stick, eh? Athenians! Always bugger-ing up the works. Send Manes to the Agora if you need more food, and I've got a few extra kitchen slaves pulling duty just in case." He paused, a slight frown marring his forehead. "Look, I know it sucks, but there it is. Not a problem for you, is it?"

"Oh no," I lied. "No problem at all."

"Good man! Excellent! Okay, I gotta blast, but you give a shout if you need anything, you hear? Just ask for Geta. That's me."

"Right." I gave him a tight smile. "Geta."

The smile fell off my face as soon as Geta left the room.

"*Ares's hairy balls!*" I cursed roundly.

These gods-damned middle classes would be the death of me—the second death, that is. Why was I cooking for such dullards? Such ignoramuses? The upper classes didn't behave like this! They *respected* celebrity chefs! They didn't go around changing things at the last minute. Oh certainly, a good chef always prepared additional food for the odd gatecrasher or two, but for *twelve* more people?

"By Apollo's pimply ass!" I swore again, yanking at my hair. "How in Hades am I supposed to feed twelve more people?"

Roast lamb was to be the star attraction of the evening, the culinary centrepiece around which the entire banquet would revolve. The gods have very specific laws regarding sacrificial animals, the most important being that all edible parts of the animal *must* be consumed on the evening of and in the house in which the sacrifice takes place. To quote the latest self-help scroll currently circulating around the Agora: no leftovers, no doggie bags.

Any chef worth his sea salt knew to prepare fewer dishes for a banquet such as this in order to avoid the egregious sin of leftovers. I was worth considerably more than sea salt. I'd planned a lovely menu with eels and scallops and mullet steaks and cheeses, but I'd purchased only modest quantities of these, counting on the lamb to fill everybody up. For twelve (*twelve!*) more people, there simply wasn't enough food to go around. I cursed again, louder this time.

"I can't work like this!" I cried, throwing my arms out. "These people don't respect my craft! I'm an *artist*, not a taverna cook!"

Hermogenes kept his attention studiously on the greens, knowing better than to say anything. Lysander's kitchen slaves were suddenly much too busy to meet my eyes.

Still muttering curses, I grabbed up a slate and started scribbling. It didn't take me long. I am, after all, very good at what I do.

"All right," I said finally. "Hermogenes, why are you still chopping vegetables? I need you to go to the Agora. Take that Manes with you. *You!*" I called to a kitchen slave. "Can you wield a knife? Take over from him. Not like that, imbecile! That's too fine! I don't want them pulverized!" I turned back to Hermogenes. "Here's the list. Find Krysippos. Tell him I'm calling in a favour. If he still has some of those Boeotian eels, get them. If not, ask for his best congers. And I'll need more mullet."

"What if he's out of eels?"

"Then bring me some bass, but make sure they're fresh! And hurry! Who knows how much longer he'll be in the Agora today!"

"I'm on it, Chef!" Hermogenes assured me before scampering out the door. "No worries!" he called back, his voice echoing through Lysander's house.

No worries for him, perhaps, but plenty of headaches for me. I turned my attention back to the kitchen and began ordering slaves to work.

Ladies!

Are you ... planning an orgy?
The designated dildo-carrier for a religious festival?
Or just looking forward to another quiet evening at home?

BREAD DILDOS ARE HERE!

They're new! They're hot! They're even edible!
And at *PHARSALIA'S BAKESHOP* we can accommodate
all sizes from the small Virgin Loaf to the popular four-foot
Ceremonial Ka-blooie. Just think! No more size-related
disappointments! No more chafing from leather!
Bread dildos come in soft, crusty, or whole grain
(for that little something extra).
Having a friend over? Try our specialty: THE DOUBLE HEADER.
Double the heads for double your fun!

PLACE YOUR ORDER TODAY!

Why pay for a set of expensive leather dildos? Whether you
need just one or a baker's dozen, bread dildos are a fraction
of the cost of leather ones! We take bulk orders for that
special orgy and—yes, ladies—discounts do apply!

*Send your slave to PHARSALIA'S BAKESHOP and
place your order today! Located in the Agora, third
stall from the statue of Aphrodite Ourania.*

Satisfaction Guaranteed!

Special discounts apply to widows and citizens of Lesbos.
Please note preparation of the Ceremonial Ka-blooie requires
three working days' notice. Day-olds available upon request.

Chapter 10

"Who is the chef here? I, I am the chef! *You*, you are nothing! A goat with brains! No, a goat has more thought in its head than you could ever dream of."

"I were just trying to help, guv."

"Help? *Help!* Great Zeus and Hera! If I need your 'help' I'll ask for it. Did I ask for it? No, I did not. I told you to—"

"Where d'you want these, then, luv?" a woman's gravelly voice interrupted me.

I spun around and the idiot slave who had almost ruined my appetizers twisted out of my grasp and beat a rapid retreat. I scowled after him before turning my attention to the visitor.

She was short and stout, with broad shoulders, and her arms were muscled and ropy from years of working bread dough. She avoided the heavy cosmetics that most women her age misused, but she liked to wear bright colours that did not suit her and today's eyeball-haemorrhaging pink chiton was no exception. Thumb-sized silver phalluses dangled ostentatiously from her earlobes. Physically, she was not an attractive woman, but her dark eyes were always smiling and the crow's feet, which crinkled at their corners, were testament to her habitual good humour. Much amused her, but very little surprised her. If I made my living baking bread dildos, I'd probably see the world in the same way.

"Pharsalia!" I exclaimed in real pleasure. "Aren't you a ray of sunshine on a gloomy day." I snapped my fingers, directing Hermogenes to help her divest herself of her carrying basket. "But, since when do you deliver the dildos yourself?"

"*Oof,* ta very much, I'm sure," she said, shrugging the heavy basket off her shoulders and into Hermogenes's waiting arms. "All me slaves are off running deliveries this morning," she replied. "I'd nobody else to send, did I? The Panathenaea's one of my busiest times, luv."

"Tell me about it," I commiserated with an empathetic sigh. "Still, you shouldn't have to run your own deliveries. Surely you could have hired somebody."

"Oooo … don't you worry your lovely head about it. Does me good to get out and about once in a while, and Lysander's one of me best customers." She leaned towards me and lowered her voice conspiratorially. "Numbers don't lie, Pelops. And me numbers tell me his Cresilla prefers a nice crusty loaf to himself—bit of a disappointment in the sleeping couch, if you know what I mean. She's got a standing order every four days. And she always buys day-olds for her slaves. A right thoughtful mistress she is. No, I don't mind providing more personal service for a customer like that. Besides," she added with a wicked gleam in her eyes, "Lysander's paying through the arsehole for the bloody privilege, isn't he?"

"Always the businesswoman," I laughed. "Come, have a seat. Tell me, how are things with the shop?"

Pharsalia plopped onto a stool and tweaked her pink chiton decorously around her ample thighs. "Booming, bloody booming. I'm not sure what all you lads are up to, but my guess is not much!" She laughed crudely.

"It's because we're all pining away for you," I told her. It was common knowledge that Pharsalia had forsworn men since she'd started baking bread dildos. If nothing else, the rumour was fantastic advertising for her product. According to Hermogenes, however, Castor the Macedonian had been spotted hanging around the bakeshop recently, and there were, apparently, several wagers as to whether or not Pharsalia would renounce her dildos in favour of his hairy charms. So far, it appeared she had not yet succumbed.

"Oooo, Pelops!" She chortled, whacking my arm and probably leaving a bruise. "Always the charmer."

I sketched an exaggerated bow and offered her a cup of watered wine.

Pharsalia accepted the cup with a grateful smile, took a healthy swallow, and smacked her lips noisily. "Ah, that hits the spot, it does. It's a bloody scorcher out there. So, how's the chef business, then?" She looked pointedly at the direction in which the disgraced slave had fled.

I pulled a face. "A slave with delusions of grandeur," I explained. "He thought he could make an appetizer. He thought wrong."

Pharsalia had begun to play absently with one of her silver penis earrings, a vaguely disturbing sight. She shook her head at my words and *tsk*ed. "And what about that sodding Sicilian? Is he still giving you a bad time of it?"

"Always."

"Did you know Praxilla's husband hired him for their daughter's wedding feast last week?"

My shoulders slumped. Another coup for Mithecus.

"I did not know that," I said, trying not to sound too sour.

Pharsalia stopped fingering her earring and reached over to pat my hand comfortingly. "Now don't you worry your sweet self about it, luv!" she reassured me. "They'll never hire the stupid sod again. I should know, I was there, if you please. I may be a poor relative, but Praxilla invites me to all the celebrations. Wish I'd sent my regrets for that one though. Great Zeus's arsehole! I had the shits for days afterwards—and I wasn't the only one! Crappy way to spend your wedding night, if you know what I mean." She snorted inelegantly. "Some sodding Phidias of the kitchen he turned out to be."

I clucked in sympathy at her experience, though her story cheered me.

"He'll be losing business over that one," she predicted, sipping her wine. "Praxilla's got the biggest gob in Greece and she'll be putting it to good use. You mark me words, himself'll have a job finding work once word of this gets 'round. But enough about Mithecus the not-so-magnificent. Look at you! You're doing well for yourself. Lysander, eh? That's a plum job."

"It is," I agreed. "Or at least it would be if he hadn't changed the terms." I told Pharsalia about the additional guests.

She shook her head sympathetically. "That's his Cresilla, that is."

"What do you mean?"

"I mean it's just like her, luv."

"She makes a habit of this?"

"Well, let's just say Cresilla's a true daughter of Athens, through and through."

"What does that have to do with it?" I asked, mystified.

Pharsalia leaned towards me and dropped her voice to a whisper. "She doesn't hold with foreigners."

"I'm a foreigner," I said a little defensively.

"Oooo, I'm not talking about you, luv. You're lovely." She patted my arm. "I'm talking about the bloody hetaeras, aren't I? Lysander likes foreign women at his dinner parties and it sticks in poor Cresilla's craw something awful. I still can't decide whether it's that he gives other women what he won't give her, or that the other women are from away. Bit of both, I imagine. Either way, she can't do much about it, being a good Athenian wife and all. So what does she do? Makes him work for it, that's what. Demands her own party at the last minute. And no expense spared either. Flowers, food, music, dildos. The whole sodding works. And the poor bugger has to come through."

"Why?" I asked, refilling her cup.

"She brought a huge dowry with her, didn't she? Lysander

would be half the citizen he is today if it weren't for Cresilla's coin—and he's ambitious. Climbing the social ladder like a sour grapevine, he is. He wouldn't want to see that lovely dowry go skipping out the door and back to her father's house. So..." She shrugged philosophically and slugged back her cup of wine before continuing. "Cresilla says 'jump' and Lysander hitches up his chiton."

"Except that I don't see Lysander hopping around the kitchen preparing more food for this party."

"Isn't that always the way, luv?" Pharsalia shook her head. "Isn't that always the way?"

Chapter 11

As tradition dictated, Lysander and his guests were all present in the courtyard when the time came to sacrifice the lamb for the feast. I recognized Damokles, the foreign chariot racer, by the green victory ribbon he'd woven through his perfumed locks. He smiled widely and a great deal and appeared quite taken with himself. I noticed him frequently touching his hair ribbon as if assuring himself it was still there. He seemed very popular with the hetaeras who fluttered around him, giggling. There were several other men I recognized, all among Lysander's middle-class peers. The only exception to this was the grey ghost I'd noticed the previous night at Xenarchus's party. I was a bit surprised to see him there, and wondered who had brought him. He avoided my eyes, probably ashamed to be seen wearing the same tired grey chiton two days in a row.

Lysander's wife and her cronies were also present, heavily

veiled, of course, and despite the suffocating heat, wrapped tightly in colourful himations. Upstanding Athenian women rarely appear in public, festival times being the exception to this rule. They stood by themselves off to one side of the courtyard. Cresilla was an unusually large woman, easily taller than her husband and in possession of, as the diplomats would put it, big bones. I noticed that, while his wife was present, Lysander kept his distance from the hetaeras and flute girls (who, at this point in the festivities, were also heavily veiled and wrapped) and I hid a grin, recalling what Geta and Pharsalia had told me regarding her jealous nature.

All in all though, the group seemed a relaxed, happy party, already smiling and chatting amongst themselves. They were even happier when I produced the red-figure amphora of Thasian wine. It was an older vintage, very rare, very expensive—when one was not chummy with the god of wine. It was nice to have friends in high places. Lysander didn't piss purple (as far I could ascertain) but his eyes did widen and his thin face stretched into a wide grin.

"Pelops!" he exclaimed, clapping me on my bad shoulder. It hurt, but I hid my discomfort behind a modest smile.

"It is nothing," I murmured. "A mere appetizer to the delights of the dinner table. A treat for your esteemed guests."

"A treat? Oh ho! That's quite a treat!" Lysander was practically purring.

The guests echoed his sentiments and I began anticipating the evening's tips. The wine gave off a heady scent of apples when I poured the libation. Phormio was named symposiarch. I didn't know anything about him, but he seemed a stable sort—an impression that was confirmed when he dictated the ratio of wine to water. Two-sevenths wine to every five of water. Dionysus probably wouldn't have approved, but he wasn't there. One of the serving girls produced a kylix and the wine was strained, appropriately watered, then served. Judging from the surprised smiles and enthusiastic smacking of lips, it tasted as good as it smelled. An auspicious beginning to the festivities.

And then, it was time for the sacrifice.

A slave girl offered a basket of barley seeds first to the men, then to the women. Each person scooped up a handful of seeds and threw them to the ground, the act signifying their direct participation in the ritual. Solemnly, Hermogenes led the beribboned lamb into the courtyard.

It was a healthy beast, young and plump, its coat free from blemish. When I sprinkled the woolly head with purified water, it nodded, showing its assent to be slaughtered. And when I took the knife to its throat, the blood spurted skyward before falling to the ground in a gushing stream. The flames at the altar claimed Athena's portion. All was just as it should be.

And then, it wasn't.

My first moment of uneasiness came when I began to butcher the animal. The meat was fine and of good colour, but the entrails! The entrails were strangely twisted, as if some force had stirred them into chaos. I could have remarked on them—I *should* have remarked on them—but thanks to the Thasian wine, the party was in full swing and I did not want to cast a pall over the festive atmosphere. And so, I said nothing.

As I prepared the meat for roasting, I tried to reassure myself that the twisted entrails were nothing to worry about. The colour and texture of the organs had appeared normal. There had been none of the lumps or strange growths that might betoken disaster. Perhaps the creature had simply eaten something that hadn't agreed with its digestion.

As afternoon faded into evening and nothing untoward happened, I even managed to convince myself that this was so.

The banquet preparations had gone smoothly—so well, in fact, that I'd even had a few moments to climb the ladder up to the flat rooftop where Hermogenes and the household slaves were gathered to watch the torch race.

"Here, Chef!" Hermogenes called. "I saved you a spot. You can see 'em clear as day from here."

I nodded my thanks and pushed my way to his side. Like Hermogenes, all of the younger male slaves sported green victory ribbons in their hair. Almost, I wished failure upon the self-satisfied charioteer, though if Damokles did not win his race, then the streets of Athens were likely to be rendered impassable from all the green hair ribbons discarded by disappointed fans.

"*Oi!*" one of the kitchen slaves squealed. "Look at 'em go! Hestia's tits! They're moving, they are!"

The runners were coming in along the Panathenaic Way, beardless boys on their way to becoming bearded men. They came from the altar of Eros at the Akademia bearing flaming torches aloft and clad in nothing but a thin layer of olive oil. In the darkness, the torches bobbed (along with other things) like fireflies spanning the route. These young men—striplings, really—made their way first past the Dipylon Gates and then into the potters' district, where fun-loving spectators tradition- ally gathered to smack any lagging buttocks. From there, the runners continued through the Agora and up the hill on their way to the Acropolis. We could hear the roar of the crowds as they passed and not a few runners, who had seemed to be trail- ing behind the others, sped up noticeably as they ran the gaunt- let of "slaps of the Kerameikos."

Two torches were slightly ahead of the others. The crowd shrieked encouragement. Even Lysander's slaves were shouting from their rooftop vantage point. On the final slope, the two torches bobbed beside each other for several heartbeats until one torch, brave and bright, pulled ahead of the other. Some- thing must have happened to the second runner. Perhaps he stumbled on the slope. His light seemed to flicker, then it went dark. The first flame continued bobbing along its way, well ahead now of the others. At the peak of the Acropolis, the tiny light paused, then suddenly billowed into a massive bonfire as the winner finished the race by lighting the sacred fire on Athena's altar. The city went wild.

Caught up in the excitement, I cheered and clapped and stamped my feet with the rest of the rooftop spectators. Athena ought to be pleased. It had been a brilliant race, exciting and well-run. And a happy goddess made for happy mortals—and happy mortals would be hungry mortals.

"All right, let's go, people!" I had to raise my voice to be heard. "That's our cue! Back to the kitchen!"

"Come on, you lot!" Geta took up my call. "Listen to the chef, eh! Back to work! The master'll be home soon, won't he? And he'll be looking for his supper. Come on! Manes, get yer finger out of yer arsehole. Let's go, go, go!"

Lysander and his guests had gone to the Hephaistion to watch the race. It was the best viewing point in the city (if one did not wish to partake in the Keramcikan slaps) and, for most, it had the added attraction of being right in the centre of the enormous street party that would follow. But if there's one thing the middle classes are noted for it's their pride, and Lysander was no exception. Far be it from him to dance and sing the night away beside mere craftsmen and peasants. Instead, he and his class-conscious chums would return to the house for an evening of fine dining, excellent wine, and hetaeras whose greatest attribute was not their conversation.

Between the steward and myself, we got all the slaves off the rooftop. I followed the last one down the wooden ladder and retraced my steps to the kitchen. The kitchen staff were still enthusing about the race, their eyes sparkling with excitement, laughing and relaxed. But there were sauces to be stirred, eels to be poached, walnuts to be toasted, and sesame pancakes to be fried and set to soak in honey. Lysander might be middle class, but he paid well and I preferred to keep it that way. In Athens, complaints of poor cooking are grounds for not paying the chef.

"Oi! They're coming, guv—I mean, Chef! I can see their torches!" A small undergrown slave shouted the words across the kitchen.

"All right, people!" I clapped my hands. "I need servers! Where are my servers? First tables. Let's move!"

The serving girls lined up to receive their platters. They were all young and attractive in colourful chitons held together by not quite enough pins. I sent up a quick prayer of thanks that Lysander had provided his own dishes for the evening. And that was the last time for a while that I was able to think about anything other than food.

It was still early on in the feast when I was approached by one of the dinner guests.

The appetizers had been enjoyed, the eels had been poached in wine and cherries and were waiting to be served. The lamb was roasting on the outdoor hearth. A small boy had been set to turning the spit, though he had a tendency to turn it too quickly when he wasn't paying close attention, which appeared to be most of the time. I'd stepped outside to check on him—again—wondering if a sharp rap on the knuckles might slow him down, when I spied a shadowed figure looming over the boy.

"You there!" I called out testily, thinking it was a slave shirking his duties. "Leave him—oh!"

The man had turned around. By the torchlight, I could now see his fine clothes and the flowered garland of a dinner guest perched on his head.

"Forgive me … please!" I stammered. "I thought … well, I did not realize a guest was out here."

He stepped away from hearth. "You are the cook?" he asked.

"The chef, yes." I nodded. "Pelops of Lydia at your service, sir."

"Pelops. Yes, excellent." He stroked his beard with fat,

sausage-like fingers. "Pelops. From Lydia. Yes, yes, I've heard of you."

He moved closer and I stepped back instinctively. He was unusually fat for a Greek, but his shoulders were as massive as his belly was round and his face had a sly, crafty look to it. His eyes were odd, a pale grey rather than the dark brown of most Athenians.

"I need to speak with you, my friend," he whispered, sliding a hairy arm around my shoulder. "About the dinner, you understand." Briefly, the smell from his armpit fought against the much sweeter fragrance of the flowers from his garland. The armpit won.

"The ... dinner?" I asked, trying to ease away.

He felt my movement and squeezed my shoulder more tightly. It was my bad shoulder and I winced as skin pinched against hard ivory.

"I need a favour," he continued. "And ... I'm willing to pay." He opened his hand and I saw the flash of silver coins. "Look, good Athenian owls! Eh? What do you say to that?" He bounced the coins on his palm.

"I don't understand," I said, bewildered. "Lysander is paying—"

"I know what he's paying you for!" the man interrupted with a hiss. "Eels poached in wine with sour cherries, roast lamb stuffed with garlic and plums, sesame pancakes soaked in honey. Oh yes, my friend. I know exactly what he's paying you for. But what *I* need,"—he lowered his voice and bounced the coins again—"what I need is for you to serve the dishes *hot*. Eh?

What do you say?" In the light of the hearth fire, his eyes glinted strangely, almost like the silver coins he held in his hand.

I frowned at him, offended now as well as puzzled. "I always serve my food hot."

"But can you serve it hotter? Right off the fire, like. Look, man! Look at these lovely owls. And all for you, if you do as I ask!"

"Philoxenus?" Lysander stepped into the courtyard. "Are you out here?"

The fat man—Philoxenus—dropped his arm from my shoulder and stepped away smartly. The owls disappeared into a fold in his chiton.

"Ah, I thought I heard your voice," Lysander said. "But what are you doing out here, my friend? Come, Theoclea is about to start playing." He paused as he saw me standing there. "Pelops?"

"Just checking the lamb, sir. It's almost ready."

"Excellent! I look forward to it immensely. Your shellfish were worthy of the gods themselves."

Bowing low, I thanked him and the two men returned to the andron. Before he passed through the curtain, Philoxenus paused and gave me a long look, rubbing his fingers and thumb together meaningfully.

"What was he on about, then?" Hermogenes piped up behind me.

Bemused, I shook my head. "I haven't the faintest idea," I told him.

"Crazy bloater," Hermogenes snorted.

I shrugged it off.

Despite the ineptitude of the spit boy, the lamb was crisp and brown, redolent with garlic and rosemary, and it was ready for carving. I had far too much to do than to spend any more time wondering about Lysander's guests.

Throughout the evening, I'd heard the rise and fall of conversation and the occasional honeyed laugh of the hetaeras. I had it on good authority that Neaera was, in fact, present this evening, though I had not yet seen her myself. During the sacrifice, the women had been far too bundled up for me to identify any individual—even one who looked like the statue in the Agora. But the food servers had all got an eyeful, and they were buzzing with talk of her.

"She's lovely, she is!"

"Oooo, that skin! Just like a summer flower. And her hair! goes all the way down to her bum."

"And that purple number she's wearin' must have cost a bleedin' fortune. There's not many can lay out coin for cloth like that. Dyed with them crushed snail shells, it is. Priciest cloth at market."

"From what I hear, she can afford it."

"Well, if I had a nice plump arse like that, maybe I could afford one too!"

"Only if you could do The Lion, luv!"

My ears perked up at this last comment, but nobody elaborated on what exactly The Lion was and whether it was on a cheese grater or not. For obvious reasons, I was not about to ask for clarification.

Normally, a hetaera of Neaera's stature would be quite beyond

Lysander's means. She was rich enough to maintain her own household, which was ostensibly owned by Strepsiades (a feeble old citizen who would, it was commonly believed, send himself swimming down the Styx if he ever attempted to do more than just pay for her house). Neaera was one of the few hetaeras who could pick and choose her lovers, and she was much in demand, so much so that men considered it a social coup to have her grace their symposion.

According to his exceedingly loquacious slaves, Lysander had been determined to have the famous woman at his Great Panathenaea party. Cognizant of the fact that he himself was not inducement enough to secure her attendance, he had invited a foreign chariot racer to his symposion. Hermogenes's hero, Damokles, son of Iobates. Apparently, everyone in Athens (except myself) knew that Neaera had a weakness for fast horses and muscular shoulders. And, from what the slaves were saying now, Damokles seemed to have a weakness for white skin and well-rounded buttocks.

"Aphrodite's tits! He's all over her, he is."

"Hands're dippin' into her chiton more than they're in the food."

"And the wine! He's gettin' her pissed right proper."

"Did you see the boss's face? He'd like to have a go at her himself, he would."

"Well, tip a few more cups into her, luv, and they all can play Racehorse."

The party was, apparently, going well.

A little too well, perhaps, for my purposes. I was beginning to despair of approaching Neaera—at least while she was still relatively sober. My only introduction was through my culinary creations. The servers had informed me that first tables had been much appreciated. Perhaps Lysander, like Xenarchus, would summon me to the andron for compliments. It would, after all, be the elegant thing to do. And when I went in, a murmured question in a shell-shaped ear, a request for an audience was all I needed.

I waited. And waited. If Lysander wasn't up on his self-help scrolls, I'd have to think of another strategy. I waited a little longer, hoping for a summons or, at the very least, for a little divine inspiration.

What I got was decidedly different.

Between the banquet preparations, the odd encounter with Philoxenus, and a last-minute request for a special vegetable dish from the demanding Cresilla, all thoughts of the early morning omens had been banished. Inexcusable, really. I am not a seer, but I do have some facility for divination—indeed, I would never be able to work as a professional chef if I could not sacrifice an animal and read the signs in its entrails. I should have heeded the portents. Should have. Could have. But somehow, had not.

I had arranged to set aside my amphora of olive oil in Lysander's storeroom rather than in the kitchen with all its attendant chaos. Now, as the time for dessert approached, I found myself in need of more olive oil for the sesame sweetmeats. Fetching oil would normally be a slave's job, but all the kitchen slaves were busy with other tasks and, as the general household slaves had already proved themselves incompetent, I decided to fetch it myself. For obvious reasons, I was twitchy when it came to my olive oil.

I had just entered the poorly lit storeroom when suddenly my eyes registered movement. I froze and peered into the gloom, holding my lamp lower to the floor. There! There it was again. Movement. Silent, sinuous.

Great gods, it was a *snake!*

I sucked in air with a noise that was more gasp than breath.

A snake was in the house!

It was purely harmless on a physical level—just a small garter snake—but as an omen, it was one of the worst. Everyone knew snakes were companions of the dead. A sudden chill skittered up my spine as all the evil portents of the day fell into place. The crow's flight, the unlucky stumble on the doorstep, the lamb's twisted entrails. And now a snake in the house! Signs from the gods were rarely so clear. I stood motionless with horror, certain that terrible tragedy was waiting to strike.

I do not know how long I stayed there, holding my breath, waiting. A minute? An hour? A month? It was the muted sound of laughter that released me from my stasis.

"Get the oil, Pelops," I muttered through clenched teeth. A cold sweat had broken out on my brow. "Just get the oil and get back to the kitchen. You can tell Geta about the snake after you get the oil."

The reptile had slithered off into the shadows. I forced my feet to walk towards the back of the storeroom. My breath was tight in my chest. Lamplight fluttered and jumped.

And it was by this flickering light that I finally laid eyes on Neaera.

She was every bit as exquisite as Lysander's slaves had described. Every bit as lovely as her statue in the Agora. And she was as dead as a swordfish steak.

Chapter 12

It was Neaera, all right. I knew it at once. Her skin was pale, her feet small and delicate in their dainty sandals, and her lifeless body was clad in the pricey purple chiton so admired by the slaves. She lay folded over the rim of a large cauldron, the sort of waist-high pot used for preparing vast quantities of soup. Behind her, lying on its side on the floor, was my amphora of olive oil. I saw at a glance that its entire contents had been slopped into the cauldron. Neaera's long dark hair floated eerily in the golden liquid.

She had been drowned in olive oil.

"*Holy Hera!*"

I turned at the exclamation. The steward, Geta, stood in the doorway, stunned, his mouth hanging open in shock. His outcry brought more slaves. They crowded into the tiny room, crying out in panic and horror. Hermogenes wormed his way through them to my side. His eyes were wide and frightened. He tugged at my chiton, but I couldn't hear what he was trying to say to me over the cacophony. I found myself unable to move.

"What in Hades is going on here?" Lysander demanded furiously, shoving his way through the crowd of slaves. "I'll have you all whipped! How *dare* you interrupt—" he broke off with an inarticulate cry. "Great gods! Neaera? *Neaera!*"

The dinner guests came running. Before I knew it, the storeroom was filled with men crying out and tearing their hair. Half-clad flute girls clung to each other by the doorway, their painted faces pale and frightened.

"Neaera!"

"Oh gods! Gods!"

"What happened?"

"What does it mean?"

One of the dinner guests stumbled against me, crushing my toes. I think it was the chariot racer. The sharp pain released me from my stasis. Together with Hermogenes, I began rudely pushing my way past the shocked and grieving men. We appeared to be the only ones able to keep our wits. With their cries still piercing our ears, we tried to lift Neaera from the cauldron. She was slippery with oil and her body slid from Hermogenes's grasp, sloshing oil over our sandals. Geta joined us then, his apple-red cheeks now a pale, sickly green. Between the three of us, we managed to hoist her out of the cauldron and lay her gently on the floor. The olive oil formed a golden puddle around her corpse.

By the lamplight I could see the purple chiton twisted around

her limbs, the fine linen now soiled and torn. Her long fingernails were jagged. Dark bruises on her neck told the rest of the
tale.

I knelt beside her and placed my hand on her breast, hoping
to feel a heartbeat, however feeble. A futile move.

I caught Hermogenes's eye and shook my head once.

"There's no breath in her, is there, Chef?" he said faintly.

I sat back on my heels and passed a hand across my face, leaving an oily streak. "No," I agreed. My voice sounded tight and
strained. The men had fallen silent, their cries finally silenced by
the realization of what this death meant. "She's dead. Drowned."

My words fell like stones into an endless pit, swallowed up by
the darkness of horrified silence. Murder is rare in Athens, most
Athenians being far too fond of litigation to settle their differ-
ences in more violent ways. But, more importantly, murder is
not just a crime against the victim, it is a crime against the gods
themselves. Whoever killed Neaera had committed the ultimate
act of sacrilege, and by doing so, had exposed the entire community to the vengeful wrath of the gods.

Chapter 13

The symposion ended, of course.

Once Lysander recovered his senses, he and Geta promptly got rid of guests and hired help alike. Nobody complained. Damokles was first out the door, nearly sprinting in his eagerness to be gone. He'd even lost his green hair ribbon. The others were a little slower, but just as determined. Most quit the house in utter silence, though I heard one man praying fervently to Zeus's incarnation as the patron of hospitality and guests.

"Protect me, Zeus Xenios," he begged. "Defend me from the Kindly Ones. Keep me safe. Protect me, Zeus Xenios. Defend me from the Kindly Ones. Keep me safe."

Hermogenes and I were loading the donkey with cooking utensils and pots when Geta stopped by.

"Pelops," he said, then hesitated as if he wanted to ask me something.

I paused, waiting.

"Hurry home," he said after a moment. "Stay safe."

I gave him a long look before nodding. "You too."

"You have the things to purify yourselves?" he asked.

I tied the last bundle on to the donkey. "Yes."

"Good man. I've never—" he began, then broke off. "Zeus on a stick!" he swore. "I hope I never see anything like that again."

"I know what you mean," I agreed.

He stepped back and gave the donkey a thump on its flanks.

As Hermogenes and I started down the street, I spotted several priests sprinting grimly towards Lysander's house, their slaves wild-eyed and scared behind them. The purification rituals would be extensive, complex and, likely, useless. Until Neaera's killer was found, nobody in Athens would rest easy. Already the city felt different. A hush had fallen over the street— a silence that seemed to spread as I paused to listen.

"The Kindly Ones'll be flying tonight," Hermogenes said in a small voice.

I shuddered at the thought of them, but hid my concern from Hermogenes. "Less talk, more walk," I said tersely. "We've got a long way to go."

"But—"

"We'll purify ourselves as soon as we get home," I promised. "Just get moving!"

We quickened our steps, eager to be home and cleansed of the foul crime that had touched us. News of the murder hadn't yet reached the rest of the city—though that would only be a matter of time.

The Agora was ablaze with torches. The press of singers and dancers was hot and close. Hermogenes clung to the hem of my cloak as we pushed our way through. It was testament to the depth of his fear. Normally he would have lost himself in the crowd, reappearing back at the house several hours later smelling of cheap wine and claiming that he'd been looking for me.

We paused only once on our way home, when I spied a familiar face. She was tall, handsome rather than beautiful. And she was dancing with a crowd of merry women, all of them wearing flowers in their hair. Oleanders, I believe. She appeared to be smiling happily, but she plucked at my cloak as I passed and when I turned to look more closely, I could see her grey eyes were dark and troubled.

I stopped dead and Hermogenes scraped my heels with his sandals as he bumped into me. In the presence of the goddess, I barely felt it.

"Hurry home, Pelops," Athena said gravely. "Purify yourselves. Chaos approaches and I would not have you caught in it."

She turned back to the dance before I could reply, but as I watched she seemed to grow in both stature and coldness. Lovely and terrible at the same time. I needed no further encouragement.

"Hurry!" I shouted back to Hermogenes, and I started pushing rudely through the crowd, making my way toward the Dipylon Gate. The donkey balked. I yanked hard on its rope, cruel in my haste. It was not accustomed to such treatment, but my panic must have communicated itself to the beast, for it jumped forward, an odd little hop, before resuming its trotting gait.

"Who was that?" Hermogenes demanded breathlessly.

"Never mind! Save your breath and run."

With so many gathered in the Agora, we could only run in fits and starts. Great Zeus and Hera, had all of Athens turned out for this festival? And then, finally, we were through the worst of the crowds. I began to run in earnest. Hermogenes dropped a spoon and started to skid to a stop.

"Leave it!" I snapped. "Go, go!"

I didn't breathe easy until we reached the Herm outside our house whose carved smile seemed reassuring. But before I could open the door, we heard the distant sounds of celebration suddenly turn to cries of panic and pain.

I fumbled with the door latch. Over the cries I could hear another noise. A strange, unearthly shrieking. I shuddered and flung the door open.

"Wha ... what's going on, Chef?" Hermogenes squeaked, his voice high and wavering. The voice of a mere lad. Sometimes I forgot how young he was.

"I don't know," I told him honestly.

"Is it the Kindly Ones?"

"Perhaps."

Without ceremony, I dumped my load of crockery and utensils in the vestibule. Hermogenes stood there stupidly, still holding his bundles in trembling hands. Gently, I took them from him and let them fall to the floor.

"Go in to the courtyard," I ordered, speaking softly. "Strip down and stand by the altar. Put your clothes on the drying rack. I'll bring the things we need."

"But the donkey—"

"Leave her here," I said over my shoulder. "She'll be fine. We'll take care of her afterwards."

The men's rooms were empty, as were the kitchen and the storerooms. Gorgias and the slaves were out celebrating the start of the Great Panathenaea. I hoped he was nowhere near the Agora.

With prayer and fire and water, we purified ourselves, washing the stain of murder from our bodies and spirits. For once, the water behaved as it should, neither evaporating away nor suddenly becoming too hot or cold. Myrtle-scented smoke rose in the air, carrying away the corruption, and we peeled sea onions till our fingers were raw and our eyes burned with tears. But I could still hear the cries coming from the Agora. And those terrible, terrible shrieks.

We prayed for a long time.

"To sleep now," I told Hermogenes once we'd finally finished. I wrapped him tightly in a clean cloak. He was shivering, swaying back and forth, he was so tired. "We've done all we can. It will be alright."

He nodded dumbly and turned toward the storeroom where he had a pallet. Then he paused.

"Chef?"

"Yes, what is it?"

"Who was that woman? The one in the Agora?"

"A friend," I said briefly. "Just a friend."

Purification for Prats

If you have been unwise or unlucky enough to be associated with death in any form, it bloody well sucks to be you, doesn't it? No more gadding about in public places! No more entering sanctuaries for you! You reek of filth and corruption and all manner of nasty things. And you're about as welcome as a farting Spartan at a dinner party.

Sound like a nightmare? It is! Fortunately, EUKRATES is here to help with this simple but effective Five-Step Program.

You will need:

- ✓ Water, preferably from the Nine Wells
- ✓ Myrtle wood for fire, additional branches for smoking
- ✓ Fire
- ✓ Sea onions
- ✓ Eukrates's *Prayers for Pinheads**
- ✓ Fig branches
- ✓ An ugly beggar

Instructions:

Step One: Under an open sky, fire up a nice blaze of myrtle wood and strip down to your birthday chiton. Drape your discarded clothing on a drying rack. Begin to pray (see Eukrates's Prayers for Pinheads).

Step Two: With water from the Nine Wells (or, in a pinch, from the sea), fill an entire amphora of water to pour over your head and hands. Really drench yourself. Don't skimp, even if it's cold out. Suck it up, mate! You're scrubbing away corruption. More is better! And remember to keep on praying!

Step Three: Once you're thoroughly soaked, bundle a few myrtle branches together and use the blaze to light them on fire. When they begin to burn, blow them out. Bathe yourself in the smoke, paying particular attention to the hands and hair. When you start to feel like a side of pork, it's time to tuck the smoking branches under the drying rack so your clothing can be purified too. Are you still praying? Good! Don't stop now!

Step Four: Congratulations, you're almost there! Now it's time for the sea onion. Carefully peel an onion, skin by skin until nothing remains. To get rid of every speck of that stubborn filth, peel two or three onions. Burn the peels on the myrtle wood fire and pray, pray, pray. Please note: Steps One to Four are adequate for most stains of corruption. For more troublesome stains (i.e., those involving possible visits from the Kindly Ones), proceed to Step Five.

Step Five: Find an ugly beggar. Dress him in a fine cloak and feed him your best figs, barley broth, and cheeses. Dress him and feed him, but don't go getting chummy. As soon as he's done eating, that's your cue to bring out the fig branches and sea onion leaves and start whipping! Don't forget to pray while you whip that ugly beggar up and down the streets of Athens. Really give it your all here. You don't want the Kindly Ones to come calling, do you? Keep on whipping him with branches and onions as you chase him through the city and across the boundary stones. Once he's out of the city, you may stop praying (and whipping) and resume a normal life.

Chapter 14

The Kindly Ones are, in fact, nothing of the sort, though only a fool would risk their notice by referring to them by their true name. Their origins are ancient, going back to the time when the Titan Kronos castrated his father with a jagged-toothed sickle. When Kronos tossed his old dad's genitalia into the sea, Aphrodite, the goddess of love and desire, was born from the sea foam.

Something entirely different emerged from the droplets of blood.

The three are said to resemble women, but they fly on black, leathery wings. Their bodies are corpse-white. They appear garbed in long black mourning robes or sometimes, and more alarmingly, in shorter hunting attire. Their eyes run with blood, dark and terrible, and their cries are said to drive a man to insanity. They are anger and vengeance, netherworld goddesses who avenge crimes against the natural order, crimes against the gods. They are the Erinyes. The Angry Ones.

And they were flying over Athens.

I could hear their cruel screams, could imagine them swooping and diving over the crowds with their brass-studded scourges. They would flay the skin from guilty and innocent alike, pitiless in their righteous fury.

Hermogenes had fallen into an uneasy slumber. He twitched and moaned on his pallet. Strabo and Lais had found their way back home, and they huddled in the storeroom with him, their eyes wild and staring. Despite my exhaustion, I could neither sleep nor relax. Gorgias was still out there, somewhere. I paced back and forth across the small courtyard for what seemed an eternity, listening to the sounds of distant screaming, to the exhalations of my own heavy breath.

When I heard the rattle of the latch, I sprang towards the door.

"Gorgias!" I cried as he stumbled into the vestibule.

His chiton was filthy, his cheek torn and bloody. "Ansandra?" he demanded hoarsely.

I stopped, horrified. "Isn't she in the women's hall?"

Gorgias tore past me, taking the stairs three at a time. He ran across the upstairs balcony to the women's hall at the back of the house.

It had never occurred to me that Ansandra might have gone out to the festival, that she might have been caught up in all this. When Gorgias emerged seconds later with a white-faced Irene right behind him, I knew Ansandra was not there.

"She … she went over to Nico's house," he said, stumbling down the stairs, his eyes blinking rapidly at nothing. "She wanted to celebrate the festival with his daughters. She was supposed to spend the night with them. She—" he choked, unable to continue.

I put my hand on his shoulder. "What happened?"

Gorgias scrubbed at his cheek, smearing blood across his face. His hand was shaking. "Nico's wife took them all to the Agora. For the dancing. But Ansandra—" his voice tightened, "—Ansandra ran off and they lost her."

"What was she thinking, taking the girls to the Agora at this time of night?" Irene exclaimed angrily. "With all the drinking and carousing and—"

"Enough!" I cut her off with a savage gesture.

Gorgias's face had begun to crumple. "She didn't go back. She didn't go back to Nico's house. So I came here. I thought … I thought she might have come home." His voice broke. "Zeus Almighty, Pelops, if she's out there…"

"We'll find her," I told him with a certainty I did not feel.

Irene looked at me, her mouth pursed tight, her eyes wide with fear.

"I can't lose her," Gorgias pleaded. "I can't lose her too."

"You won't! We'll find her," I said again.

The last thing I wanted to do was leave the relative safety of the house, but Gorgias and Ansandra were family. My real family. I could not stay at home while Gorgias searched for his daughter.

"We'll go to the Agora," I told him. "That's where the party was. That's where she'll be. We'll go there and we'll find her."

"Yes. You're right." He closed his eyes, took a deep breath, and straightened. "You're right. That's where she'll be." His eyes flew open. "But the Kindly Ones! Gods help us, they're out there, Pelops! They've got scourges and—" he broke off. "We're going to need some weapons."

Without another word, he spun around and ran to the storerooms.

There was another rattle at the door. Ansandra! I dashed into the vestibule and flung open the door, Irene hot on my heels. A bundle of colourful veils fell against me. I recognized the turquoise himation immediately.

"Zeuxo!" I grasped her shoulders. "Great gods! What are you doing out? Are you all right?"

"Pelops," she sobbed, clutching at me. "You're alive!"

"Zeuxo, I'm fine," I assured her. "But you! Why did you go out? Are you hurt? Weren't you supposed to be at Kallikrates's symposion?" I turned her this way and that, trying to see if she'd been injured. Her body was vibrating with tension.

"I was," she gulped. "We could hear the screaming from his andron."

"Great Zeus and Hera! Why didn't you stay there?" I was appalled.

"I couldn't! I had to see … I had to make sure that…"

Just then, Gorgias strode into the vestibule. Instantly I felt all the tension flow out of Zeuxo's body. She sagged against me and uttered a brief prayer of thanks.

"Is she hurt?" Gorgias asked, not unkindly. He was carrying two of the picks the slaves used to dig clay from the clay pits.

Picks against scourges?

"Where is your spear?" I demanded, aghast. "Or your sword? Or your armour, for that matter? I thought you were a hoplite! I thought you fought with Archestratus in Potidaea!"

"I was," he said mildly, though his eyes glinted at me. "I did."

"Then where are your weapons?"

"Sold." He bit the word off. "After the plague."

I closed my mouth, silenced by realization. I knew Gorgias had fallen on lean times after the plague, but I had not known he'd been obliged to sell his soldier's gear. When I'd volunteered to go with him to the Agora to find his daughter, I'd thought we'd be properly armed. I'd thought we'd have *swords*.

Picks against scourges. I did not like the odds.

"Is she hurt?" he asked again, gesturing to Zeuxo, who still wept in my arms.

I shook my head, distracted. "No, just frightened, I think."

"Good. Let's go, then," he said. He was all business now, hard and resolute.

"*Go?*" Zeuxo gasped, horrified. "Out there? Gorgias, have you gone totally insane? Do you have any idea—?"

"My daughter's out there," he told her curtly, passing one of the picks to me.

"By all the gods!" Her voice fell to a whisper. "*Ansandra*'s in the Agora?"

"It looks that way. We're going to find her."

She didn't even pause. "I'm coming too, then." All of a sudden, she was just as decisive as Gorgias.

It brought him up short.

"*What?*" he exploded. "Don't be daft! Do you even know what's out there? What's *flying* out there? You are *not*—"

She stopped him with a finger square in his face. "Don't try to tell me what to do," she hissed fiercely, her eyes flashing even in the dim light. "You said it yourself, Ansandra's out there. Three sets of eyes are better than two, aren't they? And *you're* wasting time!"

She was stubborn, I gave her that. And loyal and brave. I only hoped she wouldn't suffer for it.

Gorgias capitulated. He had little choice in the matter and even less time to spare.

Moments later, the three of us slipped out of the house, Irene's warnings to stay safe still ringing in our ears. Swiftly, we began making our way through the dark streets of the Kerameikos towards the Agora.

"They come from above and behind," Gorgias murmured as we paused in the shadowed entrance to the marketplace. "They're fast and they're loud. Watch their scourges. They're covered in metal. They'll—" He broke off and cleared his throat. "They'll take the skin right off you."

Zeuxo's eyes were wide with apprehension, but she listened carefully to Gorgias, nodding once when he'd finished. Her silver earrings were shaped like little owls in honour of Athena. I hoped they would bring us luck.

For the first time since I'd met her, Zeuxo was out in public without a cloak. She'd left the turquoise himation back at Gorgias's house and she'd tucked the long skirts of her festival chiton under her belt, leaving her lower legs free. As I watched, she pulled her hair back with quick, deft movements and tied the curls into a severe knot. Her wide mouth was set and determined, she was stripped down and ready for action. She bent and picked up a sharp stick. It looked ridiculous in her jewelled hands, but somehow I didn't feel like laughing.

I shifted my grip on the pick and gave her a tight smile, wishing fervently—and not for the first time—that we were armed with more than digging tools and sticks.

A full moon hung over the city, casting its silvered light on the destruction. It was eerily silent, the hush punctuated only by muffled sobs and soft cries. The Agora was unrecognizable. Broken pottery and shattered stands littered the normally tidy grounds. Cloaks, veils, wreaths, and flowers had been trampled into the mud, lost or discarded in the general panic.

But worst of all were the bodies.

Splayed obscenely amidst the devastation, there were more of them than I'd thought possible. Citizens, slaves, freedmen. Wives and flute girls. Even, here and there, the smaller forms of children. All lay face down, backs stripped bare of skin, blood running black in the moonlight. The metallic tang of it was heavy in the air.

At first I thought they were all dead, but as we watched I could see them moving, struggling desperately to crawl to safety. Not dead then, but at the very least, gravely injured. My first impulse was to stop and help them, but we had to find Ansandra. Great gods, if she was out there and wounded…

I swallowed bile, sour and hot in my throat. I nodded to

Gorgias as he gave the signal to move out. Zeuxo made a little noise, but did not hesitate to follow.

We crept along the edges of the Agora, crouched low against a possible attack from above. Pale, terrified faces peered out at us from the remains of stalls and from under broken carts. The sounds of weeping seemed louder.

The air felt unnaturally warm, thick, and cloying without even a hint of a cooling breeze. I checked the sky obsessively. It was clear for now. Quiet too. But I knew better than to think The Angry Ones had gone.

"Ansandra!" Gorgias called softly.

"By the Spring House," Zeuxo urged, her voice low. "Most of the women were celebrating there. If she got caught out in this, that's where she'll be hiding."

Gorgias gave a brief nod of acknowledgement and altered his course towards the Spring House.

Still calling Ansandra's name, we clung to the shadows of the plane trees, stumbling every so often on the wreckage, squelching in puddles of mud or piss or worse. I caught a whiff of Zeuxo's perfume. An incongruous note of lavender over the heavier choking smell of fear. To my right, I could see the unfinished Law Court, and the dark shapes of crying, huddled figures cowering against its bare bones.

And then, we came to the centre of the Agora. No more plane trees. No more concealing shadows.

Neither Gorgias nor Zeuxo even paused. As one, they ducked out into the bright moonlight, making directly for Spring House. Gorgias was jogging now. I followed quickly but more cautiously, my heart thumping irregularly in my chest. I'd been killed before. I had no desire to repeat the experience.

I heard it before we were halfway across the clearing.

A strange new sound. It drowned out the other noises, the groans and weeping. It started low, like the throaty growl of a wolf, before rising to an eerie wailing moan. A grue skittered up my spine. Frantically, I searched the night sky. I couldn't see anything! And then the noise rose again, higher and higher, until it tore the fabric of night with a rasping shriek. Fury! Madness! Vengeance! The scream went on and on, flaying the very spirit from my body. I cried out.

And then, they fell on us.

I dove to the ground just as the first creature attacked. Leathery wings grazed my neck and I flung myself to one side, avoiding the cruel scourge by a hair's breadth. A stench of putrescence rolled over me, the dank smell of disease and rot. I gagged and tried to thrust the metal rod into the creature's body. But the Angry One shrieked and darted away from my feeble attack. It snarled, the sound rising as the creature rose in the air above me, readying itself for another attack.

Gorgias had thrown Zeuxo to her knees. He stood over her, muscles bunched, metal pick clenched in his hands. Two of the Erinyes flew at them. They were clad in short hunting skirts, black serpents writhing around their torsos. Their terrible eyes flashed with fire, and they laughed as if drunk on the destruction. He struck one of them, sending it veering off to the side. But the other swept in with its brass-studded scourge and Gorgias screamed as it tore a long strip from his back.

"Gorgias!" I cried.

Just then, the creature above me plunged down with a strangled screech. I lurched up to meet it, clutching the pick and bracing myself as Gorgias had done, but instead of flaying me with its scourge, it grabbed hold of my pick and flung it far behind me.

I was defenceless.

The creature landed and strode towards me. For the first time, I got a good look at it. I wished I hadn't.

Ostensibly female, its body shape was somehow wrong. Torso oddly elongated, limbs too slender, muscles and tendons too sharply drawn. The creature moved jerkily on the ground, more insect-like than human. Its leathery wings trailed in the mud, and dark blood ran from its glittering eyes down its pale hollow cheeks. The stench of the creature was thick in my nostrils. Grinning obscenely, it opened its mouth—far wider than a mouth should open—and growled again. Deep and rumbling. I knew what was coming.

The sound rose, moaning, wailing. Wavering up the scale to that terrible shrieking crescendo. *Great gods, that cry!* Like the tortured scream of some wounded animal!

I clapped my hands over my ears and sank to the ground, my knees buckling under the onslaught. My sanity shredding. Dimly, I was aware of the creature looming triumphantly over me, drawing its arm back, preparing to flay the flesh from my body.

I closed my eyes.

Chapter 15

"Not so fast, bitch!"

There was a muffled whump followed by a startled screech. When I opened my eyes, the Angry One was gone, replaced by a man so large in stature he would tower over me even if I hadn't been hugging the ground like a flatbread.

He was a splendid specimen, all bulging muscles and bronze armour. His head was bald, his neck non-existent, and he had a scar above his ear that extended down one well-sculpted cheekbone. He was built like a marble shithouse and looked as tough as hoplite boot leather. A long spear was in his hand, shining silver in the starlight. An eagle owl perched on his shoulder, its eyes staring down at me with a baleful orange glow.

The man spat on the ground, and even that seemed tough. For a split second, everything froze. The Erinyes, the man and his fierce-eyed hunting bird, even the small background movements of the wounded. All motion stilled. All sound faded into silence.

And then, with a suddenness that snatched my breath away, the owl took wing, streaking towards the three Erinyes. They screamed defiance, but the bird never faltered. Talons extended, it slammed into one of the creatures, tearing a long gash in its neck. Without pausing, the owl launched itself off the first creature and onto the second. Feathers flew as they collided, but the bird's knife-sharp beak found its mark. As the second creature squealed and clawed at its now non-existent eye, the man's silver spear took the third neatly in the stomach.

The Erinyes howled. Terrible, tortured ululations. Ink-dark blood ran from their wounds, spraying in all directions as they writhed in pain and fury. I cowered down even further. Blood splattered against my arms, burning wherever it touched. I cried out, the sound lost in the endless ocean of that terrible noise. I thought I should go mad or die. In that moment, I swear I heard the watery growl of the River Styx, felt its cold, dark waves lapping at the edges of my failing spirit. And then, suddenly, unbelievably, the creatures turned, still screaming, and flapped awkwardly away.

"Ha! That's right, you sodding motherfuckers! This one's ours," the man bellowed after them. "So, piss off!"

He paused a moment, watching until their black shapes disappeared into the night. Then he turned his gaze to the Agora, looking around at the carnage. His eyes glittered strangely as if he relished what he saw, as if he were pleased and not a little aroused by it all. If I hadn't already recognized him, I would have known him by his reaction.

"Ares," I gasped, still lying on the ground. "Your timing is impeccable."

"Pelops." He greeted me and offered me a hand up. He looked at my torn, muddied chiton and frowned. "Fuck me! You've had a time of it."

"It's not been fun," I agreed a little breathlessly.

"Cock-sucking Titan spawn!" He horked and spat in the direction the Erinyes had flown. "Think they're too fucking good for rules."

He rolled his massive shoulders back and shook out his arms vigorously. "I mean, don't get me wrong," he added with a lopsided grin. "I like a little blood and gore as much as the next god—maybe even a bit more, yeah?" The god of blood-lust winked and gave me a friendly jab in the ribs. "But hey, when the fucking word comes down, you don't see me standing around saying bugger that, do you?"

"Uh, no," I replied uncertainly. "No, I wouldn't think I'd see that."

"Damn right you wouldn't. There are rules—even for fuck-ing gods. Those sodding goat fuckers were told to leave your pan-frying arse out of things! They were given the fucking word, just like everyone else. Too fucking good for rules, are they? Well…" He cracked his knuckles ominously. "I think it's time someone taught The Flying McBitch Sisters a lesson in fucking manners."

I thought at first perhaps the Erinyes had succeeded in

scrambling my brains with their terrible shrieks. I was having difficulty grasping the meaning of Ares's words.

"You mean … are you saying the Angr—I mean, the Kindly Ones. Are you saying they were told to leave me alone? *Me?*" I almost fell back on my knees.

"Well, sure as shite I didn't come to Athens for the fucking party. I'm not that fond of my sodding sister." Ares shrugged. "What can I say? Word came down from the Big Guy. Apparently, we fucking *owe* you for that shoulder." He snorted a bit. "Me, I'd've called us even a long time ago, but hey, I'm just the fucking heat. I don't give the bloody orders, do I?"

"I … I guess not."

"No, I do not." He nodded. "But by my own hairy bollocks, I fucking well follow them!"

"Uh, yeah. Right. Thanks. I, uh … I really don't know what I would have done if—"

"Ah, shut it." Ares waved it off. "Wasn't my call, was it? Besides, you're not half-bad. For a mortal, that is. And you know, it really wasn't any fucking skin off my back." He brayed with laughter at his own wit.

"*Damn!*" I swore as memory came crashing down with that visual. "Gorgias!"

Forgetting the foul-mouthed god, I spun around and staggered back to where I'd last seen my friend.

Despite his wounds, Gorgias had regained his feet. Blood covered his shoulders and back. His left arm was a mangled mess, hanging uselessly at his side. He stood unsteadily, wobbling and cursing. Something seemed to be wrong with one of his legs. On his right, Zeuxo was either trying to hold him up or hold him back. I couldn't tell which.

"Lend us a hand!" he cried to me through gritted teeth. His voice was almost unrecognizable. "I've got to … I've got to get to the Spring House!"

Ares had come up behind me. "What the fuck's he banging on about?"

Gorgias looked at him and blinked uncomprehendingly.

"His daughter," I explained. "We're looking for his daughter."

"Well, you won't be finding her at the fucking Spring House, I can tell you that," the god said, frowning as he examined a spot on his armour. "She's under the wine seller's stall. You know the one."

"She's all right, then?" I demanded, perhaps not as respectfully as I should have done. Fortunately, Ares didn't seem to notice.

"Right as rain." He gave an offhand shrug. "Whatever the fuck that means." He looked up from his armour and brushed off his hands. "Well, kids, time for me to be pissing off." He glanced up briefly and the eagle owl swooped down and landed on his bronze-clad shoulder. "It's been a fucking slice and all, but I've got places to go, people to see, and bugger knows what else to do."

Ares started to turn away, then paused. "And Pelops, do us a favour, yeah? Watch your ass around the Erinyes. They're older than fucking dirt—way older than any of our lot, not counting Aphrodite, of course. We don't go noising around about it but technically, they don't *have* to listen to the Big Guy. So, don't go fucking about with them, right? At least not till I get a chance to beat some respect into the skanky-assed bitches."

"I won't," I promised. "Thank you."

But he was already on his way, striding briskly across the Agora. The groans of the wounded were markedly louder wherever he passed. For a moment, I thought I could see the flickering forms of his twin sons, Deimos and Phobos, the lion-headed gods of terror and panic, matching steps with their father. Then I blinked and they were gone. As the god of slaughter disappeared into the shadows of the ruined marketplace, I could hear him whistling a jaunty tune.

Chapter 16

"Stay here," I ordered Gorgias.

He started to protest.

"I know exactly where she is." I touched his arm gently. " I'll bring her back to you."

I sprinted off. Gorgias was in no shape to follow.

I found Ansandra huddled under the wine seller's stall, the wine seller himself standing grim guard over her. Miraculously, his booth was undamaged, his goods still intact, though perhaps that wasn't surprising, given his nature.

"Pelops," Dionysus greeted me as I approached. His mouth was a thin line, his expression devoid of all its usual merriment. "I seem to have found something you lost."

"Pelops?" A muffled voice emerged from under the stall.

I bent down to peer under the counter.

"*Pelops!*" Ansandra gasped, scrambling to her feet.

She flung herself into my arms and I rocked back on my heels, fighting to keep my balance.

"Where's my dad? Is he okay? I'm sorry! I'm so sorry I ran off. I didn't know. I didn't! I'm sorry! Is Dad okay? Why didn't he come with you?" Her face and hair were filthy, her festival chiton in much the same shape. She wasn't crying, but her eyes were far too wide and far too bright. Her whole body was trembling.

"Your dad's grand," I assured her, stroking her tangled hair. "Shhh. He's a bit banged up, but he'll be fine. He *did* come, Sprout. He and Zeuxo are waiting for us just across the market. I'll take you right over to them. But are you all right? You're not hurt, are you?"

She buried her face in my shoulder and shook her head. I lifted my eyes and met Dionysus's sombre gaze.

"Thank you," I told him gratefully. "Thank you for keeping her safe."

He inclined his head.

I'd already turned to go when Dionysus spoke again. "Hurry home," he called softly. "They may not be done yet."

It was the second time that night a god had told me to hurry home. Without hesitating, I lifted Ansandra up and began jogging back to where I'd left Gorgias and Zeuxo. I ran past shattered stalls and dodged around piles of unidentifiable debris, conscious the whole time of the warm weight in my arms and my own wildly beating heart. Ansandra clung to me like a limpet, her body convulsing with shivers. I tried to shield her from the worst of the sights, but there were a lot of them. And I couldn't cover her ears.

I heard Gorgias's cry of relief before I saw him.

"Daddy!" Ansandra shrieked, wiggling out of my arms and darting towards him.

He swept her up with his good arm.

That was when she started crying. "Daddy!" she choked. "You're hurt!"

"It's nothing, luv. Just a bit of a scrape," he told her, tears running down his face. "I'm fine. It's nothing."

She wept in earnest now, babbling incoherently, her fingers plucking at his chiton. Great wracking sobs shuddered through her slight frame.

"It's okay, honey," he said over and over again.

Gorgias rocked Ansandra back and forth, his wounds forgotten in the need to comfort his child. I found myself oddly touched by the sight. My own father would never have behaved in such a way. Tantalus had not believed in showing affection of any kind—for which my ivory shoulder was daily proof.

"It's okay now," Gorgias murmured, reassuring her. "I'll be fine. You'd need more than a bunch of rubbishy Kindly Ones to take out your old dad, yeah?"

Zeuxo had stepped back from their reunion, her expression unreadable, her arms wrapped tightly around herself as if for comfort.

I touched her shoulder to get her attention. "We've got to go," I told her.

Her eyes widened at my tone, but she nodded her understanding.

"Gorgias," I said.

He was oblivious to me.

"*Gorgias!*"

He looked up blankly.

"We need to go," I repeated. "Now. Fast."

Sense returned to his eyes and with it, fear. He glanced up at the sky apprehensively then swivelled around until he found Zeuxo. "Right," he said, turning back to me. "Let's move, then."

Ansandra was still crying.

"I'll carry her," offered Zeuxo. "Pelops, you're going to have to help Gorgias. The great bugger's twisted his knee. He can hardly walk."

The less said about the journey home, the better. I don't think the Kindly Ones returned to Athens that night—at least I heard no more of their dreadful screams—but fear licked at our backs almost as effectively as their cruel scourges. We stumbled and staggered back to the house, clumsy in our eagerness to achieve its relative safety.

Zeuxo's arms gave out just shy of the Dipylon Gate and Ansandra had to walk the rest of the way home. Stumbling along behind us and drooping with weariness, she had stopped crying, too exhausted to do anything more than shuffle one foot in front of the other.

I was in no position to help. Gorgias had twisted his left knee so badly, he could barely put weight on it. I had to support him on that side—the same side laid bare by the Erinyes' metal-studded scourges. It was not a pleasant journey for me. It must have been excruciating for him. We were both reeling like drunkards by the time we fell through the door and into the front vestibule.

Irene took immediate charge of Ansandra and Zeuxo, hustling them both up the stairs as soon as we arrived.

"There's hot water and fresh drying cloths," I could hear her saying to them. "I've had the water heating since you left, enough for a bath if you've a mind for that. And look at the state of your clothes! We'll be lucky to use them for rags, won't we? Well, better the clothes than the body, that's what I say. No, Ansandra, put them here. I'll deal with them later. Now don't you go worrying about your father, pet, he'll be fine. Pelops will do what needs to be done, won't he? First things first, we need to get you cleaned up. Look at you, you're all but asleep on your feet."

Her monologue faded as the three of them disappeared into the women's hall and, presumably, the bathing room. It was a good idea. We all needed to clean up. Gorgias, however, was going to need more than hot water and a strigil.

Even without lamplight, I could tell his colour was bad. His chiton was torn, dark with filth, and his skin was marble-white beneath it. My own clothing was wet and sticky with his blood. Leaning heavily on me, he limped into the courtyard and collapsed onto the bench with a ragged groan.

"Lie down," I told him.

"I can't," he said through gritted teeth. "My bloody back!"

"I'm sending for Menon."

"*Menon!*" He half rose in protest, then fell back onto the bench with a strangled cry of pain. "You're bloody joking!" he gasped.

"Tell me you're joking! That pigeon-chested little tosser is—"

"The only doctor we can afford," I cut him off. "Look at yourself! You need a doctor, Gorgias."

"I'll go to the sodding Asclepeion, then."

"And how do you propose to get there?" I argued. "The Temple of Asclepius is too far away. Unless, of course, you want me to strap you upside down over the donkey and drag you halfway across the city through all that chaos and debris. I'm sure it would do your back a world of good."

He scowled blackly at me.

"Look," I said, dropping my voice persuasively. "The Temple's too far and it's too expensive—"

"But they don't charge—"

"A fee. I know. But eventually, you'll have to show your gratitude, won't you? A sculpture of all the happily healed body parts? Look at you. You're a mess! You'd have to dedicate a whole statue of yourself. Frankly, I haven't got the coin for it, and I'm quite sure you don't either."

He didn't answer me.

"Besides," I rubbed my eyes wearily, all the strain of the last few hours finally catching up with me. "The priests are going to have their hands full after what happened tonight. There were a lot of people hurt."

I sighed and straightened up with an effort. "I'm sorry, my friend, but I'm afraid Menon's our best bet. He's a self-important little prat, I'll grant you that much, but at least he knows what he's doing most of the time."

Gorgias was probing at his knee, sucking his breath in sharply each time he touched it. "You'll never get the bloody bugger out of his house," he grunted pessimistically. "Not tonight. Not with Themselves flying about."

I rose and tried unsuccessfully to brush some of the filth from my chiton. "Oh, I've got a few ideas," I assured him and turned away.

"Pelops."

I paused and looked back over my shoulder.

"Bring us some wine, will you? And..." His mouth worked, and he seemed to be struggling to find words. "Ta, yeah?" he said finally, his voice low and ragged. "Thanks for coming out. Thanks for finding my daughter."

I smiled and nodded tiredly. "You're welcome."

Chapter 17

I found Lais and Strabo in the storeroom with Hermogenes. They were wrapped in oat-coloured blankets and huddled around a small, inadequate lamp. Its weak light did nothing to hide the strain on their faces. As I stood in the doorway, three sets of wide eyes glinted up at me with a combination of fear and wariness.

"Up!" I ordered, not unkindly. "Strabo, Lais. Both of you. Come, you're to fetch Menon."

Naturally, they protested.

"Sod that!"

"Are you out of yer gourd, man? 'Ave you seen what's flyin' about out there?"

"We never meant to break yer olive oil. It were a mistake—"

Losing my temper, I cut them off with a couple of well-placed slaps.

"Silence!" I snapped, raising my voice over their howls of protest. "This has nothing to do with my amphora! I've not gone mad, but 'what's flying about out there' has flayed half the skin off your master's back!"

That shut them up rather effectively.

I heard Hermogenes gasp.

"They got the Boss?" Strabo rumbled in a deep voice perfectly matched to his massive physique.

I nodded curtly. "He needs a healer."

"I could go," Hermogenes offered, visibly swallowing his reluctance. "It's not far. And I can run faster than these two dirty great buggers." He gestured toward them with all the disdain of youth. "You know I can!"

"No." I shook my head. "I know you're fast, Hermogenes, but I'm going to need you here. Gorgias is a mess. You and I need to start cleaning him up. Strabo and Lais will go. Besides, knowing Menon, he's likely to require some ... persuading."

At that, Strabo lumbered to his feet and poked the still-protesting Lais with his toe. "C'mon, Lais," he said. "Shut yer gob. The Boss's hurt. Let's go fetch the leech, then."

Lais was relatively new to the household, but Strabo had been with Gorgias for years. Certainly long enough to appreciate the value of a good master—and Gorgias was a very good master. Fortunately, Strabo was also the larger of the two slaves. Yanking the reluctant Lais to his feet, Strabo marched him smartly down the entrance hall to the front door.

"Don't take 'no' for an answer," I ordered as I handed them a couple of torches. "Go into his rooms, if you have to. Check under the sleeping couch if you can't find him. And make sure he brings his medical bag."

"Sleeping couch. Medical bag," Strabo repeated dutifully, his thick features scrunched up in concentration.

"Break his bloody door down if you have to!" I called after them as the light from their torches disappeared down the street. "And hurry!"

Though Menon was the closest thing this part of the Kerameikos had to a doctor, I had no fear that he'd be out tending the victims of tonight's horror. In addition to his fairly impressive medical knowledge, Menon possessed an even more impressive sense of self-preservation. He was far more likely to be cowering under his sleeping couch or quaking behind his disciples than out applying salve and bandages to the wounded. It was the reason I sent Strabo and Lais to retrieve him. The two slaves were as big as oxen and twice as stupid. They would follow my instructions to the word, and obstacles such as locked doors, furniture, and obstructive disciples would be nothing more than pesky annoyances to them.

I sent Hermogenes to the kitchen for hot water and rags, then I went to see if Gorgias had passed out in his geraniums.

It was some time before Strabo and Lais finally returned with Menon. By then, Hermogenes and I had managed to clean the worst of the filth and blood from Gorgias (who had stubbornly managed to hang on to consciousness), though I'd decided to leave his back for the healer. I'd also broached the amphora of Thasian wine that Dionysus had given me and, although purists might have had an issue with the ratio of wine to water, the drink was helping to dull some of my friend's pain.

As for myself, I was beyond exhaustion at this point, running on little but nervous energy. I couldn't help feeling that Gorgias's injuries were somehow my fault, that even though I'd done my best to purify myself, he had somehow been tainted by my corruption—and that the Erinyes had been drawn to him because of it. The more rational part of my mind knew this for false logic, but I found I could not entirely dismiss it. And so I hovered around him like an over-solicitous slave, plying him with wine at every perceived opportunity.

I'd stationed Hermogenes by the Herm in front of our house to wait for the doctor. An unnecessary precaution, as it turned out. I heard Menon coming down the street long before Hermogenes was able to spot him through the gloom.

"How dare you treat me like this! This is outrageous! Your master will hear of this! He'll have your hides for ass cloths for this insult!"

I rushed to the door, ready to lend my assistance should it prove necessary. It was not. The two slaves arrived with Menon wedged firmly between them. Lais seemed to be favouring one leg and Strabo now sported a long scratch across his forearm. It appeared Menon had put up a good fight.

The physician was a short, very thin individual. The sort of man who made up for his lack of stature with a towering ego, at the same time that he begrudged his body the pleasures of a good meal. Normally, he had all the foppishness of a flute girl and smelled like he'd bathed in perfume, but tonight he arrived with his chiton askew and his carefully coiffed hair tangled and mussed. A darkening bruise on his cheek was further testament to his lack of enthusiasm for this particular commission. But despite his general state of disarray, he still managed to reek of violets.

"Where are your disciples?" I inquired, looking in vain behind them. Menon never went anywhere without his two apprentices.

"Ask them," Menon replied icily, indicating Gorgias's muscle-bound slaves.

"You never said nuffin' 'bout helpers!" Strabo protested.

"We never knew we was s'pposed to bring those buggers, did we?"

"Great Zeus and Hera," I swore, pinching the bridge of my nose.

"You never said!"

"We never knew!"

"Be quiet!" I snapped, cutting them off with a chopping gesture.

Menon had been silent throughout this exchange. He did not remain so.

"So, you're the one who gave the orders for these pox-ridden idiots to come collecting me, are you? What makes you think you have the right to treat me—me!—like the lowest root cutter? I was a student of Hippokrates himself! And I'll have you know that I have well-placed friends—*very* well-placed friends—and they won't be pleased when I tell them of this outrage. Just you wait until—"

"Enough! Spare me the drama, Menon. I know your history. You were a slave until, what … six months ago?"

"I was a free man before the battle of Salamis!" he interrupted shrilly.

"And a slave after it. What's your point?"

"I still practised medicine! I was a well-paid slave!"

"Granted. But you were a slave all the same. I know you finally managed to purchase your freedom with all your earnings. But as for well-placed friends? If they were placed so advantageously, then why did it take so long for you to raise the money?"

He began to wilt visibly.

"Could they not induce their own well-placed friends to come to your aid?" I inquired. "And if your standing is so high, why are you not practising your profession in the Asclepeion with the rest of the priest doctors? And *please*." I withered him further with a scathing look. "You're no student of Hippokrates. Every quack with an herb garden makes the same claim. You really ought to come up with something a little more creative." I paused. "Are we done now?"

Menon opened and closed his mouth like a fish out of water, but no sound emerged. A silence that was predictably—and regrettably—short-lived.

"That doesn't mean you have the right to treat me like this!" He found his voice, which, though lacking much of its former arrogance, was just as shrill.

I ignored his complaints and steered him, still sputtering and protesting, through the vestibule, down the hallway and into the courtyard. My friend was hurt and in pain. I had no more patience for Menon's attitude. But as soon as he laid eyes on Gorgias, the physician's tirade fizzled and died as medical curiosity overcame affront. It was one of his few redeeming qualities.

Menon began examining his patient, turning him this way and that, clucking and *tsk*ing, as he catalogued the injuries aloud.

"Hmm ... a scourge, yes? Yes. Studded with metal, I think. Yes. Very nasty. Very nasty, indeed."

He did something that made Gorgias jump.

"*Ares's balls!*" Gorgias swore. "Have a care, you dodgy git!"

I tensed up, poised to shove the leech away from my friend if he tried to hurt him again.

But Menon paid no attention to either his patient's curses or my threatening posture.

"Not deep, though," he muttered to himself. "No, not too deep. That's good, yes? Yes. We clean it out, and wrap it up. Cannabis leaves steeped in water, I think. And clean linens for wrapping."

He pulled thoughtfully at his thin beard. "The problem will be in rebalancing the humours, but ..." He shrugged. "That is what I do, yes? Yes."

Menon kept mumbling to himself as I looked over his shoulder.

"Ah, and what is this?" He poked at Gorgias's shoulder, his movements quick and birdlike. "Hmmm ... a dislocation, I think. Yes, yes, a dislocation. Easy to fix! Painful, but easy. I will need strong arms to hold him. Yes, very strong arms—especially as I am missing my disciples."

Menon slid me a darkly resentful look.

"I'll have Strabo hold him down," I told him.

He sniffed and turned back to his patient.

"What about my knee?" Gorgias asked tightly. His face had paled even further under the physician's less than tender ministrations.

Menon recoiled, offended that a patient would actually dare to question him. "It is a twisted knee," he said shortly. "What do you expect when you go traipsing about on nights such as these?"

"I can't stand on it."

"Well, of course you can't!" he snapped. "Did you, perhaps, miss the part where I said it is twisted?"

Gorgias face darkened.

"Fine, fine, fine." Menon waved his arms impatiently. "I'll bind it up for you, yes? You'll be able to walk on it in a day or two. How are your bowels? Are you troubled with wind?"

"Leave my sodding bowels out of it, you!" Gorgias exploded, before collapsing back on the bench with a cry of pain.

"Perhaps we should just concentrate on his injuries, shall we?" I intervened, barely hanging on to my own temper. "And leave his inner workings alone. The man is injured, not ill."

Menon sniffed. "Very well," he said. "Send for this Strabo, then."

For such a small, slight man, Menon proved remarkably strong. He popped Gorgias's shoulder back into place with a practised yank. Gorgias, of course, bellowed like an ox and very nearly threw off Strabo's hold. Menon seemed to enjoy himself more than was strictly necessary. But he gave Gorgias a strong tea of willowbark to reduce the pain, and his hands were gentle as he washed out the terrible wounds left by the scourge and bound them with clean strips of linen. Gorgias fell asleep on the bench before Menon was finished.

"You must keep the wounds clean and change the bandages daily," he told me as he washed up in the fresh basin of water that Hermogenes had brought for him. "I will leave you some cannabis leaves for steeping. Boil the water and put in a handful of leaves. Let it cool and use the liquid to clean the wounds, yes? Yes. Very easy to remember. I'm sure even you can do it."

I let that slide.

He gestured at my arms. "You may use the same thing to wash those. To make certain they do not fester."

Surprised, I looked down at my forearms. Where the Erinyes' blood had splattered me, there were several raised welts, almost like cooking burns. I'd been so focused on Gorgias's wounds, I hadn't noticed my own injuries. Now that I had, they suddenly began to pulse and throb.

"Your friend has lost much blood," Menon continued, drying his arms with a piece of old linen. "So his humours will be too dry. Give him broths to increase the wetness. See how he shakes even in his sleep? Chills without fever. Give him hot wine to combat the cold. But not too much, yes? With wounds like this, the hot humour can become very strong. You must send for me if this happens. And I would appreciate it if you would not send those two louts to collect me."

"I was not confident that you would risk coming out tonight without them."

"And I would not have, if I'd had any say in the matter," he said snippily. "Only a fool would go out with the Kindly Ones flying."

"Some of us," I said, "did not have that choice."

Athens's Emergency Services

What to do in the case of:

—————— Medical Emergency ——————

1. Visit the temple of Asclepius. Bring pajamas.
2. Make your prayers to Apollo the Healer and Asclepius the Physician. Sleep overnight in the temple. Wait for the god to visit you in a dream.
3. Describe your dream to the temple physicians. They will interpret it for you and prescribe a course of treatment that may include baths, purgation, dieting, or mild gymnastics.
4. Express your gratitude to the gods by dedicating small votive tablets or statues depicting the formerly diseased or injured body parts.
5. If the costs of a temple visit are beyond your means, seek the advice of a private health practitioner. Beware of disguised or outright quackery.

—————— Fire, or the Breath of Hephaestus ——————

1. Rally a group of neighbours and a goodly number of buckets.
2. Using the nearest fountain, form a line and pass buckets of water along.
3. Make your prayers to Hephaestus the Firecrafter. Throw water on the flames until extinguished.

— Burglary, assault, or any other personal crime —

1. Report the crime to the Scythian archers. It is their job to guard public meetings, keep order, maintain crowd control, and assist with making arrests.
2. Make your prayers to Sharp-Sighted Athena before carrying out a criminal investigation. Remember, as a citizen of Athens, any investigation is up to you.
3. Make the arrest.
4. Should the criminal be convicted and fined, collect your half of the fine as a reward for your service to the community.

*PLEASE NOTE, EMERGENCY SERVICES ARE NOT AVAILABLE OUTSIDE CITY WALLS

ATTACK BY KINDLY ONES!!

1. STANDING WITH LEGS SHOULDER-WIDTH APART, BEND AT THE HIPS BRINGING YOUR HEAD TO YOUR KNEES.
2. EXTEND NECK AND HEAD THROUGH YOUR LEGS.
3. MAKE YOUR PRAYERS TO ZEUS THE PROTECTOR.
4. KISS YOUR ARSE GOODBYE.

Chapter 18

"Go," Irene ordered, making shooing motions with her hands. "See herself home. I'll watch Gorgias."

Her tone was kinder than I'd ever heard it, her whole demeanour one of friendly affection. Could it be that by helping Gorgias find his daughter, I'd slain The Gorgon?

"And what about Ansandra?" I asked.

"Don't you worry your poor head about Ansandra," Irene chided. "I've set her to the loom, haven't I? Not that I'll be able to use the cloth for anything more than rags the way she weaves, but it'll keep her out of mischief while I keep an eye on himself."

"He felt hot to me," I said, still unwilling to leave my friend. "He's sleeping, so it's hard to say, but his forehead seemed warm."

"If that's the case, I'll send Strabo for the leech, won't I? Go!" She all but pushed me out of the room. "Life sails on, even with us wishing it would slow down a bit. Herself has a contract tonight and she's got to get ready. And so do you, if I don't miss my mark. Let me look after the master. I've been doing it for years, haven't I?"

Still astonished at the change in her, I allowed myself to be bullied out of the room. Gorgias lay restlessly on his sleeping couch, oblivious to our conversation. The room reeked of steeping cannabis and various other herbs which Irene had used to dose him during the night. I hated to leave him like this, but Irene was right. Life would not stop just because the Erinyes had taken to the skies. Celebration of the Great Panathenaea would continue—nobody would risk offending Athena by doing otherwise—though I suspected the festivities were about to take on a vastly different tone. I would have liked to keep Gorgias company, but I had a symposion dinner to cook and Zeuxo needed to get home to make her own preparations for the evening.

"Damage control" was how she described it when I caught up with her in the kitchen. "I'm to be main flute girl at The Parthenon Pair's symposion tonight," she explained as she passed me a small cluster of red grapes. "It's a big deal, Pel. A lot of the girls were hoping for it. Tiny—Iktinos—was kind to ask me, and I don't want to disappoint him by showing up looking like a harpy."

I popped a grape in my mouth and chewed as I considered her words. She did look tired and worn this morning. Her face was pale, except for the shadows around her eyes, and there was a shallow scratch across her cheek that I hadn't noticed the night before. Her right arm sported a nasty bruise that must have been painful. I had no doubt that she'd clean up nicely once her slaves had at her, but right now, without all the cosmetics and jewellery and fancy clothes, she just looked young and somehow vulnerable. I thought she was all the more beautiful for it.

"You could never look like a harpy," I told her sincerely.

Her mouth quirked up at one side in a crooked smile, but it soon faded.

"How's Gorgias this morning?" she asked, playing absently with her grapes instead of eating them.

I made a face. "I *think* he's going to be okay, but what do I know?" I shrugged, suddenly losing my own appetite. Even in the fresh light of day, I still felt responsible for what had happened. I pushed the grapes away. "He might be getting feverish. He had a bad night. But Irene's kicked me out so I can see you home. She says she'll send for Menon if she needs to."

Zeuxo's face was stricken. "You should stay with him! I can see myself home. What if Menon won't come for Irene? What if—"

"Irene's been looking after Gorgias for years," I told her. "She knows what to do. Strabo will go for Menon if he's needed. And as for seeing yourself home? Don't be ridiculous! I won't hear of it. Hermogenes and I will take you to your door. I need to pick up my fish from Krysippos anyhow. You're not the only one with a contract for tonight. And it seems I must somehow find myself more olive oil before the week is out."

Zeuxo frowned. "More oil? Again? Didn't you just replace one?"

I realized then that Zeuxo had no idea of my part in last

night's tragedy. Briefly, I described Lysander's symposion and its tragic ending.

"Great Hera!" she breathed when I'd finished. "Pel, have you been to the priests? To have had contact with a corpse—especially one to have met such an end! You must get purified!"

"I did. I am," I said, laying a reassuring hand on her arm.

She flinched and I snatched my hand back.

"Zeuxo," I began, then paused to take a calming breath. "Hermogenes and I took care of it as soon as we got home. It was the first thing we did. Myrtle, sea onions, the whole treatment. Don't worry about me."

She passed a hand across her eyes. "How can I not? Pel, this is terrible."

"What's terrible?" Ansandra asked, coming into the room. She was cradling Kabob in her arms.

I turned to look at her, opened my mouth, then closed it again as I took in her appearance.

Ansandra was a changed girl this morning. Clean, for the first time since I'd known her, with hair freshly brushed and—wonder of all wonders—arranged in a style involving curls and ribbons. Instead of her usual grubby tunic, she was dressed in a pale green chiton, which matched her hair ribbons. If Zeuxo looked more youthful this morning, Ansandra looked older. But it wasn't just her physical appearance, I realized as I examined her more closely. The events of the night before had matured her, and the expression on her young face was serious.

"What's terrible?" she repeated, then fear quickened in her eyes. Kabob squawked in protest as she inadvertently tightened her hold on him. "It's not Dad, is it? He's still okay, isn't he? Irene said—"

"Your dad's fine!" I hastened to reassure her. "He's going to be fine. Irene's watching him and I've told her to send for Menon at the slightest hint of fever. Zeuxo and I were just talking about business. Nothing to worry about. Come here, you."

She came to me and I put my arm around her. The quail muttered and clucked. "Don't worry, Sprout," I said, giving her a comforting squeeze. "We're not about to let Charon take your old dad just yet. Right?"

Ansandra snuffled noisily and nodded.

"By the way, nice hair," I told her, tugging gently on a lock of it.

She looked pleased. "Zeuxo did it for me."

"She's good."

"The best!" Ansandra agreed.

"Speaking of fancy hairstyles," I said, turning to Zeuxo, who had been watching our conversation with an enigmatic smile "I need to get you home."

Ansandra disengaged herself from me. "You're leaving now?" she asked Zeuxo, crestfallen.

Zeuxo crinkled her nose. "I have to, honey. I've got to work tonight."

"But you'll be back, right? You won't have to work for the whole Panathenaea?"

"I'll be back," Zeuxo promised her solemnly.

I walked Zeuxo back to the house that she shared with several other flute girls, Hermogenes trailing along behind us. Although the cleanup crews had obviously been working since before dawn, there was still a lot of rubbish lying in the streets. Zeuxo clasped my arm, sobered by the evidence of so much destruction. At the sight of each crushed wreath of flowers and each clump of bloodied cloth, she clung a little tighter.

I was affected by the sights as well—indeed, no feeling man could have been otherwise—but I was also very aware of Zeuxo's warm body pressing against my own, her soft breast against my forearm. And when we arrived at her door and she offered me that lovely lopsided smile and kissed me sweetly on the cheek, it was everything I could do not to glow.

"You will be all right, Pel, won't you?" she asked anxiously.

"I promise." I smiled down at her. "I've been purified. I'll be fine."

I bent my head and ventured another kiss. "Now go. Get ready for your party."

She gave me a last, uncertain smile, then nodded once before disappearing into her house.

I took a deep breath and turned away. Hermogenes was sliding me a knowing smirk.

"To the Agora," I ordered before he could say anything. "Come, we haven't got much time."

The artistic competitions were scheduled for today and I would be cooking dinner for Timon that night. A grain merchant with artistic pretensions, Timon was (according to Hermogenes, who had it from Timon's slaves) set to bore his guests to tears with lengthy recitations of his own mediocre poetry. Fortunately, the evening's entertainment was not my problem. The feast that would follow this performance, however, was a different matter.

Krysippos had promised to procure some shark-belly steaks for me. Timon was middle class, so the meal would not be as elaborate as the one I'd prepared for Xenarchus, but I wanted to try out a new recipe at tonight's symposion. First, I would season the steaks with a dry rub of spicy cumin seeds, oregano, and a generous pinch of salt. Then, I would brush them lightly with olive oil and grill them over low embers until the outsides were crispy and the insides tender and sweetly succulent. Test batches had been outstanding. If it went over well tonight, I planned to serve it at Xenarchus's second symposion.

The second symposion.

The thought almost stopped me in my tracks. In all the chaos and upset, I had almost forgotten that the entertainment for Xenarchus's second symposion—an event that was to take place a mere seven days from now—was most assuredly my problem. With Neaera dead, my only living link to her hetaera sister had effectively disappeared. I would now have to find time to attend Neaera's funeral in the hopes that the elusive Daphne would emerge from wherever she was hiding in order to pay her final respects to her sister. My mood soured at the thought, and I scowled to myself.

I do not like Athenian funerals. Gorgias believes this is because they remind me of my own narrowly avoided funeral rites, but I rather think it's the actual nature of them that bothers me more. A lengthy procession fraught with grieving friends and family and (in this case) clients, which always ends around an elaborate funeral pyre surrounded by all the aforementioned friends and family and clients tearing their hair and beating their chests and wailing as if their souls were being squeezed from their still-breathing bodies.

We do not grieve like this in Lydia. Lydian funerals are more respectful, more introspective. Quieter. No, I do not like Athenian funerals, but if I wanted to find Neaera's sister, I would have no choice but to attend one.

These dark musings occupied me down all the twisting streets that lay between Zeuxo's house and the marketplace.

"Ares's balls! That's a bloody mess, that is!" Hermogenes exclaimed as we entered the Agora.

Still frowning, I looked up.

Hermogenes had not been with us the night before. He hadn't witnessed the destruction of the Agora, which explained his horrified reaction upon seeing it. To my eyes, however, the cleanup crews had been remarkably efficient. Much of the debris from the shattered stalls and broken benches had already been cleared away or, at least, shifted to one side. Most of the torn awnings and discarded clothing had been collected and bundled up. And here and there, slaves armed with besom brooms were busily sweeping the remaining litter into larger, more transportable piles.

In the centre of the marketplace, slaves were loading the debris onto three massive ox-drawn carts. The oxen waited placidly, their coarse-haired tails rhythmically flicking away the swarms of green flies that had come to feast on the rubbish. A small, florid-faced foreman stood in the middle of all this, bellowing commands to which nobody appeared to be listening.

"Come on, you bunch of toad-buggering shite-eaters!" he shouted at them, his accent betraying his Samothracian origins. "Move! We've got to set up the racetrack yet, don't we? You! Sosias! You looking to have some bum-fucking javelin tosser ram his spear up yer arse just because you didn't clean up properly? Then pick up that wood! Ares's hairy balls! What kind of pathetic crew did I end up with? Too busy eating shite and buggering toads! What in the name of the Twelve Gods and all their hairy armpits did I do to deserve a crew like this?"

Although the athletic events weren't scheduled until the next day, tradesmen were busy setting up stands for the crowds that would come to watch the Panathenaic competitions. I could hear the carpenters shouting and hammering and calling instructions to each other. Amidst the cleanup efforts, the stands and bleachers were already beginning to take shape. There was industry enough, but the mood was subdued, with none of the smiles and cheerfully bawdy songs that usually marked any festival preparations.

The foreman continued to curse at his work force.

"Excuse me," I interrupted his seemingly endless tirade. "Have you any idea where the fish sellers have set up?"

The man turned to stare at me incredulously. He looked vaguely familiar, though I couldn't imagine where I'd seen him before. "Where the fish sellers have set up?" His voice had risen an octave. "Where the fish sellers have set up! Hestia's butt cheeks! Do I look like I want to buy a fucking fish?"

"No," I said mildly. "You look like the only person who has a handle on this sorry mess." I spread my arms to encompass the marketplace.

The man closed his mouth and regarded me for a long moment. Then, "By Aphrodite's jiggling jugs!" he exploded. "Finally, a man of perception!" He grabbed my hand and pumped it enthusiastically. "How right you are! Name's Pisistratus. Call me Piss 'cause I don't take it. What I say is what I mean. And I *am* the only one who knows his head from his arsehole in this clusterfuck. Archons had me up at the crack of dawn to take care of it. Right after they voted to chase old Xanthius out of town, bless his warty old hide."

Hermogenes and I exchanged glances.

"They found a scapegoat already, did they?" I asked casually.

"No choice. Not with Neaera being killed during the Great Panathenaea and nobody knowing who did it. I tell you, no one wants the Kindly Ones coming 'round for another go at us all." Piss shuddered at the thought. "No sirree Basileos! Same sort of thing happened eight, nine years ago. Fellow was killed during the Apaturia. Bloody Kindly Ones came every night for damn near a week, till city council thought to run some poor beggar out of town. No, the ekklesia met at first light and they were feasting old Xanthius before the sun was much higher in the sky. Kinda sorry he ended like that. Never seemed to do much except bother the bread-wives, and they're a bunch of harpy-tongued bitches anyway, but he was one ugly beggar. Can't argue with that. They thrashed him up and down the streets over an hour ago. Surprised you didn't hear it."

"I was sleeping in," I said. "It was a bad night."

"It was a bad night for all of us," Piss agreed. "Could have been worse, though. Only two dead, from what I hear. Not counting the hetaera, of course."

"Two? That's all?"

Piss nodded. "And *they* died when the crowd stampeded. Guess the Kindly Ones were more interested in punishing than killing. Lots of injured, though. Whole city stinks of meds."

The garrulous foreman was right, I realized, suddenly aware of the pungent smell of steeping cannabis infusing the fresh morning air.

"Let's just hope Xanthius took all the bad mojo with him," Piss said, turning his eyes back to his crew. "Sosias! I swear to you, it'll be me shoving a spear up your arse if you don't pick up the pace!" He turned back to me. "Look, I gotta get back to work. You're Pelops, aren't you? That fancy-ass chef from Lydia."

I nodded, surprised that he'd heard of me. "That's right."

"Heard you make a mean roast lamb."

"Uh, thanks."

"You're out of my price range, of course, but you got a good rep. Don't worry. You should be able to get through this shit as long as you keep your head down."

"Get through what? What are you talking—"

"Sosias! Get back to work! This is the Great Panathenaea, you spawn of a one-eyed goat, not some pansy-assed toad-bugger-ing festival!" He started striding toward his recalcitrant worker. "And you! Pyrrhias! Get a shovel and start cleaning up after these oxen. Can't have the athletes sprinting through shit pies, can we? And you three! What do you think you're doing? No never mind! Don't answer that. You're too stupid to know and I'm too smart to care. Listen up, people! I want everybody's arse over here, on the double! That means now!"

"Pisistratus!" I called to him. "Piss, wait! What did you mean? What do I need to get through?"

"Only a few fish sellers out today," he shouted back over his shoulder. "Over by the South Stoa. Can't miss 'em."

"Wait!"

But his crew closed around him and Hermogenes and I were left looking after him uneasily.

"Maybe he heard you were at Lysander's house last night," Hermogenes offered.

"That's what I'm afraid of," I said. "Come on, let's find Krysippos."

Chapter 19

Krysippos was by the east side of the South Stoa, right beside the Spring House. So, it appeared, were half the men in Athens.

Gathered around the statue of Neaera, they wept and wailed, tearing their hair and clutching at the figure as if it were fashioned of flesh and blood rather than bronze. Dirge singers were already in place, chanting their sorrowful melodies. I saw Lysander swaying and moaning along with several of his dinner guests from the night before, their brown hair grey from the ashes they'd sprinkled on their heads. There were other men I recognized too: Alcibiades, the sculptor Kritias, Iktinos, and Kallikrates. Even the hoary old statesman Palladas was there, the ashes on his head indistinguishable from his thinning white hair. Neaera had, apparently, been loved by many.

The chariot racer, Damokles, was present too. By far the most dramatic of the mourners, he was beating his chest and tearing at his cheeks and wailing louder than the rest of them put together. I did notice that he'd managed to overcome his grief long enough to tie another green ribbon around his head before he'd come out. Or perhaps one of his slaves had done it for him.

"What a wanker," Hermogenes muttered to me, watching his hero's antics with a disappointed sneer.

Krysippos overheard and grunted his agreement. "Still, what do you expect from a foreigner?" he said philosophically.

Offended, I drew myself up, but Krysippos noticed my reaction before I could say anything.

"Don't go getting your cock in a knot, my cook friend," he said, holding up a white hand. "You Lydians are more like Athenians than any chariot racer from Thessaly. Just look at how he's carrying on! You'd think he was her best beloved, rather than the poke of the party."

I glanced back again at Damokles and caught sight of one of Lysander's other guests. The strange man. The one who'd tried to bribe me to serve the food hot.

"Do you know that man?" I asked, pointing him out to Krysippos. "The fat one standing just next to Alcibiades."

"Him? That's Philoxenus," Krysippos replied. "Why?"

"What do you know about him?"

Krysippos shrugged and began to wrap my shark steaks in large leaves. "He likes to eat. But you could tell that just from looking at him." He curled his lip in disgust. Gluttony was not widely admired in Athens.

"But who is he? What does he do?"

"He owns a large farm in the north. Cabbages, I believe. But why are you so curious about him? Surely such a man holds no interest for a chef like yourself—unless you mean to cook for him."

"He was at Lysander's house last night," I explained. "For the symposion. He was behaving very oddly."

"Lysander?" Krysippos's pallid face suddenly went even paler. "Lysander, son of Prodicus? Are you telling me that *you* were the chef that night? At the party where Neaera was killed?"

Hermogenes screwed up his face and clapped his hand over his eyes.

Too late, I realized my mistake. "I—"

"Here! Take your steaks. No, no. Put your money there on the counter and be off with you. There are many customers waiting. You must make room for them. I cannot sell fish if customers cannot get to the counter. Yes, goodbye. Thank you very much. Yes. Have a nice day."

Wordlessly, I laid a few coins on the counter. Krysippos eyed them as if they were serpents, finally taking a corner of his chiton and scooping them into a pouch without touching them. I gathered up my leaf-wrapped shark steaks and put them in the basket Hermogenes was carrying. We turned to leave. There were no customers waiting.

"What do you bet he scarpers off to the nearest temple to get purified," Hermogenes said scathingly while we were still within earshot.

I quelled him with a glance. "He's right to be cautious," I said. "He doesn't know we've been purified."

"He never asked, did he?"

I couldn't argue with that.

"Come on," I said tersely. "Let's get out of here."

Before we left the area, I glanced back once more at the grieving mourners. One stood apart from the others. A greying man in a grey chiton. He leaned against the laurel tree next to the Spring House as if for support. He wasn't weeping or wailing or tearing at his hair, but his face was haggard and his eyes were full of anguish.

Another small crowd had gathered on the opposite end of the Agora by the altar of the Twelve Gods. But far from being a group of olive oil sellers (as I'd hoped) or even another group of mourners (less desirable, but still acceptable) the men clustered around an all-too familiar figure in a bright yellow chiton, listening intently to his words.

The Sicilian stood on a pedestal in reality as well as in his own mind. His arms were flung out, his eyes shone with fervour, and his voice rose easily above the murmuring of the crowd and the background clattering of construction work.

"The gods have spoken!" Mithaecus cried. "Hear me, good citizens of Athens! You are all asking today why the Kindly Ones came last night. Why they flew over our fair city with their horrible scourges and hideous shrieks. Why did they see fit to punish us? What heinous crime was committed to loose such an ancient evil upon us all?"

The crowd was nodding and muttering.

"Tell me, how many of you were injured last night? Or had loved ones wounded in the attack? How many of you saw your sons and wives terrorized by the bat-winged arbiters of justice and vengeance? Tell me, what did we do to deserve that?"

"Tell us, Mithaecus! Tell us!" shouted one of his sycophants.

"It were Neaera!" yelled a voice from the crowd. "Somebody done her in, didn't they?"

Mithaecus paused and laid a thoughtful finger on the side of his nose. "Neaera, yes," he mused aloud. "She was killed last night. Murdered most foully. But people have been murdered before and the Kindly Ones did not fly. No, my friends, we must dig deeper to discover the real truth."

I had a very bad feeling about what was coming.

"I have been digging deeper," Mithaecus told the growing crowd. "I, Mithaecus the Sicilian, the greatest chef in Athens, the Phidias of the kitchen, I have been digging deeper into this mystery. And I have discovered why the Kindly Ones saw fit to emerge from their lair."

He had them and he knew it. He paused and looked down, as if composing himself. The crowd waited breathlessly.

"Where was Neaera when she was killed?" he asked.

"At the house of Lysander, son of Prodicus," one of his sycophants shouted.

"At Lysander's house." Mithaecus nodded. "And what was going on at Lysander's house last night?"

"A symposion!"

"A symposion," he agreed. "A typical dinner party to celebrate the Great Panathenaea. And, pray, who was cooking for this symposion? For it certainly was not myself." He brushed imaginary lint from his chiton.

"Pelops!" a sycophant cried. "It was Pelops the Lydian! He was chef at Lysander's last night!"

The crowd shifted and muttered. This must have been what Piss had been warning me about.

"Pelops. Indeed. Pelops of Lydia." Mithaecus curled his lip. "An ... adequate cook, I suppose."

I ground my teeth together. Hermogenes quivered beside me and I clamped down hard on his shoulder, holding him in place.

"An adequate cook, but a sacrilegious man!" he thundered. "Pelops of Lydia boasts of his special roast lamb. He boasts of its modern flavours, of its uniqueness in a city of tired cuisine. Pelops of Lydia stuffs a tender young lamb with plums and herbs and that is modern. That is unique. But Pelops of Lydia roasts the lamb in its own skin!"

The crowd gasped.

It was nothing I had not heard before. Mithaecus had attempted to discredit my roast lamb months ago, standing up and denouncing it in the Agora much as he was doing today. But his descriptions had so inflamed the Athenians' gastronomic sensibilities that the dish had become my most frequently requested culinary creation. No, his accusations of sacrilege were nothing new. The only difference now was that this time, people were taking them seriously.

"In its own skin, I tell you! Sacrilege! Now maybe they do things differently in the barbaric land of Lydia, but here in the good city of Athens, every citizen knows that the skin of a sacrificial animal should be given to the gods. Every citizen knows that the skin and the leg bones and a piece of the fat should be burned on the fire for the gods to enjoy. But Pelops of Lydia roasts lamb in its own skin!"

The crowd was buzzing now, like a swarm of angry bees. I hunched down, afraid of being recognized.

"And what do you think Pelops of Lydia cooked at Lysander's special Panathenaic symposion?"

"Roast lamb!"

"Roast lamb," Mithaecus agreed. "Roasted in its own skin. Depriving the gods of their rightful share. My friends, Neaera may have been killed, but it was Pelops who offended the gods. It was Pelops who brought down their wrath. And it was Pelops who—"

"Ho, there!" A voice boomed out from behind me. "Coming through! 'Scuse me. Pardon me. We've got ox-carts coming through!"

The crowd turned, distracted from the climax of Mithaecus's carefully prepared speech. It was Pisistratus and his work crew with the debris-laden carts.

Mithaecus turned a furious eye on them. "Take your beasts by another route," he ordered peremptorily. "We're holding a meeting here!"

"And I'm getting the Agora cleaned up for the athletic competitions," Piss said just as snottily.

Mithaecus stepped down from his pedestal. "What's the matter with you, slave? I told you to take the carts another way!" The Sicilian's face had darkened. One of his sycophants sidled up and tried to whisper in his ear, but Mithaecus brushed him off.

Piss had stopped in front of Mithaecus. The oxen kept

plodding on obliviously, but the work crew looked back and forth between their foreman and Mithaecus, clearly amused by the exchange. Their smiles enraged The Sicilian even further.

"I have every right to be here!" Mithaecus cried shrilly. "The public needs to know about this menace! This is disseminating information! This is democracy in action! This is—"

"Where my ox carts need to go." Piss was short, but he was heavily muscled. Puffing out his chest belligerently, he added, "And this is the way they're going. Sorry to make you blow yer wad early and all, mate, but city council's given me a job to do and, by the Twelve Gods and all their hairy armpits, no poncy-assed foreigner in a piss-coloured chiton is going to stop me. Now are you going to get out of my way, or am I going to have to give you a nice purple bruise to go with your fancy outfit?"

Pisistratus may have been a slave, and therefore of lower standing than a foreigner of The Sicilian's stature, but at the moment, he had all the power of the archons behind him and Mithaecus knew it. Face red with fury, The Sicilian stepped back, and the crowd started to break up.

Hermogenes and I had been watching from the sidelines. As Piss turned to follow his ox carts, his eyes met mine and he winked once, solemnly. Then he looked away and started bellowing at his crew to get moving and how in the name of Hestia's butt cheeks did they think the oxen were going to know where to go if they weren't guiding them and how in Hades had he ever ended up with such a crew of goat-fucking idiots.

"Hear me, good people of Athens!" Mithaecus tried desperately to regain the crowd's interest, but whether distracted by the confrontation or suddenly remembering other errands, most of the men continued to move off. Keeping our heads low, Hermogenes and I skulked away with them.

"He has a point though," a pinch-faced man was saying to another. "The skin belongs to the gods. Always has."

"Maybe." His friend shrugged. "But Mithaecus has been banging on about this roast lamb for months now. If Pelops of Lydia was such a blasphemous son of a bitch, then why haven't the Kindly Ones come 'round before this to give him what for? No, I'd say they flew last night on account of Neaera being killed. Imagine, doing somebody in during the Great Panthenaea! And her that invented Lion on the Cheese Grater, no less! That, my friend, is sacrilege."

The man looked unconvinced. "So you don't think Mithaecus has a point? About the skin?"

"Nah. Not a chance. The Kindly Ones don't work that way. You piss 'em off, they don't wait for months before having a go at you. Mark my words, Mithaecus is just trying to take down a rival. You'll see. I tell you one thing though, that slave with the ox carts sure had it right. I always thought The Sicilian's chiton looked like someone had taken a good long whiz on it."

Both men laughed and began to saunter off.

I took careful note of my defender's face before he moved out of sight. If I should ever have the great good fortune to cook for him, I would ensure he got the fattest eel, the sweetest pastry, and the most succulent slice of roast lamb.

Chapter 20

"Well, we've had a busy morning here," Irene informed me as soon as I walked into the house. "First off, the leech has been and gone. *He* said the master was doing well enough, that he's got a fever and we're to give him cooled willow bark tea to keep it down."

She helped me out of my cloak and sniffed disdainfully. "*He* didn't even change the master's bandages. Left that for me to do, the lazy good-for-nothing. If you ask me, bringing him in a second time was a waste of good money, to say nothing of the first time. I've known about willow bark long before *he* was knee-high to the scrawny chicken he looks like. Good common sense, it is. I didn't pay him. Told him you or the master would settle up later. *He* didn't seem very happy about it, but I told him that just because he knew a few things about herbs and bones and the like didn't mean he could go squeezing money out of a sleeping man lying on his sick couch. He'll get paid when he gets paid. That's what I said. Strabo saw him to the door."

"I see."

"And after the leech slimed his way out of here, Meidias came sniffing about. With two of his lads, no less. What you're doing consorting with the likes of that one, I'll never know. A nasty piece of work, he is. He'd as soon spit at you as look at you. "

I sighed. I was going to have to do something about Meidias—and soon. Xenarchus had been generous and there had been plenty of tips that night, but I'd since had unforeseen expenses in the form of olive oil, and Lysander had not yet paid me for his disastrous symposion. At this point, I was loath to collect the debt. I did not need further association with that particular event. This meant, however, that I did not have the ready coin to pay Meidias.

"I owe him money," I told Irene.

"Well, pay him then and get him off our backs. Imagine him having the nerve to come 'round here and tell us what for." She pursed her lips in disapproval.

"I will," I told her. Just as soon as Timon paid me, I added silently.

But then, as if I'd spoken the words out loud, Irene sniffed and said, "And then we had that slave come 'round, you know, that tall bent fellow. Timon's man."

My stomach sank. "Timon?"

Irene nodded. "He's gone and cancelled on you, hasn't he? His slave said he was hurt something terrible in the Agora last night. Seems he's too sick to hold his symposion. What's this world coming to when an honest man can't go to market without the Kindly Ones tearing a strip off him? Why I remember when—"

"Cancelled?" I broke in. "Are you certain? Cancelled. Not postponed?"

"Cancelled. That was word he used. His man never said anything about setting a different time and he scuttled out of here before I could even think to ask. I tell you, slaves these days have no manners. In my day…"

While Irene prattled on about the golden days, I considered the reason Timon had given for his cancellation. It could be true. Many had been injured the night before. It was possible he'd been forced to cancel his symposion due to injury.

But Hermogenes didn't believe it.

"Chef, if you think Timon's hurt, then I've got a temple to sell you. Cheap!" he said hotly. "That's Mithaecus, that is! He's probably been hanging about the Agora since first light, trying to set people against you. That … that toad-buggering shite-eater!"

"You watch your tongue!" Irene snapped.

Hermogenes flashed her a dark look. "It's not right, Chef," he urged. "You've got to do something about him. Send Strabo. Or even Lais. You've got to do *something*! That Sicilian bastard's going to get people all worked up and then others'll start cancelling and Meidias will send his goons 'round again to get the money for his dishes and how are you supposed to pay him if nobody'll hire you to cook for the Panathenaea and—"

"Hush your mouth!" Irene cut him off with a sharp slap to

the face. "Pelops doesn't need to hear you yammering on. He knows his business."

Hermogenes stopped, but his expression was unrepentant.

"Put the fish in the ice pit, Hermogenes," I said quietly. "I can use it tomorrow for Iphicrates's symposion. I'm going to check on Gorgias."

Hermogenes looked like he wanted to say more, and for a heartbeat, I thought he would. But instead he snatched up the basket of fish and slammed out of the room, grumbling audibly to himself. I ignored him.

"Will you be wanting some lunch, then?" Irene asked, an expression of uncharacteristic sympathy on her face.

"No. Thank you." Not trusting myself to say anything more, I turned and left the kitchen.

Gorgias was still awake when I entered his room.

"You look moderately awful," I told him.

"I feel like total shite," he grumbled.

"I heard Menon was back."

Gorgias scowled. "I swear the next time I see that sodding little bugger, I'll wring his scrawny neck. Look! I'm bruised all over what with him poking at me like I'm a bleeding lump of clay. And there's him enjoying it the whole time. Nasty bugger."

"Trust me, you were already bruised all over."

He grunted irritably and started picking at one of his bandages. "You saw Zeuxo home, then?"

"I did," I nodded. "Safe and sound."

He chewed his lower lip for a few seconds. "You know, I damn near throttled her when she said she was coming with us last night," he said at last. "And when Themselves started in at us, I almost had a bloody heart attack thinking she'd get a strip torn off her. But even with all that, I was glad she was there."

"She's certainly very brave," I agreed, allowing some of my own admiration for her to show.

He was silent for a moment, then he chuckled. "You know she took a whack at them with that little bit of a stick she'd picked up."

"What! You're joking!"

Gorgias shook his head, smiling in remembered disbelief. "Right after they got me with the scourge. I'm flopping on the ground like a sodding fish out of water and I look up and there's Zeuxo standing and screaming at them like a bloody harpy. Then she tried to have at them with the stick. I tell you, it damn near made my hair stand on end. If that hoplite hadn't shown up with his spear, we'd have been done for."

"Uh … right, the hoplite. Good on him."

"You can bloody well say that again. But, Pelops," he said, pausing a moment, as if struggling to find the right words. "Having Zeuxo there, it really made a difference. Did wonders for Ansandra too. You know, to have another woman there for her."

There was a faraway expression on his face I'd never seen before. My stomach clenched.

"I went to the Agora this morning," I said, changing the subject abruptly.

Gorgias blinked, then brought his attention back to me. "How's it looking, then?"

"Better." I shrugged. "The cleanup crews have been working

since dawn. Most of the debris has been cleared away now, though I imagine there'll be a fair number of shop owners needing new stalls."

"I don't doubt it."

We were quiet for a moment.

"Pelops," he began hesitantly. "Strabo tells me the Kindly Ones flew because Neaera was killed last night. Murdered during Lysander's symposion."

"It's true." I nodded glumly. "I found her body."

His eyes widened and he sat up, wincing in pain. "Great Zeus's arsehole! Why didn't you say something last night?"

"There wasn't time, was there?" I said defensively. "You staggered in and Ansandra was missing and we ran out to find her. And then—"

"I got myself torn up by a sodding Kindly One," Gorgias finished.

"That's about it."

"Have you been purified?"

"Of course!" I waved it off. "Hermogenes and I took care of that as soon as we came home."

"Ah." Gorgias leaned back again against his cushions. His eyes had become overly bright and there were red splotches coming out on his cheeks. "Good. That'll be the end of it then."

"Mmm," I said noncommittally.

"And the news from the Agora? Did they find the killer yet?"

I shook my head. "No. Though they did find a scapegoat."

He considered that for a moment. "Good," he said. "That should take care of that."

"Let's hope so."

He fell silent then. I fidgeted a little, wrestling with the question of whether or not I should tell him about The Sicilian's slanderous activities and Timon's subsequent and suspicious cancellation. Gorgias made the decision for me by closing his eyes. In seconds his breathing had deepened and he was asleep.

I sat with him for a while, my thoughts whirling around like a second coming of the Kindly Ones. The longer I thought about it, the less inclined I was to believe Timon had been honest with me. At least one man in the Agora—two, if you counted Pisistratus—had not believed me responsible for last night's attack, but what of all the others? Mithaecus's accusations were insidious enough to cause even a calm, rational man to consider them. What then of a man who had seen his city terrorized by the Erinyes? How many more cancellations was I going to receive? Was I still a person of importance in Athens? A man in demand? Or was my career over before it had truly begun?

I stood suddenly, needing to move, to distract myself from these grim thoughts. Gorgias stirred and mumbled but didn't wake. Quietly, I left the room and headed down to the kitchen. There were things I could be doing for tomorrow's symposion. Elaborate dishes I could begin preparing. Iphicrates would not regret hiring Pelops of Lydia to feast his dinner guests. Iphicrates would be astounded and amazed at the sumptuousness of the new, revised menu. Iphicrates's Panathenaic dinner would be the talk of the town, renowned throughout all of Athens, and less fortunate men would fall to their knees and weep because they had not thought to hire me for their symposions.

But Iphicrates would never know of the gastronomic delights I might have prepared for him, or of the social accolades that might have awaited him. When I came downstairs, I discovered that Iphicrates, like Timon, had cancelled.

A Taste of Lydia

PELOPS'S ROAST LAMB WITH PLUMS

---

* 1 lamb, properly sacrificed with intestines, organs, and fleece removed and skin remaining
* aromatic wood (olive, oak, apple)
* best quality olive oil
* sea salt
* pepper
* fresh rosemary, several large bunches
* whole garlic cloves
* plums, pitted and chopped

Glaze
* wine vinegar
* crushed garlic
* mustard seeds, finely ground
* plums, pitted and chopped
* fresh rosemary, chopped
* honey
* sea salt

---

1. Start the fire at midday.

2. Sprinkle the inside of the lamb liberally with salt, pepper, and olive oil and rub in. Affix lamb to a sturdy spit. Stuff the body cavity with a mixture of chopped plums, garlic cloves, and bunches of rosemary. Sew the body cavity closed.

3. Rub the entire lamb with a mixture of half olive oil, half wine vinegar. Sprinkle it with more salt and pepper.

4. At midafternoon, place the spit over the fire and spread the coals so they are under the shoulder and thigh, which are the thickest parts of the animal. Begin to roast. At first, the lamb must be turned quickly in order not to burn. Once the fire settles and the lamb is golden all around and the skin is starting to crisp, you may slow the turning. Replenish wood as needed. Baste occasionally with more olive oil.

5. Prepare the glaze by combining all the ingredients in a good-sized pot. Bring to a boil and simmer until the plums are soft and the mixture has thickened.

6. Cooking time for the lamb will depend on the size of the animal. When done, the skin on the legs and chest of the lamb will crisp and crack open. The colour should be a deep brown and when you stick a knife into the thigh, the juices will run clear.

7. Once the meat is cooked, baste the lamb all over with the glaze. Continue to turn the spit and baste with the glaze until the glaze is a rich brown. Do not burn.

8. Remove lamb from fire. Let stand on a carving surface for a while, then carve. The meat should be a delicate pink on the inside. Combine the stuffing with any leftover glaze and serve on the side.

Chapter 21

Enough was enough. Mithaecus was becoming … inconvenient. It was time to take advantage of my friends in high places.

I arrived back at the Agora as the festival crowds began to appear for the midafternoon break. The Panathenaea's much subdued swearing-in ceremonies had taken place in the Theatre of Dionysus earlier in the day, as had the first rounds of the poetry competition. Now the spectators swarmed into the Agora seeking to moisten dry throats or partake of grilled fish from one of the many braziers set up around the grounds. A few were discussing the quality of this year's recitations, but most, unsurprisingly, spoke in hushed tones of the events of the previous night. Official proclamations had been issued from all corners of the marketplace. The citizens of Athens were being instructed to carry on with the festival. All ceremonies, all athletic events, all parties were to be held as usual so as not to risk offending Athena. The mood in the city was distinctly unfestive.

Lining the southeast corner of the Agora were a number of stalls with purple-red awnings, their owners standing ready to sell cups of overpriced wine to the parched festival attendees. But even in this traditionally rowdier venue, conversation was muted and few seemed terribly thirsty. I found Dionysus's stall in its usual place between the Tholos and the Bouleuterion.

The god of wine looked glum as he leaned on his counter, surveying the cheerless crowd. His expression did not change when he saw me.

"Pelops," he said without his usual genial smile. "I've been expecting you."

I nodded, unsurprised.

He heaved a sigh and pushed himself off his counter. "Come on in back, then." He gestured with his beard towards the purple curtain behind the counter.

I eyed it doubtfully. Dionysus wasn't exactly a lightweight god, and his stall butted right up against the wall surrounding the Tholos. Any room he had in back could not be very spacious. I needed to talk to him, yes, just not quite that intimately. But the god of wine had disappeared behind the curtain and he clearly expected me to follow. Sighing inwardly, I ducked past the cloth and promptly stopped dead.

I poked my head out again, looked at the exterior of the stall, then pulled it back in and goggled at the sight in front of me.

The room was huge—impossibly huge, easily ten times the size of an average andron. The floors had been painted with a leaf motif and the walls were exquisitely decorated with frescoed scenes of happy people making wine and even happier ones drinking it. Silver bowls of flowers perfumed the air, warmth and light came from several bronze braziers around the room, and there was music playing softly in the background, though I did not see the musician. All this I noticed later. For now, I had eyes only for the four purple-cushioned dining couches—and the gods that were reclining on them.

The atmosphere was subdued, to say the least. Zeus, Hermes, and Ares lounged on the couches, their expressions morose. Hermes plucked disconsolately at a lyre, while Zeus nibbled steadily from a dish of toasted nuts. Ares was cleaning his fingernails with a large knife. As I stood there gaping, Dionysus draped himself over the fourth couch and picked up a wine cup.

"Told you he'd come 'round, didn't I?" he said to his father, with the air of someone who had completed a difficult task.

Zeus rumbled into his beard and popped another nut into his mouth. "Pelops," he greeted me. "It's been a while. You're looking well—all things considered."

"Father Zeus," I managed to say. "I … I was not expecting to see you here."

His eyes were the colour of storm clouds and his dark hair was shot through with streaks of white. His shoulders were massive, his legs thickly muscled (though his knees were as knobby as I remembered them). As I greeted him, Zeus belched and scratched his belly. I noticed that he'd gotten a little paunchy since I'd seen him last.

"Only place that's safe, right now," he shrugged.

Ares snorted and flicked a fingernail cutting on the floor.

"Uh, safe?" I ventured.

"From the wife," Zeus said moodily. "And my sodding daughter. Great Me on a stick! You'd think I'd killed the mortal myself the way those two are carrying on. I mean, why is it my fault some walking bollocks went and buggered up her festival? It's not like she won't have another one next year."

"But this is the *Great* Panathenaea, Dad," Dionysus reminded his father. "She won't get another one of those for four years, will she?" He sounded quite gleeful about it.

"One year! Four years!" Zeus waved it off impatiently. "What's the sodding difference? We're gods, son. Time is different for us."

"Tell that to fucking Athena," Ares said.

I passed a hand over my eyes. My knees felt wobbly but there were no more couches, and even if there had been, I could not sit in the presence of gods. I glanced down at the floor and noticed the leaves that had been painted on it were undulating as if fluttering in a gentle breeze. Disconcerted, I looked up at the frescoes on the wall. They, too, were moving, the painted figures cheerfully crushing grapes and lifting buckets and quaffing wine. One figure appeared to be vomiting all over his painted sandals.

Completely unsettled now, I brought my attention back to the gods with some difficulty.

"So ..." I began. "Uh, you ... you don't know who killed Neaera, then?"

Zeus's eyebrows drew together in a frown. "Do I look like I

know who killed the mortal?" he demanded imperiously. His eyes flashed lightning bolts, their blue-white light flickering on the ends of his eyelashes before dissipating into the air with a faint crackle.

I cowered back. He might be getting bit flabby around the middle, but Zeus could still be crushingly imposing when he put his mind to it.

"Great Me!" he was ranting, his eyes still flashing dangerously. "Why is it always my problem? Who did this, Zeus? Why did they do that, Zeus? Can you sort this? Who killed the mortal? Why did my festival get ruined? How do we stop the Erinyes? Give me a break! I'm not all-knowing like sodding Odin, am I?"

"Um … Odin?" I asked weakly.

"Dude up north," Hermes explained as he poured himself more wine. "Only has one eye, but he's supposed to know everything."

"Ha!" Zeus barked with laughter. "Doesn't seem to know he's got bird shit all over his shoulders though, does he? Stupid tosser." He leaned to one side and let fly a divine fart. "Whoa. Left cheek sneak." The smell of roses suddenly permeated the air.

I looked from Zeus to Hermes helplessly.

"Odin likes ravens," Hermes piped up as if that explained everything.

"Of course, if I was all-knowing like old Bird Shit for Brains, I wouldn't be in dutch with the wife so often, now, would I?" Zeus brooded on that for a few moments.

If he wasn't so constantly tempted by mortal women, he

wouldn't be in trouble with his wife so often, but there was no way on Olympus or Earth that I was going to say that to him.

"This isn't fucking getting us anywhere," Ares said at last.

"Agreed," Dionysus said, setting down his wine cup. "Pelops, you came to us. What can we do for you?" He paused and made a face. "Keeping in mind, of course, that we're stuck here until…" he paused delicately, searching for the right words.

"Until fucking Athena grows some bollocks and learns to suck it up," Ares broke in. "And Hera right fucking behind her."

"Don't talk about your mother and sister that way," Zeus ordered.

"Half-sister," Ares corrected him.

The two gods fell to bickering.

Dionysus pushed himself up off his dining couch and walked over to me. "What do you need, Pelops?" he asked, resting a sympathetic hand on my ivory shoulder.

"I … I need help," I stammered. "With another chef. He found out I was cooking for Lysander when Neaera was killed. He's been accusing me of sacrilege and basically blaming me for the Kindly Ones' attack."

Dionysus drew himself up. "Bollocks!"

"Maybe so, but people are listening to him," I said seriously. "I've lost two contracts already. I tell you, Dionysus, Mithaecus would like nothing more than to see me run out of town like an ugly beggar—and he's halfway to achieving it!"

"Mithaecus?" Dionysus had stiffened. "Mithaecus of Sicily?"

Zeus and Ares broke off their argument and turned to look at us. Hermes's bright eyes had gone wide.

"Yes," I said cautiously. "Why?"

All at once, the gods seemed unable to look me in the eye. They squirmed and shuffled and cleared their throats and suddenly found the moving wall frescoes endlessly fascinating.

"It's not my lamb, is it?" I asked, sick with apprehension. "Is Mithaecus right? Does it offend you?"

"No, no," Dionysus denied, still refusing to meet my eyes. "No, the lamb's lovely."

I waited a few moments.

"The skin makes it nice and crispy on the outside," Hermes offered.

"And I like how it tastes with all those plums inside," Zeus agreed. "Nice touch, that."

There was more silence.

"Then … why…" I struggled to find the right words.

"We can't touch him," Dionysus said finally, sliding an uneasy look at his father.

Zeus drew his eyebrows together in a ferocious frown and started picking at a bowl of plump olives.

"The Sicilian, I mean," Dionysus continued. "Mithaecus. We can't touch him."

I opened my mouth, but no words came out.

"His mum did a favour for Hera," Hermes explained. "A long time ago. So Hera, in her divine gratitude, promised to watch out for him. For all the rest of us, that means nooo touchy."

"Nooo touchy," Dionysus agreed solemnly. "I've been on Hera's bad side once already, thank you very much. She can be … creative when she's in a snit." He shuddered, but didn't elaborate.

I still didn't know what to say.

"Why do you think Mithaecus is so successful, anyway?" Hermes asked.

"Sure as shit, it's not for his cooking," Ares said with a snort. "Stuff goes down like a fucking rock."

I was too busy trying to get my mind around what the gods were saying about Mithaecus to be gratified by their opinion of his cooking.

I turned to Zeus, my only hope now, and took a deep breath. *You're the king of the gods,* I wanted to cry. *Help me!*

But before I could say anything, I caught movement out of the corner of my eye. Ares was trying to get my attention.

I looked at him and he shook his head warningly. Cocking his head to one side, he gestured at Zeus with his chin and mouthed some words. It looked like he was saying "pussy-whipped."

Zeus still had his eyes fixed firmly on his bowl of olives. Ares made a whipping motion with his hand.

I opened my mouth, then closed it again. Zeus may be king of the gods, but he was still hiding out from his wife in the back of a wine stall. Defeated, I let out my breath slowly.

"But if there's anything else we can do…" Hermes said, trailing off suggestively.

"Or if some *other* asshole is trying to fuck with you…" Ares rolled his shoulders back and began cracking his knuckles one at a time.

Dionysus clapped me on the back. "Then you know where to come," he said much too heartily.

"Thanks." I tried not to sound ungrateful. "Thanks a lot."

Chapter 22

What good was it having friends in high places if they wouldn't help you when you needed it? It wasn't as though I'd ever asked them for a favour before! I had never asked the gods for anything!

I never asked to be remade out of stew. Never asked for an ivory shoulder, or a talent for the culinary arts, or for help in establishing myself in Athens. I had certainly never asked for Poseidon to fall in love with me—or to obsess about me so thoroughly after I'd turned down the offer to become his lover. I had never asked for any of it! It had all been their idea! But now, when I really needed some help, the gods had turned me down flat.

Fuming at the bitter injustice of it all, I stumbled through the Agora, paying little heed to the activity around me. I sailed past food stalls without pausing to examine their wares. I bumped into festival-goers who started to berate me for my carelessness before taking one look at my thunderous expression and beating a hasty retreat. I wandered with no thought as to where I was going or what I might do when I got there. I only knew I did not want to go home. Gorgias was too sick for me to ask his advice, Irene's new-found sympathy was far too cloying, and Hermogenes would try to harass me into solving my problems with brute force.

Besides, when I went home, clients cancelled on me.

The sun was just starting to set by the time I finally stopped to take in my surroundings. I'd fetched up at the far end of the Agora, in the long afternoon shadows which stretched behind the unfinished Law Courts building. The crowds had thinned considerably. Most had already headed to wherever they were spending the night. Nobody wanted to be out in the open once Nyx covered the land with her dark cloak.

In this less desirable part of the Agora, there were still a few stalls set up here and there, mostly second-rate shops hawking third-rate wares. I spied Lamachus squatting like a fat toad under his tattered green- and gold-striped awning.

The sight jogged my memory. I had no idea what had happened to the batch of olive oil that Neaera had drowned in. Not that it mattered. I could never cook with oil that had been contaminated by a dead body. I'd be thrashed out of town in much the same way that ugly beggar had been run off. I was going to need more olive oil, and it appeared Lamachus was the only oil seller left in the Agora.

During festival times, things tend to get a little rough when night falls, and many a stall had been looted or vandalized when wine flowed too freely and tempers got out of hand. All the respectable sellers simply close up shop for the duration of the festivities. Less respectable sellers close when the sun goes down. But today, even the dodgiest shop owners had gone home well before darkness arrived. Lamachus was the only merchant stupid enough or desperate enough to stay open right up until night's shadows fingered his wares.

"Good evening to you, good sir," Lamachus oozed, jumping to his feet as soon as he saw me approaching his shabby stall. "And may I say, what a pleasure it is to see such a fine cook as yourself once again gracing the environs of my humble boutique. Especially after such a terrible, terrible tragedy." His small eyes were bright and knowing and he rubbed his fingers together greedily as if anticipating the feel of coins between them. He knew exactly why I was there.

"Olive oil," I demanded, not even bothering to be civil. "The best you've got."

Given my other tasks, purchasing more olive oil was low on my list of priorities, right after dealing with Mithaecus, trying to keep my remaining clients, salvaging my reputation, and finding a hetaera who did not wish to be found. But right now obtaining olive oil seemed my only achievable goal.

Unfortunately, Lamachus, it turned out, had none of the half-decent oil I'd purchased from him previously. Between overblown compliments and cringing apologies, he brought out the only amphora of any size that he had left—a sad, undecorated vessel barely bigger than a mini amphora. I eyed it dubiously. It might see me through to the end of the festival, provided I had a light hand with it. Of course, if more clients cancelled, I'd be able to slop the stuff around as much as I wanted. Savagely, I cut off that train of thought.

I asked Lamachus how much it was. He named a price as ridiculous as it was offensive. I asked to taste it. He poured a bit of oil into a shallow dish. It was more green than gold and the scent was unappealing, verging on rancid. I dipped a finger in it and brought it to my mouth. It was not good.

Still, what choice did I have?

We haggled, but Lamachus sensed my desperation and bargained meanly. Clenching my jaw so hard it ached, I counted out my last coins into his eager, sweaty palm.

If the gods hadn't turned me down earlier, I might have been tempted to ask them to intervene. Or, at least, to change the oil into something more palatable. But there didn't seem much point in asking them to do anything for me now. I turned my back on Lamachus's triumphant smile, my mood more foul than ever. I settled the amphora in my arms and headed in the direction of home. The sky was red now, it was past time to be getting inside.

But I hadn't gone more than a dozen paces when a dusty-sounding voice greeted me by name. "Ah, Pelops," he said. "How fortunate. I've been looking for you."

Startled from my black reverie, I looked up at the man in front of me. Or rather, at the *men* in front of me.

They were standing directly in my path, two bulky, heavy-browed individuals on either side of a smaller man. The man in the middle was nondescript. Average height, average weight, average features, hair cut short, beard well-trimmed. The sort of man you'd never glance at twice were it not for the massive silver caduceus hanging from a leather thong around his neck. He was the only man in Athens who still wore bling, the trend having ended some years previously. One of Zeuxo's roommates maintained that the enormous pendant was to compensate for deficiencies elsewhere, but I couldn't attest to that one way or the other. Regardless, this man obviously cared little about what was in style, or how people might regard his fashion choices, or what flute girls thought of the size of his genitals. If I were as rich as Meidias, I probably wouldn't care what people thought of me either.

"And here I've been trying to find you, too," I lied.

"Indeed? Then you have my money," Meidias said in his dry, disinterested voice. He sounded distracted, as if part of him were still back in his warehouse listening to the cheering clink of his coins as they were polished and counted.

"How fortunate for you," he continued. "And yet, how very tedious for me to have to seek it out in this manner. I am not accustomed to doing business in the middle of the street." He paused to stretch his mouth into a small, cold smile. "But in your case, I will make an exception."

"Ah, yes, very good of you, I'm sure," I began. "But as for the money … there is a slight problem."

"Indeed," he said again, the smile disappearing so thoroughly I might have imagined it in the first place.

His two burly slaves perked up like household dogs at an overladen feast table.

I coughed uncomfortably.

"Perhaps you have some dishes for me, instead," he suggested. "To replace the ones now missing from my inventory."

"I'm afraid not," I admitted with a regretful smile. "You see, I've had a few setbacks—nothing serious, of course! But there was an accident with my olive oil—well, two accidents, in actual fact—and, as a result, there were some unexpected expenses that—"

Meidias narrowed his eyes at me. "Accidents with olive oil do not concern me," he interrupted.

I closed my mouth.

"Unexpected expenses do not concern me. Broken dishes concern me. Unpaid bills concern me. Men who are accused of sacrilege, whose clients are cancelling, and who do not appear to have the means to pay their debts concern me." He did not seem distracted now.

I gulped.

"What is that in your arms?"

I showed him the amphora. "Olive oil," I explained. "So I can fulfill my other contracts. And thereby make enough money to pay you, of course."

His eyes flickered down to the amphora, then back up to my face. Thoughtfully, he fingered his silver caduceus. The winged staff was the symbol of Hermes, god of merchants, trade, and, not coincidentally, thievery. "Am I to assume you have not lost all your contracts, then?" he inquired.

"Only two of the lesser ones," I answered, praying that it was true. "The Sicilian is lying, I'm no blasphemer. My other clients are intelligent enough to recognize envy when they encounter it."

He regarded me for a long moment before nodding.

"I am a reasonable man," he said finally. "As well as a generous one. You have until the last day of the Panathenaea. You may come to my warehouse at the Piraeus to settle your account then."

"My wealthiest client has booked me for the final day," I protested.

"Then you may come the following morning at first light," he conceded. "But the price is doubled."

Doubled! The word almost burst past my lips. With an effort I choked it off. "I'll see you then," I said instead.

Meidias nodded to his goon slaves and they stepped to one side to let me pass. But as I began to make my way past them, the larger slave hooked his fat foot around my own and dropped me face-first into the dirt. The amphora of olive oil sailed out of my arms and landed with a crack on the hard ground.

"Clumsy," he *tsk*ed with a nasty laugh.

Ignoring him, I scrambled over to the amphora.

Please gods, don't let it be broken, I prayed.

But before I could reach it, the other goon saw where I was headed and with a cruel grin, he gave the amphora a mighty kick. The clay vessel went skittering across the road, stopping only when it smacked into the base of a marble statue of Perikles. Even then, it did not appear to have broken. The jug was either made of sterner stuff than I'd thought, or the gods had decided to take pity on me.

"Oops, I'm sorry," the second goon said insincerely.

"And what in the name of the Twelve Gods and their hairy armpits is going on here, then?" a booming voice demanded.

I looked up to see the foreman, Pisistratus, standing with his hands on his hips, his crew of slaves arrayed behind him. Beside him was another man I recognized. It was Geta, Lysander's steward. Now that I saw them together, I realized why Pisistratus had seemed so familiar to me. The two men were like two snap peas in a pod.

"I'll not have you shite-eaters messing up my Agora," Piss was bellowing at Meidias's two slaves.

"And who the fuck are you?" The larger goon curled his lip and loomed ominously over the shorter man.

Undeterred, Pisistratus thrust his chest forward aggressively. "The name's Pisistratus, mate. I know it's a big word, but try hard to remember it. Hestia's tits, man, I'd even spell it for you if I thought there was a mortal's chance in Hades you'd be able to read it."

The man frowned, not entirely sure if he'd been insulted or not.

"Look, I'll talk in small sentences so you can understand. It's the fucking Panathenaea." Pisistratus spoke slowly, insultingly. "Athletes will compete here tomorrow. If there's garbage lying around they might trip. An athlete with road rash on his naked bollocks is bad. It's my job to make sure that doesn't happen. And that means no garbage, no animal droppings, no litter, *no fucking anything cluttering up my grounds*!" he thundered, and paused to look meaningfully at my amphora still lying on the ground. "Have I made it simple enough for you?"

"Shit shoveller," the goon jeered.

"That's right," Piss agreed pleasantly. "And by Great Zeus's bung hole, I'm seeing a couple of turds that need shovelling right now."

It took them a moment, but they got there.

"Who you calling a turd?" the smaller goon demanded, flexing his muscles.

"I thought I'd made it clear I was looking at one." Pisistratus spat on the ground, unimpressed. "You got a problem with me, shit for brains? Take it up with city council. Now by the Twelve Gods and their plump pink arses, piss off and stop messing up my Agora! Or do I need to call the Scythians?"

At the mention of city council and the Scythian archers, the two goons suddenly looked uncertain. Nobody wanted to mess with the authorities—especially slaves, whose testimony in the Law Court was admissible only if extracted by torture. Blustering and posturing, they turned to follow their master, laughing rudely as they moved off. Meidias had continued on his way, not even bothering to wait for them.

And then, Geta was beside me, offering a hand. "Need some help?"

"Thanks," I replied.

He hauled me to my feet and watched as I brushed off my scraped knees and shook the dust from my chiton.

"You okay?" he asked.

"I'll live."

The few men still lingering around the Agora had gathered to bet on the outcome of the altercation. Now that the entertainment was over, they began to disperse, coins clinking as money exchanged hands. Pisistratus thanked his crew and sent them off to their dinners.

"What by the Great God's hairy bollocks possessed a smart man like you to have dealings with the likes of Meidias?" he asked, joining Geta and me.

I shook my head wearily. "No choice," I said. "He rents dishes. I needed some, and they got broken. I haven't paid him yet."

Pisistratus's eyebrows shot up. "He's roughing you up over bunch of *dinner plates?*" he asked incredulously.

I nodded. "And serving platters and bowls and there were a few wine kraters, too."

He shook his head in disbelief. "You chefs live a strange life," he observed.

I limped over to my amphora. Miraculously, it still appeared to be intact, its undecorated sides free of fractures. I let out my breath in a gusty sigh of relief—a sigh which turned into a pained grunt as I bent over to retrieve the jug. I was going to be sore for the next day or two, but at least my olive oil was safe. Truly, the gods must be watching out for me.

I was lifting the amphora off the ground when its neck suddenly snapped off in my hand. I cried out, scrambling to adjust my grip, to somehow protect the precious contents inside. But even as I did so, the entire vessel split, falling away into several large pieces. Oil flowed over my hands and spilled to the ground, forming a greenish puddle.

"No!" I gasped. "*No!* Fuck! Fuck, fuck, fuck!"

Even Pisistratus looked impressed.

"What in Hades did I do to deserve this?" I cried. "It's not *fair!*"

"In case you hadn't noticed, life is unfair, my friend," Pisistratus said mildly. He pulled his mouth to one side, considering the broken amphora. "Still, from what my little brother here has been telling me, you seem to have had a run of bad luck these days. You piss off Tyche or something?"

"Have you been purified?" Geta asked at the same time.

"Of course!" I snapped, tired of people asking me the same question. "I did it myself as soon as I got home. Myrtle, sea onions, the lot."

"Maybe you should go to the temple," Piss suggested. "Peeling onions and smoking yourself with myrtle is all very well and good, but for something like this? Best get the professionals to do it. That's what Geta did. And look at him. I don't see any toad-buggering turds shoving him around the market."

"It's true." Geta nodded. "About the temple. The whole damn household went to the priests. Had no choice. Lysander wasn't about to piss around. Not with his career being on the line and herself on at him like a harpy all night. Oh, she wasn't happy with him. No sirree, Basileos. It'll be a cold day on Mount Olympus before he has another foreign hetaera at his dinner table if his wife has any say in the matter. It was the Missus who insisted we all go to the temple for cleansing. Had us out even before the sun was done rising. Can't say I disagreed with her, either." Geta shook his head slowly. "Go to the priests," he urged.

"They'll do you up proper," Pisistratus agreed.

I looked from one brother to the other. Both were nodding encouragingly.

"You know," I told them, "I think that might be the best idea I've heard all day."

Piss looked up at the rapidly darkening sky. "Best wait till morning, though," he advised me. "In case the Kindly Ones decide old Xanthius wasn't enough."

"How likely is that?" Geta asked dubiously.

His brother shrugged. "Straightforward murder's one thing, isn't it? But the hetaera was cacked the first night of the Great Panathenaea. That's a jab at Athena if I ever saw one. So, yeah. I'd bet good silver owls we've not seen the arse end of them."

Pisistratus was right.

The Kindly Ones screamed over Athens again that night. This time, people knew better than to go outdoors.

Chapter 23

It might have made the most sense to go to the Temple of Zeus for cleansing. After all, one of his epithets was Zeus Katharsios, God of Ritual Purification. But his new temple, in the south end, was still unfinished, his old temple was halfway to the Piraeus, and his altar on the Acropolis was inaccessible to mere foreigners such as myself who were not permitted past the Propylaea, the gateway to the Acropolis. Besides, even in his roles as Zeus Alastor, Avenger of Evil Deeds, or Zeus Xenios, the Protector, he had not shown any particular inclination to either protect or avenge me. Why, then, would he bother to purify me? So rather than seeking out Zeus in any of his less-than-helpful incarnations, I went instead to the Eleusinium to have a word with the only god who actually owed me a favour.

The main temple for Demeter, goddess of agriculture, giver of laws, upholder of order, and nibbler of shoulders is actually located in the town of Eleusis, a full day's journey from Athens northwest along the Sacred Way. Fortunately for me, at some point in the past, a quick-thinking priest came up with the brilliant idea to open an urban branch of the temple. You can find The Eleusinium a block east of the Panathenaic Way, right before it reaches the Clepsydra fountain and the Court of the Pythion, which stand at the north-eastern foot of the Acropolis.

Demeter is a popular goddess, and the Eleusinium is considered one of the holiest sites in Athens—apart from Athena's temples on the Acropolis, of course. Because of this, the grounds in front of the temple are thick with statuary—offerings, for the most part—including a huge winged serpent, numerous marble pigs, and a particularly fine bronze horseman.

Hermogenes and I arrived at the gate before the sun had fully risen. The sky was achingly blue, heralding another scorching day. It was already quite warm, and the bronze horse was covered in a pale coating of road dust, dulling his usual bright lustre. Images of wheat and barley were everywhere, and gigantic sheaves of golden grains stood guard on each side of the gateway, lending a rich country pungency to the air.

The goddess was not in when Hermogenes and I came calling. I was relieved, though not terribly surprised. Demeter's deep and abiding desire to make amends for what had been, after all, an understandable mistake was as disconcerting as it was overwhelming. As such, and despite her generally sunny nature (Demeter really *is* as nice as you'd think), I far preferred her absence to the awkward, if heartfelt, apologies she always offered when present. I suspect she felt much the same, for she was rarely home when I called. Shame and guilt, it seems, do not come naturally to gods.

Her priests were in, however, and once I told them who I was, what I needed and why, they were more than willing to help me out. I'll say this for her, Demeter always made sure her priests knew to lend a hand whenever I required aid. It was gratifying to know that I still had at least one friend in high places.

The acolytes took charge of Hermogenes, while the priests led me to the altar outside the temple, where the head priest stood waiting. There they stripped me, washed me, and prayed over me before bringing out a suckling pig for the sacrifice. Ignoring the animal's struggles, the head priest deftly slit its throat with a bronze knife and held the pig over my head, letting it pump out its life blood directly over my head and hands. Then there was more washing and more praying, several rounds of it, until finally every last speck of blood and corruption had been scoured from my flesh.

I felt renewed.

They dressed me in a fresh white chiton. The cloth was rough against my scrubbed skin. An acolyte offered me a cup of barley water mixed with mint and honey, a drink sacred to Demeter. I swallowed it in a single draught, the honey sweet against my tongue, the mint cool in my mouth and throat. I handed the cup back to the acolyte and, with a final invocation, the priests pronounced me pure.

Hermogenes and I emerged from the temple grounds blinking in the late morning sun. I felt as wobbly as a newborn lamb

and I assumed Hermogenes felt the same for he was uncharac-
teristically silent. I did not see Pharsalia until she tugged on the
back of my chiton.

"Now that's a fine idea, luv," she said, indicating my white
clothing and all that it implied.

Her own chiton was a bright yellow-green monstrosity today.
It was edged in a darker green, which did not quite match the
paler colour, and it had been secured at the shoulders with two
gold phallus pins, each pointing perkily skyward.

"I had meself done yesterday," she was saying. "Soon as I
heard the news."

"I wish I'd had your foresight," I said wryly. I wondered why
she'd made the trek up to the Eleusinium today if not to be purified. Politely, I did not inquire. "Are you heading back now?" I
asked instead. "Shall we walk together?"

"Sounds a treat, luv. I'd appreciate a bit of company."

We set out with Hermogenes trailing behind us. I'd only
taken a few steps before I realized Pharsalia was limping. I
stopped dead.

"But, what's happened to you?" I asked, concerned. "You're
hurt!"

"It were the Kindly Ones, weren't it?" she said, screwing up
her face. "The first night they flew. Got caught in the panic, I
did. Twisted me foot something awful."

"Pharsalia! That's terrible."

"That's life," she said philosophically, gesturing me to keep
walking. "I'm no fool. I kept me doors shut tight as a virgin's
thighs last night."

"You and all of Athens." I offered my arm. "Here, at least let me help you."

She took it gratefully. "Ooo, ta very much, I'm sure." She looked up and fluttered her eyelashes.

I chuckled despite myself and we continued on.

"Did you ever see her that night, luv? Neaera, I mean," she asked.

"See her? I found her," I replied. "Drowned in a pot of my olive oil."

"Great Zeus's arsehole! No wonder you're all in white then."

"And freshly scrubbed. I had Hermogenes done too. For good measure." I looked around to see where my slave had gotten to. He was dawdling several blocks behind us, swinging his market basket as if it were a discus. He'd produced another of the ubiquitous green victory ribbons from somewhere and had tied it around his freshly washed mop of curls. I noticed his white tunic was already starting to look a little grubby.

"Who do you think done her in, then?"

I turned back to Pharsalia and frowned in thought, realizing this was the first time anyone had asked me that question.

"I've no idea," I answered slowly. "I suppose it had to be one of the men at the dinner. I can't think that a slave would have done such a thing—and Geta, Lysander's steward, keeps a pretty close eye on them all. Damokles, maybe? Or one of the other men she was ignoring in favour of him. Maybe even Lysander himself. The slaves thought he wanted a go at her, but Damokles wasn't sharing."

"Oh, that shouldn't have been a problem." She waved it off. "Not with Lysander being the one who hired her."

I lifted one shoulder in a shrug. "Maybe Neaera wasn't interested in him."

Pharsalia slid me a knowing look. "Luv, a hetaera's *always* interested—especially if the man with the bump in his chiton's the one with the coins in his hand."

"Right," I conceded sheepishly and we walked a few more steps.

"You know, there was another man there," I said at last. "A fat one. Philoxenus. There was something … off about him."

"Off?"

"Well, for one thing, he was trying to bribe me."

"Bribe you!" Pharsalia was startled. "What for?"

Troubled, I shook my head. "I'm not entirely sure. He wanted me to serve the food hot. Hot! As if I didn't know any better. As if I were some taverna cook!"

Pharsalia patted my arm soothingly.

"He even flashed a handful of owls at me."

It was her turn to shake her head. "That is passing strange," she agreed. "But what does it have to do with Neaera?"

"I don't know," I admitted. "Except that he was odd and he was there the night she was killed."

I was still thinking about possible suspects when a donkey cart clattered past us, kicking up clouds of hot dust. I covered my mouth and nose with a corner of my chiton. Pharsalia clung more tightly to me. I suddenly became aware of the sheer strength in her arms. Her muscles were hard from years of hauling heavy baskets of grain and flour and kneading mounds of bread dough. This was a woman who could never be described as soft and yielding. She was probably stronger than I was. She was certainly stronger than some of the men who had dined at Lysander's table that night. In order to drown Neaera, someone had held her head under the oil, presumably while she was struggling. Was a woman strong enough to do that?

"What about a woman?" I asked once the dust had settled and we could breathe again. "What was the wife's name again?" I asked. "Cresilla?"

Pharsalia gave me an indecipherable look. "That's right. You don't think she killed the hetaera, do you?"

"Well, I thought perhaps—"

Pharsalia was shaking her head vigorously. "No, no. Cresilla would never stoop to that."

"But you told me she was a snob," I argued, warming to the idea the more I considered it. I remembered Cresilla. She was a large woman whose strapping frame had been apparent even under cover of her heavy veils and himation. "You said she was a good daughter of Athens and that she disapproved of Lysander bringing foreign women to his symposions. Remember? That's why she was demanding all those last-minute changes to the menu—to make him pay for it. Neaera was from Thessaly. I know there were separate parties that night, but at some point maybe Cresilla went to the loo and spotted Neaera. Or maybe Neaera had gone for a pee and they bumped into each other. Maybe Cresilla had too much to drink and was overcome by a fit of jealousy. Maybe she lured Neaera into the storeroom and—"

"Listen to yourself, luv! Jealous? Cresilla?" Pharsalia snorted inelegantly. "She doesn't much care where Lysander pokes his spear as long she's got a few of me bread dildos to keep herself company. 'Course she disapproved of her husband's choice of hetaeras, but only because they were foreign. Not because she was jealous."

"They?"

"All the hetaeras that night were foreigners. Didn't you know?"

"Oh. No, I didn't."

"Well they were—and a slyer bunch of sneakyboots you won't find anywhere. Not exactly a big happy guild, is that. It's them were envious of Neaera. Too popular for her own good, that one. If it were a woman who done her in, it's much more likely to be one of the other hetaeras than the lady of the house. And besides, what good daughter of Athens would do such a thing during the Great Panathenaea?"

I had no answer for that and we continued on our way in silence, thinking our own thoughts. I was loath to let Cresilla off the hook so easily, but Pharsalia's reasoning was sound. And I highly doubted whether any of the other hetaeras could have committed the crime. Jealous though they may have been of Neaera, Lysander liked his women small and delicate. All the hetaeras present that night had been slight, diminutive women, selected more for their ability to mix wine and fornicate than for any more physically demanding talents. Which brought me back to the men at the party.

The popular chariot racer, Damokles, was an athlete. He would have been strong enough to kill her. But what motive would he have had? Annoyed at myself, I shook the thought off impatiently. Why was this my concern? It was not my place to ferret out the killer. I was chef, not citizen. I was cleansed and purified now. Done up properly by the priests. I needed to get on with my life, to see what I could do about my rapidly shrinking client list. I did not have time to track down murderers.

Hermogenes had found a stick on the side of the road. I could hear him spearing invisible enemies behind us, no doubt imagining himself on the back of a war chariot. Pharsalia stumbled a little and cursed under her breath.

"Did you get someone to look at that foot?" I asked her. "There's a leech in the Kerameikos, a fellow named Menon. He's a bit of a prat, but he's a decent enough physician—though I'll thank you not to tell him I said so."

"I know all about Menon, luv," she wrinkled her nose. "Used him meself when I hadn't the coin for any better. But now business is booming—or, it was booming—and I've the means to see meself to the Asclepion if needs be. Castor took me over to the temple yesterday."

"Castor, eh?" I slid her an arch look. Were the rumours about him and Pharsalia true? They were an unlikely couple—he was more than twice her size and three times as hairy, but stranger pairings had been known to occur.

"He's a good friend." She nodded serenely, giving nothing away. "He even helped commission a statue of me foot, you know. So I can give it to temple for fixing me up proper."

"That was nice of him," I agreed.

We stopped in front of the Herm at the entrance to the Agora, each of us pausing to touch the statue for good luck.

"Well, this is me, then," she said. "I've got to get back to the shop."

"Let me walk you there."

"Oooo, always the charmer." She fluttered her lashes at me again.

I grinned briefly, but it soon faded away. I was thinking about something Pharsalia had said. "What do you mean business *was* booming?" I inquired as we continued walking. "I thought you were busier than ever."

"Maybe before the hetaera was murdered and the Kindly Ones started flapping about," Pharsalia replied.

"What do bread dildos have to do with any of that?"

"Word got out, didn't it? Me bread dildos were at Lysander's house the night Neaera were killed."

"Your bread dildos were probably at every house in Athens that night!" I protested. "What in Hades does that have to do with anything?"

She patted me on the arm. "I know it, and you know it, luv, but it's that poxy Sicilian. He's been flapping his great gob all over the Agora, hasn't he?"

"Mithaecus!" I hissed the name, feeling my blood start to boil.

"Telling everyone me dildos are impure on account of that I delivered them meself to Lysander's that day and somehow got meself polluted in the process."

"But you weren't there when Neaera was killed! She hadn't even arrived yet! What does bloody Mithaecus"—I spat the name like a curse—"think he's doing?"

I'd stopped again, and my voice had risen. The few other pedestrians on the road looked askance at me. Pharsalia gave them a reassuring smile and pulled me forward.

"He's just trying to get back at me, isn't he?" Pharsalia said in a low voice. "He knows I don't like his dirty great self—and I make no bones about it. He thinks he lost a few clients last year on account of me. But really it was his own sodding cooking that did the trick." She chewed thoughtfully on her lip for a moment. "Of course, I *might* have let drop in a few ears that his cheese fish were pure shite," she conceded. "And maybe I mentioned here and there that his soup were as thin as goat piss and not quite so tasty."

I smiled down at her, though I was still fuming inside. "I always knew I liked you, Pharsalia."

She grinned back, but the smile faded before we'd taken more than a few steps.

"All me orders for yesterday were cancelled," she confided, an uncharacteristic furrow of worry wrinkling her brow. "I thought at first maybe nobody was wanting a bit of fun, what with people being hurt by the Kindly Ones and all. But the parties are still going on, aren't they? Nobody wants to offend Athena. So I had meself purified good and proper by the priests, and that should have been the end of it. But most of me orders were cancelled again today. That's Mithaecus, that is. Ox-buggering arse-licker! That's why I went to the Eleusinium this morning. To see if Demeter could lend a hand, her being the goddess of bread and all. I sacrificed a nice pig and brought a basket of me bread dildos as an offering."

"That ought to do the trick," I said, trying to console her.

"Let's hope so, luv. Because if it doesn't, me dildos are all going to end up as croutons. I might as well hang up me apron if that's the case. I don't like salad, me. Ta very much, but I've no desire to be a sodding crouton-maker."

"It won't come to that," I said, patting her arm reassuringly. "The women of Athens won't have it."

"I hope you're right, luv. I hope you're right."

Chapter 24

We saw Pharsalia to her shop door, but before we left, she offered us each a freshly baked bread dildo. As she deftly sliced them open and started stuffing them with cheese, Hermogenes got a rather funny look on his face, his mouth managing to appear both tight and wobbly at the same time. My expression must have shown something of my own discomfort for Pharsalia laughed uproariously when she looked at the pair of us. But the walk had made us hungry and we were too grateful for the unexpected breakfast to take offence. Once I got past the idea of it, the bread dildo *was* very tasty.

Munching happily, we set off once more. Now that I'd been purified, I needed to see what I could do about salvaging my reputation. I was going to have a word with Iphicrates.

I'd had some time to think while the priests had been praying over me. Granted, I possessed no olive oil of my own, but

Gorgias had a small amphora of the stuff sitting in the kitchen and I knew he'd let me use it. It would do for at least one dinner party, and I could try to get more tomorrow from Lamachus. I had baskets of dried and fresh fruits in the storeroom, along with walnuts, almonds, and pots of honey. In the ice pit, there were assorted cheeses, the shark-belly steaks, and a dozen quail (no relation to Kabob). If I started the pastries and breads as soon as I got home, I could still produce a decent feast for a Panathenaic symposion. Provided Iphicrates would agree to honour my contract.

But Iphicrates would not even agree to see me.

"Sorry, guv," the porter apologized, opening the door just enough to peer out at me. "I'm not t'let you in, am I?"

I stood on my toes, trying to see past him. "But, I need to speak to Iphicrates. It's important. Tell him Pelops is here."

"I knows who y'are."

"Well, then tell him I'm here, what's wrong with you, man?"

The porter shook his head. "'E knows yer here," he said. "An' I told you, I'm not t'let you in."

"But I've been to the priests!" I grabbed a handful of my white chiton and held it up. "Look! I've been purified!"

The man was staring over my head, refusing to meet my eyes. "Don't matter, do it?" he said. "'E don't want ter see you. 'E's, uh … sick. Yeh, sick."

"But I'm to cook for him—"

"'E's 'ired another cook, 'asn't 'e? To, uh…" He began shuffling his feet, shifting his weight from one foot to the other. "To … 'elp 'im get better."

"What cook? Who would he find at such a late date?"

"The Macedonian."

"Castor? Castor's not a *real* chef! He's just—"

The man slammed the door in my face.

"Stupid wanker!" Hermogenes cried, shaking his fist at the closed door. "Shite-eater! Goat-buggering tosser!"

"Enough!" I snapped, cutting Hermogenes off with a sharp gesture. I paused, then took a deep breath through my nostrils and let it out slowly. Smoothing my hair back, I turned away from the door. "Enough," I said again, more quietly this time. "We're better than this. Come, Hermogenes. We'll try Anacreon. Perhaps he will prove more enlightened."

Hermogenes and I spent the rest of the morning and part of the afternoon trudging down the dark, narrow streets of Athens. There were four days left of the Great Panathenaea, which meant three more clients to visit—not including Xenarchus, who I suspected wouldn't bat an eyelash if I'd strangled fifty hetaeras with my own hands as long as I produced Daphne for his end of the festival party.

But Anacreon was "sick" too. So was Sostratus. Leucippus refused even to open the door, though it was clear from the muffled voices behind it that someone was in. I had no doubt that a message would be waiting for me at home informing me he'd fallen victim to the same sudden illness that afflicted my other clients.

By the time we'd been around to all these houses, I felt like I'd walked halfway across Athens and back with nothing to show for it beyond sore feet, a parched throat, and a now grimy white chiton. Glumly, I headed home, Hermogenes scuffing along behind me.

He was pouting. It was the first day of the athletic competitions and he was eager to go to the Agora to cheer on his favourite athletes. I could think of few things I cared to do less, so I'd refused his request to attend. But as we started to detour around the marketplace, I reconsidered. I had no feasts to prepare. In fact, I had nothing whatsoever to do, except track down the elusive Daphne, and as Neaera's funeral wouldn't be held until later that afternoon, I wouldn't be able to search for her sister until then.

I stopped for a moment, staring at nothing. Then I sighed and pinched the bridge of my nose. "Fine," I relented. "We'll go, then."

"Really, Chef?" Hermogenes perked up. "The wrestling should be starting soon. Are you sure? I mean, I know you're not really in the mood, but Glykon is competing against Saurus and, you know, that Saurus is nothing but a dirty great wanker. He's—"

"Enough!" I held up my hand to interrupt his chatter. "Let's go before I change my mind."

He closed his mouth with an audible snap, and I turned to go back to the Agora. Hermogenes danced along beside me.

I regretted my kindness almost immediately. The midafternoon sun beat down directly over the Agora, and the still air was heavy with the sickly sweet smell of warm wine, the fetid reek of poorly grilled goat, and the sour stench of a thousand sweating men. I could feel the perspiration running freely down my own back and I paused to mop my face with the corner of my chiton. It was as hot as Hephaestus's forge out there.

I spared a moment of pity for the athletes. By tradition they competed in the nude, so at least they weren't sweltering under a chiton. Even so, I would not want to exert that kind of effort in this sort of heat. I shuddered a little, thinking of the last race, which would be run, for amusement's sake, in full battle armour.

Undeterred by either the heat or the press of people, Hermogenes was busily pushing his way through the throng in search of a better view. I trailed behind him reluctantly.

The crowd felt odd. For one thing, the spectators were surprisingly well-behaved. They clapped for the winners, but there was none of the usual jeering at the less-favoured athletes, and few seemed to be gambling on the outcome of the events. It was the most subdued festival I'd ever attended.

Hermogenes had disappeared into the crowd. Annoyed, I stood on my toes trying to spot him. I couldn't even see a sign of his passage.

I scowled. It was just like him, always buggering off on me. He was a slave, for Zeus's sake! He was supposed to stick close in case I required anything. All of a sudden, I was furious with him.

I was hot, sweaty, thirsty, and depressed. My head was pounding. I'd lost all my olive oil. I had to find a hetaera who didn't want to be found. I owed a man with large slaves money I did not have. And because a filthy flea of a man was slandering me, my illustrious career appeared to be going up in smoke. I didn't care who won the wrestling event. In fact, I didn't much care about any of the athletic competitions. I decided to go home.

But Tyche, that unsteady goddess of fortune, had not quite finished kicking me in the bollocks. Before I could quit the crowd, an over-excited spectator sloshed his wine—an inferior vintage—down the front of my chiton, and another man stepped back suddenly, crushing my toe under the heel of his sandal. As I wrenched away from him, I slipped and fell in a puddle that had not been there a moment ago. Courtesy of Poseidon, no doubt. I cursed under my breath. Had he no love left for me, then? No fond feelings for all the years I'd grown up with him? Or any appreciation for all the recent prayers and sacrifices I'd offered to him, for that matter?

Apparently not.

To make things worse, insult was added to injury when I limped from the Agora, muddy and dishevelled, only to see Mithaecus the Sicilian breezing past on his way to his next assignment. He was garbed in a crisp, clean yellow chiton, and he was surrounded by his retinue of fawning disciples, all of them carrying baskets of spoons and ladles as well as his famous red-figure dishes. Mithaecus himself carried nothing. Instead, he wove carefully through the very edges of the crowd, holding his nose in the air and his hands in front of him as if they were sacred offerings. He frowned just a little when he spotted me, but instead of pausing to trade insults, he simply looked down his nose at me—a brief, pitying sort of glance—before hustling his slaves off toward the richer section of town.

The message was clear. I was no longer important enough to notice.

Litigation for Lunkheads

Ask Anacreon ...

Dear Anacreon,

I hired a professional chef to make a fancy dinner for my festival symposion, but now I want to cancel the contract. How can I do this without getting sued?

— SIGNED, Out-to-Lunch

Dear Out-to-Lunch,

You didn't mention if the chef you hired is an Athenian or a foreigner. This makes a big difference. If he is an Athenian, he would be well within his rights to take you to court. If such an event should occur, you would then have to come up with a sound legal reason why you cancelled his contract. This could prove tricky depending on who the chef is and whether or not members of the jury were sympathetic to him (or wished to secure his services for themselves). It is very possible you might find yourself paying a hefty fine, as well as the original cost of the commission.

However, if the chef in question is a foreigner, no such considerations need trouble your mind. His legal rights are severely limited and he can only bring suit through a patron citizen. Such a situation has occurred so rarely, few are even aware of its possibility. In other words, should your chef be of foreign extraction, feel free to cancel at will.

A note of caution: if you decide at a later date to hire the services of this foreign chef, you may find him less than amenable to your proposals. As such, it may be far better to feign illness or injury rather than simply cancel his contract outright. Thus you may excuse the cancellation based on unforeseeable circumstance.

Chapter 25

And all they had me do was play the ruddy flute!" Zeuxo's voice was low, her tone uneasy.

"What's going on?" I asked, stepping into the courtyard. I'd shaken the worst of the road dust off my chiton, and I'd rearranged the folds to hide the mud and the purple wine stain. I hadn't felt any more respectable for doing so, but when I realized Zeuxo was there, I was glad I had taken the time to do it.

I found her in the courtyard with Gorgias and Ansandra, enjoying a cup of water in the afternoon sun. Gorgias reclined on his favourite bench by the geraniums. Ansandra was fast asleep against him, Kabob dozing in her arms. Zeuxo was seated under the shady portico. She looked odd somehow. I paused, trying to identify what was different about her, then realized she was dressed simply. No fancy jewellery, no elaborate hairstyle, a plain, muted blue chiton instead of one of her finer garments.

Gorgias raised his eyebrows at the sight of my white garb. "Well, look who's gone and gotten himself fluffed and buffed, then."

"And purified to a turn," I agreed, trying to sound chipper in front of them. "You're looking better."

"The fever's gone. I think I'll live," he said with a lopsided grin. "Though I'm not sure Ansandra believes me." He dropped a gentle kiss on the top of her head. She didn't move.

"Sticking close, is she?"

"Her and the quail," Gorgias said wryly. "If she has to go anywhere, she leaves Kabob to keep me company. Little bugger snuggles in like I'm his bloody mum. I'll be all over in bird shite before the end of it." He didn't sound like he minded too much, and despite his words, there were no visible droppings on him.

Smiling, I joined them, seating myself casually beside Zeuxo.

"So what's wrong with playing the flute?" I asked her. "I've heard you. You play beautifully."

She slid me a dark look as she poured a cup of water and passed it to me.

"What?" I protested. "It's true!"

"Maybe so," she said. "But I do a lot of other things beautifully, don't I?"

My already parched mouth went a little dryer at the thought. I swallowed the water down in one draught.

"And all they were interested in last night was my flute," she said, pouring me a second cup

"At Iktinos's symposion? They only had you play the flute? But I thought you were—"

"The main flute girl. Yes, that's what Tiny promised me," she said bitterly. "But when it came time to auction off my services, they bid on Theoclea instead."

Bewildered, I said, "But Iktinos adores you! Why would he toss you over for Theoclea? You're a hundred times more talented and a thousand times more beautiful. I don't understand."

"All the flute girls paired up last night, except me."

I could see how much it cost her to admit it. I didn't know what to say.

"I was left twiddling my flute and wondering when the Kindly Ones would bugger off for the night so I could go home."

"Did … did Iktinos give you a reason?"

Zeuxo didn't respond. Instead she looked down at her hands, her lower lip trembling ever so slightly. It was Gorgias who answered my question.

"It was Kallikrates's doing," he said.

"Kallikrates? Why should he care who Iktinos has at his symposion?"

"Well, they *are* business partners—"

"So?"

"So, Kallicrates saw Zeuxo walking with you the other morning, didn't he? And when he went to the Agora, I guess he got an earful from Mithaecus about you being there. You know, when Neaera was killed." He paused for a moment, letting it sink in.

When it did, I gaped at him. "Do they think Zeuxo has been tainted by association? Corrupted just because I walked her home? *Because we're friends?*" My voice had risen.

"Sorry, Pelops." Gorgias shrugged uncomfortably.

"That's preposterous!" I exploded.

Ansandra stirred and mumbled in her sleep. Gorgias frowned at me.

"Kritias cancelled me for tonight as well," Zeuxo said in a small voice. She was still looking down at her hands.

I choked off my outrage with an effort. First Pharsalia and now Zeuxo! Even my friends were affected by The Sicilian's jealous rivalry. I seethed inwardly, wishing him immured in Hades right beside my snake of a father.

"I'm so sorry," I told Zeuxo after a moment. "I ... I don't know what to say."

She looked up at me then, her eyes bright with unshed tears. "It's not your fault." She shrugged, the slight tremble in her voice at odds with the easy gesture. "It's Mithaecus, isn't it. I wouldn't mind so much, you know, if it were only a couple of contracts here and there. But the fees are so much higher during the festival, Pel. And the tips! I was counting on them. I've got bills to pay. But you don't get tips for blowing the flute, no matter how well you play. And if nobody wants to hire me for anything else ... well, I'm not sure what I'll do."

I'd never seen her look so worried. I touched her hand gently and she managed a small, unhappy smile.

"Look," I began, thinking fast. "I've been purified by the priests now. There's not even a whiff of corruption on me anymore. The biggest problem now is—"

"Mithaecus," Gorgias spat the name out quietly.

"No," I contradicted him.

Even Zeuxo looked surprised at that.

"It's not Mithaecus himself," I explained. "It's what he's telling people."

"What? That you were there the night Neaera was murdered? So were a dozen other men, not including the slaves."

"Ah yes," I nodded. "But none of them is accused of sacrilege."

"Sacrilege?" Zeuxo squeaked.

Gorgias's frown deepened, his eyebrows scrunching together to form one bushy black caterpillar.

"It's not just that I was there that night. Mithaecus is telling anyone who'll listen that I'm *responsible* for the Kindly Ones' attacks," I explained. "He says they're flying, not because Neaera was murdered, or because it happened during the Panathenaea. No, he's telling everyone they're attacking because I roasted lamb in its skin instead of offering the skin to the gods."

"That piss-sucking little goatfucker!" Gorgias sputtered, following up with a description of Mithaecus as vulgar as it was apt. Oblivious, Ansandra slept on, which was probably just as well. Kabob, however, raised his head and fixed Gorgias with a beady, reproachful look. Gorgias lowered his voice. "Why would anybody listen to him?" he demanded.

"They're scared, aren't they?" Zeuxo answered, her tone soft. "The scapegoat didn't work. The Kindly Ones are still flying, and nobody knows who killed her, so Pel is…"

"The next convenient scapegoat," I finished glumly.

"But, Mithaecus is…" Gorgias began.

"Wholly despicable," I said. "And a pig's ass to boot. But people are listening to him. Zeuxo's not the only one with cancelled contracts."

"Ah, bollocks! Another one's gone and cancelled, then?"

"Gorgias, they've *all* cancelled on me. I've no contracts for the festival at all. Except for Xenarchus, of course, and every time I hear a knock at the door, I half expect it to be his snotty slave come to tell me I've been axed."

Gorgias swore again. "What are you going to do, then? You can't just let that bastard Sicilian get away with this shite!"

I took a deep breath, realizing only now the one course of action left open to me. "I'm going to find out who killed Neaera," I told them.

"How the chuff does that help you with Mithaecus?" Gorgias demanded, dubiousness written all over his face. "Not to mention it's not your responsibility, is it?"

"Look, I know I'm not a fine upstanding Athenian citizen. I *know* it's not my civic duty to investigate Neaera's murder."

And even if I found the killer and he was hauled up in front of the Council of the Areopagus, I wouldn't be able to collect half the fine—which was really a shame as it was bound to be considerable, given the circumstances.

"But think about it," I urged. "As soon as the killer's discovered and jollied away for whatever well-deserved punishment the Areopagus devises, the Kindly Ones will take themselves off, and then ... then my old friend Mithaecus—"

"Won't have a pot to piss in," Zeuxo finished, a satisfied gleam in her eyes.

"Well, he won't have any reason to accuse me of sacrilege," I amended.

"He'll be left with his thumb up his arse." Gorgias practically cackled in delight. "All this time he's been banging on about your lamb, and all this time, your clients have been secretly panting for a taste of it, the greedy bastards. Once the Kindly Ones bugger off to wherever they live when they're at home, and everyone realizes you're on the up and up, then all those clients will come crawling back, foaming at the mouth for a bit of your roast lamb and plums."

"You'll be able to name your price!" Zeuxo enthused.

"If you're smart, you'll make them pay through the arsehole for the privilege," Gorgias advised. "And that goat-buggering Sicilian will just have to eat it, won't he?"

"That," I told them, "is the plan."

In light of my new resolve, Zeuxo agreed to attend Neaera's funeral with me.

In addition to the elusive Daphne (who I hoped rather than thought would attend the ceremony), every man who had been at Lysander's symposion would be in attendance, as well as anyone else who had known Neaera well enough to kill her. It was an unparallelled opportunity.

Gorgias didn't think anyone would speak to me, and he was probably right—especially if they'd been listening to Mithaecus—but Zeuxo would know things about the mourners even Hermogenes couldn't tell me, and her insights would be invaluable.

To my intense irritation, Hermogenes had not returned by the time we left.

Neaera's final rites were being held late that afternoon.

Funerals normally take place two days after a death, but because
the deceased one's shade lingers until the rites are performed,
it had been decided to light Neaera's pyre as soon as decently
possible. Nobody wanted her vengeful shade wailing about and
whipping up the Kindly Ones' already destructive ire.

Because of the festival crowds, we had to take several
unplanned detours to get to the house that Strepsiades had kept
for Neaera. As a result, we arrived just after the funeral procession had set out to escort the body to the waiting pyre outside
the city walls.

Neaera travelled the first leg of her chthonic journey on a
mule cart piled high with flowers and greenery, the aforementioned Strepsiades having, presumably, forked out the money
for such an extravagant display. She'd been decked out in a purple chiton, similar to the one she'd died in, and her best jewellery adorned her fingers, hair, arms, and neck. A honey cake
had been set in her lifeless hands, an offering for Cerberus who
guarded the entrance to the underworld. Ahead of the bier
marched the flute players, blowing their mournful melodies.
The spot immediately behind the litter was usually reserved for
relatives. I saw a large group of women, each wearing the traditional black himation, all crying and keening their grief. We
stood to one side to let them pass. I thought at first one of them
might be Daphne, but Zeuxo disabused me of that notion.

"Aphrodisia, Timarete, Theano," she began naming them.

They were the flute girls of Athens, the lower-class hetaeras,
even one or two of the higher-class hetaeras. Neaera's colleagues
and rivals coming to bid her a last goodbye.

"How did they get on with her?" I asked, remembering Pharsalia's comments about them all being sly sneakyboots. "Neaera was awfully successful. Were there any jealousies?"

Zeuxo flashed me a disbelieving look. "Pel. We're human."

"I know, but—"

"If you get that many women in a room together, the feathers are bound to fly, aren't they? But if you're asking me if Neaera attracted more than her fair share of it, the answer's no—in spite of all the talk of her being nymph or half-nymph or whatever it was she was supposed to be."

"Excuse me?" I asked, startled. "Neaera wasn't human?"

Zeuxo shrugged and rolled her eyes. "Well, that's what Harmodia said, but then she's always going on about the other girls. This one's too skinny, that one has spots on her face, her tits are like fried hen eggs on the drying rack. Neaera was just her latest target. But Neaera was beautiful and talented. She chose her own lovers. She invented Lion on the Cheese Grater. It didn't leave Harmodia much to complain about, did it?

"So she started telling everyone that no human could be that beautiful, only a nymph. And that nymphs and the like shouldn't be allowed to compete with humans. That it's not fair to the rest of us." Zeuxo made a face. "But Harmodia's nothing but a nasty jealous cow. She'll say—or do—anything if she thinks it'll get her some attention. You know, she once scratched Cassandra's face so badly, 'Sandra tried to sue her for loss of wages."

"Really?"

"It didn't go anywhere, of course, but 'Sandra ended up losing her clientele, while Harmodia had men panting after her, all hot and bothered on account of her being so wild. I wouldn't believe a word she says, and honestly, Pel, I try to stay out of it all."

"I don't blame you," I told her with a mock shudder. "I had no idea."

"Thought we were one big happy family, did you?"

I blew my breath past my lips and shook my head slowly. "I guess I've never really thought about it." I scanned the group of women again. "Which one is Harmodia?"

Zeuxo pointed her out. The jealous flute girl marched with the other flute girls and hetaeras from Lysander's party, all of them clumped together in a small cluster towards the back of the larger group. Although they were crying and moaning theatrically enough, most of them appeared to be truly shocked, and more than a little saddened by what had happened. A few of them even looked angry. Harmodia, on the other hand, was so pale and expressionless, I couldn't tell how she might be feeling about it all. But as soon as I laid eyes on the doe-eyed beauty, I knew it didn't really matter. The woman was tiny—almost as small as Ansandra. There was no way on Olympus or Earth that Harmodia would have been strong enough to hold Neaera's head in the olive oil. She didn't even look strong enough to hold up her own bitter resentments. I would have to search elsewhere for the killer.

The last few veiled figures fluttered past us.

"What about the sister?" I bent my head to whisper the question. "Do any of this lot look like they're related to Neaera?"

Zeuxo scanned the women again, frowning a little in concentration. "I don't think so," she murmured doubtfully. "I recognize every one of them."

After the women came all of Neaera's male acquaintances. There were a lot of them, which was not surprising for a woman in her profession. Damokles, the foreign chariot racer, was front and centre, wailing and moaning like a fourth Kindly One. His face was twisted, and tears flowed like twin rivers down his cheeks. Whether his grief was real or simulated, I could not say, but he, too, was wearing a black mourning cloak, and I noticed his colour was bad and his trademark green hair ribbon was drooping sadly.

A withered, bent old man came next, leaning heavily on his slave's arm. Strepsiades, Zeuxo informed me, Neaera's philanthropist patron. Other mourners followed. I recognized many of them. The men of Athens had turned out to pay tribute to the inventor of Lion on the Cheese Grater. As they followed Neaera's bier out of the city, they wept and groaned, though not all as theatrically as Damokles. Toward the end of the procession, the second of Lysander's guests appeared. I touched Zeuxo's arm to get her attention.

"That one," I told her. "In the blue himation. He was there. And the taller man beside him."

"Aratus and Isaeus," she named them. "Aratus is the shorter one. A friend of Lysander's from when they were boys. He's a market inspector now. Not particularly important and not usually the sort Lysander hobnobs with."

"Pharsalia told me that Lysander was a bit of a social climber."

Zeuxo snorted delicately. "That's an understatement. The man drinks water and pisses wine. I'm surprised he invited Aratus to his symposion, though I suppose if they were close as boys..."

"What about the taller one? Isaeus."

"A banker," Zeuxo said. "That's probably why he was invited. He's filthy rich—and therefore important in Lysander's eyes— but all he cares about is money. Look at the way he's staring off into the distance. He probably came out today because his slaves told him it would look bad if he didn't. But I'll bet you a hundred drachmas he's traipsing along wondering how high he can raise his interest rates this month rather than sparing a thought for poor Neaera lying there."

I raised my eyebrows a little at her vehemence. "Are you all right?" I asked softly.

"Fine." Her tone indicated she was anything but. "Who else was there?"

There had been twelve men dining that night, including Lysander. Zeuxo was able to name almost all of them for me. For the most part, they were bankers and money changers, merchants and mine owners. Some, like the sculptor Kritias and his lover Charmenides, I could name for myself, having cooked for them at Xenarchus's symposion. They marched along with the rest of the procession, holding hands and looking sombre. They did not weep or wail.

"Those two are far too involved with each other to be interested in a hetaera," Zeuxo dismissed them.

"Even the one who invented Lion on the Cheese Grater?"

Zeuxo gave me an amused smile. "Oh, Kritias wouldn't be at all interested in that."

"Really."

"No," Zeuxo agreed distractedly. "Not his cup of tea at all, I imagine. You know, I'm rather surprised Kritias was there that night. He usually travels in more refined circles."

"Maybe he didn't get any other invitations." I shrugged, trying to think of a way to bring the conversation back to Lion on the Cheese Grater.

"Maybe he heard you were doing the food."

I smiled down at her and squeezed her arm gratefully. Then I caught a grey blur out of the corner of my eye. It was the symposion ghost. He was trailing along behind the rest of the procession, his shoulders bowed, his eyes on his feet. Long hair flowed down his back. Unbelievably, the man was still wearing the same tired chiton that had seen him through two symposions that I was aware of, not to mention an afternoon of active grieving in the Agora. He must be poor indeed to have only one set of clothing.

"What about him?" I asked Zeuxo. "That older fellow in the grey chiton."

Again, Zeuxo was dismissive. "Oh, that's Peneus," she said. "He came back to the city a couple of months ago."

"Came back?"

"He was away. Corinth, I think. I don't really remember. He's as poor as a temple mouse, though he seems to know everybody in Athens. Shows up at a lot of the parties, at any rate. He's a bit of a professional ghost, really—but he never bids on any of the flute girls."

"That doesn't mean he didn't want any of them. Perhaps he was overcome with lust for Neaera."

"Perhaps," Zeuxo said doubtfully. "But he's been at a few

symposions I've worked, and he's never shown any interest in any of the girls. Aphrodisia was assigned to him one night as the pity fuck. But he wouldn't have any of her, would he? She thinks he's like Kritias. You know, a cushion-biter."

"Ah. So, no go on the lusting after Neaera."

"Probably not," she agreed.

Just as Zeuxo and I were about to join the tail end of the procession, a fat man came puffing up, sweating and red in the afternoon heat. It was Philoxenus, the man who had tried to bribe me at Lysander's house. His beady eyes darted around to see if anyone had noticed his tardiness, then he started wailing and moaning and slapping his fat cheeks as he joined the line of mourners. Zeuxo and I fell in several paces behind him. The back of his dark green chiton was stained with sweat and every so often, I caught the rank whiff of him. I tugged on Zeuxo's arm and we fell further behind.

"What do you know about Philoxenus?" I whispered, gesturing with my chin.

"Who?"

"The fat one in front of us."

Her lip curled with distaste as she took in the sight to which we were being treated. Philoxenus had either lost his himation in his hurry to join the procession, or he had been too hot to wear one in the first place. He sported only a thin linen chiton, which was now plastered to his more than ample body, having been thoroughly soaked in the sweat of his exertions. Through it, we could see his rolls of excess flesh jiggling repulsively.

"A bit of a bloater, isn't he?" she said quietly.

"Yes, but what do you know about him? What kind of man is he?"

She shook her head. "I've no idea, Pel. I didn't even know his name until you told me. Why are you so interested in that one?"

I pulled my mouth to one side. "I'm not entirely sure," I said. "He was behaving very oddly that night. He tried to bribe me to serve the food hot."

"Hot?"

I shrugged, indicating my own puzzlement. We walked for a while in silence, listening to the sounds of grieving.

"Well," Zeuxo said finally, her eyes still on the wobbling sight in front of us. "From the look of him, my guess is he'd be more interested in food than women, but you never know, do you? I can tell you one thing though, a man like that wouldn't be popular with the girls. I mean, look at him! He must weigh as much as an ox. Who would want that pounding away on top of them? You're liable to be squashed like a tiny little insect, aren't you?"

She gave a delicate shudder. "Flute girls wouldn't have a choice, but Neaera, she'd be different." A note of envy had entered her voice. "She was wealthy enough to be able to pick and choose her clients. And if I were that wealthy, I sure as shite wouldn't have anything to do with a gouty meat sack like that."

We followed along in silence for a while.

"What was Neaera doing at Lysander's symposion?" I asked curiously. "If she was rich enough to choose. I mean, I know he fancies himself quite the toff, but when it comes right down to it, Lysander's really only jumped-up middle class."

"But smart for all of that," Zeuxo said. "Smart enough to invite the chariot racer. Neaera liked chariot racers. And Damokles, he was from Thessaly, same as her."

I hadn't made that connection. "You think they knew each other?" I asked.

"It's possible, isn't it?"

I thought about that as the procession snaked through the twisting streets of Athens, out the Piraeic Gate and past the city's boundaries. I was still thinking about it as we stopped in a quiet field— quiet except for the flute players still piping their mournful dirge. A handful of men, Damokles among them, carefully lifted the bier off the mule cart and placed it on the funeral pyre of dried sticks and aromatic cedar. The black-cloaked mourners, some of them still weeping, formed a loose circle around the pyre. And then, with the help of his slave, Strepsiades lifted a pine torch in shaky hands. Grunting with the effort, he threw it on the oil-soaked wood. There was a roaring *whoosh*, and the pyre ignited, flames leaping up to the sky. A wave of heat rolled over the mourners.

I happened to be looking at Peneus when Strepsiades lit the pyre. The grey man had been standing to one side, as far from the pyre as he could be and still be considered part of the ceremony. But when the flames shot up, he flinched visibly and took a step back. On his face was something that looked almost like fear.

"Look at them!" Zeuxo exclaimed.

Reluctantly, I pulled my gaze from the ghost and his strange reaction.

"They don't give a damn, do they?" Her tone was as bitter as ashes.

That more than anything distracted me from Peneus.

"Who? What do you mean?"

She gestured sharply at the circle of men. "Them! All of them. Look at them crying and carrying on. But they didn't care about her, did they?"

Her dark eyes had filled with tears. Concerned, I pressed her hand between mine.

"Not one of them could tell you what her favourite colour was," she said in an undertone. "Or what kind of music she liked to hear at home, or whether she preferred house cats to quails. They didn't know what made her sad or happy, or what she thought about when the stars are out and everyone else is asleep. They only cared about what she could do for them." She sounded disillusioned now, and sad. Unbearably sad.

"She was a hetaera," I ventured.

"She was a person!" Zeuxo flared.

"But it was her job to please men," I said, struggling to say something that would make her feel better. "All those other things, the music and the stars, those are things you share with friends. Not clients or colleagues."

"I know." Her shoulders slumped as the fight went out of her. "I know, Pel. But it doesn't mean it's right. I look around and I doubt—I really doubt—whether any of these people were her friends. It makes me wonder if she had any true friends. Is it even possible for a hetaera to have friends?"

"I'm *your* friend," I said.

But she turned her head away and did not answer.

Uncomfortable with the ideas her questions had raised, I

looked up to scan the group of mourners—and found myself being examined in turn.

Philoxenus was on the other side of the pyre. He stared fixedly at me, and his tiny eyes, almost hidden in the folds of his fat cheeks, were calculating. He was wearing several silver rings, his sausage-like fingers bulging out over the metal bands. He played with his jewellery absently and as he continued to stare at me, a small smile began to twitch at his lips. The light from the fire reflected eerily in his eyes and for a moment it seemed as though his orbs were made of flames themselves.

Chilled and discomfited, I averted my gaze and looked instead at the other mourners. They were talking quietly amongst themselves now, glancing first at the dying pyre and then at the sun as if gauging the time it would take for the fire to die down completely. Once it did, they would chant Neaera's name three times in farewell before hastening back to the city and the safety of their comfortable homes. Everybody wanted to be indoors before night fell. Before the Kindly Ones came again.

And then my eyes found the chariot racer.

He was standing closer to the burning pyre than anyone else. He had stopped weeping now, but his shoulders were bent as if under a tremendous weight. In the light of the dying flames, his eyes seemed dark and sunken, and there were lines on his face that had not been there two days ago.

Zeuxo, it appeared, was wrong. Neaera had had at least one friend at her funeral. And as soon as the Kindly Ones had finished their night's dark work, I intended to have a word with Damokles of Thessaly.

Chapter 26

Before retiring for the night, I'd made plans to be up and out the door early the next morning. It was the day before the Panathenaic chariot races and I wanted to catch Damokles before he went off to prepare his horses for the big event. But by the time rosy-fingered Eos had spread her saffron draperies across the sky, I realized I had an additional task.

Hermogenes had not come home last night.

I had been annoyed when he hadn't arrived back by suppertime. What if I'd needed him for something? What if Timon had changed his mind and I had suddenly found myself with a feast to prepare and no slave to help me? This was not acceptable behaviour. But as the skies grew darker and the time of the Erinyes drew nearer, I found my anger gradually metamorphosing into concern.

I tried telling myself that he had probably hooked up with

some friends to watch the athletic competitions and drink away the afternoon. He'd lost track of time—as he always did—and when he'd realized how late it had grown, he had probably found himself a safe place to hole up until dawn heralded the end of the Erinyes' attack. And, for that matter, why was I so concerned about him? He was just a slave—and an undergrown, scrappy one at that. And yet, I spent the darkest hours of that night padding back and forth from my sleeping couch to the front door to watch for him.

The eerie wails of the Kindly Ones rode wild on the night air and every so often, I felt a deeper note thrum through the very core of my body and I knew they hovered directly overhead.

I kept very still during those times, hidden in the shadow of the open door, not even daring to breathe. And then a fetid whoosh of hot air rolled over me from above and the ominous beat of their wings faded into the distance like retreating war drums.

I knew Hermogenes had enough sense to hide himself from their cruel attacks—after all, he'd seen first-hand the damage their scourges could inflict—but I couldn't rid myself of the notion that he'd somehow been injured and was unable to get under cover. I do not think I slept.

Hermogenes did not return at dawn.

Gritty-eyed and bleary, I left for the chariot racer's house before the rest of the household had even begun to stir. I chose a long, roundabout route, but though I kept a sharp eye out, there was no sign of my slave either in the dark, narrow streets or in the sun-washed Agora.

He was just a slave.

In Sipylus, I'd had hundreds of slaves. They came and went, subservient faces blurring into anonymity. This one was no different. There were thousands like him in Athens. I could replace him in a heartbeat. My stomach began to churn oddly at the thought, and I wondered if I should have taken the time to eat breakfast. I arrived at my destination, weary and not a little distracted. But one look at the chariot racer's face, and my own problems suddenly seemed inconsequential.

If anything, Damokles looked worse than he had on the previous day. His face was pale, almost gaunt, and his eyes were dull, the lids red and swollen as if he'd been up all night weeping. He clutched his black mourning himation around him as if it were the middle of winter rather than high summer. He was not wearing a green hair ribbon today.

"You found her, didn't you?" He rose to greet me as a slave escorted me into his courtyard. His voice sounded weak and quavery. "I remember, you were the cook that night."

"The chef, yes," I answered, then fell silent. In the face of such obvious suffering, I wasn't sure how to begin my inquiries. But Damokles seized the initiative.

He cleared his throat several times before he spoke. "You must have seen something," he said, his voice tight and strained. "I mean, you were the chef. You were probably in and out of those gods-cursed storerooms." He paused, passing a hand over his face. "I keep thinking about it. She said she had to go to the privy. But she was gone much longer than she should have been. I thought ... I don't know, I thought maybe the food had messed up her stomach, or something. Did you see her? You must have seen something—anything!"

Ignoring the comment about the food, I shook my head regretfully. "Not a thing. In fact, I came here today to ask you the same question."

"Me?" He seemed surprised. "Why would I have been poking around in Lysander's stores? You think I was there? You think I was in the *storeroom*?" His voice began to rise in anger and red blotches started to come out on his pale face.

He straightened, massive shoulders rolling back, equally massive chest thrusting forward. The mourning himation slid from his shoulders, pooling on the ground like black blood. "Are you saying *I* killed her?" he asked quietly. There was a dangerous glint in his eye.

All of a sudden, I was overwhelmed by his sheer physical strength. This man—this athlete—was at the peak of his prowess. He drove chariots. He threw spears. If he wanted to, he could snap me like a twig.

"Of course not!" I hastened to say. "Don't be absurd. You were clearly very close to her."

He deflated as quickly as he'd flared.

"Close to her," he repeated numbly.

"The slaves said you and she were together that night," I said delicately. Actually the slaves had been quite a bit more explicit than that. "They said that Lysander seemed jealous."

"You think Lysander did her in?" The thought clearly startled him.

"I don't know," I admitted. "I'm just starting to look into all this."

"Why?" he said bluntly. "Why do you care? She wasn't anything to you."

"No," I admitted. "But my reputation is. There's a man, you see, a rival chef who is trying to blame me for the Kindly Ones' attacks."

Damokles snorted in derision. "Heard about that. Pure horseshit! But what can you expect from a Sicilian? Not exactly the fastest ponies in the stable, are they?"

"I couldn't agree more, but there are those who think Mithaecus has a point. And my reputation is suffering because of it."

The chariot racer still looked suspicious. I needed his help with this. As far as I could tell, Damokles had been Neaera's only real friend. The only person who knew the woman as well as the hetaera. If he refused to speak to me, I was afraid my task would be over before it even began.

Part of any chef's job is convincing people that they would like to eat what you would like to cook. It's not that we're dishonest *per se* (except for Mithaecus, of course), but if I've got too many tuna steaks on my hands, then it's up to me to convince my client that he absolutely adores tuna steaks and can't possibly live another day without trying my special recipe for them. Now, I have no idea whether the client even likes tuna, but the fish will turn if it isn't used and so, it is included in the feast. And if the client is less than thrilled with the succulence of the dish? Then my job becomes suggesting, in the most delicate and diplomatic fashion, that it was, in fact, his taste buds which were at fault, having been perhaps adversely affected by the inferior vintage of the wine he had so rashly quaffed at lunch.

But in this particular case, I suspected delicacy and diplomacy would not get me far. Which left only honesty. I took a deep breath and plunged ahead.

"Look," I said. "I'll be up front with you. I think it's terrible that a woman like Neaera would be sent down the Styx in such a fashion. I didn't know her, but everything I heard about her was positive. She was beautiful, talented, and very good at her job. But I'm trying to find her killer because if I don't then Mithaecus will convince all of Athens that the Kindly Ones are attacking because of me. Not only will I never work in this city again, but the Athenians will probably end up thrashing me up and down the streets before tossing me over the boundary stones and telling me never to darken their gates again.

"I am a celebrity chef. Where else am I going to go? Sparta?" I pursed my lips and held my nose in the air. "The Spartans would only recognize a good meal if it was served up on a dead Persian. Corinth?" I snorted and rolled my eyes. "Please. A backwater town, no better than a hopped-up farming village. Their highest culinary achievement is the peasant loaf. The colonies? They're all too small and too far away from anything. No, I need to be here in Athens. And that means I need to discredit whatever The Sicilian has been saying about me. Completely and irrefutably."

Damokles considered my words for several long moments. As the silence dragged on, I began to regret my honesty. I was just about to open my mouth again, though I had no idea what else I might say, when Damokles broke the silence.

"Fair enough," he said simply. "What do you want to know?"

I let my breath out explosively, not realizing until then that I'd been holding it. Damokles gave me a small, humourless smile.

"Have a seat," he offered, gesturing me over to a bench. He clapped his hands. "Wine," he told the slave who answered his summons. "And figs."

The slave nodded without speaking and bent to pick up the himation, which still lay in a black puddle on the floor. He made as if to place it around Damokles's shoulders, but the chariot racer waved him off impatiently and the slave scuttled away with the cloak.

Gratefully, I settled against the cushions. Damokles chose an adjacent bench, unconsciously arranging himself to present his best side to me. His fit of temper had restored much of the colour to his face, and his eyes were now sharp and inquisitive. Without the black himation wrapped around his body, he looked more like the famous chariot racer again. All that was missing was the green victory hair ribbon.

Damokles's courtyard lacked an herb garden and he had only a cistern rather than a well, but the household altar had been decorated with fresh flowers, the furnishings were surprisingly well-made, and someone had planted small trees in a set of fine red clay pots. For a foreigner, he'd done well for himself—especially for one who hailed from an enemy state.

All the benches had been carefully positioned to face a tall wooden shelf. It stood on the north side of the courtyard so as to be shaded during the worst heat of the day. Arrayed on it were dozens of black-figure amphorae.

Unlike most amphorae, these had flat bases so they could be displayed without the use of stands. The exquisitely decorated designs were various takes on chariots, horses, and men riding on both. They were Panathenaic amphorae, prizes won during Athena's festival, and they contained olive oil.

The state kept a register of sacred olive trees descended from the very tree that Athena had gifted to the city so many years ago. Located outside the city walls on the grounds of the Akademia, olives from these trees were harvested, their oil used only to fill the special amphorae awarded to the winners of Panathenaic competitions. It was the best olive oil in the whole of Greece. I examined the amphorae covetously. Only a few of them had been broached.

"So, what do you want to know?" Damokles asked again.

Reluctantly, I tore my eyes away from his victory amphorae. "Everything and anything," I told him after a moment. "I never even had the pleasure of meeting her."

"She was adorable," he said immediately. "Everybody thought so."

Not everybody, I almost said, but I bit the words off before they could escape.

"She liked the finer things in life," he continued, not noticing my near gaffe. "You know, music and dancing. And the clothes and jewellery!" He shook his head in fond remembrance. "She'd spend a fucking fortune on them without even blinking! It was unreal. She was vain, but not stuck up, you know? She liked men, and men ... well, we liked her. She had these great eyes. She was always a looker, you know, even as a kid."

So, Zeuxo had been right. They had known each other before. Damokles's slave came in with a wine krater and cups as well as a bowl of ripe purple figs. He mixed the wine with herbs and water and poured us each a cup. Leaving the krater and the bowl of fruit on the table between us, he bobbed his head and retreated to the shadows of the courtyard, waiting there in case his master might require him again. Damokles had fallen silent.

"You grew up together?" I prompted, selecting a fig from the bowl. I bit into it. It was perfectly ripe, the pink inner flesh juicy and neither too sweet nor too tart. I wondered which vendor had sold them to him.

"Yeah," Damokles nodded, taking an absent sip of his watered wine. "In Thessaly. We lived in the same block of houses. In the potters' district. My dad was a potter, you know. And Neaera's mom painted amphorae for him. She was pretty good by Thessalian standards. The Athenians probably wouldn't have thought much of her designs. And, of course, her stuff couldn't hold a lamp to these beauties." He gestured negligently to his shelf of prize amphorae, calling my attention to them on the off chance I had not already noticed them.

I made the appropriate noises of admiration and he beamed proudly before he suddenly recalled the reason for my presence. His face twisted and his eyes grew bleak again. I averted my gaze.

"I'm surprised you and Neaera met each other," I said after a tactful silence. "From what I've seen here, girls are kept quite segregated from boys—at least boys from a different family."

"In Athens, they are," Damokles agreed, his voice a little hoarse. He cleared his throat before continuing. "But Thessaly's smaller. More laid-back about that kind of thing. It's a poorer city, you know. And when all you're doing is trying to make sure there's fish on the table, you don't give much of a shit about who your kids are playing with. Besides, Neaera was a wild child. Not like her sister."

I paused in the middle of tasting my wine and lifted my face from the cup. "You knew Daphne too?" I demanded, realizing that I should have guessed as much.

"You know Daphne?"

"I've been searching the city for her for days now."

"What are you talking about? Daphne's in Athens?" He seemed genuinely surprised by it.

"So I've been told. I've got a client who's looking for her."

"A client? Daphne's no chef."

"Ah," I paused and rubbed my nose. "He's looking for a hetaera. Not another chef."

Now Damokles was utterly perplexed. "What are you talking about? Daphne? A hetaera? That's impossible!"

I spread my arms to indicate my own uncertainty. "That's what I was told."

"It's ridiculous," he said forcefully. "She's worshipped Artemis ever since she was a kid."

"Well, that would explain why she's supposed to be a virgin," I said dryly.

The elusive and probably mythical virgin hetaera.

I could see that Damokles was upset by the idea, but I'd been around long enough to know that life didn't always work out the way you expected it to. Sometimes you were forced into situations you'd never thought to experience. I had certainly never dreamed I'd be a chef. And Zeuxo. What of her? Beloved child and cherished wife, yet she'd lost both husband and parents within weeks of each other and had been forced to become a flute girl in order to survive. Surely she had not spent her girlhood dreaming of being a flute girl. Perhaps Daphne told a similar story.

"Daphne in Athens? That's just fucked up," Damokles mused to himself, though I could tell from the tone of his voice that he was considering the possibility. "Why would she come to Athens? Neaera always wanted her here, but Daphne hated the place. Thessaly was more her style. Smaller, poorer, wilder—like wilderness, I mean. Daphne always had a thing for wild animals and places. Just like Artemis. No," he said, sounding decisive now. "No, if Daphne had been in Athens, she would have been at her sister's funeral. Nothing would've stopped that. Nothing! Your client's full of shit."

It was a possibility. Xenarchus had told me Daphne was from Megara rather than Thessaly. If he was mistaken about her hometown, perhaps he'd been misinformed about her presence in Athens. I rubbed my eyes wearily. If Daphne was not in Athens, then I had no hope of procuring her for Xenarchus's symposion. I cut off that line of thought. I'd consider it later—after I figured out who might have killed her sister.

"You said before that Neaera was a wild child," I said, after a long moment. "Wilder than her sister?" Perhaps Neaera's reckless nature had carried through into adulthood. If so, she may have attracted attention from certain undesirable elements.

"Oh, yeah." Damokles smiled as he looked inwardly at his memories. "She was like a wild creature sometimes. Always getting into trouble. Her mom couldn't control her at all. "

"Her father?"

"Nah," Damokles shrugged. "He lived outside the city. It was weird, but he was kind of a dick, if you ask me. Never wanted a kid and pretty much ignored Neaera. Of course, the flip side of that was he spoiled Daphne rotten when she came along. Always sending presents or inviting her to visit or some other damn thing. You can imagine what that does to the other kid. I mean, it's one thing if your dad treats you both like shit, but to play favourites like that?" Damokles paused and shook his head. "So Neaera ran wild and nobody really cared. You know, I remember there was one time when we…"

As Damokles regaled me with stories of a young Neaera's wilder escapades, I couldn't help but think of the similarities between her and Ansandra. It gave me an oddly uncomfortable feeling. Ansandra was wild too, but I did not want to see her grow up to be a hetaera.

Eventually, Damokles fell silent, lost in pleasant memories of happier times.

"About that night," I said into the quiet. "At Lysander's party. What can you tell me about your dinner mates? Did you notice anything strange? Anything that struck you as being the least bit odd?"

But Damokles had noticed nothing.

The dinner party had, apparently, been just that, a convivial evening with fine food, wine, and music. Though he had, he admitted, perhaps imbibed more than was strictly good for him and so some parts of the evening were, understandably, a little murkier in his mind than others. But he maintained Lysander was an excellent host, and if he'd been envious of Neaera's preference in dinner partners, then he, Damokles, had not been aware of it.

Of the other dinner guests, the chariot racer had only positive things to say, though he informed me that quite a few of them had boasted literary pretensions without also possessing any of the necessary talent to display them.

"The banker was the worst, though!" Damokles made a sour face.

I searched my memory. "Isaeus?" I ventured, remembering that Zeuxo had said he was a man much concerned with money and little else.

"That's the one," Damokles agreed. "Thinks he's a poet, of all damn things. Him! Sweet Athena's arse, you should have heard the crap he was spouting. 'The leaves fall to the ground, I crush them under my sandals, I am alone, so alone.' I mean, what the fuck is that? Neaera couldn't stop laughing. Had her face pushed into my shoulder so nobody would see. And all the other guests falling all over themselves, talking about how his use of imagery was brilliant and how he's ahead of his time and how they can't believe he wasn't selected to be part of the poetry competition." He snorted in derision.

"Maybe they'd all had too much to drink as well," I said diplomatically.

"No question," Damokles shot back. "But that doesn't mean the guy's poetry wasn't utter horseshit."

I conceded the point.

"You said Neaera found him amusing. Do you think he realized that?"

Damokles opened his mouth to deny it, then paused to reconsider. "You think he was pissed at her?" he asked instead.

"It's possible. If he's the sort of man who doesn't take criticism well."

Damokles chewed on his lower lip for a while. "She wasn't doing a great job of hiding it," he said finally. "We'd all of us had a lot of wine at that point. I couldn't tell you if Isaeus noticed or not. To be frank, I was too busy trying not to piss my own self laughing. His poems really were crap. Like something a mopey-arsed youth would have scratched out when he was feeling sorry for himself." He shuddered theatrically.

I picked up another fig and rolled it between my fingers. "Still," I said thoughtfully, biting into it. "If he'd been angry enough and drunk enough ... wine can be notorious for making lions out of mice. He might have followed Neaera to the privy, confronted her about his poetry, she laughed, he lost his temper and—"

"I'll kill him," Damokles said flatly.

"What?"

"I'll murder the son of a bitch!"

Appalled, I held up my hands in a soothing gesture. "Slow down. I'm not saying it actually happened. You understand me? This is pure speculation at this point. Did you notice who else left the room while she was gone?"

Without hesitating, Damokles shook his head. "I've thought

about it over and over again," he said. "But there were guys coming and going all night. The wine was flowing freely and so was the piss. I can't remember who got up when."

"Ah," I said, disappointed. "Well, who else did Neaera speak with?"

He looked at me askance. "She was the hetaera of the party," he said as if to a child. "She talked to everyone."

We both went silent for a while. There were no more figs in the bowl and the wine krater had long since been drained dry. I was just about to take my leave when Damokles spoke again.

"You know, now that I think of it, there was one other guy—a fat one—who seemed ... I dunno, weird."

"A fat man. Philoxenus?"

"You know him?"

"Barely. He does stand out in a crowd."

"I've never seen anyone so humongous." Damokles curled his lip in disgust. "And Hestia's tits, all the guy did was eat! He barely even spoke to anybody. Though I guess I should be glad he didn't try reciting poetry," he conceded. "Otherwise we might have been treated to 'Ode to a Steamed Clam' or some other horseshit. But really, it was like the guy hadn't seen food in a month. His hands were in the plates before the slaves even had a chance to put them on the table. And he was shovelling it all into his mouth so fast, I thought for sure he was going to choke. He wasn't exactly savouring the flavours, if you know what I mean."

I winced.

"The guy's a total savage. If he hadn't won the lottery for city council, nobody would invite him anywhere." Damokles threw his hands up as if to wash himself of any responsibility for the vagaries of life.

"What did you find so odd about him—apart from his obvious gluttony, of course?"

"Well, he was sitting beside us—Neaera and me. She was trying to charm him, but he wasn't having any of it. Can you believe it? A woman like Neaera! And when the cheese plate came out and everybody started saying the usual stuff about Lion on the Cheese Grater, Philoxenus just shoved half a cheese in his face and asked us what in Hades we were talking about! He'd never even heard of it! Un-fucking-believable! And here the Lioness herself was sitting beside him! If that isn't weird, I don't know what is."

"Shocking," I murmured.

"Neaera even offered to give him a demonstration, seeing as he was so innocent and all. And guess what? He turned her down flat!"

"No!"

"Oh yeah. She may have been a bit pissed at him, now that I think about it. She went kinda quiet after that. And a little while later, she said she had to visit the privy, and then … well, you know what happened after that."

I pulled my mouth to one side as I pondered it. "Would she have looked on someone like Philoxenus as a challenge?" I asked finally. "You said she was vain, that she liked men. Perhaps a man who showed no interest in her…" I let my voice trail off suggestively.

Damokles regarded me, his expression a mixture of outrage

and revulsion. "You've got to be fucking joking!" he exploded. "The guy's as big as a shit cart—and about as appealing!"

"I'm not saying she would have been attracted to him," I said soothingly. "More that it might have been a matter of professional pride. You know, the only man in Athens not drooling over her. If she'd encountered him when she was out of the room, and then tried to engage his interest…"

I could tell from the look on his face that the very idea offended him. Damokles seemed to forget (or perhaps he did not want to remember) that hetaeras—even beautiful, famous ones—had their professional reputations to consider. And that hetaeras didn't always get to service only handsome young athletes.

Well, I was not going to be the one to remind him of it. I dropped the subject and soon after that, I pushed myself to my feet and said my goodbyes. I wished him luck in the chariot races the following day and he promised to contact me if he remembered anything else.

I walked home slowly, sunk in thought. Damokles had given me much to consider.

Chapter 27

By the time I gave the Herm in front of our house a perfunctory pat and pushed open the front door, my thoughts had covered everything from jealous flute girls to pretentious bankers to the fat Philoxenus and his appallingly poor grasp of priorities. So it almost came as no surprise when I heard his name as soon as I entered the house.

"Philoxenus!" Hermogenes was exclaiming loudly. "What did that fat bastard want?"

Hermogenes was home.

An unexpected wave of relief washed over me. He hadn't been killed by the Kindly Ones, after all. I closed my eyes and made a silent prayer of thanks to whichever gods had seen him home safely. Then, feeling better than I had in a long while, I tossed my cloak over a wall hook and went to see if he'd been injured.

"He's wanting to hire the Chef for tomorrow night's supper,"

I heard Irene telling him. "His slave left good silver owls too. A down payment for services, if you please. That's better than anything else that's come 'round here lately."

"But ... but it's not on," Hermogenes sputtered indignantly. "Philoxenus is a right wanker! You can't trust him. The Chef, he doesn't know. He doesn't understand—"

I heard a smack. "He understands enough! It's good money, that is. And him with all his clients cancelling because of that poxy Sicilian. The fat man's the only one who'll hire him now, so you'll be keeping that loose tongue in your mouth or I'll know why."

I followed their voices to the courtyard. It was hot and blindingly bright in the midday sun, the heat tempered only by a faint breeze wafting in from the east. But the breeze brought something more than a welcome relief from the day's heat. Before I could step out of the shadows, the sour stench of stale wine engulfed my nostrils and stopped me in my tracks. I paused and examined my slave more closely.

Hermogenes was squinting as if the sunlight pained his eyes. His face seemed pale, his hair a tangled mess, and his previously white tunic was wrinkled and grey except where it had been stained purple from spilled drink. There was no blood on his clothing that I could ascertain, no evidence of any injuries on his person. But his whole body exuded the rank odours of old sweat and young wine. As he turned away from Irene, I could see the whites of his eyes shot through with red from imbibing whatever substandard vintage he'd managed to refrain from slopping down the front of him.

So. Hermogenes had had fun yesterday, had he? All of a sudden I was so incensed I could barely breathe. While I'd been running all over the city attending funerals, he had been kicking back watching sporting events. While I had been questioning suspects trying to find a murderer, he had been sucking down cheap wine. There I was trying desperately to recover my soiled reputation, and all he could do was carry on with his disreputable slave friends. Miserable wretch! I'd paced the house all night waiting for him to come home, and he'd been out on the town laughing and joking without a care in the world. Ingrate! He never stopped to think that perhaps people might be worried about him. That perhaps they'd be up half the night wondering if he was all right.

"Chef!" he said now, noticing me standing in the shadows. "Chef, you can't cook for Philoxenus, you can't! You'll get no joy there. He's a dirty great bloater and—"

Two strides and I was at his side. I'd never hit him before, and I didn't even realize I'd struck him now until I felt the sting of it on my palm.

"Silence!" I cried furiously.

Hermogenes stared up at me, shocked, his eyes swimming with sudden tears, his hand reaching up to touch a cheek already darkening to red.

Irene folded her arms across her chest, radiating approval but saying nothing.

"I do not need to ask where you've been," I raged. "I can smell the stench of it on you from across the courtyard. You stink! How dare you turn up in such a condition!"

"Chef, I—"

"What kind of slave abandons his master in the middle of a crowd? What kind of slave doesn't bother to come home at night? What if I'd required something? What if Timon had changed his mind? What if I'd suddenly found myself with a feast to prepare? Did you ever think of that? No, you just jollied off without a thought in your head."

I loomed over him, my face hot with anger. Hermogenes hunched his thin shoulders and hung his head.

"You keep saying you want to be a chef, that you want to be my disciple, but what kind of a disciple behaves in such a fashion? I need an assistant who will help me, not desert me to go carousing about town! How is that helpful? Well? And then to have the nerve—the balls!—to turn up in this condition!" My voice dripped with disgust. "How *dare* you behave like this!"

"I'm sorry, Chef. I'm so, so sorry," he mumbled contritely.

Sorry! I'd paced the house all night and all he could say was sorry? I'd spent the night listening to the Erinyes scream, feeling the thrumming of their wing beats in my bones, and he was sorry? I'd trudged down dark streets and poked around in filthy alleys searching for him, and all the while, he had been sleeping off a taverna crawl on some flea-infested pallet. I felt my whole body suffuse with fury. Hermogenes was *sorry*, was he? Well, I'd give him something to be sorry about! No slave of mine was going to behave like this!

Hermogenes cringed down, his unruly mop of curls hiding his expression from me. But before I could raise my hand to strike him again, I saw two fat tears plop down one after another onto the packed dirt of the floor. Hurriedly, he scuffed at the marks, hiding them from my gaze. I hesitated.

Taking a deep breath, I looked up and caught Irene's eyes. She'd edged away from us, the bright sun casting her features in stark relief. Trepidation had replaced approval, and her wrinkled face looked fearful. To her right, Kabob foraged in the garden, cooing and chuckling, oblivious to the human tensions around him.

I heard another small noise. At first, I thought it was the quail, then I realized it came from Hermogenes. I listened and it came again. A quiet stifled sob.

Such a small, vulnerable sound.

All at once, my fury bled away, leaving me feeling limp and drained. I closed my eyes and felt my shoulders drop. With a sigh, I scrubbed at my face.

"Irene," I said quietly.

She jumped at my voice. "Yes, master?"

Master? Since when was I "master" to her?

"I understand Philoxenus wants to hire me."

"Yes, master. He sent his slave 'round first thing this morning. He wants you for a feast."

"When?"

"Tonight."

"*Tonight!*" I burst out.

She cowered back and I raised my hands in placation.

"Tonight?" I said, consciously moderating my tone. "Are you sure? That doesn't give me much time to prepare."

"He brought a slate," she said helpfully, bobbing her head.

"It's not a full menu—his slave said you were allowed to be creative with the rest—but it lists the dishes he's asking for specially. Begging your pardon, master, but I had a quick glance at it, and I think we've got the ingredients for all the dishes he's after—apart from eels and a suckling pig, and Strabo could easily go to the Agora for those if you'd like. You might have to skimp on the olive oil though, we've barely got a jar left and I'm afraid it's not as nice a pressing as you're used to."

"It will have to do," I said absently, my mind already occupied with the upcoming symposion. "Thank you, Irene. It was kind of you to check the stores. And where is this slate?"

Hesitating a little, Irene passed it to me, retreating as soon as it was secure in my hand. I scanned the menu.

"How many people has he invited?" I inquired, surprised at the number of dishes.

"Four."

"For all this food?" I was incredulous.

Nervously, Irene nodded again. "That's what his slave said. There was to be four at table."

"Eels, suckling pig, hen eggs, shark. These are all expensive dishes. Did he say how much he was paying?"

Irene named a figure as low as it was insulting.

"*What!*" I exploded.

She shrank back. "It wasn't my fault!" she cried. "His slave waltzed in here snooty as can be, didn't he? Said his master was paying fair price for a chef nobody else wants to hire. I didn't tell him yes or no. You could still refuse it."

I clenched my fists, my fingernails digging savagely into my palms. My blood felt like it was at a rolling boil. The sunny garden now seemed tinged with red. I aimed a vicious kick at an unsuspecting basil plant, refraining only at the last moment from punting it into oblivion.

I wanted nothing more than to take Philoxenus's slate and throw it back in his gluttonous face. But thanks to the pox-ridden Sicilian, the only other client I had for the foreseeable future was Xenarchus. And if I didn't unearth his precious Daphne, I highly doubted whether he'd let me off unscathed, let alone pay me. The hard truth was I needed Philoxenus's money. Meidias was not going to wait forever.

"No," I said after a very long moment. "No, I don't have a choice, and Philoxenus, the greedy bastard, knows it."

Irene nodded, then hesitated.

"Yes? What is it?"

"If you please, master, his slave said you and Hermogenes were to eat before you come. I guess he's not wanting to pay for your meal. He'll be making arrangements for you to stay the night—you know, on account of the Kindly Ones—but he never said anything about breakfast and if he was planning on feeding you."

"I see." My scowl deepened. Only the most miserly of clients insisted on such a thing. I railed inwardly at the thought of cooking for such a man.

"Very well!" I shook it off with difficulty. "I'm going to need some help. Send Strabo to the Agora. He's to go to Dromon for the pig and Krysippos for the eels."

I paused, remembering the last time I'd spoken to Krysippos.

"And tell him not to say who they're for," I added. "If Krysippos asks, he can tell them they're for Gorgias. Now what are you about? Are you busy with Gorgias? Can you give me a hand this afternoon?"

Irene gave me a startled look. I'd never asked for her help before. "Ansandra's with him now," she said. "If you need me, I can help."

I thanked her and she scurried off to start gathering my things. Only then did I turn my attention to Hermogenes.

My young slave hadn't so much as shifted from his previous position. His head still hung with shame and his bony shoulders were still hunched up in anticipation of a beating. I sighed and laid a gentle hand on his back. He jumped and quivered under my touch, but kept his eyes trained on the ground.

"Come, Hermogenes," I said softly. "We have work to do."

Dinner Parties for Dummies

A HOST SHOULD:

1. Go to the public toilets to socialize. It is from here you will issue your dinner invitations. Take a slave along to deliver them for you so that you may concentrate on displaying your aptitude for conversation, thereby dazzling your guests well before the big day.

2. Consider carefully the quality of your guests. Select only those who possess a certain knowledge of art and culture, or a talent for sophistry, or those whom you wish to impress or to whom you owe an invitation. Do not neglect to reciprocate a dinner invitation within a reasonable period of time. Should you disregard this obligation, you will soon find your evenings spent dining alone in sprat bars.

3. Hire the best cook you can afford. It has become common practice to demand that a cook and his slaves eat before they arrive so you do not have to bear the expense of feeding them. Although some find this behaviour acceptable, it is, in fact, niggardly and vulgar. By offering to feed the cook and his retinue, you will both appear magnanimous and secure his gratitude, thereby obtaining a vastly superior meal for your special symposion.

4. Visit the baths on the day of the banquet; a smelly host is a selfish host. Bring at least one slave to wash you and another to ensure delinquents do not pilfer your clothing.

5. Begin your party in the afternoon and see it through till it ends late at night. Do not yawn pointedly or feign illness in order to end the festivities early. The resulting savings in food and wine will not be worth the sharp decline in your reputation.

6. When your guests arrive, be sure to escort them through your atrium so they may best admire your fountains and grape vines.

Be modest in your response to their praise. While acknowledging their compliments, downcast eyes and a demure smile would not be out of order.

7. Have your slaves remove the guests' shoes, place flower garlands on their heads, and offer them drinks. Make sure the same level of attention and service is offered to all, even the poor friend, or "ghost," who might accompany one of your guests. Tyche, the goddess of fortune, can be capricious and many a ghost has gone on to rise to great heights. They will remember small kindnesses shown to them when their fortunes were less exalted.

8. Exercise caution in choosing a symposiarch. Many a dinner party has been cast into ruin by the appointment of an inexperienced or (worse!) reckless symposiarch. Remember, drink enhances desire at the cost of performance.

9. Provide entertainment for your guests in the form of: a) conversation (now is the ideal time to trot out your knowledge of obscure legends; if all else fails, an in-depth discussion of Homer is always stimulating and impressive); b) music and recitations (hire the best flute girls and poets you can afford); c) sexual gratification (see above regarding the flute girls. If possible, hire hetaeras and dancers as well. If this is beyond your budget, ensure your most attractive slaves are clean and on display).

10. Do not dominate the conversation. By all means, take the opportunity to display your knowledge of sculpture and poetry, but be wary of tiresome artistic pretensions.

11. Do not be ostentatious about your wealth by changing clothes numerous times during the course of dinner. Although it is possible you may become sweaty and thus leave yourself susceptible to chills, it is unlikely that this would happen several times throughout the evening. Limit yourself to one chiton change only.

12. Do not attempt to fool your guests regarding the quality of wine by affixing a fake seal.

13. Do not poison your guests.

Chapter 28

"Excuse me, Chef, what should I do with the collards?"

"Chop them up as fine as you can. Have you toasted the nuts yet?"

"No, Chef."

"You! What are you doing with that pot?"

"I were just moving it—"

"Imbecile! Idiot! When you're moving a pot of boiling water, you tell people if you're coming behind them! Do you want to risk burning someone?"

"No, guv—I mean, Chef. Sorry, Chef."

"Hermogenes! Make sure these idiots know how to behave in my kitchen."

"Yes, Chef."

"And you, whatever your name is, have you ground the spices for the shark steaks yet?"

"No, Chef."

"Well, why not? Great Zeus and Hera, people! We've got less than three hours left and only five dishes are ready! You've got to move faster than this, or I swear I'll chop the lot of you into stewing meat and serve you to your master for first tables."

"He'll do it, too," I heard Hermogenes say seriously to one of the kitchen slaves. "He's from Lydia, you know, it's in their blood. Haven't you heard the stories? One of their barmy old kings took the cleaver to one of his own slaves—*No, no, he likes the greens cut this way, they won't fry up right if you do them like that*—dinner guests didn't even know it, did they?—*Get that cheese away from the oven, it'll melt if you leave it there*—nobody knew till they were done eating. And then they all found out they'd eaten—" He dropped his voice. "—roast slave!"

It wasn't entirely accurate—I'd been son rather than slave, and I'd been fashioned into stew instead of a roast—but I smiled grimly as Philoxenus's kitchen slaves bent to their assigned tasks with a much renewed sense of purpose.

The feast preparations were not going well.

Half the dishes hadn't even been started yet and the other half were behind schedule. The oven had gone out before the barley rolls had finished baking, two of the cheap earthenware pots had cracks in them, and the greens had had worms and had to be replaced. All in all, there were too many dishes, not enough time to prepare them, and not nearly enough skilled slaves to create any kind of culinary magic. Philoxenus's kitchen slaves weren't totally useless, but they'd clearly never worked with a chef of my exacting standards. Oh, for a team of nimble-fingered and quick-thinking Hermogeneses! The knowledge that Mithaecus had a whole team of professional chef assistants did nothing to improve my mood.

Of Philoxenus himself, there had been no sign, though all afternoon a young house slave had been in and out of the kitchen, preparing bowl after bowl of boiling water for her master. I couldn't imagine why he would need so much hot water, unless he was attempting to bathe, but then why not simply heat a cauldron of water and pour it into a bathing tub? It made no sense, but I had little time to speculate on the matter.

I sautéed and seasoned and shouted out orders. I ran from courtyard to kitchen to storerooms and back again. I mixed ingredients and rolled out honey-sweetened pastry dough and crumbled soft goat cheese and lamented the inferior quality and rapidly dwindling quantity of my olive oil. I shouted some more. Sweat ran freely down my face.

It was after I'd sacrificed the suckling pig that my fortunes appeared to turn. I had finished wrapping the leg bones and a piece of fat inside the skin for the gods' portion, when change arrived in the form of a gift that was as surprising as it was welcome.

I was dressing out the pig when a strange slave arrived at the door asking for me. He was carrying a large and mysterious cloth-wrapped bundle when Philoxenus's steward escorted him into the courtyard. The man waited politely for me to finish my work.

I had already prepared the stuffing—a special filling made up of wine-soaked bread crumbs, garlic, onions, fresh sage leaves, and sea salt. The pig was almost ready to go over the flames. I gave the body cavity a last rinse, and directed Hermogenes to take the carcass into the kitchen for stuffing. Then I turned my attention to the waiting slave.

"Yes?" I said somewhat impatiently, as I rinsed the blood off my hands. "What can I do for you?"

"You are Pelops of Lydia?"

I nodded. "The very one."

"A gift for you," he said, extending the cloth bundle.

Mystified, I held my arms out to accept it, my eyebrows raised in inquiry. He passed it to me, and my eyebrows climbed further at the weight of it—and its bulbous shape.

"But what—?" I began.

"From Damokles of Thessaly," the slave explained. "There's a message too." He handed me a small slate the size of my hand.

Awkwardly, I shifted the heavy bundle to take it. It was a short, simple note, the letters neat and precise. It read:

> For Pelops,
> Thanking you in advance.

This was followed by the letter Delta, which had been embellished with a spoked wheel at its base (presumably to represent a chariot). What on earth could Damokles be sending me? I passed the slate to Hermogenes, who had returned from the kitchen, and as I did so, the bundle made a sloshing sound. My breath caught in my throat. Eagerly, I tore away the cloth wrapping. Could it be?

Yes! It was one of Damokles's Panathenaic amphorae.

Greedily, I ran my fingers over its fine lines, admiring its gorgeous design. It had been painted with a scene from the great festival's chariot race. Two black horses flew across the image as if winged, while a man in a chariot, his white chiton whipping behind him, controlled his steeds with tautly held reins. It was an exquisite piece of pottery.

But what it contained was even better.

Pure cold-pressed olive oil. Golden sunlight made liquid. First pressing. From the sacred grove of Athena at the Akademeia. Only the ripest olives were harvested. Only those perfectly formed and without blemish were selected to extract the oil which would fill the Panathenaic victory amphorae. There was no finer olive oil in all of Greece. And I had been gifted with an entire amphora of it.

Overwhelmed, I paused to clear my throat. "This is ... this is a magnificent gift." I cleared my throat again. "Please be so kind as to express my deepest gratitude to your master."

The slave grinned and bobbed his head. I found myself wanting to slip him a generous tip, to allow him to share in the sudden bounty he had brought me. But I didn't even have an obol with me, let alone a silver owl. Still, I had not yet met a slave who was not perpetually hungry.

"Tell me," I said, steering him toward the kitchen, "are you fond of pastries?"

At last the feast was ready. The appetizers were beautifully arranged, the suckling pig was roasted and ready to be carved, and the shark-belly steaks awaited only a final searing over the flames. The eels bubbled in wine sauce in the oven, and batter for the sesame pancakes stood ready beside the frying pans. The honey, which would be drizzled over them, was warming with a curl of rare cinnamon bark to give it a spicy, exotic flavour. I examined each dish carefully, lovingly. All had been exquisitely prepared, brought to sublime perfection by the addition of Damokles's victory olive oil. Surely, Philoxenus could not help but be impressed by it all.

My client swept into the courtyard shortly before his guests arrived. I was by the outdoor hearth, brushing the pig with a final coat of the melted duck fat that I'd infused with herbs and salt. Philoxenus waddled over to the hearth, his rolls of fat wobbling. An acrid wave of body odour arrived a moment later. I dropped my gaze to hide my surprise and held my breath. It was a poor host, indeed, who did not bathe for his guests.

"You will serve the food hot?" he asked, though it was more instruction than inquiry. His eyes flickered strangely, reflecting the orange flames from the hearth fire.

"The slaves will bring each dish out the instant I take it from oven or flame," I said, having expected the request all afternoon.

Philoxenus licked his lips, greedily eying the pig. He lifted his hand as if to wipe non-existent crumbs off his face and I noticed his plump fingers were curiously red, almost purple. He caught me looking at them and quickly dropped his hand, hiding it under a fold of his chiton.

"I will expect no less," he said haughtily. "And if I am not disappointed, there will be tips."

The fat miser! Even with tips, I would barely break even on this dinner. I nodded, not trusting myself to say anything.

He stood beside me for a long moment, inhaling the smell of roast pig so vigorously, he was practically ingesting it on the spot. It seemed like an opportune time to further my investigations into Neaera's death.

"I wonder if I might ask you a question," I began diffidently.

"Yes? What is it?" He turned his attention back to me, annoyed at the interruption.

"I'm curious about the other night. At Lysander's house."

All of sudden his expression became closed, his grey eyes wary. "A tragedy," he said curtly.

"Yes. Yes, it was. But ever since I found her, I've been wracking my mind trying to remember if anyone was behaving oddly that night."

"You found the hetaera?"

He seemed startled, which surprised me in turn. Hadn't all of Lysander's guests appeared in the storeroom once I'd made my grisly discovery? I thought back to that night. I'd found her body. Geta had come to the door and cried out. The slaves had all come running, followed by Lysander and his dinner guests. I searched my memories, but now that I thought of it, I could not recall seeing Philoxenus among the crowd.

"I, uh … I'm wondering if you noticed anything strange," I stammered, thrown off by the realization. "About your dinner mates. Maybe someone was behaving oddly, or maybe changed their clothes at some point in the evening."

"Clothes? Why would I pay attention to anyone's clothing?" he demanded irritably.

"I just thought you might have noticed if anyone had left—"

"And why do you care? Trying to collect half the reward if you find the killer?"

"Well, that had crossed my mind," I admitted. "But I'm far more interested in clearing my name. Mithaecus is saying—"

I broke off, realizing too late that this was the last thing I should say to a man who had taken full advantage of my misfortunes. The greedy Philoxenus would not want to see my reputation restored—and my prices along with it.

"I noticed nothing," he said shortly—and predictably— before turning on his heel.

He strode from the courtyard, moving much faster than a fat man ought, leaving me behind with the pig, cursing my own stupidity.

And then, the dinner guests arrived. Three of them—an unusually small number for a symposion. As I watched the men stroll through the courtyard, each more slender than the last, I thought that Philoxenus must have been hard-pressed to find such thin tablemates. In addition, two of the men had the poor colour and shadowed eyes indicative of some sort of intestinal complaint. Most of the food Philoxenus had requested was very rich. I doubted he intended to poison his guests, but he certainly had not taken their dietary needs into account when he'd made his requests.

There were no musicians present, and no flute girls or hetaeras had been invited. No gatecrashers showed up at the door, and no ghosts accompanied the dinner guests to share in the bounty. Philoxenus's slaves removed the guests' shoes, but the flower garlands they set on their heads were already wilting. Yesterday's blossoms, no doubt. I wondered if Philoxenus had used fake seals on the wine amphorae as well. I wouldn't have put it past him.

I waited until the men had settled themselves in the andron, then I called the servers to the kitchen and began sending in the food. It was Hermogenes who commented first.

"Zeus and Hera!" he exclaimed after returning from the andron. "He's a great greedy bugger, isn't he?"

I didn't normally use Hermogenes to serve food, but there were so many dishes and too few slaves, so I'd sent him in with the huge casserole of eels.

I raised my eyebrows in inquiry. "What do you mean?"

"He's snatching food right off the serving plates. Before we can even get them set down!" Hermogenes's tone was one of outrage. "He almost tipped the whole dish of mullet. And when I brought the eels in, he grabbed at them. With both hands! Slopped wine sauce all down the front of me, he was in such a sodding rush."

I looked at his chiton and saw he was telling the truth.

"But, that dish was straight from the oven," I protested.

"I know! Even with a cloth, I near burned me hands just carrying it in. How he could touch food that hot, let alone be stuffing it in his gob..." Hermogenes threw up his hands, incredulous. "He must be made of fire, that one."

"He always eats like that, don't he," a soft-spoken slave piped up behind me.

I turned to look at her. It was the same girl who had run in and out of the kitchen all afternoon preparing bowls of boiling water. She was a tiny thing, even more undergrown than Hermogenes, though I would not have thought that possible.

"Really?" I said.

She nodded solemnly. "Yeh, he'll beat us if th' food's gone cold." And then in a smaller voice, she added. "He don't hold nothing back neither, if he's in a mood." She twitched a fold of her chiton over her arm, but not before I saw the livid bruise on her flesh. Black mottled with purple and red. It must have taken a considerable amount of force to leave a mark like that. "He likes 'is food ter be right burnin'."

"I see," I said gravely. "Well, there'll be no beatings tonight. If he wants the food any hotter, he'll have to stand over the fire and eat it directly off spit."

"Oh, he's done that afore," she assured me.

I gave her a dubious look. "Really?"

"Yeh, we all thought he was going ter roast hisself, didn't we." She sounded disappointed that he hadn't.

I glanced around. The other house slaves were listening and nodding. For the first time that day, I examined them closely. They all, to a body, appeared to be underfed, and many bore visible signs of their master's ire.

"Well then," I said dryly. "I guess we'd best get the pig carved and into the andron or we'll have the other pig joining us here in the kitchen."

The adult slaves chuckled, and the small girl offered me a shy grin.

First tables had come to a successful end and I'd sent in fruits and cheeses and piping hot sesame pancakes for second tables. Only after this was I finally called into the andron for compliments. Philoxenus was a cheap bastard who had taken full advantage of my unfortunate situation, but I knew I had outdone myself with the feast tonight (inspired, no doubt, by the superior olive oil) and I hoped that he would see fit to reward me for it.

Philoxenus was reclining on his own dining couch, having left his guests to share one between them. I thought it inexcusably rude of him, but in truth, had he attempted to share, there would have been little room left for anyone else. My client barely fit his bulk on the couch as it was. He lay against the cushions, the great mound of his belly ballooning over the edge like bread dough left too long to rise.

"Ah, the chef!" he boomed heartily, not bothering to conceal the rumbling belch which accompanied the acknowledgment.

He smiled, his strange eyes almost disappearing in his bulging cheeks. The room was overly warm, and his face was puce from the heat. His smell had not improved. Sweat glistened in the creases of his flesh. It made me hot just to look at him. He had a self-satisfied, smug sort of look on his face. That made me hot too, though with anger rather than temperature, as I recalled once again how little he was paying me for tonight's culinary creations.

"A fine feast," he told me. "Quite excellent. I could not be sure if your cooking the other night was a fluke."

I bristled, but he bulled on.

"Ah yes, my friends. It happens. And more often than you

might think. The chef's offerings of one night are but peasant food the next. But not with Pelops of Lydia. Eh? You are, it seems, everything they say you are. Well done, Chef. Well done."

He clapped his hands together, his arm fat jiggling with the motion. His dinner guests nodded and clapped politely, though they had no words of praise for me. In fact, all three still had uneaten food on their plates and one of the men looked decidedly peaky. The rich food had clearly not agreed with him.

I managed a stiff smile, almost but not quite impressed with the way Philoxenus could compliment and give offence at the same time.

"And for you, my fine chef, a token of our deepest appreciation, eh?" With a flourish, Philoxenus held out his fist and pressed some coins into my hand. "A fine feast," he said again. "Very fine indeed."

I paused for a moment, but the dinner guests did not seem inclined to follow their host's example. Without looking in my palm, I permitted myself a small smile, before bowing my way from the room. But once I was in the courtyard, the smile dropped from my face. The coins had felt small in my hand. I'd hoped that I was just imagining it. But by the torchlight, I could see the sad bits of metal I held in my palm.

There were five of them. Obols. The lowest denomination of coin. One obol would get me a loaf of bread. Two would hire me the services of the oldest, lowest kind of prostitute. Five obols didn't even make one drachma! Five drachmas would have been an acceptable tip. Ten or twenty, even better. But five *obols*! I had never been so insulted in my life!

The uncultured boor! I wanted to take his base coins and fling them at his fat feet. I wanted to storm from the house, never to darken his kitchen again. But now that I was in the courtyard, I could hear the distant shrieks of the Erinyes, and I knew they were flying over Athens once more.

I closed my fist on the obols and took several deep breaths. I couldn't leave the house, not until morning. Not until the Kindly Ones had finished their nightly rampage. And I couldn't even throw Philoxenus's money back at him, no matter how insulting the tip. With Meidias on my back, I needed every obol I could get.

"Chef?" Hermogenes said tentatively. "Are you out here, then?"

I took another breath through my nostrils and let it out slowly. "I am," I replied. "What is it?"

"I've seen to our room," he said quietly, knowing there was something wrong, but not wanting to ask what it was. "It's ... well, it's not much, but I've made it as comfortable as possible."

"Thank you. I'll be in shortly."

He bobbed his head and went back to the kitchen.

I stood silently for a while, listening to the sounds of the night. From the andron I could hear voices rising and falling in conversation. From the kitchen, there was clattering and splashing and murmured orders as the house slaves began the task of cleaning up after the meal. The Erinyes had moved farther away, screaming their terrible cries on the other side of the city. For the moment all was quiet around me.

I felt more despondent than angry now, utterly depressed at

the way things were turning out for me here in Athens. I couldn't seem to get a break—even with all the alleged help from divine sources. The truth was, if I didn't discover Neaera's killer—and soon—I was going to find myself shipped off to Sparta or Corinth, or worse, back home to Lydia.

I shuddered at the very thought of it. To go back to my boyhood home? To the place where my father had sacrificed me to his ego? No. I would just have to double my efforts. Find Neaera's killer and try to recover my reputation.

I would *not* go back to Lydia!

With these thoughts dogging my steps, I went back into the house to find Hermogenes and see what kind of accommodation Philoxenus had offered us for the night.

The room was miniscule and had, at some time in the recent past, housed a goat. I could still smell its distinctive musky odour, though Hermogenes had done his best to sweep the place out. He'd fashioned us a couple of pallets on the floor and had even laid down some fragrant rushes to try to cover up the smell. A small oil lamp provided weak light.

"Best I could do, Chef," he said, spreading his arms in apology.

All of a sudden, I was weary to the bone. "It's fine," I sighed. "And it's far better than skulking through the streets hoping the Kindly Ones don't find us before we can get home."

We lay down and settled ourselves for sleep. Hermogenes blew out the lamp.

"I heard Anacreon hired Castor for his symposion," Hermogenes said into the darkness. "That makes two, with Iphicrates."

I was silent for a while. "Good for Castor," I said finally.

"Not so good for Anacreon or Iphicrates, yeah? Castor can't cook like you."

"No," I agreed. "I think his clients will be disappointed. Maybe they really will get sick."

"Serve 'em right, the sodding buggers."

"Castor's a nice enough fellow."

"But his tuna steaks! There's a bad business. I mean, he puts honey on them. Honey!" Hermogenes made retching noises. "That's ill-conceived, that is. "

I smiled a little. Since he'd come under my wing, Hermogenes had become a bit of a food snob.

"Well, let's hope that Anacreon and Iphicrates regret their decision. I suppose it's too much to hope that word of tonight's excellent feast will get out. I don't think the guests finished more than a plate of food between them."

"No," Hermogenes agreed. "Not with himself troughing his way through dinner. That's enough to put anybody off their feed. What a wanker, yeah? Snatching food off the plates like that? I've never seen the like."

"Nor I."

"And, Chef, you just watch. He won't be telling anyone about your cooking either. I saw the way he was looking at you. Like you were a fish steak or something. Greedy bastard. He'll want to keep you all to himself."

A grim thought.

"You know, Corinna says she's seen him put his hand right in the fire and not feel a thing."

"Corinna?"

"That house slave. The little one."

"The one he hits when the food isn't hot enough for him?"

"Yeah."

"I can't believe he beats his slaves over something so inconsequential," I said, frowning to myself. "Did you see the marks on her arm? I'm surprised she was able to carry anything. What kind of man treats his slaves like that?"

The kind of man who commits murder? I didn't say the words out loud, but I was beginning to wonder about Philoxenus. He was a greedy drachma pincher, and it was clear he could be violent when crossed. And where had he been when all the guests were milling about the storeroom that night?

"That's nothing," Hermogenes said blithely. "You should've seen Ante."

"Which one was Ante?"

"Oh, she's not one of Philoxenus's slaves, she belongs to Lysander."

"Lysander!" I opened my eyes in the darkness. Without lamplight, I couldn't even distinguish shadows, let alone shapes. "Lysander beats his slaves?"

"Not him exactly, but he lets his friends have at them, doesn't he?"

"Really? I thought that was considered poor behaviour here."

"I guess." I could hear him shift around on his pallet. "But I met up with Ante yesterday at the Agora when I went to see the wrestling match…" He broke off, remembering belatedly how much trouble he'd gotten into for doing so. "Anyhow," he rushed on, "she was all over in bruises, wasn't she? From the night we were there. Not from Lysander, but from one of his mates. That rich bugger."

"The rich one—the banker? Isaeus?"

"That's him," Hermogenes agreed. "Ante said he wouldn't have a flute girl. Wasn't interested. But he wanted a slave, so she got assigned to him."

"What happened?"

"He took her in one of the storerooms, didn't he? Bastard beat her till she was black and blue. Never even had a poke at her. Guess he just wanted to hit somebody."

"Great Zeus!"

"Some men are like that." I could hear the shrug in his voice. "They like to take out their frustrations on a slave."

"What did Lysander do?" I asked.

"Nothing. It's his banker, isn't it? And I guess he had more to things to worry about, what with Neaera being killed and all."

"But still, to beat another man's slave. And so badly!"

"She's just a slave, Chef."

Just a slave. The words resonated. He said it as if that explained everything. And perhaps it did.

In Athens, slaves are servants, scribes, bakers, porters, factory and farm workers, miners, even cooks (though a slave would never be trusted to prepare a formal feast). Slaves are everywhere, but they have few rights. They cannot marry, they cannot enter the public assembly, or the gymnasium. Even the word for slave means "man-shaped thing." And although a slave cannot be put to death by his owner, there is nothing preventing that owner from beating the slave to within a hair's breadth of Charon's ferryboat.

Few, of course, go so far. Slaves can be expensive and most are exceedingly useful. And, of course, there is public opinion to consider, which, though condoning a certain amount of corporal punishment, nevertheless frowns on crude brutality. That Isacus would treat a slave—and another man's slave, at that—so cruelly said much of his character. And he had taken this slave into a storeroom to mete out his punishment. Neaera had perished in one of Lysander's storerooms. Was there a connection?

And what about Philoxenus? Damokles said he'd ignored Neaera all evening, even going so far as to refuse a free round of Lion on the Cheese Grater. How strange was that? And he beat his slaves beyond what was socially acceptable. I was a chef—a famous one—but even I wouldn't beat a slave so ruthlessly just because the food had cooled. And why hadn't he come running with the rest of the guests when Neaera's body had been discovered?

Philoxenus and Isaeus. Both violent men. Both at Lysander's house the night Neaera had been killed. I couldn't imagine what motive either might have had for killing a hetaera, but perhaps men of this sort did not require a motive. Just a stimulus.

With such thoughts in my head, sleep eluded me. The pallet was uncomfortable, the room smelled of goat, and Hermogenes was snoring like a drunken ox. I plumped up my cushion and rolled over yet again.

Eventually, of course, Morpheus did find me. And just before I fell off the edge of sleep and into unconsciousness, surprisingly, the single thought in my head was one of regret that I had struck Hermogenes.

Chapter 29

I had the opportunity to question another of Lysander's dinner guests the following morning. And I met with just as much success as I'd achieved with Philoxenus—though for very, very different reasons.

Hermogenes and I had quit Philoxenus's house well before dawn had finished spreading her golden robe over the sky. The rank smell of goat and the growl of Hermogenes's snores had kept me awake for the first half of the night, with troubling thoughts and simmering anger at Philoxenus's parsimony bringing wakefulness to the other half. I was ready to go home.

Hermogenes grumbled about leaving before breakfast, but I ignored his complaints and handed him a heavily laden basket of utensils and supplies. I would carry the precious amphora of olive oil myself.

"Come," I said, settling the amphora firmly against my chest and holding it with both hands. "We'll pick up some barley rolls on our way through the Agora."

"Just barley rolls?" he asked, a plaintive note creeping into his tone. He'd sucked in his cheeks, trying to appear thinner and even more waif-like than he already was. "I could murder some figs, me."

"We'll see," I told him with mock severity. "I'm not made of money, you know."

Shouldering the heavy basket manfully, he allowed a small groan of effort to escape. My lips twitched, and Hermogenes gave me a cheerful lopsided grin. He knew I was a soft touch when it came to food.

Philoxenus's house stood in an inferior neighbourhood in the southwest quadrant of the city, so Hermogenes and I needed to cross the length of the Agora in order to get home. We slogged down several narrow, dingy streets and squished our way through one particularly unsavoury alley before we finally hooked up with the wide, gravelled expanse of the Panathenaic Way. We entered the market by the Mint.

The Great Panathenaea's athletic competitions were over. All that remained were the equestrian events and those would take place outside the city walls. In the Agora, the spectator stands had not yet been dismantled, but many of the small market stalls would be open soon, their owners trying to take full advantage of the daytime shoppers, now that the Erinyes had rendered any night trade impossible. Because of the Panathenaea, everything was in a jumble with leftover stands and festival debris, and shops not set up in their accustomed locations. I gave

Hermogenes a handful of obols and sent him off in search of rolls and fruit for our breakfast, bidding him catch up with me once he'd made the purchases.

I, myself, wanted nothing more than to get my olive oil home safely. I wouldn't breathe easy until I had done so. But as Hermogenes scampered off, I happened to glance over to my left, and there by the Spring House, I spotted another of Lysander's guests. It was the grey ghost, Peneus.

There was nobody else at the Spring House yet. It was too early for most people to be up and about. Peneus stood, almost hidden, in the early-morning shadows of the bay laurel tree he seemed to favour. He still sported his dreary grey chiton. He wasn't reading or eating or even washing out his grubby clothing. In fact, he didn't appear to be doing much of anything at all. He was merely standing, one hand on the tree. Still and quiet, his gaze turned inward.

I settled the amphora of oil more securely in my arms and began to make my way over to him.

His head turned in my direction, as if he had somehow divined my intention, and he watched without speaking as I made my way to his side. His grey eyes were curiously devoid of expression.

"Good morning, sir," I greeted him politely. Given his obvious poverty, I doubted he was deserving of the appellation, but it never hurt to overestimate a citizen's social standing.

He waited several heartbeats, then inclined his head in response. A man of few words, it seemed.

"I am Pelops of Lydia," I began. "A chef."

"I know who you are," he said with another inclination of his head.

I had never heard him speak before. His voice was arresting, deep and rich, yet oddly musical with a dark rippling undertone. I wondered if he was a singer, then discarded the thought. Culture-conscious Athens would never let a talented singer fall into such a state of want.

"Can I help you?" he asked, interrupting my thoughts. His grey eyes regarded me with distant disinterest.

"I hope so," I said, putting on what I hoped was a sincere smile. "You're Peneus, aren't you?"

His eyes grew wary and he nodded without speaking.

"You see, Peneus, I've got a bit of a problem. With another chef."

He waited, not even raising an eyebrow in inquiry. He certainly wasn't making this easy for me.

"Mithaecus—The Sicilian—is blaming the Kindly Ones' nightly visitations on … well, on me. Because of a dish I prepared. You've probably even heard him whinging about it yourself. He's been in the Agora denouncing me for days now. He says the dish is sacrilegious. But, you must see, the Kindly Ones don't care about a bit of roast lamb. They're here because Neaera was murdered."

The man jumped at her name. His eyes were no longer distant.

"You were there that night," I continued. "Did you happen to see—"

"I saw nothing!" Peneus shouted, his face darkening.

I blinked, taken aback by his response.

"I'm not accusing you of anything," I added quickly.

"What gives you the right to ask such questions? Who are you?"

"I told you, I'm Pelops of Lydia, and—"

"Leave me alone!"

"But I just … I need to know if you saw anything strange. I'm trying to find out who killed—"

"I told you to leave me alone!" he hissed fiercely, his voice no longer musical. "I saw nothing! Nothing!"

I was bewildered by his intensity.

"But—"

"I tell you, I saw nothing of the filthy whore!" he cried with a furious glare.

And then, the edges of his shape began to blur.

At first, I thought my eyes were playing tricks on me. Lack of sleep and the early-morning light combining to fog my vision. I blinked hard, but the problem was not with my sight.

As I watched incredulously, Peneus's features began to soften and droop, pulled down as if by some strange force. His hair began lengthening, growing at an unnatural rate until it reached the ground, where it pooled around his rapidly widening feet. And his face! It was growing paler by the moment. Bleaching, fading, until his skin was the same drab grey of his chiton and I couldn't tell where one began and the other left off.

In less than two heartbeats, the man's form had lost all cohesion. And with a long, hissing snarl, he dissolved.

Just *dissolved*.

I gaped in disbelief.

Completely amorphous now, more liquid than solid, he

swirled around my feet, faster and faster. I leapt back as if scalded, though his waters had not touched me. I did not want to know what would happen if they did. He surged towards me again, and again I retreated. Seething and foaming, he began to spin, forming a dizzying whirlpool. A boiling vortex of fury. I backed away until I bumped up against the laurel tree, unable to take my eyes off him, even to flee. Then, the waters seemed to shiver, suddenly coalescing into a bubbling, churning mass. It began to grow. Spiralling higher and higher. Stretching, elongating, until it towered over me. Taller, even, than the columns of the Spring House.

Great Zeus and Hera! I mouthed the words.

In the blink of an eye, it snapped down towards me. I recoiled, smacking my head against the tree trunk. The water began whipping back and forth and around itself, an angry, writhing tentacle. It lunged towards me again. I cried out, flattening myself against the tree, aware that its protection was dubious at best. The tentacle seemed to hesitate.

One heartbeat. Then another. And another.

It hovered less than an arm's length from me, its water rippling in the early morning sunlight. Wide-eyed, I stared at it, not daring to move. And then, with a suddenness that snatched the breath from my chest, the creature known as Peneus turned and plunged to the ground.

I darted behind the tree as the waters splashed out in a fan. But the creature was no longer attacking. Churning and seething, it gathered up all the droplets of itself. And with a last furious growl, the angry amorphous mass swirled down the water pipe beside the laurel tree and disappeared.

The Athenian Bureau of Scythian Archers (ABSA)

THIS WEEK'S **WAR ON CRIME** MOST WANTED LIST ...

ARGOS PANOPTES

WANTED FOR: Public indecency, voyeurism.

DESCRIPTION: Unusually tall and extremely strong. Body is covered with one hundred eyes (colour: brown), at least one of which is always open and alert. May be bearded.

SCARS AND MARKS: Unknown.

ALIASES AND NICKNAMES: "Lashes" Panoptes.

NOTE: Often seen loitering outside public bath houses. Difficult to catch unaware. Multi-archer **ABSA** team may be required.

MEDUSA GORGONES

WANTED FOR: Defacing public property, erecting unauthorized statuary.

DESCRIPTION: Youngest of the infamous Gorgones Sisters. Winged, with a broad head, snakes for hair, and swine-like tusks. Eye colour: unknown. Hair colour: green.

SCARS AND MARKS: Multiple double puncture wounds on face, neck, and shoulders.

ALIASES AND NICKNAMES: Pig Tooth, Scales, The Rock.

NOTE: Use extreme caution. Special issue **ABSA** HazMat armour is not effective. Do not look directly at this creature's gaze.

** UPDATE**

Attention all **ABSA** employees

There have been several unsubstantiated sightings of a giant, moving water "tentacle" in the Agora. It is unclear whether a new threat has arrived in the city, or if these sightings are a product of mass hysteria and/or Panathenaic overindulgences.

Updates will be posted as new information is discovered. Be on the alert. Should you witness such a phenomenon, proceed with caution.

(artist's rendering)

Chapter 30

I was out of my depth.

Demanding clients, I could handle. Sullen slaves, I could manage. I could cope with rival chefs and dishonest oil sellers and jealous flute girls and ovens that went out before the barley loaves had finished baking. Men who turned into giant water tentacles when they got angry were an entirely different story. For that I was going to need some divine aid.

I collected Hermogenes and, ignoring his repeated queries as to the whiteness of my complexion, I hustled him back to the Kerameikos. Somehow, throughout the encounter with Peneus, I had managed to hang on to my precious amphora of olive oil. As soon as we got home, I set it gingerly in a protected corner of the kitchen and instructed Hermogenes to guard it with his life. Then I crammed a barley roll in my mouth, grabbed up a handful of figs, and went to see Dionysus.

On the surface, it was an odd decision. Frankly, he hadn't been much help the last time I'd approached him, but I was hoping for more from him this time around. I rather doubted that Peneus was associated with Hera, and if this proved to be the case, then the god of wine should be free to help me out—or at the very least explain a few things to me. Like who exactly was Peneus, how in Hades was he able to turn himself into a water tentacle, and was he, in any way, shape, or form, collaborating with my old nemesis, Poseidon?

While I was at it, I had questions about Philoxenus, too. There was something distinctly off about that man—apart from his greed and his cruelty. Something I couldn't quite put my finger on. He made me uneasy. And his tolerance for heat and flame bordered on the unnatural. If Peneus could dissolve into water, what could Philoxenus do? Just how many non-humans was I dealing with here?

Clearly, I needed help of the non-human variety. And if Dionysus started hemming and hawing and shuffling his divine feet, then I would rub my ivory shoulder absently and allow a small sigh to escape my lips. The god of wine wasn't clueless. He would get the hint.

But, as it turned out, theatrics were unnecessary—at least for now. When I arrived at his wine stall, it was not Dionysus who stood behind the counter.

"Hey, baby!" the man hooted at a passing slave girl. "Nice tits! More than a mouthful's a waste, eh? How's about you and me have a little go 'round the Agora, eh? Eh?"

His long hair had slipped from its thong and was frizzing

out in a wild starburst around his face. His flattened nose was shiny with sweat, his dark eyes were wild, and through his mass of hair, I could see that the tips of his sharply pointed ears were flushed crimson with drink. An astonishing number of empty amphorae littered the ground beside the shop.

A satyr was manning the wine stall.

"Hey, where ya going, baby?" he called to the woman, aggrieved. "Lookie what you're missing!"

In a single bound, he leapt onto the counter, displaying a supremely impressive erection under his chiton. With a lascivious grin splitting his face, he shook his phallus back and forth, his hips gyrating obscenely. The grubby chiton covered his horse tail, the very tip of which I could see dangling down behind him.

"Eh? Eh? Look at this! I can even balance a wine cup on this puppy!" he cackled gleefully, suiting action to words. "Bet your boyfriend can't do that! Eh?"

The object of his desire, a young dewy-faced slave girl, blushed pink and hurried away, her basket held in front of her like a shield.

"Maybe next time, eh, darling?" he shouted after her. Laughing, he retrieved his wine cup and drained it dry. Smacking his lips lustily, he wiped his mouth with a prodigiously hairy arm and looked around, his eyes alive and sparkling.

"Anyone else?" he demanded with another significant shake of his anatomy. "What? No takers? Your loss!" He hopped off the countertop and sloshed more wine in his cup.

Nobody appeared to notice that he was not human, but then,

everyone seemed to be going out of their way to avoid eye contact with him. Cautiously, I stepped up to the stall.

"You want a go, mate?" The satyr wiggled his eyebrows at me. "You're a bit flat up top for my taste, but hey, I'm not averse to a little walk on the wild side if—"

"No," I said firmly. "No, I don't want a 'go.' I'm looking for Dionysus. Do you know where he is?"

The satyr shook his head. "Got me. I'm just watching the shop."

"Well, do you—"

"How about you?" he called out to a plain-faced older woman. "I can carry my pipe-case with this momma! Wanna see? Maybe you can blow my pipe for me, eh?"

"Do you know when he'll return?" I interrupted.

"Hooooo, look at the booty on that one!" He whistled, his attention distracted by a passing flute girl. He leapt up onto the counter again. "Hey baby! Wanna play Archimedes screw? Eh? Lookie here, I've got *aaall* the equipment."

Unimpressed, the flute girl rolled her eyes disdainfully and passed by without replying.

"She'll be back," the satyr assured me with boundless confidence. "You'll see."

"Do you know when he'll return?" I repeated.

The satyr looked down at me blankly. "Who?"

It was only with great effort that I managed to hold on to my temper. What had possessed Dionysus to get a satyr to work his stall?

"Dionysus," I said again. "Your boss, presumably. Do you know when he'll be back? I need to speak to him."

The satyr shrugged. "He never said."

"Well, tell him Pelops needs to see him. It's urgent."

"Yeah, sure. No problem. Hey baby! Fancy a bonk? A little snog? A bit of how's your father, eh?" And he was off again. This time it was aimed at a bread-wife, one of the wizened old crones who sat in the Agora selling barley rolls and giving away insults.

"How's me father?" She chortled, her raisined face crinkling up in amusement. "Me father's stiffer than that limp sprat you call a pecker, seeing as he's been dead these forty years."

"Who're you calling limp?" The satyr was bouncing from one foot to another. "Lookie here, baby!" He yanked his chiton up to his chin. "Stiff as a temple column, that is! I could balance your bony ass on this sucker!"

"Ha! I've seen bigger cocks on a goat."

"And you've tried 'em to know 'em, eh?"

The bread-wife and the satyr traded insults, each cruder than the last. I waited, hoping to have another word with him, to get some assurance that he would pass on my message, but they were enjoying themselves far too much to stop anytime soon.

Finally, I gave up and left. I had no faith in the satyr's ability to carry out my request. All it would take was a nice bosom to jiggle by and the lascivious satyr would forget all about my message to Dionysus.

It looked like I was going to have to deal with the Water Tentacle myself.

"An obol for your thoughts." A familiar voice hailed me just before I quit the Agora.

"I'd never cheat a friend so badly," I said, turning to join her. "Believe me, my thoughts aren't worth that much."

She was dressed for the market in a sky-blue chiton, her shoulders and head covered with a darker blue himation. She carried a large basket laden with produce, and the feathery fronds of carrot tops tickled my arm as I ventured a quick peck on her soft cheek. Zeuxo's lopsided smile brightened the day, more than making up for any rival chefs, miserly clients, and dissolving men.

"How are you?" I inquired, smiling back at her. "It feels like I haven't seen you in ages."

It was true. I'd been so preoccupied with my own problems that I hadn't sought her out—hadn't even realized until now that I had not seen her. Totally unforgivable on my part.

I searched her face. It was clean and fresh, younger-looking without the flute girl makeup, but there were shadows in her eyes and, when her welcoming smile faded, there was a small, sad droop to her generous mouth.

She dropped her gaze and shrugged. "The same," she said quietly.

"Contracts?"

She shook her head. "Not a one."

I opened my mouth to apologize, but she cut me off before I could say anything.

"And don't be falling all over yourself apologizing either!" she ordered, shadows fading in the face of her irritation. "It's not your fault, is it? There's nothing to be done about it, and ... well, just think of all the sleep I'm catching up on now." She offered me a wry grin, but her flashing eyes forbade me to say another word about it.

I hesitated, then smiled back uncertainly. "All right," I said.

"Good. Now if you really want to help out, you can carry this sodding basket home for me." She passed it over with a groan of relief.

My eyebrows shot up when I realized how heavy it was. "What in Hades have you got in here?" I asked, trying to peer past the carrot tops.

"Soup."

"Soup?"

"Well, the things to make it. I've been all over the Agora already. There's a nice ox bone, dried peas, some herbs, and the veg."

"How did you find the market today?" I asked carefully, thinking about my own experiences in it.

"Find?"

"Did you notice anything strange?"

Zeuxo shot me an odd look. "Like what?"

"Nothing." I shook my head. "Never mind. So, you're making soup, are you?"

"For Gorgias." She nodded. "To help him get better. My mum used to make oxtail soup. She always said it would cure what-ever ails you."

"Ah," I said, suppressing a twinge of jealousy. Zeuxo had never made soup for me. "Well, it sounds lovely. I'm sure that will set him up nicely."

"How's he doing, then?" she asked. "Last I saw, his shoulder still looked like raw meat." She shuddered delicately. "It's not gone and turned bad now, has it?"

"I don't think so."

As we strolled back to Zeuxo's house, we spoke only of Gorgias and his injuries. She seemed so genuinely concerned about him that I began to wonder if he was suffering more than I had realized. With everything that had happened in the last few days, I hadn't paid much attention to him either. I certainly hadn't made him soup—probably because anything I tried to do with water generally turned into a disaster. But still, I could have made him *something* special. I was, it appeared, a poor excuse for a friend. I resolved to rectify the situation as soon as I got home.

I carried Zeuxo's heavy basket right into the tiny courtyard of the house she shared with several other flute girls. Clouds of pink and purple flowers enlivened the space. Zeuxo's doing. None of her housemates had any interest in gardening. There were even some herbs sprouting up among the blossoms. A girl after my own heart.

Nobody else was home that morning. The other flute girls, untainted by the stain of my friendship, were all still out on contracts or over at the public baths preparing for tonight's round of clients.

"How are you set for money?" I asked, setting the basket down on a small table.

Zeuxo had removed her himation. She draped it over a wall hook, then lifted one shoulder in a careless shrug. "I'll get by," she said, smoothing back her hair. But she did not meet my gaze.

"Let me help."

She turned and looked at me. The shadows were back in her eyes. "With what? Your slate's just as empty as mine."

"Not true," I contradicted her. "I had a contract last night."

Her brow furrowed and she shook her head. "One contract, Pel! It doesn't mean—"

"And another for tomorrow," I lied glibly.

Her frown began to fade as she looked at me, hope warring with concern.

"I've got the coin," I urged. "Truly. Let me help you."

She hesitated for a moment longer, then her expression cleared and she gave me a wide smile that almost stopped my heart. "Pel, that would … that would be brilliant!" she breathed. Her shoulders seemed to drop as the tension left her body. "It's the rent. Aphrodisia's on at me, and I just haven't got it."

"Well, now you have," I told her firmly. "How much do you owe?"

She named a figure.

"I'll bring it by tomorrow."

"Pel, I don't know what to say. You're a sweetheart. Thank you!"

Zeuxo put her soft hand on my arm, reached up and gave me a gentle kiss on the cheek. I felt my face flush, while other parts of my body started to quiver.

She stepped back and grinned up at me, relief written plainly on her face. "Now, be off with you," she said with mock severity. "I'll never get this soup made with you loitering about."

"I could help."

"Oh, no." She shook her head, smiling warmly to take the sting out of her words. "I'll not have a celebrity chef hovering over my shoulder while I'm trying to cook. I'd bugger up the works for sure, and even if it didn't taste like total shite, I'd probably end up poisoning poor Gorgias, and then where would we be?"

I laughed.

"I'll see you this afternoon, though," she said as she walked me to the front door. "I'll bring the soup 'round as soon as it's done."

"Do you need help carrying it?" I asked. "I could always come back."

"I'll be fine," she assured me. "Thank you, Pel. For everything."

And with that, I had to be content.

I had a lot to think about as I retraced my steps home. My problems had not disappeared. I still didn't have any contracts. I still hadn't figured out how to deal with a man who could turn himself into a water tentacle. I was still being slandered, cheated, cancelled on, and harassed. And now I needed to find enough money to help Zeuxo pay her rent. But despite all this, there was a spring in my step that hadn't been there earlier this morning, and my heart was lighter just knowing that I'd see her again that afternoon.

I heard the commotion while I was still picking my way through the side streets. By the time I reached the Herm, which marked the crossroads to the Panathenaic Way, the noise had resolved into the cheers of a crowd of small boys and slaves. They lined the main street, waiting breathlessly for the chariot racers to pass.

It was the first day of the Great Panathenaea's much-antici-
pated equestrian events. All adult spectators had left the city at
first light in order to secure a place in the hippodrome, which
explained why the Panathenaic Way was lined mostly with small
boys. As I took my place among them, the first of the charioteers
swept past in a flurry of trotting hooves and snapping reins. The
boys went wild.

I counted fourteen chariots in all, each pulled by a team
of four horses. The chariots were simple affairs from a design
standpoint, being essentially small wooden carts with two
wheels and an open back. But they were highly embellished
with brightly painted scrollwork and bits of beaten copper and
silver to give them some shine. The horses needed no such
adornment. They were superb examples of their kind. Perfectly
proportioned, coats gleaming in the morning sun, they pranced
along, snorting and nickering, tossing their manes in anticipation of the race to come.

Hermogenes would be sorry, indeed, that he'd missed this.

The final chariot in the procession was driven by none other
than my friend Damokles. A wealthy-looking citizen, probably
the owner, marched on his right. On his left, a gaggle of wide-
eyed youths (all sporting green hair ribbons) crowded together,
jostling one another in their excitement. Surrounded by these
sundry admirers, Damokles held his horses to a regal walk. The
four enormous black stallions had been decked out in silver-
studded tackle, perfectly matching the black and silver chariot
they pulled.

Damokles stood tall, chin raised proudly in the air, turning his head first one way, then the other, so all could gaze upon his countenance. I never would have hailed him at such a juncture, but he turned his eyes toward me, and instantly he was reining in his team and beckoning me over.

"How do you like my ride?" he asked, giving his chariot a proud pat.

"Nice," I replied. "Very nice."

"Come on up."

"On the chariot?" I was startled.

"Yes, on the chariot! I need to talk to you and I can't stop here." Holding the reins with one hand, he reached down with the other and hauled me up beside him. The green-ribboned youths glared at me with envious eyes. The owner frowned. Damokles ignored them all. Snapping the reins sharply, he got his horses moving again. The chariot lurched forward and I grabbed on to the side of it, fighting to keep my balance. Chariots were not popular in Lydia. I had never ridden on one before.

Damokles was wearing the traditional charioteer's garment, a blindingly white, sleeved sort of tunic, which fell to his ankles and was secured high at the waist with a green belt, which (not coincidentally) matched his hair ribbon perfectly. Two straps crisscrossed in the back to prevent the cloth from ballooning out during the race.

"I must thank you for the magnificent gift," I said a little breathlessly. "The olive oil is exquisite!"

"It was nothing." He waved it off, though I could tell that my appreciation pleased him. "So tell me, what have you found out?"

I pulled my mouth to one side, considering what and how much I should tell him.

"Damo-kles! Damo-kles!" A cluster of young boys were chanting his name.

Damokles turned to bestow a gracious smile on them.

"Keep in mind, I've only started," I began carefully. "But it does seem that your friend was not universally liked."

He bristled at this.

"No reflection on her own fine qualities, I'm sure, " I hastened to add. "But several of the dinner guests that night were less than impressed by her credentials, and I know for a fact that one of the other hetaeras had been calling for her retirement."

"Retirement? Good gods! Why?"

I shrugged (a difficult thing to do when one is riding in a chariot). "Apparently, she thought it wasn't fair to the rest of the girls on account of Neaera being a nymph or naiad, or some such thing. Not human, at any rate, if you can believe that."

"But, I thought you knew." Damokles left off waving at his admirers to turn his attention to me. "Neaera's father *wasn't* human."

"What?" I exclaimed. "What was he then?"

"A nature god of some kind or another. I never met him."

"Oh." I digested that for a moment. "So Neaera and her sister were…"

"Not quite human," Damokles finished my thought. "But, you'd never know it to look at them."

We rode in silence for a few heartbeats. Damokles continued to smile and wave at the boys.

"It seems Harmodia had it right then," I mused aloud.

"Harmodia?" Damokles made a face. "Harmodia's the one who was bitching about Neaera? That figures. She's been jealous of Neaera for ever. Retirement! What a load of horseshit!" He paused before adding thoughtfully, "Harmodia couldn't have drowned her though, she's just a little tiny thing."

"I know," I agreed. "But I thought she might have enlisted someone a bit more robust to do the job. Perhaps a favourite client."

"Horseshit!" Damokles scoffed. "What man in his right mind would get mixed up in a cat fight?"

I conceded the point.

"Hurry," Damokles said, clamping a strong hand on my shoulder. "Tell me what else you found out. We're almost at the gate, and I can't run a race with you clinging to the side of my ride."

I shuddered at the thought.

"I want to know about these men who were 'less than impressed by her.'"

"You already know about Philoxenus." I ticked him off. "But you may not know that he was the only one in the house who didn't come running when I discovered Neaera's body. I, for one, would like to know why. And the banker—Isaeus—is a violent, unpleasant sort of man. I don't know yet what he thought of Neaera, or if he knew she was making fun of his poems, but he was in the storerooms that night."

"Really," Damokles rumbled with an ominous growl. "What was he doing there?"

"Beating one of Lysander's slave girls black and blue, from what I understand," I said. "Did he stop with that? I don't know."

The chariot racer's expression darkened.

"Now, don't do anything rash," I warned, after a quick glance at his face. "I'm just guessing. He may have had nothing to do with Neaera's death. I will try to find out more about him."

Damokles's fists had clenched on the reins, the knuckles whitening. In his face, I could see the desire for vengeance struggling with the need for caution. The horses threw up their heads in protest, rolling their eyes backwards as if to see what had gotten into their driver.

"Damokles!" I said sharply.

He flattened his lips grimly, but I saw his grip on the reins loosen. The horses shook their heads and settled down.

"Who else?" He rasped after a moment.

"Peneus," I said promptly.

Damokles scowled. "Who in Hades is Peneus?"

"The ghost."

"Oh. Right. The man with that awful grey chiton."

"The very one," I agreed. "I tried to question him early this morning, but he behaved ... strangely when I broached the subject."

It was a bit of an understatement.

"What did he say about her?"

"Nothing complimentary," I replied. "He called her a filthy whore."

His eyes flashed dangerously. "Really. And what exactly did this ghost think—"

"Damokles!" All of a sudden, the chariot owner was beside us. He did not look happy. "Come!" he ordered imperiously, awarding me a cold glare at the same time. "We must hurry. It's past time. You're going to be late!"

Damokles's face twisted in frustration, but he gave a quick nod to the man before turning back to me.

"End of the line," he said.

"I know," I nodded. "We'll talk again soon. Good luck with the race today."

His face was suddenly full of determination. "I'll win it for her," he told me. "Gods willing."

He didn't bother stopping the horses. With one hand, he grabbed hold of my upper arm and swung me expertly down from the chariot. "Keep me informed," he called back to me. "*And keep looking!*"

And with that he turned to face the waiting crowds. He urged his horses to a brisk trot, kicking up clouds of dust in his wake. As he rounded a curve in the road, I could see the ends of his green victory hair ribbon fluttering behind him like a war banner.

Chapter 31

I heard the rumble of male voices as soon as I came through the front door. My first thought was that a couple of Gorgias's potter friends had come to keep him company while he recovered, and I was struck anew with guilt over my recent neglect of him. But when I went to greet them, I discovered his guests were a little more exalted than the usual Kerameikos crowd.

My friend was entertaining in his courtyard. The early afternoon sunshine was pleasantly warm, the air not as stifling as it would be later in the day. Gorgias lay on one of the benches, Dionysus and Hermes were sprawled on each of the other two. Dionysus was feeding a cluster of small green grapes to Kabob, who cooed and clucked in obvious enjoyment as he gobbled them up.

It was Gorgias who spotted me first.

"Pelops!" he boomed. "We've been waiting for you!"

Gorgias did not seem to know who—or specifically, what—these guests were. Either that, or he was remarkably comfortable around gods. He reclined against a tall stack of pillows, one hand loosely holding a cup of wine, the other still-bandaged hand trailing in the geraniums beside him. His face was suffused with merriment. He did not look like he was suffering. In fact, all three of them looked like they were having a right jolly time of it.

"Come, sit! Join us!" Gorgias threw his arm out expansively, sloshing half his wine down the front of him.

I wasn't sure how the gods had introduced themselves so I didn't greet them by name, contenting myself merely with a polite nod to each. Dionysus shifted to make room for me on the bench. I settled beside him and he passed me a cup of wine.

"Thasian," I observed, after sniffing the sweet apple fragrance of it. "Very generous of you." I held up my cup and inclined my head. "Cheers."

"Your mates here have been keeping me company," Gorgias said with a hiccup. "We've been getting right chummy. Bloody hilarious, they are. Have they ever told you the one about the flute girl and the fish seller?"

"Oh, yes," I said. "And the flute girl and the cheese seller, and the flute girl and the oil seller, and the flute girl and—"

"Well, why the chuff haven't you ever brought them 'round before?" he demanded testily. "I can think of a few nights I could've used a good laugh."

"Oh, we don't live in Athens," Hermes told him before I could answer. "We heard Pelops was looking for us, so we came in specially."

"Ah, you don't, eh?" Gorgias scratched his belly and suppressed a belch. "That's too bad, is that. So where's home, then?"

"The mountains," Dionysus said with a straight face.

"Mountain folk. Is that where you get all those jokes from?"

"Nothing to do up there but tell jokes to your mates and bugger the sheep," Hermes agreed with a mischievous grin.

Gorgias snickered, spilling more wine on his chiton in the process. His colour was better than I'd seen it since he'd been injured, though that was more than likely due to the wine. I watched as Dionysus leaned over and refilled his cup to the brim. Gorgias drained half of it in one swallow.

"So, Pelops," Dionysus began. "Silenus tells me you were looking for me."

"Silenus?"

"My employee."

"Ah, the, uh…" I paused, glancing over at Gorgias. His eyes were closed and he was brushing his fingertips across the geranium petals. "… employee," I finished. "Right. Silenus, eh? Quite frankly, I'm astonished he remembered I stopped by."

Dionysus chuckled at my tone. "Ah, he's not so bad," he said, waving it off. "Sales go down when he's at work, but he takes his pay in stock, so it all comes out even in the end."

"Indeed. You must be paying him very well, judging from what I saw."

Dionysus laughed again, not at all offended. He was probably thrilled that another soul was lost to drink. Still, he *had* come out in response to my request.

"I need help," I began without preamble.

Dionysus looked suddenly uncomfortable. "I told you," he said in a low voice. "Mithaecus is—"

"This isn't about The Sicilian."

He closed his mouth and sat back. "Oh. Well, then. What's the trouble, eh?"

"Peneus."

"Who?"

"A dinner guest—the ghost, actually. From the look of him, he's not got two obols to rub together. He was at Lysander's house the night Neaera was killed."

"You think he did her in?" Dionysus asked intently.

"I ... I honestly don't know. But this morning, I ran into him—he likes to hang around the Spring House—and I tried to talk to him about it. About the night she was murdered. All I wanted to do was ask if he'd seen anything strange. But he started shouting at me, and then he..." I paused, sliding an uneasy glance toward Gorgias. "Well, he dissolved. Right there in front of me."

Gorgias opened his eyes and blinked owlishly at me.

"What do you mean, he dissolved?" Hermes asked.

I turned to look at him. "I mean, his face started melting and he turned into a giant water tentacle. Then he splashed down the water pipe and buggered off."

Dionysus and Hermes exchanged long looks.

"And then there's another dinner guest," I said, my voice rising as all my frustrations came to a head. "He was also at Lysander's house. A fellow named Philoxenus. He appears to have a remarkable tolerance for fire. His slaves say he can put his hands in the flame and not feel a thing. I cooked for him last night—and even that was odd, because, as you know, nobody in Athens will hire me right now." I couldn't help a note of reproof from creeping into my tone. The gods did not seem to notice. "So why did Philoxenus hire me? And why is he so obsessed with hot food?"

Dionysus looked troubled, and Hermes appeared downright solemn.

"You see what happens when we're kept out of the loop?" Dionysus grumbled to him. "Bollocks! If bloody Athena weren't so sniffy about her sodding festival—"

"We still would have been stuck on the Mount," Hermes interrupted. "Hera would have seen to that, D. You know she would."

"Aye," Dionysus agreed sourly. "But look what happens when we're not about. Things go all to cock."

Gorgias had stilled. His eyes had gone as wide as dinner plates.

"So, what's going on, then?" I asked the gods. "Who—or what—are these men? Is Poseidon involved in this? I need to know what I'm dealing with here."

Dionysus chewed on his lower lip thoughtfully. "Well, it wouldn't be old Fish Arse," he said. "Not here. Not now."

"Why not?"

"The festival," Hermes explained. "Poseidon wouldn't come to Athens during the Panathenaea. Not after the city picked Athena over him to be patron god."

"But ... that was ages ago!"

Hermes shrugged. "He holds grudges."

I grimaced and fell silent. I was all too familiar with Poseidon's grudges.

"Your mystery men don't sound familiar to me," Dionysus said. "But then, I'm more about the satyrs and maenads, aren't I?" He grinned crookedly, before his face grew serious again. "Can you tell me anything else about them?"

I pressed my fingers against my eyelids for a moment, then sighed and began telling them everything I knew about both men, about the dinner they'd attended, and about their contact with the dead hetaera. The two gods mumbled and muttered and exchanged highly significant looks, but were unable to come up with anything concrete.

"I got nothing," Dionysus said finally.

"But, we'll see what we can find out," Hermes chimed in. "You can trust us."

I looked away and didn't say anything. Having friends in high places was not proving to be especially helpful—either to my investigations or my career.

"How's business going, then?" Dionysus asked, reading my mind.

"Poorly," I said, trying not to sound too bitter.

They were gods, they could tell I was unhappy.

"You've got *some* work, surely!"

"One client," I conceded. "Though it's possible Xenarchus will change his mind—along with everybody else."

Dionysus and Hermes exchanged odd glances.

"Xenarchus. I see." Dionysus said, stroking his beard thoughtfully. "Huh."

I sat up straighter and gave him a sharp look. "Yes, Xenarchus. Why?"

He waved it off. "No reason, no reason. I'm sure, uh … *Xenarchus* will be very happy with his supper. Very happy indeed. Well, look at the time!" He pushed himself to his feet, yawning and stretching theatrically. "We should be off. Places to go and all that."

I regarded him suspiciously, but he refused to meet my eyes. Thanking Gorgias effusively for his generous hospitality, Dionysus and Hermes gathered themselves up and were out the door in record time.

"We'll let you know what we find," Dionysus called back as he disappeared down the street. "I promise!"

I closed the door behind them and made my way thoughtfully back to the courtyard.

Gorgias was sitting up now, his back straight as a rod. He seemed a little wild around the eyes.

"Are you all right?" I asked, concerned.

He nodded without blinking. "Fine, thanks." His voice was higher than normal. "So, uh … those were gods, yeah? Your, uh … your mates."

"That was Dionysus and Hermes," I confirmed with a sigh.

"Ah, yeah. Dionysus. Yeah. Okay. And Hermes. All right."

I waited.

"Uh—" he paused and cleared his throat "—shouldn't they be glowing or some such thing?"

"Glowing?"

"You know, with divine light."

"Gorgias, they're *gods*. They don't need to glow. You can tell they're gods just by looking at them." The memory of Nicander's symposion flitted across my mind. I hadn't recognized Dionysus or Hermes that night.

"It just seems like they should glow," he said defensively. "How are we supposed to recognize them if they don't glow? What if we didn't know it was them? What if we said something stupid? Or sacrilegious? What then, eh?" He opened his eyes very wide, then pushed himself creakily to his feet and began lurching up and down the courtyard.

"What did I say before you got here?" he demanded. "Did I say anything stupid? Anything offensive? Great gods! What if I said something wrong?"

"Gorgias, relax!" I assured him. "I'm sure you didn't say anything offensive. You're fine." I caught his arm and steered him back to his bench. "Sit down before you fall down. Come on, I'm sure they could glow if they wanted to. They probably weren't in the mood. Here, have a drink." I passed him a cup.

He gripped it without drinking.

I put my hands on my hips and gave him a severe look. "Gorgias, drink your wine," I said. "It's Thasian."

Slowly he raised the cup to his lips and gulped from it. "I still think they should glow," he mumbled into his drink.

I stood over him until he finished his wine.

Gorgias did manage to rally when Zeuxo arrived with her soup, though I noticed him glancing surreptitiously and frequently at the benches on which the gods had rested their exalted behinds. But Zeuxo was in a happy, sparkly mood, and she had him laughing and sipping soup in no time.

As for myself, I assuaged any lingering guilt over my neglect of Gorgias by whipping him up a batch of my cheese and fig appetizers. They were a delicious complement to Zeuxo's savoury oxtail soup, and Gorgias devoured both with grateful gusto.

Ansandra and Hermogenes joined us, as did Irene, Strabo, and Lais. There wasn't enough soup for everybody, but I made a second batch of fig appetizers so everyone could have a snack. Bellies were full, the wine was flowing, and Zeuxo and Gorgias were vying with each other to see who could come up with the most outrageous pun. All in all, it seemed a merry little party.

I, on the other hand, was somewhat less than jovial. Oh, I wished I could have joined in their light-hearted banter, enjoyed Zeuxo's scintillating company, but I found myself far too distracted—and not by thoughts of Peneus or Philoxenus or even the thrice-cursed Sicilian. It was Xenarchus who was first and foremost in my mind.

Xenarchus. My last remaining client. My final chance to reclaim and restore my reputation. My one chance to save my failing career. But Gorgias had once described Xenarchus as shadowy. He'd said that nobody seemed to know much about the man, beyond that he was rich. And now it seemed Dionysus knew him. But not only that (which would have been worrying enough), the god knew him by a different name.

It did not, I suspect, bode well for my future.

A Taste of Lydia
PELOPS'S CHEESE AND FIG APPETIZERS

---

* Fresh figs
* Fresh goat cheese
* Fresh mint leaves
* Salted pork, very thinly sliced
* Olive oil
* Mount Hymettus honey
* Sprigs of fresh thyme

---

1. Set honey in a pot over a very low flame. Add sprigs of thyme and allow the herb to infuse the honey.

2. In a bowl, mix fresh goat cheese with chopped mint leaves.

3. Insert a knife into each fig and hollow it out with your thumb. Fill each fig with a small spoonful of the cheese mixture.

4. Wrap each fig loosely with a slice of the salted pork, folding to secure the edges. Brush lightly with olive oil. Grill over a hot flame, turning frequently until the pork is crisped.

5. Place in a serving dish and drizzle with the warmed honey. Serve immediately.

Chapter 32

Hermogenes!" Ansandra's scream rang out from the vestibule. "Irene! Pelops! Come quick! Hermogenes is hurt!"

I was out of the courtyard in a heartbeat, Gorgias right behind me. The remains of our breakfast lay scattered and forgotten on the benches. I could hear Irene clattering down the stairs, and Strabo and Lais lumbering in from the workshop.

Hermogenes was propped against the front door frame. His small body was bruised and scraped, bleeding from any number of places. Ansandra was trying to pull him into the house.

"Help!" she cried as he staggered off balance.

I dashed to his side, supporting his slight frame before it could hit the ground. "It's all right, I've got you. Ansandra, I've got him. Irene!"

"I'm here."

"Get water and rags. And some wine too! Ansandra, clear off one of the benches in the courtyard."

Gently, I lifted my young slave and carried him into the courtyard. He was surprisingly light in my arms. I'd sent him to the market for grapes. He had only been gone a short while. What could have happened?

Ansandra cleared a bench by shoving everything onto the floor. Kabob eyed the half-eaten barley rolls with undisguised greed. I sat Hermogenes down. His head had fallen forward, his mop of dark curls obscuring his face.

"Hermogenes, what happened?" I asked intently.

He looked up at me then, and I sucked in my breath at the sight of him. Blood and snot flowed freely from his nose. A savage cut sliced across his upper lip. One of his eyes was swollen shut, and his right cheek was a pulpy mass of blood and flesh and filth.

He was shaking uncontrollably. I could tell that he wanted to cry, though he was trying to suppress the sobs in front of Ansandra.

"What happened?" I asked again, softly this time.

"Meidias," he croaked, his voice catching in his throat.

My lips tightened at the ragged sound.

"Chef, he said it was a reminder. He—" Hermogenes broke off, coughing.

I laid my hand on his shoulder in wordless apology. "Don't try to talk anymore," I told him. "Here, lie back. I've got you."

"Here's rags and water, then," Irene said, standing behind me. "Strabo, Lais. Out! You're not needed here. Back to work with

361

the both of you. We'll see to him. And you, Ansandra. Get that quail of yours and get him out of here. Yes, I know you're worried about Hermogenes, but Pelops and I will see him right and we can't do it with you hovering about and getting underfoot. You and Kabob can sit with him when we're done."

"Go to the kitchen, honey," Gorgias murmured. "Maybe you could fix him a bit of a snack for when he's feeling better, yeah?"

Ansandra lingered, unwilling to leave.

"Go!" Gorgias ordered more firmly.

Ansandra left and Irene and I started to work.

In silence, we washed the filth and grime from Hermogenes's small body, cleaning out the blood-caked scrapes, and binding the worst of the wounds. Most of the blood had come from his nose, but I was afraid that his cheek had been broken, the bone smashed by one of Meidias's vile slaves. I began cleansing it with the same cannabis wash that we'd used on Gorgias. Hermogenes had remained stoic throughout our ministrations, but when I began picking out the bits of rubble and dirt from his cheek, he began to whimper, a steady track of tears streaming from his eyes.

"Easy, lad," I told him. "I'm almost done. The good news is the bone looks sound enough."

And so it did, though the flesh was cruelly torn and bruised. Meidias's goons must have sent him skidding across the road. I clenched my teeth at the thought.

I was aware of Gorgias standing behind me for a while, but when it was obvious we needed no extra help, he patted my shoulder once and hobbled off in the direction of the kitchen. I worked quickly but gently, concentrating only on the task at hand, ruthlessly suppressing any thought as to why such a task was necessary in the first place. But even as Irene and I worked to bind Hermogenes's injuries, my mind must have been wrestling with the problem. By the time we'd finished with him, I knew what I had to do.

In Athens, beating another man's slave is merely considered bad form. It is not illegal, or even immoral. No court in the city would convict Meidias for doing so—especially when I owed him money. The law was not on my side. And so, there was only one possible response to his "reminder."

I waited until Hermogenes had been poulticed and bandaged and sent to his sleeping pallet, until a lavender compress had been placed on his swollen eye, and a cup of willowbark-laced wine set beside his hand. I waited until he drifted into uneasy slumber, and Ansandra and Kabob had been settled beside him for company. Then I wrapped up my amphora of victory olive oil, tiptoed quietly past the others, who had returned to the courtyard to exclaim over Meidias's brutality, and I slipped out of the house.

I knew Castor the Macedonian would buy my oil—no chef in his right mind would ever turn down such an opportunity. The oil would more than cover the cost of what I owed Meidias. It would even pay for Zeuxo's rent. Today, I would sell my victory olive oil to pay my debts. But as I marched purposely down the streets, the sight of Hermogenes's battered face hovered in front of me, and I vowed that someday, somehow, I would punish Meidias for what he had done to my slave.

Castor answered the door himself.

"Pelops!" he exclaimed in delight, throwing the door open as if it were the most natural thing in the world for me to come calling. "You honour me. Come in, come in."

"Thank you." I stepped across the threshold and into his abode.

It was a small house, poorly constructed, with few touches of grace or elegance to elevate it beyond its impecunious state. The life of a second-rate chef was clearly not a lucrative one. I'd been banking on Castor to have enough coin for my needs, but looking around at his shabby surroundings, I was assailed by sudden doubts.

Still beaming happily, Castor ushered me into a tiny courtyard, dwarfing the space with his enormous form. Indeed he was so large and his house so small, I thought he must overwhelm every one of the home's cramped rooms. It wasn't just that he was unusually tall, but he had the physique to go with his height. He was not fat, but his legs and arms were as thick as tree trunks, sturdy and solid. His shoulders were positively massive, and they were covered all over in a pelt of curly, reddish-gold hair the same shade as his beard. According to Hermogenes, it was commonly believed that his mother had mated with a bear to produce him. I had my doubts about that, but who really knew what sorts of shenanigans those Macedonians got up to high in their northern lands?

"Please, sit!" Castor rumbled, motioning me to a greying wooden bench. "Would you care for a cup of wine?" He rubbed his hands together in child-like anticipation. "Or perhaps some grapes?"

"Nothing, thanks," I said a little too curtly. If I hadn't sent Hermogenes out for grapes this morning...

Castor's face fell, bringing me back to the job at hand.

"Although," I temporized, "if you've got a spot of water handy, I wouldn't say no to it."

The Macedonian brightened and hurried off to fetch me a cup of water. I glanced around at his garden. It was small, but his basil plants were lush, his oregano thick and fragrant, and the deep green fronds of his dill weed stood at almost chest height.

He was back quickly, an unadorned clay cup full to the brim with cool water.

"Thank you," I said, taking a grateful sip before setting the cup down beside my chiton-wrapped bundle. "Look, I won't take up too much of your time," I began. "I come bearing ... opportunity."

As I explained the reason for my presence, Castor's blue eyes grew rounder and rounder. When I unwound the cloth to reveal the victory amphora with its exquisite decoration, his face split into a wide grin. His smile widened even further when I pried off the plug and let him sniff the heady aroma of the amphora's contents. His whole body was quivering at the thought that he might possess such riches.

I was familiar with the feeling.

I shared Castor's delight with the precious olive oil, fully comprehended his excitement over all the elaborate plans that were now racing through his mind. All the dishes he would prepare that would be immeasurably improved by using the rare oil. But knowing that I had held such a gift only to be obliged to

sell it to another chef—and one who served the lower classes!—
was bitter, bitter.

He asked me how much I wanted for it. I countered with
the request that he make me an offer. He pondered it for a long
moment, his brow scrunched together in thought, then he made
me a surprisingly fair offer. It was enough both to pay Meidias
off and to help Zeuxo with her rent. I agreed without haggling
and gave the amphora a last, regretful pat before handing it over
to its new owner. The clink of Castor's silver owls did little to
cheer me up.

"Normally, I wouldn't have enough coin to pay half that," he
admitted, holding the amphora against his broad chest as carefully as one might hold an infant. "But I'm afraid I've benefited
somewhat from your misfortunes." He shifted uncomfortably.

"I know," I said. "It's all right, it's not your fault."

"No," he agreed. "But I still feel badly."

"Don't," I advised. "Tyche is a changeable goddess. I'm sure
my fortunes will improve eventually."

"That's what Pharsalia always says."

"She is a wise woman," I told him.

"And cute, too," Castor said with a fatuous smile.

I blinked a few times. "Right," I managed.

I took my leave of him shortly afterwards. Castor was a nice
enough fellow. It wasn't his fault that he'd managed to pick up so
many of my contracts after the clients had cancelled on me, or
that I'd been forced to sell him my magnificent olive oil. Nevertheless, I found it impossible to celebrate his good fortune.

And I was already regretting parting with the oil.

I emerged from Castor's house, noticing only now that the day was cloudy and grey. I considered walking straight to the Piraeus, making the trek to Meidias's warehouses to pay him his money, but my mood was dismal and I did not trust myself to face him just yet. So I decided to call on Zeuxo first and give her the coin for her rent.

I was scuffing my way to her house, listening morosely to the dull, chain-like clank of the pouch of silver owls at my side, when those fortunes I'd mentioned to Castor earlier suddenly took an unexpected turn. I had rounded the corner of one of the narrow streets which led to Zeuxo's neighbourhood, and had just offered a glum pat to the Herm that stood sentinel there, when I saw the unmistakable glow of Mithaecus's bright yellow chiton coming down that dark passageway.

Miraculously, he was free of sycophants, or any other kind of companion for that matter. It was midday. Nobody else was around. Just he and I, moving through the gloom, our sandals making soft sucking noises as they squelched through the refuse on the street. His head was down, he had not yet noticed me. I could feel the hands of The Moirae, the Fates, pushing us inexorably toward one other.

Mithaecus had been a skewer in my side ever since I'd arrived in Athens. He had slandered me, undermined my successes, ridiculed my cooking, and tried to ruin my reputation with his vicious rivalry. Hermogenes had been beaten up, Zeuxo had lost her contracts, Pharsalia's business had taken a serious hit, and I had been forced to sell one of the princeliest gifts I'd ever received.

All because of this Sicilian.

I trained my eyes on him, watching his approach as intently as a hunting cat watches its prey. I could tell the instant he saw me. He stiffened, his weasel eyes darting around the street, his head coming up sharply at the realization that he was without his usual fawning retinue. He kept coming, though his steps slowed, his nose automatically going in the air as he drew nearer to me. I could tell he was preparing to greet me with one of his haughty nods.

"Well, well," he sneered with all the respect accorded a weevil in the barley flour. "If it isn't the disgraced cook. Heading off to the next assignment, are we? A fancy dinner for the dildo-maker perhaps?"

I didn't say anything to him. Not a single word. Not even when he named me cook instead of chef. But as we drew abreast, I clenched my hand, hauled back and with all the strength of the past week's anger and frustration and fear and fury, I sent my fist crashing into his spiteful, hated face.

Hera be damned, I thought recklessly.

I felt his nose crunch, then squish flat under my fist.

He cried out, a high girlish scream. I took a sharp, fierce pleasure in the sound—and even more satisfaction in the slippery feel of his blood on my hand.

Still without speaking, I turned from him.

Mithaecus had fallen to his knees, his sandals sunk in the filth of the street. His yellow chiton was splattered with red. He was shouting something at me, but the victory cheers in my head drowned out his pathetic mewling. I walked away and left him there, paying not the slightest heed to his words.

I continued on to Zeuxo's house, my steps markedly lighter than before. The sun had come out again, and the air felt clean and crisp, as if washed by a cool rain. I took deep, cleansing breaths, delighting in the refreshing feel of it coursing through my body. With every step I took, the silver owls clinked musically in their cloth pouch, and I found myself grinning cheerfully at the merry sound.

I felt better than I had in a long, long time.

Chapter 33

I'm getting married."

They were not the words I was expecting.

"Did you hear me, Pel? I said I'm getting married."

I blinked, opened my mouth then closed it again. A freshly caught fish gaping at its unexpected fate.

"Gorgias and I," she said. "We're getting married."

I heard her words, but I couldn't make sense of them. I looked around Zeuxo's tiny courtyard, trying to ground myself in the familiar sight. There were the pink geraniums and the purple hyacinth she'd planted. There were the benches with their matching pink and white cushions. There was the silver pile of Castor's drachmas I'd brought so she could pay her rent.

"Gorgias?" I wasn't sure whether or not I'd said it aloud.

"We'll be married this Gamelion. During the full moon. I don't know how these things are done in Lydia, but here in

Athens, Gamelion is sacred to Hera. And the full moon is the luckiest time of the month," she explained. "I want all the luck I can get, Pel. It is the second marriage for both of us."

I was drowning. I must be drowning.

"Gorgias?" The name managed to seep past my collapsed lungs.

Zeuxo looked at me, a slight frown marring her brow.

"Yes, Gorgias," she said a little impatiently. "Why not?"

"But ... Gorgias?"

"He's kind," she said simply.

Kind? I was kind!

"He's funny. He makes me laugh."

I was funny. Didn't I make her laugh?

"He's strong and handsome."

I was strong. I could lift heavy cauldrons. I could carry baskets of fish and grains. And while my profile could never be described as Grecian, I wasn't hard on the eyes. I was handsome enough.

She put a soft hand on my arm. "He's a good man, Pel."

I dropped my gaze and covered her hand with my own. I was a good man too. I looked up at her, my chest aching, struggling with the effort of pushing breath in and out. But in her eyes, I saw only loving concern for a friend.

A friend.

"He loves me," she said, her voice tinged with wonder.

Loved her? Great Zeus and Hera, didn't she know *I* loved her! I'd loved her since the first moment I'd set eyes on her. It had been at Xenophon's symposion. She had been dressed in pale green, the colour of sage leaves in the sun. Her dark curls framed her heart-shaped face. I could still hear Xenophon introducing her. "And this is Zeuxo," he'd said proudly. "The loveliest woman in Athens." She'd chuckled at his tone, and her gorgeous eyes had smiled at me.

"And I love him," she said quietly, bringing me crashing back to the present. Those gorgeous eyes were now dark with emotion. Her expression had clouded. "I know he'll never forget Helena, but ... I hope I can make him happy too. He deserves it, Pel. Gorgias deserves to be happy."

Did he now? Gorgias? A potter whose only goal in life was to make wine jugs? I was a celebrity chef! A man in demand! I had far more wage-earning potential than a mere potter! If all went well, in a year or two, I'd be able to offer more than some shabby old house in the Kerameikos.

A house he had shared with me.

The thought brought me up short. Unwillingly, I remembered how Gorgias had taken me under his wing and into his home. I remembered all the help he'd given me when I was starting out. All the advice. All the shared meals and late-night cups of wine. He had shown me the first kindness I'd known in Athens and thousands more since. I wanted to hate him—I *needed* to hate him—but I couldn't. He was my friend. He was my brother.

I looked down at Zeuxo's hand again, so small and white, trembling on my own. She was right. Gorgias deserved to be happy. They both did. I waited, breathing, just breathing, while the last vestiges of my world crumbled around me. Then I looked back at her and gave her hand a comforting squeeze.

"You're right," I said gruffly. "He does deserve to be happy."

Her face cleared and suddenly her smile was as radiant as Helios's golden chariot. She leaned forward and gave me a fierce hug. It almost undid me. I wanted to tell her I was happy for her too. That Gorgias wasn't the only one who deserved happiness. But I couldn't. Not now. Not yet.

"Dear Pel!" she exclaimed affectionately. "You're always there for us. What would we do without you?"

"Eat underdone eels and overcooked greens," I said promptly, with a pale imitation of my usual insouciant tone.

Zeuxo didn't notice. She laughed and gave me another happy hug.

I was a good man too. But not, apparently, good enough.

Chapter 34

Her name was Obole.

Obole didn't cost much more than her name implied. I found her in one of the little houses of Aphrodite by the Dipylon Gate. It was one of the older stalls, decrepit and squalid, much like its proprietress. A filth-crusted curtain provided a measure of privacy for those who required it. I did not care much one way or another.

I grappled with her until the sweat ran freely down my back. Until I was panting with the effort. It was sweltering outside and even hotter in the stall, the heavy air thick with the stench of rancid sweat and old semen. I didn't care about that either.

Locked together in frenzied lust, we crashed from one side of the rickety stall to the other. Dirt, dust, and worse rained down on us, sticking to the sweat on our bodies. Dislodged from its vantage point, a spider plopped down on her shoulder and scuttled off. I ignored it. In rage and pain and frustration, I spent myself in her.

"Oooo, sure you don't want another go then, luv?" she cackled when I'd finished. "You're a strong one, you are. And Obole likes it rough, yeah." She wiggled her bony hips suggestively and contorted her greasy face in her best come-hither look.

Revolted, I recoiled from her.

She clutched at me with skeletal fingers. "Now, don't go leaving Obole all alone," she whined. "You look like you could afford another round."

I shuddered and looked around me with clearer eyes.

Several of the wall boards were freshly cracked. *Had I done that?* Slivers of harsh sunlight now sliced into the thick gloom, illuminating the squalor within. I could see cobwebs blurring all the corners of the tiny room, the bloated bodies of well-fed spiders dark smudges against the paler grey of the aging wood. The pallet we lay on was grimy and stained, little better than the dirt floor it sat on. Obole herself should never have been viewed in such unkind light. Breasts thin and stretched, skin sagging and wrinkled, she was older than I'd realized and almost as greasy and loathsome as her environment. I curled my lip at the sight. She was utterly repellant. But there were purpling marks on her arms that hadn't been there before, and her thin chiton was torn in several places.

I swallowed a sudden upsurge of bile, disgusted as much with myself as with what I saw. A good man, was I? What kind of a man spent his seed in a place like this? What kind of man would treat a woman like this, even if she were the lowest sort of prostitute? I used to be a prince! I had been raised better than this. I *knew* better than this. How had I fallen so far?

Sickened, I stood up and yanked the filthy curtain open, desperate for the taste of fresh air on my tongue. Obole squawked as the grey fabric tore in my hand.

Ignoring her shouted curses, I pulled my chiton on and threw a handful coins at her. It was more than ten times what she charged. It was more than I could afford.

It didn't matter.

I wasn't a good man—I'd proved that this afternoon. But maybe it was time I tried to be a better one.

Hermogenes found me just as I stumbled from the malodorous stall. He'd put on a clean tunic, but his bruises and cuts were dark and dreadful in the harsh sunlight. He should have been lying down.

"What …Why …?" I began, trying to formulate the words. "You should be…"

Hermogenes stepped up to take my arm gingerly. "Chef, it's okay," he said gently. "I had a sleep and Irene gave me more medicine. I'm okay. Well … I'll live. But, come with me, yeah? I'll take care of you."

Bemused, I allowed him to guide my steps. I felt like I should say something, make some excuse for where I'd been and what I'd done. But there was no need.

"Ansandra told me as soon as I woke up," Hermogenes said softly. His dark eyes were as serious as I'd ever seen them. "About Zeuxo and Gorgias, I mean. She's over the moon about it. Right chuffed about having a new mum, but I knew that you would…" he trailed off.

My heart spasmed and my eyes filled with tears. I blinked furiously, trying to will them away.

"Well, I came searching for you soon as I heard the news," he continued. "I'm sorry, Chef. I'm so, so sorry." On his face was a look I'd never thought to see from a slave. Sympathy. Concern. Love.

My mouth worked, but I had no words to say. I'd never told Gorgias of my feelings for Zeuxo. Greek men did not share their innermost thoughts in such a fashion. They talked about chariot racing or Homer or whether or not Sparta would retaliate for the seaborne attacks on their colonies and when that might be. They didn't talk about love—especially love for a woman. Especially love for a flute girl. Gorgias had no idea I was in love with Zeuxo. I had not told Hermogenes either, but he had guessed. It was pure irony that of all the people in my life, only my slave knew the cause of my present anguish.

A tear escaped and rolled down my cheek. It paved the way for another, and another, until a steady stream poured down my face. Hermogenes, visibly distressed now, steered me to a dark alley, and there in the shadow of a crumbling Herm, I fell to my knees and sobbed like a child.

Chapter 35

I do not know how long I sat and cried in that fetid alleyway.

"Come on, Chef." Hermogenes was tugging gently on my arm. "Let's get you to the baths. We'll get you all cleaned up. You'll feel better, you'll see. Look, I've got money for the attendants. We'll get the works. Oil, steam, maybe even a massage, yeah? That would help, wouldn't it? A nice massage? Get all the kinks worked out. You'll see."

He wiped my face with the corner of his tunic and tugged and pulled at my chiton to arrange the folds, all the while carrying on a quiet monologue. Comforting me. Reassuring me. Expecting nothing back.

Slowly, he guided me through streets and alleys and into the public baths, still speaking in that soft, soothing voice. His bony shoulder supported me as I stumbled along beside him. How could someone so thin be so staunch? He'd been beaten up just that morning, but now he was the strong one.

He paid the bath attendants and demanded fresh water, a strigil and a small jar of olive oil. He paid extra to have an attendant rinse out my chiton and still more for scented oil and a slave to massage it into my skin. He even paid for a dish of olives and grapes to be brought to me in the steam room, though the very thought of food set my stomach churning. He did everything a good disciple would do and more. And this, despite being injured. I was touched to my core by his solicitude, by his simple concern. Hermogenes wasn't just looking after a master, he honestly cared. I had not expected that from him.

At the door leading to the baths, I balked. "But ... the money," I protested. "Are those your savings?"

Most slaves had savings, either from tips they'd earned or from wages paid to them for extra chores. All coins were carefully saved to buy one thing. Freedom.

Hermogenes reached up to pat me on the shoulder. "It's okay, Chef," he assured me with a trusting grin, lopsided now because of the cut on his lip. "I know you'll pay me back when you can."

"But—"

"Go," he ordered kindly. "Get cleaned up. Don't worry, I'll be right here by the door. If you have any problems, you just give a shout and I'll be there before you can say poached eels in wine sauce."

I nodded wordlessly and allowed myself to be led back into the steam-clouded bathing room. There, with the help of the bath attendants, I coated myself liberally with olive oil, scraping it all off with the strigil until my skin smarted and pinpricks of blood rose from patches on my arms and legs. I steamed and soaked and steamed again until I couldn't detect even the faintest whiff of Obole's rancid stall or my own rage-filled lust.

Apologizing silently to Hermogenes, I gave away the olives and grapes to the bath slaves. I simply could not bring myself to eat anything just yet. But the slaves brought me cup after cup of cool clear water and I drank each down as if I were dying of thirst.

And then, a bath attendant—a huge brute of a man—massaged scented oil into my skin. His touch was surprisingly light for someone so large, but effective all the same. The oil was warm, almost hot, and it smelled of rosemary and lavender. Clean, cleansing scents. He worked his fingers down into knotted muscles, releasing tension and anger and deep-rooted hurt. By the time he'd finished, I felt as weak as a new duckling. My heart still ached in my chest, but I was finally, wonderfully clean.

Now I could go home.

Now I could hide my feelings. I could pretend that I was still whole, that my very essence had not been shredded and torn. Now I could embrace Gorgias and express my congratulations and wish him the very best with his new wife. Now I could smile at Zeuxo and tell her I was happy for her. For them. What else could I do? They were my family and I loved them—both of them.

I sighed and rolled off the bench. The bath slave held out his hand and coughed meaningfully, but I needed all my coin to pay back Meidias, so I ignored his broad hint and eventually he went off in a huff. I shrugged into my chiton, wrinkled and damp from its rinsing, and prepared to leave.

"Pelops."

I turned and saw a familiar face emerge from the steam.

"Menon," I greeted him, surprised that he would acknowledge me.

"I have yet to be paid for attending your friend," he said snootily.

"Ah, and here I thought you were seeking me out for my scintillating conversation," I replied.

IIis nostrils pinched together. "I am accustomed to receiving payment promptly."

Oh, he was spoiling for a fight. If I'd met him a couple of hours ago, I might have obliged him.

I took a deep breath, ready with a sharp retort, then I let it out in a sigh. I didn't have the energy or the inclination to fight with Menon right now.

"How much do we owe you?" I asked.

He named a figure. A very large figure. I didn't bother trying to talk him down. I still didn't feel like fighting with him and, in all fairness, he *had* come out during one of the worst nights in memory—even if he'd needed some persuading to do so. I counted out a handful of silver owls. There were just enough left to cover his fee and pay Meidias back. Good thing I hadn't tipped the bath slave.

"Here," I said, injecting some righteousness into my tone. "I hope next time, you won't require the same level of ... inducement."

All smiles now that he'd been paid, Menon let that slide.

"And how is business going for you?" he inquired with insincere civility.

"Slowly," I replied shortly.

He *tsk*ed. "I had heard you lost contracts because of what happened to Neaera."

All Athens had probably heard of it. The Sicilian was likely still congratulating himself for it—while he held cold compresses to his nose. The last thought cheered me.

"Terrible business." Menon shook his head in feigned sympathy, failing to disguise his delight in my misfortunes. "Terrible. And you were there, yes? Cooking for Lysander? A terrible business. Tell me, how did she manage to drown at a symposion? One would think such a thing would be somewhat difficult, yes?"

I regarded the small man with dislike. "She was drowned in olive oil," I said flatly. "My olive oil. Someone dumped it in a cauldron and held her head under until she drowned."

His face paled.

"Terrible!" He said again, with true feeling this time.

I began to brush by him, unwilling to talk about it anymore. He caught at my arm.

"But, Pelops," he said, a puzzled look on his face, "I still do not understand. Neaera did not drown in olive oil."

"Excuse me?"

"She drowned in water."

"What are you talking about?" I demanded sharply. "How could she have drowned in water? Who told you this?"

Offended by my tone, Menon drew himself up to his full,

insignificant height. "I know the physician who examined her body, yes? Stobiades is a colleague and friend. It was he who told me."

"Why wasn't one of the Asclepion's priests called in?"

"The Asclepion!" Menon scoffed. "The priests from the Asclepion want nothing to do with murder. The purification rituals are too costly, yes? Costly in time, costly in money. You of all people must be aware of this." He slid me a knowing look.

All Athens had probably also heard that I'd spent a small fortune on purification. Not that it had done me, or my career, much good.

When I didn't respond, he shrugged. "And so, Stobiades was brought in to make her ready for the pyre. Strepsiades paid the bill. And very prompt he was about it. So nice to have clients who pay their bills on time, yes?"

"But..." I was still trying to absorb his words. "Water? Are you certain?"

Menon nodded. "Yes, yes. Stobiades was quite clear about it. She was covered in olive oil, her clothes were drenched with it. But her lungs were filled with water."

I pinched the bridge of my nose, trying to make sense of it all. I'd found Neaera in the storeroom submerged in a cauldron of olive oil. There had been no water in the storeroom. There was a small well in Lysander's garden, but she couldn't have been drowned in that. Not with all the house slaves passing in and out of the courtyard all evening. They would have noticed anything suspicious. And she hadn't been missing from the party long enough to be drowned elsewhere. Damokles would have raised a fuss if she had. There was only one other way that water could get where it didn't belong.

I reached out to grip Menon's arm. "This water," I asked intently. "Was it salt water? Sea water?"

Menon gave me a baffled look. "Sea water? But Lysander lives nowhere near the sea. Why would Neaera have drowned in sea water?"

"Was it sea water?" I insisted.

"No. At least Stobiades did not mention it."

Deep in thought, I turned away from Menon, leaving him gaping and bewildered behind me.

My first guess had been incorrect. When Menon told me Neaera had drowned in water, my first thought was that Poseidon had killed the hetaera. But there were rules for gods—Ares had even said as much. And one of those rules was that the Sea God could only kill with salt water. Salt water. Not fresh. Poseidon had not drowned Neaera.

But now I knew who had.

Chapter 36

In hindsight, I do not know what I hoped to accomplish by confronting Neaera's killer. Indeed, I'm not sure my thoughts at that time were entirely rational. Oh, I suppose I had some notion of obtaining confirmation of my suspicions—though intuition told me I was correct in them. Perhaps on some level I hoped to make an arrest, to be awarded for bringing a killer to justice. But if I were correct, it was highly doubtful this criminal would ever be convicted and fined. Perhaps I was just looking for some sort of closure. As I said, my thoughts were not exactly coherent.

And yet, for all that, as I strode with single-minded purpose through the deserted Agora, it felt as though the coming confrontation were fated. A brisk, late-afternoon breeze had set the leaves of the plane trees fluttering, and it seemed right. A spotted bird flew across my path from left to right, and I was not surprised. A striped cat, lean and orange, darted over my feet, and it felt oddly familiar. It was almost as though all this had happened before. Or was meant to happen. And with every step I took, my anger grew. This man, this *criminal*, had killed a young woman, apparently without hesitation or remorse. What kind of creature would do such a thing?

The grey man was standing in his usual place under the young laurel tree by the Spring House. Late afternoon shadows were lengthening into twilight. The equestrian events had ended for the day, and the festival crowds had long since disappeared into whatever shelter they'd chosen in which to wait out the Erinyes's nightly attack. I'd sent Hermogenes back to the house with strict orders to stay home and stay quiet. He'd been unhappy and concerned, but I had been firm.

Peneus and I were alone.

"You're her father, aren't you?" The words burst past my lips, angry and accusatory.

He still sported the same storm-coloured chiton he'd always worn. His grey eyes watched me with quiet wariness.

"Neaera," I said. "You're Neaera's father. The nature god. A river god, I would guess."

"And if I am?" he said in his rippling voice.

"You killed your own *daughter*." It was statement rather than question. I could hear the disbelief in my voice, though why I, in particular, should feel this way, I couldn't explain. Hadn't my own father committed just such an act?

All of a sudden I burned with an oven-hot fury. Great Zeus and Hera! What was it about fathers killing their offspring? Oh, there were some good fathers out there—Gorgias was proof of that. He'd braved the terrifying wrath of the Erinyes just to bring his daughter home safely. But Peneus? Tantalus? What exactly was their problem?

"Why?" I demanded tightly, unclear even in my own mind whether I was asking it of Peneus or of my father. "Why would you kill your own child?"

He sneered at me, his features blurring and shifting. For a moment, I thought he was going to dissolve again. To leave me with my question unanswered. But I was wrong.

"Neaera?" he literally spat her name out, his whole demeanour one of unadulterated contempt. The strands of his long hair had begun to undulate, coiling around his neck and shoulders like watery serpents. "I disowned that whore years ago. She was no child of mine!"

I blinked. "Then why—" I started to say, but he wasn't listening to me.

"Selling her body to Athenians!" he hissed. "Polluting her mouldy well with the seed of their arrogant, dissipated men. Filth!" He spat on the ground. "Excrescence!"

His features had sharpened up again, but now his hair had taken on a life of its own. It snaked out from his head in a writhing aureole, roiling and churning like fast-moving water in a rocky streambed.

"She wanted her sister to do the same. Her own sister!"

"Are you talking about Daphne?" I asked, unable to take my eyes off his agitated serpent-like hair.

He paused for a moment, head cocked to one side as if

listening to something. "Yes, Daphne," he murmured, and it sounded like a soft summer rain.

He drew a long, deep breath and leaned against the laurel tree behind him. His expression had grown softer. "She was one of Artemis's most devout followers," he said with a faraway look in his eyes, his tone as warm as an embrace. His hair had calmed now, flowing down the tree trunk like a second skin. "Pure and chaste. As lovely and wild as the maiden goddess she worshipped. Her hair was as dark as a windy night, and she smelled like hyacinth."

"Then..." he paused, voice hardening, eyes frosting to ice. His fingers dug spasmodically into the tree's smooth grey bark. "Then her sister tried to pervert her. To drag her along in her own sordid footsteps." His mouth worked for a moment. "She sent messengers to Daphne, begging her to join her. And not just one or two. Oh, no. Dozens she sent! Promising her the world! A life of pleasure and contentment. Jewels, fine clothes, rich foods and wines—all would be hers if only Daphne would join Neaera in Athens. The depraved whore! And Daphne—my poor innocent Daphne—was taken in by her evil lies."

I held my breath, not saying anything.

Lost in memory, Peneus stared up at the slender, spear-shaped leaves of the laurel tree. He didn't appear to be aware of my presence any longer. Then his eyes dropped and met mine. I flinched from what I saw in them.

"She left," he said bitterly. "One rainy night. She slipped out and came to this debauched, dying city. By the time I realized where she'd gone, it was ... almost too late." He said the word "almost" matter-of-factly, thoughtfully even. It made my hair stand on end. Had he killed both his daughters?

"She was going to sell herself to Xenarchus," he explained. "One of the richest men in Athens. I couldn't let that happen. I couldn't let her sell her innocence, her purity, her devotion! And to an Athenian, no less! A swaggering, vainglorious people! Despots, each and every one of them! Dissolute and depraved. That plague should have destroyed them all. Cleansed the earth of their foul presence."

"Did you kill her?" I asked, dreading the response.

"Kill her?" Grey eyes widened in surprise. "My lovely Daphne? Don't be absurd!" He leaned back against the laurel tree and stroked the bark gently, lovingly. "I merely ... changed her form."

My gaze went to his caressing hands, following the line of the tree trunk up to its gracefully spreading branches. In belated understanding, I brought my eyes back down to his. He gave me a cool smile and patted the tree softly.

"She's still wild and pure," he said. "And as beautiful as the spring. But I hardly think Xenarchus will want to rub his filthy cock on her bark."

"No," I agreed, feeling a little sick. "I wouldn't think so."

"And now she is in no danger of breaking her vows." He shook himself free of introspection. "I wish I could take her back to Thessaly with me. My only regret will be leaving her behind in this dying city."

We stood in silent contemplation of the laurel tree. Its leaves rustled in the still air. The sound was like the restless waves of an uneasy sea. I fancied I heard a soft, sad kind of noise. A sigh maybe. Or perhaps it was just the sound of the non-existent wind in its branches.

After a while, I cleared my throat. "And Neaera?" I asked. "Did you kill her?"

"I had no choice." He gave an offhand shrug. "She arranged the whole thing, you know. She auctioned off her sister's innocence and purity for *coin*! What kind of filth does such a thing?" He shook his head. "The world is well rid of that one. I attended her funeral just to see her corpse burn. Let her rot in the underworld where she belongs!"

His callousness stung.

"What gives you the right?" I demanded. "What makes you think you can just—"

"The right of a father," he snapped.

"A father!" I shot back scathingly. "A father is supposed to *protect* his family."

"I was protecting my daughter!"

"You were protecting one of them! What about the other one?"

"I don't have another one!"

"Bollocks!" I spat. "You just chose to pretend you didn't. I know all about Neaera's childhood. I've spoken to Damokles. Right from the start you didn't want anything to do with her. You'd invite Daphne to visit you, you lavished attention on her, but never Neaera. Where were you when Neaera was running so wild? Where were you when she needed guidance? Where were you when she decided to become the hetaera you despise so much?"

His face grew stormy and his hair started to coil and writhe again. I ignored it, too involved in my own anger.

"You claim the right of a father, but you were never a true father to her. Only to Daphne. Maybe if you'd cared more about your other daughter, she wouldn't have ended up whoring in Athens!"

"What do you know?" he shrieked, enraged. "I have existed for an age and beyond. You are nothing! You *know* nothing!"

"I know a pitiful excuse for a father when I see one!" I shouted back, just as incensed. "Believe me, I have plenty of experience with those! And you—you watery bastard!—are about as bad as they come."

Peneus gave a low growl. His form began to quiver.

"Oh, no, you don't. I'm not finished with you yet!" I yelled, making a futile grab at his arm.

It was then that I caught sight of it.

It loomed silently behind the river god, half-hidden in the darkening shadows. Its pale, sinewed arms were crossed over its breasts, a brass-studded scourge dangling from one claw-like hand. Leathery wings were folded back against the strangely elongated body. Dark blood ran from terrible eyes down bleached, hollowed cheeks. It was staring fixedly at Peneus.

The fetid stench of the creature rolled over me, and I gagged. Peneus paused and glanced behind him. He froze. For a long moment nothing moved. And then the Erinys smiled.

With an inarticulate cry, Peneus jerked back, fear lending him speed. Before I could blink, he had collapsed in a great clap of thunder. For an instant, I caught sight of a writhing, ropy water tentacle, then a boiling rush of water and steam billowed up, obscuring my view.

I leapt away from the cloud, falling heavily to the ground. I couldn't see a thing! There was another desperate scream. Seething water slapped against my legs, scalding my flesh. I cried out, scrabbling away on hands and knees, frantic to escape. My skin was on fire.

But suddenly there was nothing to escape from. As I watched, heart pounding furiously, the cloud of steam shredded, then dissipated in the cool night air. And I saw that both the river god and the avenging Erinys had vanished.

Chapter 37

From the tops of my feet to just above my knees, my skin was an angry, livid red, the blisters already filling with fluid. I limped over to the Spring House, clenching my teeth in agony, pain throbbing up my legs with each uneven step. All I wanted to do was soothe the cruel burns in the cool waters of the fountains. But when I stumbled up to the closest pool, the lion-headed waterspout dried up with a vengeful gurgle, and as I watched in disbelief, the waters in the pool drained away.

"Oh, come on! No!" I cried. "Please!"

I spun around and staggered to the next pool—the larger one—but that spout had stopped running as well. The pool had started to drain too, but there was more water to empty from this one and only one drain. Without hesitating, I hopped right over the stone ledge and plunged my burning legs into the water.

Cool, blissful, blessed water. I closed my eyes in relief, silently urging the soothing liquid to do its work before Poseidon could drain it away entirely.

"Look, I'm sorry," I said to the rapidly receding waters. "I'm sorry I turned you down back in Lydia. All right? But, how could I … I couldn't … you were my *brother*!" I cried, tears coming unbidden to my eyes at the injustice of it all. On that terrible day so long ago, I had not only lost a father, I had lost a brother too.

Uncaring, the pool water sloshed and growled.

Or, perhaps, I had never really had one.

"I never meant to insult you," I pleaded brokenly. "Please. You were like family to me."

The water kept on draining. I might as well have been talking to Kabob for all the good it was doing me.

"Fine!" I spat out. "If that's the way you want to be. You ignore my prayers, accept my sacrifices without acknowledging them, and still you won't forgive me. All this time, I've been bending over backwards asking your forgiveness. But what about me? Shouldn't you be begging my forgiveness? If you want to keep holding a grudge, then I wash my hands of you—literally! No more sacrifices. No more prayers. I'm done."

At my words, the water began to churn and seethe in earnest. Dashing away my tears, I jammed my foot hard against the drainpipe. There was a sudden surge against my legs. It knocked my feet right out from under me. Coughing and spluttering, I dragged myself up and tried again to wedge my heel in the drain. Again I was sent tumbling.

I cursed. Unforgiving fish-tailed bastard! No wonder

his family didn't like him. No wonder he couldn't get a date! Drenched but undaunted, I kept at it.

He won eventually, of course. I am only mortal and he is, after all, a god. When the last of the water drained away with a spiteful gurgle, I collapsed against the stone edge of the pool, exhausted and panting. But the cooling waters had given me some respite from the pain, and after I regained my breath, I found I could contemplate my next move with more equanimity.

Now that the Kindly Ones knew what Peneus had done, they should cease their attacks on the city. And as soon as I told Hermogenes who had killed Neaera, then all of Athens would know I was innocent of sacrilege. My reputation would be reinstated and my client base restored. But there was one client who needed to be informed in person. One client who was not going to be pleased at the outcome of events.

I had to tell Xenarchus about Daphne.

Wearily, I climbed from the pool, wincing as my burned legs scraped against its stony ledge. I slicked my wet hair back and squeezed the excess water from my chiton. I felt off-balance, strange in a way I couldn't quite identify. And then it hit me. The altercation with first Peneus and then Poseidon had taken time. No longer twilight, it was true dark now. Night covered the city.

And I was out in it.

I froze, listening so hard my ears rang. But for the first time since Neaera had been killed, the city was quiet at night. No unearthly shrieks. No cries of despair. No ominous thrumming of leathery wing-beats.

I stood in the entrance to the Spring House and peered warily into the skies. They were clear, the silence broken only by the soft hooting of Athena's little owls that lived in the city. The owls had not called since the attacks had begun. Cautiously, I stepped from the building, ready to leap back under shelter in case I was wrong. But the night remained quiet and still. The Erinyes were hunting other prey.

Peneus was an old god, as wily and unpredictable as his element. He might have made good his escape from the Kindly Ones, but he would not be able to hide from them forever. They would pursue him relentlessly—all the way back to Thessaly if necessary. The murderous river god was in for a bad time, but I could not feel pity for him. After what he'd done, he deserved every moment of it.

Before making my way to Xenarchus's house, I stopped by the bay laurel tree. By Daphne. Being the victim of an unstable father myself, I felt an all-too-understandable kinship with her.

I lowered myself to the ground beside her, groaning a little as my burned legs brushed against each other. "Hi," I said, patting her bark softly. "It's me. Pelops."

The tree's leaves rustled.

"I'm sorry about your dad," I told her. "That's rough."

The tree quivered and I gave it a moment.

"Mine cut me up into stew meat. Served me to the gods for tea."

The tree had gone quiet.

"I used to be a prince, you know. I was powerful, rich, handsome."

The tree rustled again.

"Okay," I conceded, "maybe not 'handsome,' but I wasn't too hard on the eyes. And I tried to be a good person. I really did. Then my dad got hold of me. Now look at me. I'm just a clientless chef who can't afford his own dishes. I didn't even get the girl."

The thought of Zeuxo marrying Gorgias depressed me all over again. I leaned against the laurel tree and sighed bitterly. There was more rustling in the leaves above me and then, with a plop, a leafy branch fell into my lap. I looked up in surprise.

"That's very kind of you," I told the tree, lifting the branch up to my face. I inhaled deeply. The scent of the leaves was warm and spicy—not at all like hyacinth. "You know," I said after a moment, "these would be lovely in a fish stew. Or maybe simmered in a glaze for roast lamb."

The tree's branches dipped down in benediction.

We sat in companionable silence, enjoying the still moonlight. The summer night was comfortably warm, and the bay leaves filled the air with their rich perfume. Somewhere to my left, a little owl was hooting contentedly.

"Well, I guess I should go tell Xenarchus you won't be coming to his party," I said after a while. "I don't think he's going to be very happy with me."

The tree gave a regretful rustle. This time the sad sigh was unmistakable.

"I'm sorry," I said again in belated understanding. "If you want, I'll tell him you would have come to him. It might make him feel better."

The branches shifted and then another leafy twig fell into my lap. I nodded once, then gathered up the gifts and pushed myself to my feet. My blistered legs still smarted—I'd have to get Irene to mix me up a salve—but at least I wasn't doomed to live out the rest of my life as a tree.

"I'll give it to him," I promised solemnly. "And I'll come 'round every so often. See how you're doing." I rested my hand on her trunk. It seemed to quiver under my touch. "You take care now."

And with that, I set off to give Xenarchus the bad news. Before quitting the Agora, I glanced back once more at the bay laurel tree. It stood quietly by the Spring House, its leaves silvered in the bright moonlight. Wild. Lovely. Pure.

But not even remotely human.

Xenarchus took the news remarkably well.

Simos had ushered me into the same courtyard where I'd first met his master in what seemed like a lifetime ago. The superior slave was still wearing his fine orange chiton, but Xenarchus was more casually attired. Clad only in a simple tunic, he reclined on a deeply cushioned bench, savouring a last cup of wine before bed. They both knew I wasn't there to discuss the following day's menu. Simos was too well trained to smirk outwardly at me, but his eyes were alight with glee. Xenarchus's countenance, on the other hand, could best be described as grim.

Nervously, I began to recite the sequence of events. When I got to the part when I'd found Neaera's body and the Kindly Ones had begun their attack, Xenarchus gestured peremptorily to his slave.

"Leave us," he ordered.

Simos cast him a quick, disbelieving look, but that one glance at his master's face was enough to exact obedience. He drew himself up haughtily and slunk from the courtyard with as much dignity as he could muster. Before he disappeared into the shadows, he slid me an icy glare. I narrowed my eyes back at him and had the satisfaction of seeing his face purple with anger. Poncy tosser.

Xenarchus, in the meantime, had not taken his eyes off my face. "Continue," he said, pressing his fingertips together.

I did. I told him everything, from my difficulties with Mithaecus to attending Neaera's funeral in my search for her sister to discovering the true nature of their father. I did not, however, mention anything about Dionysus or Hermes (or Zeus or Ares, for that matter). They were irrelevant to the narrative, and I didn't want to seem a name-dropper. His expression was bleak by the time I told him of Daphne's unhappy fate.

"She's over by the Spring House," I finished. "Near the statue of her sister."

I stopped talking and waited.

Xenarchus frowned at his hands and said nothing. The silence dragged on.

I fidgeted restlessly. Opened my mouth to say something, then when I realized there was nothing else I could say, I closed it again.

Still Xenarchus was silent.

And then, I remembered the laurel branch.

"There is one other thing, sir."

Xenarchus looked up at me. His eyes were cold and remote.

I gulped and fumbled at a fold in my chiton. "Here," I said, offering him the laurel branch. "She wanted you to have this."

One of Xenarchus's eyebrows rose, but he extended his hand to accept the gift.

He held the branch gently as if afraid it might break should he clutch it too tightly. His eyes bore into mine. "How do you know this?" he asked, his voice gruff with emotion. "How do you know what she wanted?"

I shrugged uncomfortably, not really sure how to explain it. "We sort of understand each other," I said at last. "I had trouble with my father too."

Xenarchus went quiet again. I waited.

In silent concentration, he studied Daphne's gift for a while. And then, with mindful determination, he started twisting the supple branch this way and that. Working meticulously, he coaxed it into a more circular shape, careful not to tear off even a single one of the fragrant leaves. I watched as he wove her gift into a head wreath.

When he'd finished, he gazed upon it for a moment, then set it gently on his head. He sighed deeply and turned his attention back to me. His expression was no longer bleak, merely sad. Full of regret for lost opportunities.

"Thank you," he said.

I nodded without speaking.

"You may go."

I turned to leave, then paused. "Your symposion tomorrow—" I began.

"Cancelled." He waved it off wearily. "I am not in the mood for celebration."

"Ah," I said, trying to mask my disappointment, though I was not surprised by his decision.

"You will be paid, of course," he said. "Do what you will with the food. I do not want it." He leaned back against his cushions and closed his eyes.

I nodded again, happier at the prospect of being paid for no work, but touched by his obvious suffering. I hesitated, then spoke.

"If it's any consolation, sir," I said, "she planned on coming to you. She wanted to. She was looking forward to it. It was her father who had other ideas."

Xenarchus gave no outward indication that he'd heard my words, but I hoped the knowledge would give him some measure of peace.

There was one more person I needed to inform, one more to talk to before I could go home, and I thought perhaps he might take the news hardest of all. Upon my arrival at his house, I was escorted promptly into his elegant courtyard, where the chariot racer was reclining in the presence of his victory amphorae.

"I have news," I told him without preamble. "You're not going to like it."

Damokles sat up, his gaze sharpening. "Tell me."

"It was Peneus," I said. "The ghost. He killed her."

He stared at me, shocked into silence.

I took a deep breath and continued. "He was her father. That nature god you told me about—a river god. He killed his own daughter. He claimed it was his right."

"*What?*" Damokles surged to his feet, eyes flashing fiery retribution.

Almost, I quailed before his fury. He stood, muscles tensed and trembling, clenching and unclenching his fists.

Hoping to defuse his anger, I told him of the Erinyes, of their pursuit of the murderous river god, and of how they would not rest until vengeance was satisfied.

He did not resume his seat, did not even relax his hands. His mouth worked, though he uttered not a word. And then he let out a terrible cry, and before I knew what he was about, he spun round and sent his fists crashing into the tall wooden shelf behind him. The shelf that held his beautiful Panathenaic amphorae.

With a sharp crack, the wood splintered. The prize amphorae tumbled to the ground, shattering on impact. I cried out in protest as the best olive oil in the whole of Greece splashed across the stone-paved courtyard.

At my outburst, Damokles spun around, fists up, chest heaving. His eyes were wild. I took a step back, and then another, uncertain in that moment if he knew me. I did not dare draw breath.

For several heartbeats, he stared at me.

And then, all of a sudden, the fight went out of him. His shoulders dropped and he buried his face in his hands. He was shaking visibly.

"He will suffer for it," I assured him in the silence that

followed. "The Kindly Ones will make certain of that. And he will suffer more thoroughly at their hands than he would have at yours."

"Do you think so?" Damokles rasped, his voice ragged and broken. He looked at me, and I flinched before the anguish in his eyes.

I was silent for a moment.

"Perhaps not," I conceded at last. "But I do not think they will surrender him to you."

The chariot racer was silent for a very long time, staring off at nothing. I could see lines of pain etching themselves deeply into his face.

I thought he must have forgotten my presence, and I was about to slip away when he suddenly brought his attention back to me. "I can't thank you for this news," he said.

"I understand," I told him. "I would feel much the same were our positions reversed."

He nodded once, briefly.

I waited but it appeared he had nothing more to say. Head bowed, I retraced my steps out of his courtyard.

"Pelops."

I stopped and looked back.

"Thanks," he said simply. "For caring enough to find out."

I wanted to offer words of condolence, some gesture of sympathy, but he turned his back before I could say anything. Silently, I saw myself out and left him to his grief.

"...and he's been doing it for years, Chef!" Hermogenes said. "Practising by sticking those fat fingers of his in boiling water just to get them used to the heat. He even gargles with the stuff so he can gulp down the hottest bits."

"All so he can have the first shot at the hot food at a dinner party?" I shook my head incredulously.

"And second and third shots," Hermogenes agreed, scratching at his healing cuts. "He's a right nutter, he is. And a dirty great pig. He'll eat a whole ox so long as he doesn't have to pay for it. I tried to warn you about him, Chef. I did! A greedy-guts like that was bound to try to take advantage of your situation."

"Indeed. I should have listened to you."

Philoxenus, it turned out, was no more supernatural than I was. Hermogenes had tried to tell me about him, it was true. The morning he'd arrived home after being out all night. But I'd been so furious with him, I hadn't given him a chance to say anything. A pity. Had I known about Philoxenus and just how far he'd taken his gluttonous instincts, I might have saved myself a lot of worry. I certainly would have saved myself the headache of preparing food for his symposion—not to mention the indignity of being underpaid for the privilege. Everyone knows that slaves hear everything. I should have remembered that and listened to mine.

Which reminded me of something I needed to do.

"By the way," I said in an offhand fashion. "You're free."

Hermogenes turned and stared at me, as though I'd been speaking some form of ancient Assyrian.

His bruises had finally started to fade and his right cheek was healing nicely, though he would bear the scars for the rest of his life. He'd informed me that the scars would lend him the sort of rakish air popular with flute girls and hetaeras, though how he would know what such women preferred, he did not elaborate and I did not inquire. Ansandra seemed intrigued by the marks, so perhaps he merely extrapolated. As for myself, those scars would be a constant reminder of a debt owed. Not mine, of course. I'd gone to the Piraeus and paid Meidias for his dishes. But the scales of justice were unevenly balanced and I'd sworn a silent oath to pay him back in full for what he'd done to Hermogenes.

"You're free," I said again. "I've sorted it with Gorgias. He signed your ownership over to me and I'm giving it to you."

Hermogenes opened his mouth, but no words came out. His dark eyes stared at me, wide with disbelief. "But why would Gorgias...?"

"To celebrate his wedding." I tried to say the words nonchalantly, but something of my inner pain must have shown in my face.

Hermogenes's look shifted to one of sympathetic concern. "Does he know?" he asked in a low voice.

I shook my head once. "He knows nothing," I said too abruptly.

Hermogenes took no offence. Instead he nodded in understanding, his scarred face looking much older than his years.

I cleared my throat. "You're free now," I said a third time. "You can go anywhere you want. Do anything you want to do. Become a discus thrower, or a boxer, or even a chariot racer—anything." I paused, giving him a moment to absorb it. "But I want … that is, I would like it very much if you would stay on to be my disciple."

His breath came out in a gasp. "Chef! Do you mean it? Your disciple?"

I smiled crookedly. "Yes, Hermogenes. I would like you to be my disciple. You're quick, you're smart, you're good in the kitchen, and you've got a natural flair for cooking." *And I care about you, you little bugger,* I added, though I didn't say it out loud.

I held up an admonitory finger. "Now, there's still a lot for you to learn—"

"Oh, I know there is, Chef. It'll take me years before I can cook like you!"

"And I don't know what I can offer you in terms of wages—it will depend on how quickly my reputation can recover—but I can say that I'll pay you a fair wage, I'll teach you how to cook, and you can continue to live here until such time as you decide to go out on your own."

Hermogenes beamed, his face practically glowing with happiness.

"Thank you, Chef! Thank you so much. You won't regret this. I promise you won't. I'll never let you down!"

I clapped him warmly on the shoulder. "I know you won't," I said.

Chapter 38

"So, why don't you glow?"

We were relaxing in the back room of Dionysus's wine stall. Hermes lounged on one enormous couch, Dionysus was sprawled on the other. A much smaller couch had been brought specially in for me—a gesture that had touched me for its thoughtfulness— and I relaxed as much as I could against its rich cushionings. I was not totally at ease (indeed, no mortal could be so in such company) but I was aware of feeling distinctly mellow.

The wall frescoes were still moving, the figures performing some sort of play now, complete with actors in elaborate masks and a chorus, which appeared to be doing its best to annoy the actors. Outside, the satyr was looking after the stall. I could hear him calling lustily to the market women as they walked by. Though it was still early in the day, Dionysus's face was already red and shiny from the wine he'd consumed.

At my inquiry, he scrunched his thick eyebrows together in a frown. "Glow?"

"You know, with immortal light."

His expression cleared. "Oh, that."

I waited.

"It's a bit ostentatious, don't you think?"

"I don't know," I said uncomfortably. "You're a god. I think you're allowed to be ostentatious if you want."

"I suppose. But sometimes one doesn't want to call attention to one's self."

"Ah, you mean you're in disguise."

"I wouldn't say that. There are times I like a little glitz and glamour just like the next god, but if I went round all the time glowing with my usual divine light…"

Suddenly I was blinded by a burst of white-hot light. I cried out and threw up my arms to protect my eyes. My wine cup fell to the floor.

"You see?" Dionysus asked. "It's hardly what I'd call unobtrusive."

Cautiously, I opened my eyes. He'd returned to his normal luminescence. "I see what you mean," I said, a little breathlessly.

"We can't go pulling out the red carpet all the time," he agreed, reaching down to retrieve my cup. He handed it back to me, full of wine, though he hadn't poured any. "Best to save it for special occasions."

"Thanks." I accepted the wine. "Still, it might be helpful if you glowed just a bit. Gorgias had no idea who you were. He was all in a knot worrying that he might have said something to offend you. It might make for fewer misunderstandings. You know, fewer cases of mistaken identity."

"Like with Xenarchus, you mean?"

"Xenarchus!" I bolted upright. "What are you talking about? Are you saying Xenarchus was a … is a…" I couldn't finish the sentence. I stared at Dionysus.

There was a hangdog expression on his face. "Oops," he said ruefully.

"*Oops!* What do you mean, 'oops'?"

"You'd better tell him, D.," Hermes said, his bright eyes sympathetic.

Dionysus pulled at his bottom lip for a moment, then blew out his breath in a dramatic sigh. "Xenarchus is a god," he confirmed.

"But … but he's got a house here in Athens! He's sponsored plays and statues. He's been around for years!"

"We all maintain houses," Dionysus dismissed it with a wave. "I've got one in every city state in Greece. You know, for when I need a place to kip down for a bit."

I passed a hand over my forehead. A sick feeling threatened to settle in my stomach. "Is he … another river god?" I asked hopefully. "Maybe some obscure forest god?"

Dionysus pulled his mouth to one side. "Ah, not so much, really."

"It's Apollo," Hermes said impatiently. "Xenarchus is Apollo." Oh, gods.

"He had to disguise himself," Dionysus explained. "On account of he and Eros having a disagreement. More of a pissing contest, really. Apollo said he was a better archer than Eros, and Eros said, 'Sod that, I'm better than you any day.' You know how these things go."

"And Apollo's always been a pompous great git," Hermes interjected.

"True," Dionysus agreed, stroking his beard sagely. "Anyhow, the upshot was that Eros let fly with one of his *special* arrows. Nailed Apollo right in his ever-so-superior arse. And Apollo found himself instantly smitten with your friend Daphne."

"Fell madly in love with her," Hermes said before *tsk*ing in mock sympathy.

"But she wanted nowt to do with him, did she?" Dionysus continued with his story. "Lied to him about where she was from so he couldn't go looking for her. Right terrified, she was. On account of him being a god and all. So he figured he'd have better luck if he changed his shape. Became mortal for a bit. Until she got to know him better. From what you say, it sounds like it might even have worked—if her father hadn't taken a hand in it all." He paused. "Sorry we never gave you the heads up, yeah? But we only found out about it recently. That he was Xenarchus, I mean."

I was listening to all this with my head in my hands.

Apollo. Xenarchus was Apollo. Slayer of the dreaded Python. God of music, poetry, philosophy, astronomy, mathematics, medicine, and science—all the disciplines that separate civilized men from barbarians.

Apollo. Only one of the most important gods of the Pantheon.

And I hadn't even recognized him!

Gorgias was right. Gods should glow. Gods should let you know who they were right up front. None of this glowing-when-they-felt-festive rubbish. Gods should glow all the time so that mortals wouldn't inadvertently say something stupid or sacrilegious in front of them or—even worse!—fail them. If Apollo had glowed, I would have known who he was. I would have tried harder to find Daphne. True, she'd already been turned into a tree by the time he'd enlisted my aid, but maybe if I'd tried harder, I would have discovered this sooner. Her sister might not have died. My life might not have been near ruined. If Apollo had glowed, everything might have turned out quite differently.

But he hadn't. And I had failed a god.

"I failed a god," I said out loud.

"Ah, bollocks!" Dionysus said bracingly. "You did your best, yeah?"

"I failed a *god*."

He waved it off. "He'll get over it! He paid you, didn't he?"

I nodded speechlessly.

"There you go then. He can't be that pissed."

"But I still—"

"Leave it be!"

"But why me?" I wailed. "Why did he come to *me* for help? Why can't you all just leave me in peace? Is it the shoulder? Does Demeter think she still owes me for the shoulder? I forgive her already! I forgave her years ago! So what exactly is it about me that makes you gods say, 'Hey I know, let's bugger up this poor blighter's life'?"

"You're one of us," Dionysus said.

"What do you mean, 'one of you'? A party animal? Let me tell you something. I don't drink that much. I never get invited to parties except to cook! *And I don't even get the girls!* How does that make me 'one of you'? I mean, in what possible way does—"

"You're a god."

"I'm a … *what?*" I gaped at him.

"A god," he said again. Matter-of-factly.

Herakles himself could not have closed my mouth.

"Technically, you're a demigod," Hermes observed. "Only a quarter of you is actually divine."

Dionysus conceded the point with a nod.

"You're insane," I said, finally finding my voice. I scrambled to my feet and pointed an accusing finger at them. "You're both mad!"

"Oh no." Dionysus shook his head. "We're both sane enough. It makes sense, when you think about it. Why else would you get remade after the whole stew-pot cockup? You think we'd do that for just any mortal? No, my friend, you're a god."

"Quarter god," Hermes corrected again.

"Right."

"But…" I stopped, licked my lips and tried again. "What … Who?"

"Who was your granddad?" Dionysus finished helpfully.

I nodded, unable to speak.

"Zeus," he told me.

Zeus. I mouthed the word.

There was a long silence, then I found my voice. "How … how long have you…?" I stammered.

"Oh, Hermes and I have known for years, haven't we, Herm?"

"Ages," Hermes agreed.

I pinched the bridge of my nose. "But … why didn't you tell me?"

"It was for your own good, wasn't it?" Dionysus answered.

"Strictly a need-to-know basis." Hermes nodded.

Dionysus reached over to clout me on the shoulder. "I mean, you can't go noising about that sort of thing, eh? Tantalus as Zeus's son? It's liable to cause all manner of mischief."

"Hera doesn't look too fondly on The Big Guy's indiscretions," Hermes explained.

I stared at them.

"Think about it, man!" Dionysus said. "Europa, Antiope, Io … do I really need to go on?"

I gulped and shook my head.

The god of wine sat me back down and handed me a brimming cup. "Drink up," he advised. "It'll help settle your nerves."

I drank.

"Feel better?" he asked after I drained the cup.

I shook my head. He poured me another.

"And you're certain Hera doesn't know?" I asked shakily after I'd finished the second cup. "You've kept it secret?"

Hermes and Dionysus exchanged an uncomfortable look.

"Ah, I'm afraid not," Dionysus said, screwing up his face. "Getting back to that whole 'need-to-know' bit, I suppose you really need to know that … well, Zeus let slip to Hephaestus, who never could keep a secret to save his bollocks. It wasn't my fault! I did tell him to keep his gob shut, didn't I, Herm?"

"You did," Hermes confirmed.

"But did he listen to me? Noooooo, nobody listens to the god of wine and festivity. Oh, he's just in his cups again, they say. Don't pay any mind to him. Doesn't know his arse from his armpit, that's what they say. Bunch of bollocks!" He sniffed, then shook himself. "Anyhoo, it all came out during the Panathenaea—stupid sodding family get-togethers, I don't know why Hera insists on them—and, well, to make a long story short, she was there. You know, when Hephaestus let the cat out of the sack."

"She wasn't too happy." Hermes shook his head.

"No." Dionysus pulled his mouth to one side. "Plus, you'd gone and smacked her precious protégé in his dirty great nose, hadn't you? I'm not saying you didn't have cause, but … well, she didn't like that."

"She didn't like that at all," Hermes agreed. "Not on top of the news about your granddad. If I were you, I'd be watching my step from here on in."

I closed my eyes and sighed. Ever since I'd emerged from the stew pot, all I'd ever wanted to do was prepare food. I had dreamed of being the best chef in Athens, of having Zeuxo waiting for me at home. Of having my own dishes!

Simple dreams of a mortal man.

But according to Dionysus, I wasn't quite mortal, and all unwittingly, I'd failed Apollo and angered Hera, the very queen of the Pantheon. To say nothing of my ongoing conflict with Poseidon.

Dionysus pressed another cup of wine into my hands. "Don't

worry, mate," he tried to reassure me. "Hera hates me too. Been there, done that, and look! I'm still here." He paused and rubbed his nose uncomfortably. "Of course, she did curse me with madness for a few years and send me wandering all over the world and … ah, but don't you worry," he said waving it off airily. "Hermes and I'll watch your back for you. We're on the job, yeah?"

I opened my eyes and looked at my "guardian" gods. They were nodding and grinning encouragingly. Dionysus was giving me the thumbs-up.

I lifted the cup to my lips and drained it dry in one gulp. My troubles, it seemed, were just beginning.

Flute Girls for Fools

Are you tired of two-obol love?

Do you find the little houses of Aphrodite just a little too cramped for your comfort? Oh sure, a two-obol handshake will get your rocks off, but can you brag about it to your mates afterwards? Not hardly! Maybe it's time to invest in your happiness with a flute girl or a hetaera. But how do you know what to pay—or even what to ask for? EUKRATES comes to the rescue once again, with this list of the latest and greatest positions you could be enjoying right now! Please note that prices may fluctuate.

The Hoplite Hop — 1 DRACHMA

It's standing room only, lads! A quick "how's your father" designed especially for the man on the move. Short and sweet, but nice and cheap! Suitable for all incomes. Hoplite armour is optional.

The Bee —2 DRACHMAS

Float like a butterfly, sting like a bee. Get your stinger ready for this gem! She's the flower, you're the bee. Enough said.

The Racehorse — 5 DRACHMAS

You get to be all stud for this one! All the rage at modern symposions, The Racehorse is pretty much what you think it is, if you've spent any time loitering about near horses. Mount up and let the race begin!

Lion on the Cheese Grater — 25 DRACHM

Not for the faint of h

Acknowledgements

I recently read a book in which the author blamed a number of people for his book. In that spirit, I blame my fabulous Classics professor, Dr. Robert J. Buck, for turning me on to Greek history and mythology. I blame the Winnipeg Public Library for providing me with some of my research books, and McNally Robinson Booksellers for providing me with the rest. I suppose I should also blame MasterCard for allowing me to purchase all these books or, at the very least, my husband, who paid off the MasterCard bill.

I blame my writers group, Chadwick Ginther, Mike Friesen, Chris Smith, and Bev Geddes. Toad-buggering shite eaters, all! You will never find a more witty hive of rogues and geekery. Thanks, guys, you're the best!

I blame Sharon Caseburg for taking my suggestion for a fantasy imprint seriously, and Jamis Paulson for agreeing with her. Great things come from a sushi lunch! Let's do that again! I blame my fabulous editor, Catherine Majoribanks, for making the book even better, Sara Harms for keeping me from committing unjustifiable commacide, and Doowah Design'for the awesome cover artwork!

And finally, I blame my husband and daughter, who are unfailingly supportive of a wife and mother who closes herself in her den, mumbles about gods and chefs, and names her child after an ancient Greek city. I could probably do it without the two you, but it wouldn't be worth it.

Author's Note

When writing historical fantasy, you first start from real life, with real situations gleaned from various historical sources. Of course, you don't stick to that—it wouldn't be fantasy if you did—so you incorporate the fantastic elements as you go, tweaking facts as needed. But you start off with the real stuff.

In *Food for the Gods*, I took this quite literally. The orgy which begins the book did, in fact, take place in Athens some 2500 years ago, with the inebriated participants suddenly taking it into their heads that they were on a warship. Believing they needed to eject the ballast, they tossed various household items into the street, much to the entertainment of the neighbours. From that time on, the house was known as The Trireme.

Mithaecus of Sicily was a real person, a famous chef described by one writer as the Phidias of the kitchen. He was the author of one of the earliest treatises on cooking, and his recipe for ribbon fish is one of the earliest surviving published recipes. I do not know if he ever wore a yellow chiton or if he was, in fact, a total dick (if not, I apologize to his descendants).

Socrates, of course, lived in Periklean Athens, and though respected for his intellect, he was, by all accounts, a bit of a joke due to his unkempt appearance and flailing stride. Iktinos and Kallikrates really were the architects of the famous Parthenon, and a fellow named Philoxenus really did soak his fingers in hot water so he could snatch up the hottest, choicest morsels at a dinner party.

The statue of Neaera was real, the naked torch race and the slaps of the Kerameikos were real, a full-sized warship really was dragged through Athens as part of the Great Panathenaea. And finally, yes, the Greeks really did invent bread dildos. I swear I am not making this up. God, I love doing research!

About the Author

Karen Dudley's checkered past includes field biology, production art, photo research, palaeo-environmental studies, editing, archaeology, and Classical Studies. Needless to say, she just couldn't seem to settle on one job and sometimes thought there was something wrong with her. Then, a number years ago, an epiphany! She finally realized that what she really wanted to do was ... everything. And if you want to do everything, the best way to do it is to become a writer.

She wrote a short stack of wildlife biology books for kids before trying her hand at mystery—mostly for the satisfaction of "bumping off" people who irritate her in real life. Then after four environmental mysteries, another epiphany ... she wanted to write fantasy! So she did. Her historical fantasies, however, still include the odd corpse, which is not surprising, given the number of annoying personalities in the world. This has presented a bit of a challenge in terms of Hellenizing the names of the not-so-innocent, but a writer is, by nature, creative and such impediments are easily overcome by the determined.

Karen lives in Winnipeg with her husband, daughter, and assorted very nice but occasionally evil-minded cats.